With This Ring

With This Ring

Carla Kelly

**CAMEL
PRESS**

Seattle, WA

CAMEL PRESS

Camel Press
PO Box 70515
Seattle, WA 98127

For more information go to: www.camelpress.com
www.carlakellyauthor.com

Cover design by Sabrina Sun

With This Ring
Copyright © 1997, 2015 by Carla Kelly
First published by Signet, an imprint of Dutton Signet, a division of Penguin Books USA Inc.

ISBN: 978-1-60381-951-0 (Trade Paper)
ISBN: 978-1-60381-952-7 (eBook)

Library of Congress Control Number: 2014951998
Printed in the United States of America

To Denise and Tisha Grayson,

friends and sisters

"With this ring I thee wed, and with all my worldly goods I thee endow."

—*The Book of Common Prayer*

Author's Note

❦

GENERAL THOMAS PICTON, WHO found his way into this narrative, was a prominent officer who served ably as one of Sir Arthur Wellesley's lieutenants during the Peninsular War (1808-1814). With his brother officers—Crauford, Beresford, Pakenham, Hill, and Ponsonby—General Picton fought the length and breadth of Portugal and Spain in the struggle that ended with the Victory of Toulouse and Napoleon's exile to Elba in 1814. Picton was brilliant, eccentric, and well-known for his breathtaking profanity in a profane army. No sight was more familiar than General Picton at the head of his beloved Third Division, wearing his famous broad-brimmed top hat (he suffered from eye strain).

Picton's errors in the fog of battle that was Toulouse in no way diminished his abilities and talents. He went into battle a year later at Mont St. Jean, and was killed instantly by a bullet through his top hat during the long afternoon that was Waterloo, June 18, 1815.

General Picton plays only a small role in my story. I hope I have done him the justice he deserves. The liberties I have taken with him are those of an admirer.

Books by Carla Kelly
Fiction

Daughter of Fortune
Summer Campaign
Miss Chartley's Guided Tour
Marian's Christmas Wish
Mrs. McVinnie's London Season
Libby's London Merchant
Miss Grimsley's Oxford Career
Miss Billings Treads the Boards
Mrs. Drew Plays Her Hand
Reforming Lord Ragsdale
Miss Whittier Makes a List
The Lady's Companion
With This Ring
Miss Milton Speaks Her Mind
One Good Turn
The Wedding Journey
Here's to the Ladies: Stories of the Frontier Army
Beau Crusoe
Marrying the Captain
The Surgeon's Lady
Marrying the Royal Marine
The Admiral's Penniless Bride
Borrowed Light
Enduring Light
Coming Home for Christmas: The Holiday Stories
Marriage of Mercy
My Loving Vigil Keeping
Her Hesitant Heart
Safe Passage
The Double Cross
The Wedding Ring Quest

Non-Fiction

On the Upper Missouri: The Journal of Rudolph Friedrich Kurz (editor)
Louis Dace Letellier: Adventures on the Upper Missouri (editor)
Fort Buford: Sentinel at the Confluence
Stop Me If You've Read This One

Prologue

❦

"**P**ERCY, DO YOU KNOW what I like best about Englishwomen?" Major Sam Reed held his hand over his bishop, then moved it three squares. The lady chapel was cold, so he tugged his overcoat higher around his shoulders, wincing at the pain.

"God save us, Sam, but after all these years, you are still a terrible player." Lieutenant Percy Wilkins moved his knight and eliminated Reed's bishop with one swipe. "Check. No, tell me what is so fine about Englishwomen. It has been too many years. And for the Lord's sake, hold still. If you open that wound again, I'm not going to feel even a little sorry for you, sir."

Reed knew he didn't mean it, because his second-in-command got off his cot and peered under the overcoat. Apparently satisfied, Sir Percy resumed his position on his major's cot. "As for me, Sam, I have not seen an Englishwoman in so long that I wouldn't recognize one if she bit me on the buttock."

"You wish." Sam contemplated his bishop on Sir Percy's side of the board, not so much of a board as a campaign tablecloth blocked and stained red and black. "I like the way women here smell, like tea cakes or sugared violets." He gestured with the silver thimble that served as a rook. "Look you now: they go up and down the rows, dispensing a sip of water here, a pat on the head there. They look like they smell good, think on. D'ye think they will come to us?" He moved his rook out a square.

Sir Percy looked in the direction Sam indicated, turned back to the board, and moved his queen. "Check and mate. They won't come over here because we look too able." He lowered his voice. "Now, if you would lie back and gasp a little like this poor captain next to you, and maybe grab your belly …. Belly wounds are good. They'll be at your side in a wink." He grinned. "And gone about as fast."

Sam sighed and gathered up the chess pieces. He knotted them in one corner of the tablecloth and leaned back against the wall. "I do not need Society ladies to feel sorry for me."

"Actually, sir, I believe you do. Surely you cannot have forgotten your predicament?"

Sam glared at his lieutenant. "How could I?"

"Indeed you could not," Sir Percy agreed, his serenity an added irritation to Sam. "You need a wife in the worst way." He nodded in the direction of the ladies. "Maybe these sightseers might know of a woman …."

The major interrupted him. "She has to be a lady. That's one of the terms."

"I *know* the terms," Sir Percy reminded him. He sniffed the air around Sam. "More to the point now, you need to locate a lady with no sense of smell, who is impervious to rude noises, and who wouldn't mind a man who looks like a troll afraid of a barber."

"I can bathe, and I can shave, and when my back heals, I can stand up straight!" Sam said with some energy. And I am being testy toward the one who has done so much for me, he thought. Whether for good or bad, who can tell? Careful not to move fast, he held out his hand to his lieutenant. "Percy, I have never adequately thanked you for writing all those letters to my mother. What a lovely wife you gave me through those letters."

Percy laughed and shook Sam's hand. "I enjoyed it! Only think how my penmanship improved, and how it broke the whole battery's tedium." His face grew serious again. "I only hope I have not overdone the matter. Your mama is expecting you to arrive with a paragon of virtuous, lovely womanhood. And of course, there is that other matter." He paused, and Sam sighed. "Don't know what I was thinking, sir. Call it poetic license."

"Ah, yes, the other matter." Sam started to speak, thought better of it, then waited until he was calm. "Well, Percy, don't let me keep you. I know that your mama is eager to see your sorry self again."

His lieutenant got up from his cot and stood looking at him for a long moment. "I'll miss the guns, sir. Do stop at Quavers on your way north." Sir Percy grinned. "With a wife."

"Don't remind me!"

Through the portal that opened onto the larger chapel, Sam watched his lieutenant leave. He smiled when Percy stopped by the cots of their men, those stalwarts of the battery wounded in the last battle at Toulouse that sent Napoleon to a change of address to Elba. You've learned, lad, he thought, remembering Lieutenant Sir Percy Wilkin's arrival two years ago before Badajoz—a baptism I would wish on no greeny, he thought fervently, and not for the first time. There was a time when these heroes were objects of the lower class, eh, Percy? he reflected as his lieutenant spent a long time before the cot of their master sergeant. And then when your sergeant saves your aristocratic but inexperienced hide from one or two gross errors that artillerymen don't want to make—ah, it's a different story.

He leaned back against the wall again, careful of himself, and thought about his own sergeant, blown into froth at Talavera, and the corporals and privates whose names had faded, if not the remembrance of their gallantry under fire. He tried to lean against the wound, winced, and thought better of it. If I am to be invalided home, I had better heal quickly, he thought. This church is already becoming tiresome indeed, and Lord knows I have some heavy ground to get over lightly, as Old Nosey would say.

Face it, Sam, he told himself. You hate to ruin your record of no wounds at all during this whole long, dreadful war. It's rough to peacock about when you're hard put to stand up straight. At least your knuckles do not drag on the ground. The major drew up his knees and leaned forward on them, finding some measure of relief in that position. It was a comfort to know that the war was over.

Except. He rested in his chin on his knees and watched the ladies moving slowly up and down the ranks of the wounded, sequestered here in this drafty London church, chilly inside while May's hawthorn bloomed outside. "I need one of those in just about the worst way," he said out loud.

"Eh?" asked the captain on the next cot.

"One of those ladies," he repeated. The captain had a gut wound and wouldn't live through the week. Sam knew he could tell him anything. "I need a wife right now."

"Oh, you artillerymen," the captain murmured. "Wasn't it enough to wench through Spain?"

With some effort, Sam stood up, then leaned over and wiped the man's forehead, which glistened with the sweat of infection. "It's a long story, lad. I promised my mother a wife several years ago in a weak moment …."

"… Drunk?" the captain sympathized.

"Of course! Why else would I do that? I wrote her that I was married to a daughter of the regiment." He sat down, more tired from that small task than he cared to admit.

"What were you thinking?" the captain murmured.

"Probably that I would be dead before the war ended, so

what difference did it make what I told her?" Sam retorted. "What does any of us think during warfare?"

"That's bad."

"It's worse. My lieutenant got into the spirit of the thing, and a year later, wrote my mother that my wife and I had a child and she was a grandmama!"

There was no comment from the adjoining cot. Good God, I hope the shock of that didn't kill the poor man right now, the major thought, as he got up slowly, and leaned over the captain again. "Are you all right?"

After a long time, the man opened his eyes. His mouth creased into a smile, and his eyes were bright with both fever and merriment.

"That is the funniest thing I have ever heard, Major," the captain said. "I'm trying to figure out how to laugh without hurting everything inside me."

"So glad you're amused," Sam said as he wiped the man's forehead again. "Before I get home to Hadrian's Wall, it either has to be marriage or a double murder, and I am not inclined toward murder, even of the nonexistent."

The man was silent again, even as his grin widened. "Good luck, Major. You'll need it even more where you're going, than I will where I am bound."

"You're already confessed and shriven?" Sam asked, his voice gentle. "You're ready for what is ahead?"

The captain nodded, his eyes still merry. "More than you are, Major, more than you are. If God Almighty doesn't strike you dead for what I think you are about to attempt, some young lady will. I, on the other hand, need merely face my maker."

Major Reed lay back down on his cot. Put that way, I am in for an interesting time of it, he thought. He watched the ladies again until they loomed larger and larger and stepped into his dreams. When he woke, the cot next to his was empty, and the ladies were gone. His dilemma, however, remained.

Chapter One

∾

"LYDIA, I VOW IF you do not come quickly, Kitty will go into deep spasms! She will never find a duke or a marquis, and we will all be ruined!"

"Yes, Mama. At once, Mama."

It was impossible to ignore Mama, even heard through two closed doors. Lydia closed her book, but did not move from her perch in the window seat. She glanced at the clock. "I wonder, Kitty, what has precipitated this latest crisis, the third of the morning?" she asked out loud. "Could it be that your curling rod is misplaced, and because this is not Imperial Rome, you cannot beat your maid into a coma? Or perhaps you cannot find the ribbon we wasted four hours picking out yesterday. Yes, I am certain that is the problem."

"Lydia!"

Still she did not leave her comfortable spot. There was suddenly something so daunting about facing Kitty and Mama at the same time, both of them upset, both of them convinced that nothing could be more important than their needs. Not for the first time since their arrival a month ago from Devon did she kick herself for thinking for even one moment that life would be different here on Holly Street.

I have the vast misfortune to be an optimist in a family where one crisis follows another like waves on a beach, she considered. I even thought that London might be fun. Mama is right; *I am* a fool.

"Courage," she muttered as she stood up, took one last look out the window at all the activity in the street below, and went slowly down the hall. She imagined the scene even before she opened the door. Kitty would be in tears—not ordinary tears, mind you, but tears that clung to her long eyelashes like dew on rose petals. Her lower lip would be quivering, and her eyes would be stormy with disappointment. Lydia knew from a lifetime of experience that if she waited just one second too long to appear, Kitty would begin to breathe in short gasps, a prelude to towering, monumental hysteria.

"And we can't have that," she murmured as she took a deep breath of her own and opened the door.

Her younger sister Kitty stood in the middle of the room, surrounded by a morning's worth of dresses tried on, rejected, and left to wrinkle on the floor. Her arms were stiff by her sides, but she had not quite reached that state of irritation that led to the ruin of one's entire day.

"Yes, my dear?" she asked quietly as she picked up a discarded dress and shook it as she wanted to shake her sister.

Kitty regarded her with beautiful, mournful eyes, eyes of the sky in early evening, violet eyes already the subject of innumerable dithyrambs from besotted poets in Devon too young to know better. She took a deep breath and a sob—the perfect sob—caught in her throat. "I cannot find the ribbon, Lyddy!"

"I know that you have hidden it to do poor, poor Kitty mischief! I was telling your father only this morning that you are an unnatural child and should have been left behind!"

On a hillside like the Greeks? In Devon? Then, who would fetch and carry and smooth over everyone's spasms and indignations? Lydia thought as she turned to regard her mother. "Mama, I would never," she said quietly. "Kitty, remember that we put it in the top drawer of your bureau so you would not forget?" She went to the drawer, pulled out the length of ribbon, and handed it to her sister.

Kitty clutched the ribbon to her heaving breast, shed a few becoming tears of relief, then took a good look at the object of her distracted search. "I thought it was darker, sister," she said accusingly. She held it out at arm's length, as though it would sink its fangs into her perfect arm. "It won't do. Mama, make her take it back and choose me another."

No, Lydia thought, in that quiet place inside her mind that was hers alone. I will not return that stupid ribbon and drag myself through three more hours of shops to agonize over the merits of one color over another. I will not. "Whatever you wish, Mama," she said.

Mama, no stranger to tragedy herself, threw herself into a chair and stared at her elder daughter. "Lydia, what I wish is that you would mind the insincerity of your tones. No wonder you are twenty-two and still single." She patted her heart, that organ of affection. "With notably few exceptions, I can trace every one of my palpitations to your intransigence."

These are heavy doings, Lydia told herself as she folded the ribbon. The day is so beautiful that I do not have the strength for Mama's cardiac insufficiencies and my role in them. "I will be happy to return the ribbon, Mama." It sounded sincere to her. She meant it sincerely—anything to stave off another lecture, more accusations, and perhaps the back of Mama's hand for punctuation.

After a long pause, long enough for Lydia to feel the familiar gnawing in her stomach, Mama nodded. "Very well." She smiled at her other daughter. "Kitty, love, be a dear and step aside so Lydia can pick up the rest of your frocks and return them to the dressing room. Sit here, my dear." She patted the cushion beside her. "I have something of interest for you, and I suppose, for Lydia, too, if she can do two things at once!"

She and Kitty put their blond heads together and laughed. Lydia knew better than to look at either of them. That would only mean more laughter at her expense. It is one of the seven wonders of the world that I have any pride left at all, she thought as she carried the dresses into the next room where Kitty's maid cowered. "Best iron them quickly," she whispered as she shut the door.

"As I was walking this morning, I overheard dear Lady Walsingham remark that it was all the rage for young women of fashion and sense to go to St. Barnabas."

Kitty gave her a blank stare. "Mama, it is not Sunday," she said.

Mama laughed and touched Kitty under the chin. "You are so amusing!"

Thank goodness I did not say that, Lydia considered as she edged herself into a chair. Mama would have called me a dolt and tugged at my hair.

"A number of wounded soldiers are lodged there right now. Some battle or other …."

"Toulouse, Mama," Lydia said without thinking. "It has been in all the papers, and now the war is ov—" Mama glared at her, and she was silent.

"One battle is very much like another, and it is amazingly ill-bred to claim knowledge of any of them," Mama declared, dismissing most of history in a single sentence. "The import is this: The better sort are going to St. Barnabas to minister to the soldiers."

"Good God, Mama, you cannot be serious!" Kitty exclaimed. "We have to *touch* them?"

"Oh, no, dear, no," Mama soothed, taking Kitty's hands in hers to stop their agitated motion. "I think you merely walk up and down and look sympathetic. Possibly cluck your tongue, but surely nothing more. I have it on good authority that it is the high kick of fashion right now."

That will be onerous, indeed, Lydia considered. No wonder Kitty is concerned. I do not think Kitty understands the ramifications of sympathy, particularly since such an emotion requires the acknowledgment of others.

Kitty shuddered and drew closer into the circle of her mother's arms. "But, Mama, suppose one of them reaches out to touch me?"

They wouldn't dare, Lydia thought, then turned her head to cough so Mama would not see her smile.

Mama drew herself up straight again. "My dearest, that is why nature intended for young ladies of fashion to carry parasols. You can beat them off!"

Oh, I like that, Lydia told herself. So much philanthropy all at once must be nipped in the bud. Probably it is a good thing that soldiers are used to harsh living, particularly if they run afoul of the "better sort," as Mama puts it.

"But why, Mama, why do we have to do this?" Kitty asked as the storm warnings rose in her eyes again.

Mama regarded Kitty sorrowfully. "Because, my precious kitten, your father—drat his timid soul—never could bring himself to visit London, or even pursue acquaintances beyond the borders of our own district!" She rose suddenly and took a turn about the room, her agitation unmistakable. "We have money enough, but no one knows us! We are living in a rented house on the fringe of the best area, and your father makes no push to renew old friendships."

And if I have told him once I have told him a thousand times, Kitty love, you are too beautiful to waste on a red-faced squire's son in Devon, Lydia thought as she watched her mother take another turn about the room. Isn't that what you have always said next, Mama? See? I have memorized it.

She knew what would follow that speech, so she tried to make herself smaller in the chair. "... Too beautiful to waste on a red-faced squire's son in Devon," Mama was saying. Lydia winced as Mama directed her attention to her. "Blame Lydia, if this exercise makes you uncomfortable," she said to Kitty. "If Lydia had been even slightly less plain, *she* could have smoothed the way for *you*! As it is, you must exert yourself and be seen where it will do you the most good."

"But a church with wounded soldiers? Oh, Mama!"

Kitty, you are fast approaching the limits of Mama's endurance, Lydia thought as she watched her mother and sister. Lips in a thin line, eyes narrowing ... I know the signs. Kitty, are you really so dense that you never figured them out? Of course, the wrath comes down less strenuously on you, because you are beautiful, where I am not.

"It is an excellent plan," Mama was saying now, her tone placating. "You and Lydia will wait outside the church in our carriage until you see young ladies and gentlemen going inside. Join their party. Tag along behind them." She took Kitty by the shoulders and gave her a little shake. "Make something of this opportunity!"

"Suppose no one notices us, Mama," Kitty countered.

"Everyone notices you, my love," Mama soothed. "It is Lydia that no one notices. It must be the right people, however, to do us any good. When we go to Almack's on Friday, you will have someone to talk to," she reasoned, concluding triumphantly, "Visiting a few dirty soldiers will not have been in vain." She waited a moment. "Very well, then. The coachman will be ready for you at two of the clock."

So we are reduced to nipping at the gentry's coattails like ill-mannered puppies? Lydia wondered as she gave Mama sufficient time to descend the stairs. When she was sure Mama was down the stairs, she opened Kitty's door quietly and tiptoed to the landing. As she looked down to the main floor, she saw the door to Papa's study open. She watched, humiliated for him, as he stuck his nose out, looked this way and that for Mama, heaved a sigh that she could hear on the first-floor landing, then quietly closed the door again.

Poor Papa, she thought, and not for the first time, as she

returned to her room. He has nothing but two daughters, and his estate is entailed away to a male relative who scarcely needs it. I wish it were not so, but I believe he only waits to die, and inflict Mama on one or the other of us.

She picked up her book again, but it held no interest for her. Instead, she looked out the window, dreading, like Kitty, the visit to St. Barnabas, if for different reasons. I do not wish to tag along and encroach upon the goodwill of others, she thought. I am not nosing after scraps from the *ton's* table, or licking someone's pot, no matter how it might forward Kitty's prospects.

As she looked at the traffic in the street below, she noticed her own outline in the wavy window glass, indistinct and barely there. It was her life's story, and as she sat and looked at her dim reflection, she discovered that she did not care for what she saw. "But how do I change the people that I must live with?" she asked herself. She peered closer at the outline of herself in the glass, then reached out to touch her reflection. "Could it be that if these people will not change, then I must change myself?" she asked.

WITH VARYING DEGREES OF impatience and resignation, they waited for what seemed like eons in the family carriage outside the church of St. Barnabas. It was on the edge of London's docks, but on a quiet, little used street made all the quieter by the quantities of straw strewn throughout the entire block to muffle the sound of passage and allow a measure of peace to the suffering inmates within.

"It is a mystery to me how you can remain so content, Lyddy," Kitty complained after an entire stretch of ten minutes when no one paid any attention to her.

"My dear sister, that is why I always travel with a book. Let me recommend it to you," Lydia said as she slit open another page.

"Reading is a bore," Kitty assured her as she reexamined her nails for the tenth time in as many minutes. "Look here, my maid is so stupid. This cuticle is not pushed down as far as the others. Oh, dear! I did not notice it until this minute!"

If I throttled my sister, a jury of rational men would never convict me, Lydia thought as she glanced at her sister's shapely, perfect hands. "I think you will be able to endure this calamity until we return to the house, my dear," she commented, then turned her attention back to the book. When Kitty began to sniff and hunt about in her reticule, Lydia closed her book in resignation. "If you cry, you will frighten away any prospects you hope to see here."

Kitty sniffed back her tears, but continued to regard the offending fingernail with a mournful expression. It lasted until she noticed that there was the smallest scuff on her boots. Her lips, which one or another Devon poet had called "twin pillows of fairy repose," drew together into a tight line reminiscent of Mama. She turned her boot this way and that, muttering, "I do not know that another person is as mortally tried as I am, Lyddy."

Lydia was spared the insincerity of a suitable reply with the arrival of a barouche, the first that she had seen this spring.

She pointed out the conveyance to Kitty, who was still regarding her boots with a frown. "Look, Kitty, the game's afoot," she said. I shall keep a satiric eye, she told herself, or this whole humiliation will overwhelm me. "My dear, let us see if they are suitably gowned, coifed, and sweet-smelling. Oh, yes, let us make sure that their cuticles are pushed back, or we will have nothing to do with them," she teased.

Kitty smiled her dazzling smile. "I know the care of one's hands is of vital significance," she said with complete serenity. "How good it does me to hear you recognize the importance of it, too."

Lydia swallowed the hot words that rose in her throat. What sense would there be in scolding someone with so little evidence of a brain box between the ears? She was murmuring something suitably appropriate when another barouche drew up beside the first. More elegantly gowned young ladies allowed themselves to be handed down by equally well-dressed young men.

"Kitty, I believe there are enough of the *Haute Ton* to suit even Mama. Do let us follow them into the church."

Kitty hung back, even as she watched the parade of pastel afternoon walking dresses and modish bonnets pass their carriage. "Lyddy, you don't think I will be required to help the soldiers, do you?"

"Of course not," Lydia replied with a small sigh. "I do not think it is possible for you to do too little for them."

That answer, delivered with a straight face, seemed to satisfy her sister. Kitty allowed the footman, who had been cooling his heels beside the coachman, to help her down. With Kitty at her side, they picked their way through the moldy straw covering the street just in time to bring up the rear of the elegant party. There are none of us equipped to help even a butterfly, Lydia thought with embarrassment as they entered the church. I should rather imagine that sturdy shoes and a sensible apron would be more to the point than bonnets with feathers and shot silk fabric.

They were greeted by a veritable wall of odors that made her take a step back. Kitty turned quite pale and grabbed her arm. "Lyddy, I can't go in there!" she whispered.

One of those rare times wholly in sympathy with her sister, Lydia patted her hand as Kitty clutched her. "Then, are you prepared for an evening with Mama's flutterings and spasms and accusations if we return without making at least one or two acquaintances?" she whispered back.

"N-no," Kitty stammered, but made no move to step forward into the nave. She tightened her grip on her parasol.

Other ladies were hanging back, and none of the gentlemen looked eager to proceed. It was an easy matter to join the group.

In a moment Kitty relaxed and looked around her. "Lyddy,

we are *mingling*!" she whispered in some awe.

Some of the bolder young ladies stepped forward finally, and they trailed after them into the nave. Lydia looked around her, careful to raise her hem above the reeking straw that should have been replaced weeks ago. I would take it all out and give everyone such a scrubbing, she thought, looking at the men, some of them still stained with dirt from the battlefield. Then I would shave them and make them brush their teeth. Their clothes would be burned, of course, and their hair cut short.

Thinking about what she would do gave her the courage to move forward. She left the group, which huddled together at the sight of all this misery, and stood staring thoughtfully at the sight before her. I wonder if there is something I actually could do, she thought as, almost without realizing it, she loosened her bonnet strings and let her hat hang down her back. In another moment she had pushed up her sleeves and handed her parasol to Kitty, who, white-faced, was clutching the arm of an elegant length of Bond Street *savoir-faire.*

"Lyddy, what are you doing?" Kitty gasped.

"I don't know," she said over her shoulder. "I can't just stand here."

It appeared that the others could. With one last look at them, she started down the row toward a man who looked as though he could be in charge.

He was standing by the cot of a young man even more pale than Kitty. As she looked on, horrified, the last of his blood drained out of a neck wound and seeped into the straw. With a sigh that went on until she wanted to cover her ears, he died.

The doctor stood there, a frown on his face as he tapped a silver-handled scalpel against his open watch. "Time of death, 3:30," he said, more to himself than her. "If anyone cares."

He noticed her then, and she knew she must look as pale as the dead man, because he took her arm, sat her down on the cot next to the soldier, and pushed her head down. "Stay that way until you feel better," he said brusquely as he closed the soldier's eyes and covered his face.

"I'm better," she said finally as she raised her head, wishing that her voice did not sound so remote to her own ears.

"I doubt it," he said. He noticed the question in her eyes, because he gestured to the corpse. "I do not understand why it is, but twice his neck wound granulated and then opened. It was only a matter of time. Well, then, what am I supposed to do with you?" It sounded abrupt, but his eyes were kind.

"May I help?" she asked.

He smiled, wiped his scalpel absently on his coat sleeve, and looked at the ladies and gentlemen. "You will be the first who has offered. Damn them all! War is not a fad!" In that abrupt way she was already becoming accustomed to, he took her arm and lifted her to her feet, gesturing with his scalpel. "D'ye see that shaggy man over there? The one hunched over?"

She nodded. A man with his long hair pulled back from his face sat on a soldier's cot. As she watched, he tried to sit up straight, but only succeeded in wincing with the pain.

"That is Major Reed, Lord Laren. I want you to march up to him and tell him to go lie down, and that you will be happy, no, ecstatic, to take his place and hold that dying man's hand."

"Sir?" Lydia asked in amazement. "Will he let me?"

"Ask anyone, ask Major Reed! A surprise attack is worth a frontal assault squared and cubed. Do try, please. I'd rather not have another casualty. He may look like a troll at the moment, but he means something to me."

Surprised at herself, she did as he directed, skirting another doctor and an orderly who were trying to hold down a soldier and lance a boil. She looked down at her dress as she passed the men. To her chagrin, the material must have served as a wick while she stood by the dead soldier. Her skirt was stained with blood. Mama is right, she thought, I will never make it into the better circles, if I do not pay more attention to what I wear. The absurdity of her situation and Mama's comment served to keep her moving through the rows.

She hesitated to address the shaggy officer who sat in obvious pain on the soldier's cot. Apparently he had not noticed her presence anyway. I could probably turn around quietly right now, retrace my steps, and wait in the carriage for Kitty, she reflected. No one would notice me, because no one ever does. But I cannot. She cleared her throat.

"Excuse me, sir," she said. "The surgeon over there said I was to relieve you."

He said nothing and did not turn around for so long that she nearly retraced her steps. She repeated her statement, wondering if she should have addressed him as Lord Laren. She suspected that even someone with imagination (something Mama said she did not possess) would have a hard time seeing the shaggy man with a hunchback as a titled person.

She was about to leave. Her courage was draining away as fast as the blood from that poor unfortunate soldier eight rows over. She decided to try one more time. "Major, I …."

"I heard you. It just takes me a moment to turn around. Don't leave, please."

She came closer. Taking great care of himself, the officer shifted his whole body on the cot, rather than just his head. "Well, miss?" he asked, his words clipped, his lips tight.

She thought for a moment that she had angered him, and then she realized that he was in pain. It showed in the tightness around his mouth and the way he squinted at her, even though the room was fairly well lit. Oh, dear, she thought as she slowly untied her bonnet and set it aside. I do not know which of you is worse off.

She took a deep breath, which was a mistake in that foul room, and gestured toward the surgeon. "He said I was to relieve you here, so you could go lie down."

The officer said nothing, but she knew he was regarding her intently, measuring her. Oh, this is nothing new, she thought, with a sudden burst of confidence. People have been measuring me all my life. "The surgeon said that I could probably hold his hand as well as you can. Sir. Or Lord Laren, or whatever you choose. You are supposed to lie down now."

Again a long pause. "Make me," he said at last.

Lydia sighed. "You are going to be difficult," she observed, more to herself than to him.

"I usually am. Make me."

If I even stop to think about this, I will never act, she thought. So I will not think about it. "Very well, sir. Since you are so stubborn," she said as she sat on his lap, took the soldier's hand from his, and held it in her own.

She did not know what to expect, but she did not anticipate the laughter that rose up from the nearby cots. "Got you, Major!" one of the men said. "She's out-thought you, sir!" said another with an arm missing, who sat up to watch.

"Oh, very well," the major said, and he did not try to hide the amusement in his voice. "Lads, such an opportunity, but I will remember that I am an officer and a gentleman." The men laughed again as the major patted her hip. When she rose up in indignation, he moved out from under her. "Very well, madam, since you are so persistent." She blushed as he sniffed her hair close to her ear, his breath warm on her cheek. "And, by God, you smell better than my stinking soldiers. Sit, madam, by all means. Hold his hand tight. And then when he's dead, you can hold mine."

She couldn't think of a thing to say, so she was silent. In another moment she was stroking the dying man's hand, and then wiping his face with a damp cloth near his pillow. She felt the cot move, and heard the officer behind her get to his feet. He staggered against her and put his hand on her shoulder to steady himself. It was a firm grip.

"It's a long trip back to officer's country, lads," she heard him say behind her. "If you don't mind …." In the corner of her vision, she saw one of the more lightly wounded men move to another cot and make room for the officer. He sat down heavily on the cot directly across from her. "I'm going to keep an eye on you, miss," he said, his lips tight again. "That man's my gunnery sergeant."

As he sat hunched over, bleary-eyed, looking older than her own grandfather, she heard a commotion from the little knot of ladies and gentlemen whose presence she had almost forgotten. She looked over in time to see her sister settle into a graceful faint in the arms of another Bond Street pattern card. Drat you, Kitty, she thought.

In a moment, another of the young gentlemen was approaching her, moving warily through the rows, careful not to brush up against anything that looked like it wouldn't wash off, and holding a handkerchief to his nose. One of the men sitting close to her snickered, and the young gentleman stopped, confused.

"It's all right, sir," she said calmly, not releasing her grip on the dying man. "They fed them this morning, and they won't bite."

He blinked at her and raised his quizzing glass with a shaking hand, which made the snickering and elbow-poking around her increase. "Miss … ah, Miss …."

"Perkins," she replied. "It appears that my sister Kitty has fainted."

"Yes, Miss Perkins. Lord Harwell and I would like to return her to your home."

You fop, she almost said. You thought to come here and amuse yourself, but it is not a pleasant sight. "Oh, so kind of you," she replied. "But I shouldn't think that task will require two of you, sir. You may stay and help here."

"Oh, no! I mean … well, I mean …."

Someone clucked like a chicken, and the gentleman blushed as he backed up into a slop jar and the contents dribbled onto his shoes. "Please come with us, Miss Perkins. This is no place for a lady."

"Yes, by all means, go," the major said, leaning forward as if attempting to alleviate the pain. "You've had sufficient diversion to qualify as a regular angel of mercy, Miss Perkins, is it?" He spoke softly enough, but the challenge was unmistakable. His men looked at each other, as if as surprised as she was. No one snickered.

She thought a moment, then shook her head. She looked up at the gentleman, who was staring down at his pants in real dismay. "Sir, if you and Lord Harwell will please take Kitty home in our carriage, I will be grateful to you. Tell my coachman to return for me in an hour or two." Provided Mama isn't so furious that she makes me walk, she thought.

"You heard the lady," the major said. "Make yourself useful and scarce." The order was delivered firmly, as though the major spoke to one of his privates, and not a bright one, at that.

Without a word, the gentleman retreated down the row. He gathered up the others like chickens before a storm, and herded them toward the foyer. The major turned himself enough to watch them go. "Men, I think that will end our exhibition visits." He wrinkled his nose. "Sterling, have we you to blame for that slop jar? Do move it somewhere before Miss Perkins changes her mind and declares us past redemption." His last words came out in a gasp, and she was grateful to see one of his men motioning for the surgeon.

"I'm not going anywhere," she assured them all as she clung to the dying man's hand.

"Then, Miss Perkins, I think you'll do," said the major as he closed his eyes against the pain. "You'll do."

2

H E LET ONE OF his soldiers swing his legs up, and another soldier help him lie carefully on his side. He closed his eyes. "Mind you hold on to my gunner," he murmured.

She did as he said, holding tight to the man as she wiped his face again and looked around for more water. One of the soldiers obligingly set a basin of water close to her hand. The men—they must have all come from the major's unit, or company, or whatever they called themselves—regarded her with some interest. She observed them right back, noting their obvious concern for their officer. One of them who could walk found a blanket and covered him.

"He's a game'un, miss, but a bit weary he is," said one of the men. The others looked at her expectantly, as though wondering if she would address a strange man so far from her own class.

"I think he must be weary. What happened to him?" she responded calmly. The man whose hand she held opened his eyes, as though startled from his coma by a female voice. "It's all right. Your major's over there, and I won't leave you," she told him, even as her stomach revolted at the odd sweetish odor coming from the bandage that bound his chest.

The men looked at each other, as if wondering, after their initial success, who should speak next. The same man cleared his throat. "Oh, t'major thought 'e was Jesus Christ and tried to save us all, 'e did."

The others looked at each other and nodded. "But … what happened?" she asked.

The same soldier continued the narrative. "Nosey played his cards a little far away from his chest at Toulouse, and we got rolled up." He grinned at his mates, pleased with himself.

Lydia frowned. "Why didn't you run?" The men stared at her, and she wondered for a second if she had two heads instead of one sitting on her neck. "Well, I would," she finished lamely.

"Pardon me, ma'am, but you don't just leave your guns," he said, with a certain primness that told her she had committed a grave military error.

"And besides, we were surrounded. Nowhere to run to," said another man with one eye and a thick bandage where the other one should be. "The major, he tried to be everywhere, and got a saber smack across his shoulders for 'is pains."

Lydia flinched. "He can't stand up straight anymore?" she asked.

"Oh, he's fine in the morning, but by the afternoon, it's all he can do to stand on his pins." The man laughed. "What with that and arguing every day with Horse Guards that he won't leave until we're all assigned, he's had a merry time."

She looked at the dying man in front of her, who still regarded her with amazement in his sunken eyes. "And this man?" she murmured as she smoothed the hair across his forehead and wished she had enough water to wash him. A person shouldn't die dirty.

"He's my gunnery sergeant," the major spoke up from his cot across from her, his eyes still closed. "He followed me, or maybe I followed him, from Oporto to Toulouse." His voice trailed off. "Too full of ginger to die."

"You'll miss him, won't you?" she asked softly of no one in particular.

"Miss Perkins, I have missed each man I have ever lost, every foot of the way. Yes, of course," the major said. He looked up as the surgeon bent over him. "Oh, it is you. All I need is a little rest. It has been a long day."

Unmindful of his protests, the surgeon raised the bandage from the major's shoulder and took a long look at his back. I hope it is nothing serious, Lydia thought as still he stood there, rocking back and forth on his heels, regarding the wound.

"Sir?" she asked finally. "Will he do?"

She must have startled him. "Oh, yes, ma'am. I was merely wondering why it is that one man can begin to heal so nicely, and another ...." He glanced at the gunnery sergeant, who was muttering to himself now. "And others, no." He returned his attention to the major. "You, sir, are a hiss and a byword around here. If I receive another evil communication from Horse Guards asking me why on God's earth you are still here and not invalided home, I will personally smite you."

Major Reed still didn't open his eyes, but to Lydia's amusement, he grinned. "I told the general that as soon as he saw to my men, I would go quietly back to Northumberland and never trouble this end of the realm again. Where is the difficulty?"

The surgeon sighed and sat on the major's cot. "Lord Laren, I appeal to your good nature ...."

"I have none, sir," the major snapped, opening his eyes and fixing the surgeon with a level stare. "I want my men who are here in hospital taken care of to my satisfaction, and then I will consent to leave. There are no other conditions."

The surgeon tried again. "Sir, other officers ha—"

"I am not other officers, and this is no ordinary battery," said the major, biting off each word as though he intended to chew it. "When my men are taken care of, I will leave. Picton's Own Battery deserves nothing less."

"You are difficult, my lord," said the surgeon.

"I am. Now, sir, if you will look at this charming lady, I believe she has something to ask you. Am I right, Miss Perkins?"

You must have eyes in the back of your head, she thought. She glanced at the soldiers around her. No wonder they trust you. "Yes, actually," she said. "This poor man deserves to be clean before he dies. Can you at least change his bandage and bring me some water and a towel?"

The surgeon opened his mouth, looked at the major, and closed it. "Very well. Orderly!"

The gunnery sergeant died two hours later, during which time he called her his mother, and Grandmama, and then Teresa, who was, one of the men assured her, a good girl who followed the army. I am not that naive, she thought, but she made no comment. She wiped his face, glad that he was clean to her satisfaction. Changing the bandage had been a trial, but she clung to his hand throughout the whole ordeal, and when it was over, vomited with what she hoped was ladylike demeanor into a bucket that the major thoughtfully pushed her way.

To her relief, the gunnery sergeant was deep in another world during the last hour of his life. It remained to her to wipe his face, and then when he died, to be amazingly touched as his hand had gripped hers, and then relaxed completely in the peace that death brings. She held it another moment, marveling at the mystery before her, even as she cried for a soldier she did not know.

The men were silent, some looking away. She dried her eyes on a handkerchief that someone gave her—probably the major—blew her nose, and looked around her. "I'm sorry to have distressed you with my tears," she said as she stood up, feeling far older than her twenty-two years.

"Ah, no, miss," said the one-eyed man, who seemed to have appointed himself the spokesman. "I thinks I speaks for all when I say that gunner there would have been flattered to have a pretty mort cry all over him." He looked around at the others, and they nodded in agreement, with a certain shyness that touched her almost as much as the dead man.

So I am a pretty lady? she asked herself. Either the light is more dim than I thought, or you have not seen Englishwomen in years and years. "I could cry more," she said simply. It sounded stupid to her ears, but again the men nodded.

The major had said nothing, and she had assumed he still slept. She looked at him, and his eyes were open, regarding her with a curious expression of relief. It surprised her at first, wondering what she could have done to occasion such an emotion. She gazed back at him with a question in her eyes, and then it dawned on her that what she had done through this interminable afternoon had lifted some of the burden from his own painful shoulders.

She surprised herself further by resting her hand on his arm as he lay there, leaning close so no one else could hear, and whispering in his ear. "Major Reed, I truly think this is too much for you right now."

He nodded, and she was chagrined to see tears in his eyes, too. "I also think the men would feel better if you returned to your own cot so you could rest."

His reply was a long time coming, and she feared she had overstepped her bounds with him. "You're right," he said finally. His voice was so soft, she was compelled to lean closer. "Miss Perkins, have you any idea how wonderful you smell?"

Sir, you are a rascal, she thought, amused that he would keep her so close just to breathe her fragrance. "It is merely good milled soap, sir."

"It is far more."

He closed his eyes, and she straightened up. She spoke to the one-eyed man, "Sir ...."

"Corporal Davies, mum, not sir," he replied in a hurry, his cheeks flushed at her social gaffe.

"Corporal, could you help me take the major back to his own bed?"

"I am far away from my own bed," he commented a trifle breathlessly as the corporal and a private helped him to sit up.

"Nonsense. You said you were quartered in the lady chapel. I can see it from here," Lydia replied. The private paled under the major's weight, and Lydia took a good look at him. "Private, why did you not mention your own wound? Do sit down." She replaced the private's shoulder with her own, lifting up the major and draping his arm around her. Corporal Davies took a firm grip on the other side, and they walked him slowly down the aisle of silent men.

"I mean Northumberland, where I live," he managed to say as they walked him along. "Just beyond Hadrian's Wall." He stopped, and they stopped. "Miss Perkins, perhaps you would like it there."

She laughed. "I doubt it! A place where the sun never shines, sheets and blankets are always damp, and where people eat oatmeal three times a day?"

He smiled at her as they started in motion again. "I have a very good cook, and we only have oatmeal twice a day! Corporal, what are you grinning at?"

"You, sir," the man replied.

"Insubordination," Reed muttered, and then said nothing more. The perspiration stood out on his forehead, and Lydia knew how much this effort at nonchalance was costing him.

They laid him down on his own bed, and Corporal Davies went for the surgeon again, over his protests. "I just need to sleep," he insisted as she wiped his face.

"And perhaps a small serving of laudanum," she added, pulling his blankets up to his shoulder. "To go with your oatmeal."

She sat beside him to await the surgeon, noting how at some point during the afternoon, the sun had gone down. How long have I been here? she thought in alarm. Surely the coachman would have come in for me. She sighed. If Mama has allowed him to return. Perhaps I am to be punished for not accompanying Kitty home. She frowned, wondering how far she would have to walk.

"Are you late to an engagement?" the major asked.

Startled, she looked down at him. "I thought you were sleeping."

"With the fragrance of 'good milled soap' so close?" he teased as he gritted his teeth against the pain. The moment passed, and he stirred on his side so he could see her better. "Miss Perkins, you had better let Corporal Davies escort you home."

"I think … at least I hope … my coachman is outside."

"If he is not, Corporal Davies will see you home." He turned his head toward the small table next to the cot. "Find some coins there for a hackney."

"I couldn't."

"Do it."

As she scooped up a few coins, Lydia decided that Major Reed was not someone to argue with. I suppose it comes with command, she thought. "I will pay you back, sir," she said.

"Don't talk twaddle. You have already given me—my battery—more than we can ever repay."

She did not argue with him, especially after he closed his eyes and the sweat sprang to his forehead again. She knelt by him this time and dabbed at his face. "I wish you would not talk, and for the Lord's sake, do stay in your bed tomorrow, and leave the Horse Guards alone, no matter how stupid they are," she murmured. "You are a serious trial, Major Reed."

He nodded, but he did not open his eyes. Now you have worn yourself down to the nub, she thought, as she sat by him again on the cot. Oh, where did the myth start that officers are lazy and concerned with no one's comfort but their own? She fingered his hair, which was far too long. If I returned, I could cut this quite nicely, she thought. Mama will never allow my return, however.

She was sitting there, chin on hand, staring at the marble

slab that used to be the altar, when the corporal returned with the surgeon. Quietly, she got up and turned to go, but the major grabbed her skirt, holding her there.

"Sir!" she protested.

"Come back tomorrow," he said, and it was a command. "Corporal Davies, either see her to her carriage or see her home."

"Aye, sir," the corporal said.

The major released her and without looking back, she left him to the care of the surgeon. "Is he always so … so peremptory?" she asked when they were out of hearing.

The corporal shrugged, as if puzzled by her question. "Miss Perkins, he is an officer. I believe they are supposed to be that way."

"With *everyone*?"

He grinned at her. "We've all been a long time away, begging your pardon, mum."

A long time away, she thought as she looked around the chapel one more time. A pity more surgeons and more comfortable quarters could not be found for the men who gave so much.

There was no carriage waiting for her outside, but she had not expected it. Her mother would likely be in rare bad humor, and she would have no allies. Unconsciously she stepped closer to the corporal.

"Happen there was another need for your conveyance," the corporal suggested.

"I'm certain that is right," she said, continuing the fiction.

The corporal hailed a hackney and helped her in, climbing in after her. "Oh, I cannot take you from the hospital!" she protested. "What will the major think!"

He shook his head emphatically, then pressed his hand to his bandaged face. "No, mum, the question is, what would he think if I let you go home all by yourself? He'd have my stripes, and I don't plan to lose them again."

"Very well. It seems that I cannot argue with any effectiveness against the army," she said.

"No, ma'am," he agreed. "Good of you to realize that."

Lydia smiled in the dark. There is no question that I am in the capable hands of master manipulators, she thought. So this is the army? She cleared her throat. It was a longish drive to Holly Street and conversation was in order, even if Mama would be shocked into catatonia to know she was speaking with someone of the lowest order. She glanced at Corporal Davies, who was leaning against the window and pressing his hand to the bandage. Now, would he rather talk about himself, his commander, or his guns? She decided on guns.

"Corporal, I believe your major said you were 'Picton's Own Battery'?" she ventured. "I do not understand."

The corporal turned to look at her. "You haven't heard of Picton's Own?" he asked in amazement.

She shook her head, feeling silly. "I don't even know what kind of guns you shoot."

"Serve," he corrected. "Big'uns, Miss Perkins. Lovely ladies. Battery B, Third Division, but no one calls us that. I thinks that t'major could land a shell on the back of a Frog in a bordello, and not hurt the *puta* underneath." He chuckled. "He probably has, think on!"

"So you are valuable to General Picton," she continued, grateful that he could not see her red face.

He nodded. "After Talavera, when we saved his liver and lights, he's quick to let Major Reed play the game 'is own way." He took his hand from his face, as though the memory of victory was as good as opium. "Timing, Miss Perkins. Know your terrain, stand your ground, and hold your fire until you want to void because you're so scared. Beg pardon, mum, but that's the simple truth."

"I don't doubt you," she murmured. "I cannot imagine doing such a thing." She smiled. "It seems that I said something about running away, didn't I?"

The corporal was prepared to be generous. "We've all wanted to, one time or t'other." He leaned back, trying to find a comfortable spot in the hackney as it bumped over cobblestones. " 'Cepting the major. I don't think he is ever afraid. Northumberlanders, miss. A wild mob are those pikers beyond Hadrian's Wall."

"And yet, some call it home, I am certain," she said. "I imagine the major is eager to return to his wife and children there?"

"If he had any, he would," the corporal agreed, then laughed softly, almost to himself. "Or maybe he does."

"He's not sure?" she asked, puzzled. "That's irregular."

"Lord, Miss Perkins, it's a very long story. And he might not want me telling it," he said, putting his hand to his eye again. "I'm not sure I could do it justice, anyway." He looked out the window as the hackney slowed and then stopped. "Gor, miss, is *this* your bivouac?"

She looked out the window, too, trying to see it as the corporal was seeing it. All I see is a rented house on a street just slightly beyond the edge of gentility. A home for mushrooms, she told herself. "Yes, I am living here for the Season. Ordinarily I live in Devon."

"Came to see the sights, did yer da and mum?"

"No, not really. My parents do not take much interest in their surroundings," she said. If you can be so honest, I can at least return the favor. "I have a beautiful sister, who is attempting to find a suitable alliance."

"With one of them earls or viscounts?"

"Oh, at least," she said. When the cabdriver opened the door, she held out her hand to the corporal. "Thank you for your escort. Do take care of yourself, and try to get Major Reed to stay in his bed tomorrow."

"I thought he told you to come back," he reminded her.

"Well, yes, but …."

"Then, he'll expect you there, Miss Perkins," Davies concluded, following her out of the hackney. "And he'll be distressed if I do not walk you to your door." He paused a moment, his face going remarkably red under the street lamp, as he extended his arm to her. With a smile, she took it.

The door opened before he could knock, and there was Mama, white-faced and with a tic in her eye. Before Lydia could say anything, Mama grabbed her arm and pulled her inside. "Mama, please don't!" she began, mortified that the corporal was witnessing this. There was no chance to explain, because here was Kitty now, in tears, holding out her hairbrush and a ribbon.

"Lydia, this is the worst thing! You know I depend on you to fix my hair just so. How could you stay in that dreadful place so long, and with those uncouth people?" Kitty noticed the corporal then, shrieked, and leaped back. "One of them followed you home!"

"I am 'er escort," Corporal Davies said, his voice stubborn as he edged his way into the entrance hallway. "I had orders to get her home, since none of you thought to retrieve her."

"Insolence! What you probably have is a mind to look over our house, steal our silver, and murder us in our beds!" Mama exclaimed. "Leave immediately, or I will summon the Watch!"

"Mama!" Lydia pleaded, tugging on her arm as she started for the corporal. "He brought me home. That is all!"

"Then, he can leave immediately," Mama said. "Daughter, he stinks!"

Lydia broke free of her grasp and hurried to the corporal, who was staring at the scene before him, his hand to his eye again. "Please forgive them," she whispered as she took his arm and led him to the door again. "If it is any consolation, I am truly mortified, Corporal Davies."

The corporal nodded to her and took a wide step around the butler, who held the door open. He turned to look at Lady Luisa. "Better it 'twas me brought Miss Perkins home than t' major," he told her in a loud voice. "He'd of yanked her right out again, and probably wonder why on God's earth we fought so hard for t' likes of you." He backed down the steps and smiled at Lydia. "See you tomorrow, Miss Perkins. Mind that you be there."

"But I …."

"Ta now."

The butler closed the door before Mama grabbed her again, shaking her so hard that the pins fell from her hair, all the while demanding to know what she had been doing, and reminding her in a voice loud enough to summon Papa from his library (to which he then promptly retreated), that she was a careless, thoughtless daughter who should have been left behind in Devon. Lydia knew better than to offer an explanation until Mama was through, breathing heavily and dabbing at her forehead and bosom, as though she had run a great footrace. Lydia stood, white-faced and trembling, her hands held tight together, suffering deep in her heart not so much from her treatment, but from the humiliation that someone else had witnessed it.

"They needed me, Mama," she said finally. "Didn't you send us there to be of use?" It was the wrong approach. Mama leaped to her feet again and slapped her. "You slow wit, I sent you there for Kitty to see and be seen!" she shouted. "Dearest Kitty succeeded, but look at you! Your dress is dirty … my God, are those *bloodstains*? Don't you even care what bloodstains do to fabric? I trust you do not think for one moment I will replace that dress!" She threw herself into a chair again. "But, then, you never think, do you, Lydia?"

She patted her heart, and Lydia sighed, dreading the inevitable conclusion of Mama's fury. "And now my heart is leaping about in my chest. You will bring me to an early grave, Lydia, and I leave it to a heavenly tribunal to sort out your punishment in the world to come."

My hands will be clean, indeed, Lydia thought with sudden bitterness that threatened to make her cry. Finish it, Mama. Humiliate me some more and threaten me with God.

"My hands will be clean, indeed," Mama finished with her usual flourish.

It was over, but Lydia knew better than to give any indication of her own relief. She stood there, head bowed, hands still tight together, until Kitty held out the brush and hair ribbon, her lower lip trembling as though she had just received the verbal beating. "Sister, you know I need you to fix my hair! Why else were you brought along?"

Lydia looked at her, and then at her mother. "I did wonder why," she said. "Did either of you ever give a thought that *I* might make an eligible alliance in London?"

Mama gasped, and then began to laugh, which was worse to Lydia's ears than all the shouts and tumult. She laughed until she had to grasp her sides to remain upright in her chair. She tried to speak, then started to laugh again.

Lydia watched her. Beat me, Mama, she thought as she winked back tears. It would hurt less. She looked at her sister. "Come, Kitty, let me fix your hair," she said calmly. "I did not know you were going somewhere tonight."

They climbed the stairs together, Kitty's lovely face alive with animation now. "Lyddy, those two gentlemen who brought me home and their sisters have invited me … me! … to accompany them to Drury Lane tonight!" She touched Lydia's hand. "I do not know when I have used a faint to better purpose! It was graceful, too, wasn't it? Did you see?"

"Yes, Kitty, it was graceful," Lydia said. "Thank goodness something profitable came of your visit of charity to those stinking, wicked men."

"That's how I feel, too," Kitty said happily. She made a face. "I cannot see what possessed you to remain a moment longer than necessary, and whatever were you thinking of, to ruin your dress?"

"I can't imagine," Lydia said. She sat Kitty down at the stool in front of her dressing table.

"Next to your looks, that is your biggest problem, Lyddy

dear," Kitty said as she smiled at her reflection. "You have no imagination. You never would have thought to faint, would you?"

Of course not, Lydia thought. I was too busy taking care of a dying man. Her hands were rock steady as she combed her sister's hair.

"I thought not, Lyddy," Kitty said as she raised her chin and turned her face to this side, and then that. "Tell me, sister, which is my best side? I need to know, so I can claim the chair that shows me to best advantage."

"I rather think one is like the other," Lydia said.

"No, silly! I have studied this matter for hours in front of the mirror, and can reach no conclusion." She looked at Lydia in the mirror, her eyes anxious.

I have spent an afternoon watching a man die, and you want to know which side of your pretty face is the prettiest? Lydia thought. No wonder I am so tired. "It is your right side, Kitty," she said finally as she pulled back her sister's mass of shining gold curls and anchored it expertly with pins and ribbon. "I am certain of it."

Kitty turned her head so her right profile showed. After a moment's earnest concentration, she smiled at herself in the mirror. "You are right!" She leaped up and kissed Lydia. "Oh, this is *such* a weight off my mind!"

KITTY LEFT AN HOUR later in the company of the young gentlemen and ladies who had braved the rough society of Wellington's soldiers to spread about a little hypocrisy as their patriotic duty. From her accustomed spot at the top of the stairs, Lydia watched them go. Mama had made no mention of dinner, and she did not wish to press the issue. Lydia returned to her room, tired right down to her toes.

She stood at the window for a long moment, trying to get up the energy to remove her dress. She closed the draperies finally, wishing that when she opened them, the view would be foggy Devon. "Or Northumberland," she said suddenly. "Laying aside damp sheets and too much oatmeal, I imagine you will be glad to get home to clean air, and nothing more dangerous than Highlands cattle on your hills, Major Reed!"

It is something to look forward to, she thought as she unbuttoned her dress and stepped out of it. There were few pins in her hair; Mama had shaken most of them loose downstairs. She sat on her bed and brushed her hair, long and brown, but just brown, as her eyes were just brown, and the sprinkling of freckles on her nose just brown and irredeemable of removal. And my mouth is too wide, and my cheekbones have no character, and my forehead is too high. She brushed harder. But how fortunate I am to have Mama and Kitty to point out all my failings, she thought. Thanks to them, I have never been compelled to devote hours to mirror gazing, like poor Kitty.

Her hands were shapely, she knew, and there was nothing really wrong with her figure, beyond a tendency to overgenerosity through the bosom, which was not at all fashionable these days. My bosom was à la mode three hundred years ago, she thought with a smile. Raphael would have loved to paint me, if he could have overlooked an ordinary face. And why not? Everyone else does.

The bed was cold, but she climbed into it with a sigh, grateful she had no wounds that stank and throbbed, and no one to worry about except herself. And nothing to look forward to, she considered again as she closed her eyes. Unlike you, Major Reed. She sighed and turned over, seeking warmth where there was none. I cannot even return to St. Barnabas tomorrow to see how you are doing.

I wish I had the courage to just leave the house tomorrow morning and return to that church, she thought, then put it from her mind. Lydia, you have wished and wished for things all your life, but you have forgotten the most important wish of all, she told herself: You need to wish for a braver heart.

3

∽

SHE DREAMED OF PICTON'S Own Battery, all one-legged, one-armed, and one-eyed men in dirty uniforms hauling their guns back and forth down Holly Street, aiming and firing upon passersby. The pounding of the guns was relentless, even when she put her pillow over her head to mute the sound.

When it wouldn't go away, she opened her eyes and removed the pillow. Someone was pounding on her door. How singular, she thought. Can it be that Kitty has somewhere to go before …. She raised her head and stared at the clock beside her bed … *nine* in the morning? It cannot be. The world will end first.

"Just a moment," she called as she reached for her robe. Her slippers were nowhere in sight, so she padded barefoot to her door and opened it, then stepped back in amazement.

Her first thought was that Birnam Wood must have come to Dunsinane, except that these were flowers, beautiful flowers, more flowers than she had ever seen in one container—roses, daisies, lilies of the valley, heliotrope, violets tucked here and there, and most impressive irises. It was a conglomeration of an English garden, and she stared in stupefaction, and then delight.

"Oh, do bring them in, Mackles. Mackles?" she asked, unable to see who carried them.

The footman staggered forward and deposited his burden on the table by the window. "These are for me?" she gasped, walking around the enormous bouquet, rearranging a flower here, touching a fern there. She breathed in the conglomeration of fragrances, marveling that the total accumulation could smell so wonderful.

"No one else, Miss Perkins," the footman said. "Begging your pardon, miss, but I wanted to bring them here before …." He coughed politely. "Well, Miss Kitty might assume they were hers." He scratched his head. "I disremember when Miss Kitty had such an offering. Miss Perkins, you must have a real admirer!"

"I can't imagine who it would be," she replied honestly. "I hope there is a note. We'll probably discover that these were intended for another house."

There was a note. It was anchored in the ribbon and hidden by a fairy fern. She broke the seal and spread out the note as Mama, her eyes wide, charged into the room and plumped herself down.

"Surely these are for Kitty," Mama said.

Lydia read the note, shaking her head in amazement. "No, Mama, they are mine." She read the note out loud. " 'My Dear Miss Perkins, The men and I of Battery B wanted you to know of our gratitude for the kind service you rendered yesterday. Angels are notoriously hard to find, but you were there. Regards, etc., Major Samuel E.H. Reed, Lord Laren of Laren Hall, Northumberland, Battery B Commanding, Third Division.' He has good handwriting, Mama." She handed the note to her mother. "I am amazed."

Her mother snatched the note from her hand and read it again, her lips moving. " 'Pon my word!" she exclaimed, then read it again. "Lord Laren?" she asked.

"I believe he is an earl, Mama, although you would be hard

put to believe it," she said. "You never saw a more scraggly haired, shabby fellow."

"I am astounded," Mama said as she walked around the flowery tribute, too.

So you are astounded, Mama, Lydia thought with amusement. Here Kitty has flirted on the fringes with baronets and second sons, while an earl sends me flowers. I wonder ....

The footman, who had left the room, returned with another announcement. "Lady Perkins, there is a second bouquet in the drawing room, and it is addressed to you."

Lydia looked at her mother, barely able to contain her delight. I think I am in the hands of a thoroughgoing rascal, she thought, if that note downstairs says what I think it will. No wonder Wellington triumphed in the Peninsula; the men he leads are positively unscrupulous.

"Do let us go downstairs, Mama, and see what we find," she said. She descended the stairs calmly as Mama thundered ahead, her wrap billowing around her like a topsail. Lydia paused at the foot of the stairs as Mama, shrieking now, ran into the entranceway, suddenly rendered far less shabby by a majestic bouquet of the reddest roses Lydia could remember.

Mama fumbled at the note lying beside the roses, finally handing it to Lydia. "Open this!" she demanded. "I vow I am all aflutter!"

At least *I* am not giving you heart palpitations, Lydia thought as she picked up one of her hairpins still lying on the floor from last night's encounter, and slit open the note. She handed it to her mother, who read it, her eyes growing wider and wider. "Daughter!" she exclaimed. "This is amazing!"

"Do read the note, Mama," Lydia said.

Mama read it out loud, her voice trembling. "'My dear Lady Luisa, You are to be congratulated on the rearing of a daughter as kind and useful as Miss Perkins. One rarely meets a parent who is so willing to sacrifice a daughter for a day of philanthropy among those who serve their country. You should be praised for your sagacity. If only I had the words to tell you what I truly think of you. Regards, etc., Major Samuel E.H. Reed, Lord Laren of Laren Hall, Northumberland, Battery B Commanding, Third Division.'" Mama sank into a chair. "Daughter, I doubt there is a single rose left in any flower shop in London." She stared at Lydia, unable to say more.

I can play this right, Lydia thought suddenly as she watched the amazement in Mama's face. She picked up the rest of her hairpins from the floor until she felt sufficiently calm to look at her mother again. Keep your voice normal, Lydia, she cautioned herself. Choose your words carefully. Major Reed has given you a toss into the saddle, if you use it right. An offhand disinterested tone would be best about now.

"Do you know, Mama, it is a pity that you forbade me to return to St. Barnabas." She sighed, with what she thought was a rather good imitation of Kitty. "Ah, well. Major Reed will manage without me, as you so helpfully pointed out last night. Excuse me, Mama. I should dress, shouldn't I?"

She went upstairs quietly, leaving Mama to stare at the flowers and then the note again. This could come to nothing, she thought as she dressed quickly. Mama is not easily led. Lydia looked at her bouquet again, breathing in the fragrance so riotous and exquisite at the same time. But I doubt that even Mama has ever met someone as determined as Major Reed. She smiled. Quite possibly he gets his way even more frequently than Kitty. I shall have to ask him, provided I see him again, and he is in the right mood.

Mama was nowhere in evidence when Lydia came downstairs again. The breakfast room was empty, except for the butler, who poured her tea. The twinkle in his eyes was most pronounced, telling her without words that the tale of the early morning flowers had spread from below stairs to the attic.

"Stanton, did you see my flowers, and Mama's?" she asked as she helped herself to eggs and bacon.

"It would be hard to miss them, Miss Perkins," he replied.

The door opened then, and admitted her father. He took a cautious peek around the door before he entered the room. Seeing only her, he sighed and came in, making himself small in his chair and allowing Stanton to pour tea. After one cautious sip and then another, he relaxed.

"Papa, did you see the flowers?"

He smiled and nodded. "Do you have an extravagant admirer, Lydia?"

"No, Papa, just a poor, wounded veteran I was trying to help at St. Barnabas yesterday," she replied, passing him the eggs. "I think he was delirious."

Papa shook his head. "Men don't send flowers when they are delirious, daughter. Do have a care." He spooned eggs on his plate. "Of course, your poor mother is even now sneezing from the effects of the flowers. Such a pity," he said, sounding anything but sad.

Lydia made some appropriate comment, hardly daring to look at her parent. I shall go into whoops over Papa's sympathy, she thought. She took a few bites of egg, a drink of tea, then regarded her father. "Tell me, Papa, would it bother you if I returned to St. Barnabas?"

Startled to be addressed, he nearly spilled his tea. "Lydia, you know your mother's views on the subject." He looked down at the cup. "She was amply clear last night."

"I know, Papa, I know," Lydia said. "But how do *you* feel about it?"

As he looked around to see if anyone could overhear him, she burned inside with embarrassment for him. Oh, Papa, when did you get this way? she thought. I remember a time before Kitty was born when you played with me in the evenings and we laughed together. Was I suddenly too plain when Kitty came along?

"I won't do anything against Mama's wishes, if that is what concerns you," she assured him when the silence stretched out.

"I just wondered what you thought."

With considerable effort, as though he were hiding behind it, Papa set down his teacup. "It has been so long since someone asked my opinion on something, daughter," he said, his tone apologetic.

She looked at him, afraid to say more for fear that he would bolt from the breakfast room. With a start, it occurred to her that no one ever asked her opinion on any subject, either. Papa, you are no advocate, and someone who folds in the slightest breeze, she thought, but so am I. She put her hand over his. "Don't worry, Papa," she said finally.

"Actually, I have an opinion," he said, to her surprise. "I … I think you should return to St. Barnabas if you choose." He looked around again, as if the wall covering were listening, and leaned closer to her. "You are twenty-two, after all, and ought to know your own mind."

She beamed at him as he leaned back in his chair, exhausted, apparently, with the strain of decision. "Thank you, Papa," she said.

"You won't tell your mother?" he asked, his voice anxious.

She shook her head. "Never."

They ate in silence, Papa still unnerved by his radical disclosure, and Lydia saddened almost to tears. At least you have a library to hide in, Papa, she thought. I must be at Kitty's constant disposal, and there is always Mama to tell me my failings, should I ever forget them. She looked out the window, beyond the view. And I do not see an end in sight for me or you.

She finished the eggs on her plate, only because Mama hated waste in everyone except Kitty, then pushed back her chair. There was a pile of mending—most of it Kitty's—she had been avoiding for weeks. Obviously even Major Reed's extravagant gift of flowers had been insufficient temptation to induce Mama to change her mind.

She was rising to leave the breakfast room when the door

opened. From habit, Papa flinched, but Lydia stood where she was, her hand on the chair. Stanton entered the room first, the twinkle in his eyes even more pronounced, even though his expression was impassive as always.

"Sir Humphrey and Miss Perkins: General Thomas Picton."

"Third Division!" the little man exclaimed, with a voice strong enough to wake the dead. "Sam said I was to fetch a fine-looking woman with a serene expression." He nodded to her. "Must be you. Nobody else looks serene. Get your bonnet."

It is rude to stare, Lydia thought as she closed her mouth and dropped a small curtsy. *This* is General Picton? This little man in the indescribable coat and trousers who has not removed his top hat? She peered closer at the hat. I wonder if he cleans out stables with it, she thought. He was dressed in faded black with a military cut, and a waistcoat so loud it could only be Spanish. His face was that same mahogany as Major Reed's under his hospital pallor, as though he was too long in the sun. There was no sign of any insignia beyond an extravagant star burst of a medal pinned lopsided to his coat that looked too garish to be English. He was barrel-chested, his posture was impeccable, and he looked every inch a general, in his own strange way.

"I am Lydia Perkins," she managed, then indicated her father, who had risen as though pulled by strings. "This is my father Sir Humphrey. I am supposed to come with you?"

The general nodded. "Those were the terms." He looked at the table, and Lydia smiled. "General, would you like some breakfast?"

"I would." He sat in the chair that Stanton pulled out for him, whisked a napkin onto his lap, and helped himself to the eggs.

"Oh, I can have those warmed up for you, sir," Lydia said as she reached for the bowl.

He held it out of her grasp. "A word to the wise, Miss Perkins," he said in that staccato way of his as he spooned a liberal helping of cold eggs onto his plate. "Never take food from a soldier. I don't give a rat's ass if it is cold. With enough horseradish, I could eat a Cossack three days dead."

Lydia blinked in surprise. The general appeared not to notice his own vulgarity, nodding when Stanton held out toast and cold bacon at arm's length. He ate quickly, with a certain economy of motion that marked him as a soldier. Lydia spared him any small talk; she could not think of a thing they had in common, beyond a minuscule acquaintance with Major Sam Reed on her part.

She had never confessed to Papa, but she knew of General Picton's exploits in the Peninsula. When the war was at its height, Stanton had allowed her to look at the newspaper when Papa had finished with it. Like most of England, she had thrilled to Picton's exploits at Badajoz, Talavera, Vitoria, and most especially at Ciudad Rodrigo.

He finished breakfast in the silent room, then leaned back in his chair. "Glad you're not one of those damned chattering magpies that blight the English landscape," he said to her. "You even look like a woman of sense. Well, get your bonnet, Miss Perkins."

"But my mother …." she began, then stopped when the door opened and Mama entered. "She preferred that I not return. General Picton, this is my mother. Lady Luisa Perkins." He was on his feet in a moment to give her hand a hearty shake, and fix her with that narrow-eyed stare that must have discommoded many a subaltern. "Madam, she'll be in my charge today. You must be thrilled beyond belief to have a useful daughter. Come, Miss Perkins. An agreement is an agreement, and I require your presence."

Mama stared, openmouthed. "I do not recall that I gave …."

"Permission?" the general interrupted. "I knew that you would, madam, considering your great generosity and foresight in allowing Miss Perkins here to visit the sick and wounded yesterday," he said briskly. "Miss Perkins, do go fetch your bonnet. I will await you in the carriage. Sir Humphrey and Lady Luisa, I will see that she is deposited back here this evening without fail."

Never removing that dreadful top hat, General Picton bowed to them and left the room almost as fast as he had entered it. Mama stepped into the hall for another look, as though she wondered if he were a phantom.

Holding her breath, Lydia tiptoed to the door, then looked back in amazement to watch Mama stagger to a chair and plop herself into it without comment. Better and better, Lydia thought as she hurried upstairs to locate her bonnet and to exchange her primrose muslin for something dark and useful-looking. A quick trip down the backstairs took her to the kitchen for advice from Stanton, an apron from Cook, and a handkerchief drenched in lavender water from the housekeeper. "For when you can't stand those smelly soldiers," she explained, pressing the cloth into her hand.

The apron over her arm, and her bonnet already dangling by its strings down her back, she hurried down the hall again, pausing long enough for another deep sniff of Mama's roses.

"Daughter."

She paused, her hand on the doorknob at the sound of Mama's voice. Don't stop me, Mama, she thought. General Picton will probably lay siege to the house, and you will blame me if Kitty's callers are stopped, searched, and turned away.

Mama came into the hall. "Mind that you do not bring home any nasty contagions that will cut up Kitty's peace."

"I wouldn't dream of it. Mama," she replied, tugging up her bonnet. "I'll even try to keep myself healthy."

They traveled most of the way in silence, General Picton looking out the window, and Lydia uncertain how to engage him in conversation. If I tell him how I have followed his division's career from Talavera to Toulouse, he will think I am a shocking female, she considered, and decided that silence was prudent.

Just as they pulled up in front of St. Barnabas, she gathered together enough courage to voice the question on her mind. "General, you said that this was part of an agreement between you and Major Reed," she said. "I do not understand."

The general smiled for the first time. "Miss Perkins, Sam Reed is much too used to getting his own way. He is also stubborn, and completely unconcerned about proper channels and protocol. His paperwork is probably the worst in any army since the days of clay tablets. He will lie, cheat, and steal for his battery and barely follows orders. I never met an officer— and an earl, too, I might add—with less sense of his own importance. It is a source of continual amazement to me that anyone would follow him to the latrine, much less into battle." He paused and drew a deep breath.

"Then, I wonder that you would help him," she said.

"I will tell you why. Having listed all his failings, I can state without perjuring myself that he is the bravest, most innovative officer I command, and I have owed my life to him on more than one or two occasions." He leaned toward her confidentially. "Naturally, I would never tell him that. No sense in ruining a man."

She smiled. "A little praise never hurt a body, sir."

"Damned if I intend to start now, Miss Perkins!" the general said.

"He is most tenacious, it seems, with the idea of seeing his men placed well before he leaves them to convalesce himself," she said, prepared to overlook his profanity.

"And that is what chaps my balls, Miss Perkins," he said as the footman opened the carriage door and lowered the step. The general descended first, and held his hand out for her. "If he does not quit pestering Horse Guards with his damned requests, *I* will be in more trouble than I care to be!"

He held out his arm to her, but she stood off for a moment. "General, what is this deal you have made with the major? Perhaps I should know before I go inside."

"You won't like it," he murmured.

"I'm sure I won't," she agreed.

"I extracted a promise from him to stay in bed, if I would find a way to fetch you from Holly Street." He took her arm then. "He did mention that your parents were less than in charity with the idea."

She nodded, wincing to think of what Corporal Davies must have reported to the major after his return from her house last night. "I am glad that he finds me useful," she said.

"Or something," the general said, with a smile of his own.

They went up the stairs. She took a deep breath before entering the chapel, and let it out slowly, looking around. To her surprise, there were other women moving between the rows this morning, but they wore aprons and appeared to have a purpose, unlike the fashionable fribbles she had accompanied yesterday. And she noticed again, as she had noticed yesterday, that despite the great suffering, horrible smells, and dismal conditions, there was order.

"My division surgeon over there will tell you what he wants you to do," Picton said, gesturing toward the surgeon she remembered from yesterday. "But I suppose I had better fulfill my agreement by taking you to Major Reed first."

"Are you afraid that he will jump out of bed and break his promise if you do not, considering how insubordinate you say he is?" she teased.

"That will not happen, ma'am," Picton replied, the picture of assurance. "I took into account my experiences with his usual creativity and had Corporal Davies hide the major's trousers and drawers!"

She laughed out loud, noticing as she did so that the sound of her laughter brought smiles to the faces of the wounded who were able to respond. General Picton noticed it, too.

"By God, we soldiers like a woman's hearty laugh," he said as he released her arm to edge his way down the narrow aisle of cots. "Nothing makes my bowels cramp up like a giggle from a silly chit with more tit than brain!"

Sir, you are amazing, she thought as she followed him down the row, heading toward the lady chapel. She paused while he stopped to talk to his men, cajoling one here, patting a hand there, or standing in silence, head bowed (but top hat firmly in place) as another man took his place in death. His profanity astounded her, but the men who could, only grinned.

"My boys, Goddamn them," he said simply when they reached the smaller chapel.

As they came closer, Major Reed propped himself up on his elbow to watch their progress. Lydia smiled to herself. And you, sir, intend to extract more work from me. Well, I would rather do your dirty work today than mend Kitty's flounces.

He looked so sour that she nearly laughed, but she chose instead to hold out her hand to him. "Don't get up on my account, Major Reed," she said. "Good morning, sir."

General Picton laughed. "Manners, Sam, manners! Or would you rather not display the family jewels?"

Reed pulled the blankets higher and held out his hand to Lydia. "Thank you for coming, Miss Perkins. Sir, you are unscrupulous."

"Any time, Sam, any time." The general's countenance was serene. He turned to her and bowed. "Miss Perkins, if he makes any move to rise or even reach for pen and paper, get me word, and I will break him right down to powder monkey, and turn him out in his shirt."

"Yes, sir," she said as she removed her bonnet and set it on the altar. "And where can I reach you, if this happens?"

"Why, at Horse Guards, naturally!" he said, as though surprised. "Someone has to irritate those supercilious sons of bitches who would make water if they ever had to make war." He came closer to the major and touched his arm. "Be easy, laddie, and heal," he said, his voice almost compassionate. "It wasn't a bad bargain."

Another nod, and General Thomas Picton was gone, working his way back down another aisle. Reed shook his head. "He's a scoundrel."

"Precisely what he said about you, sir." She shook out the apron she had carried into the church and put it on, cinching it firmly at her waist. "Now, then, Major, since you purchased probably every flower in London and worked a great scheme on my mother, what will you have me do?"

"Were they pretty?" he asked as he struggled to sit up.

She took him by the arm to help. "I never had flowers before."

He stared at her. "I find that hard to believe."

"It's true," she allowed, dabbing at the sweat on his face from the simple exertion of sitting up. "Unlike you—according to General Picton—I never lie, cheat, or steal."

The major flinched. "If I could have sent someone else to retrieve you, I would have! A man has no secrets with Picton. Sit down a moment, Miss Perkins." He moved his legs. "No, right here, please."

Of course it was not proper, but the nearest stool was occupied by a soldier in the middle of a dressing change. "Very well, sir," she said as she sat on his cot and folded her hands in her lap.

She had not been this close to him before, and the morning light that streamed in through the clerestory windows showed her a fine-looking man, despite his ragged hair, whiskery chin, and hospital pallor. His hair was a marvelous chestnut color and his eyes brown like her own. His nose was almost too straight and gave him a severe appearance intensified by his thin lips. His cheeks were on the thin side, too, and she couldn't decide if that was due to his hospital stay or the unreliability of meals in Wellington's army. He had the look of a man who would fill out nicely, once he had the opportunity to put his legs under his own table again.

He wore a nightshirt that looked soft with many washings. He sat leaning forward to take the strain off his back, his knees up, his arms draped gracefully over his knees. What wonderful hands, she thought, with long fingers and veins that looked almost chiseled. Too bad his fingers were discolored.

The major noticed the direction of her gaze, and held out a hand to her, palm up. "I have played so many years with gunpowder that it is engraved upon me, Miss Perkins. I suppose it will wear off someday." He wiggled his fingers. "At least they're all present and accounted for. I've been a lucky son of the guns."

"Luck or skill, sir?" she asked. "General Picton mentioned your ability."

He made a face, tried to sit up straighter, then leaned forward again. "I'm sorry to subject you to his company for a prolonged interval, but he owes me favors, and I knew that he could accomplish my goal."

"Your goal?" she asked.

He looked her right in the eyes, his glance never wavering. "The goal of getting you out of that house and back here to work, Miss Perkins."

She looked away in embarrassment. "I cannot imagine what Corporal Davies told you."

"He said it was not a pretty sight." He touched her arm. "I blame myself. I apologize for keeping you so long here yesterday. I am sorry they were so angry, and took it out on you."

"No one compelled me to stay, sir," she replied, her voice equally quiet. "It was the first time in my life that I felt useful." She paused. I should say nothing more. I do not know this man. She looked at him, and under the whiskers, the hair, the pain, the pallor, was an expression so kind that it compelled her to continue, even before she was aware of it. "I was doing something for myself, instead of fetching and mending for Kitty, or staying away from Mama's tongue," she explained. "It ... it was nice to be wanted and needed, even if only for an afternoon." How bald that sounds, she thought, horrified with herself. And to think I just said it to a total stranger.

The major was silent, and she knew she had overstepped her bounds. Perhaps Mama is right, she thought as she got up from his cot. Perhaps I am a stupid and gawky woman who will always be a burden and an embarrassment to her family.

"I'm sorry, Major Reed," she said, not able to look him in the eyes. "Mama tells me every day that I am a trial. Tell me what it is you wish me to do, and I'll leave you in peace."

"I *am* in peace, Miss Perkins," he said quickly. "You're no trial. You could sit here all day and talk to me, but that would irritate my men, who have taken rather a fancy to you."

"To me?" she asked in amazement.

"If I am to believe their comments, Miss Perkins. I propose that you wash their faces and shave them. We're all tired of being dirty. It will be as good as medicine. And if you were to talk to them, too. Ah, bliss."

"But … but I've never …." She stopped. He gives me something to do, and I am a pain about it.

"Shaved a man? Talked to one? My dear, you may practice on me." He glanced toward the altar, and she noticed a shabby campaign trunk with the initials SER. "My kit finally arrived. Heaven knows where it was."

"What does the E stand for?" she asked without thinking.

"Elliott. Open it, Miss Perkins. You will find my shaving gear in a leather bag. If you will overlook the quantity of dirty laundry, I will overlook your supremely silly relatives."

She frowned at him, and he gazed back with a virtuous expression. "You do not know them, sir. How can you say they are silly?"

"Anyone who thinks you are a trial is silly," he declared. "Orderly! Bring us some hot water. Miss Perkins, I am yours to practice upon. If I should begin to bleed, do staunch it. I haven't come this far to perish at the hands of a pretty barber."

4

⁓

"MAJOR, I AM FAR from pretty," she told him as she went to his campaign trunk, kneeling down to open it.

"That's true," he agreed, "but if I said you were beautiful …."

"… that would be a bigger falsehood," she interrupted, lifting up a layer of shirts stained with sweat and gunpowder.

He laughed, and she looked at him in surprise. "My men think you are an angel, and protestations aside, I did hear the word beautiful once or twice."

"They were delirious," she retorted.

"Not noticeably," he replied. "I've always considered them to be observant and factual, but then, I have only known them through six years of close company."

How odd, she thought, not daring to make another comment. She found the shaving kit under a handful of letters, plus a bottle of Spanish cologne.

"Oh, that, too," he said. "I'll smell divine."

She smiled at him. "Perhaps."

"Miss Perkins, there is a rumor that an attempt is being made to locate tin tubs from somewhere. If that is the case, then the whole lot of us will be much more pleasant."

She brought the shaving kit and cologne to the major's cot. "You are an officer. Can you not find better accommodations than this wretched old church?"

"I can," he agreed, "except for this one, niggling detail. My dear, I have shared the vicissitudes of war with my battery. We have slept together under caissons, drunk bloody water from empty shells, and eaten our own tired horses. I cannot leave them until they are settled."

She looked around the lady chapel, which was not crowded with officers. "Others can, it appears," she murmured.

He handed her his shaving soap and brush, and a pair of scissors. "I am not other officers."

She could readily believe it. "Now, sir, I think we need a towel."

"None in sight. I used my last one at Toulouse on my poor gunnery sergeant. You recall him from yesterday, I believe."

She did. "Then, I will use one of your old shirts." She rummaged in his trunk again and found one with frilly cuffs that had no powder ground into it. She tied it carefully around his neck. "I think you will have to sit straighter, if you can, sir," she said. "A chair would be best, but we have none."

"And besides that, you would have to endure the sight of my hairy legs, and other accessories," he said as he stropped his razor. "You may blame General Picton."

Is there anything you won't say? she thought in embarrassment. "We will manage," she said when she composed herself. She smiled her thanks to the orderly who brought hot water in a basin, secretly enjoying the way he blushed and stumbled over his feet when he hurried from the lady chapel. "Now, sir?"

With the scissors, she cut his weeks-old beard, then lathered his face and set to work. He did not bleed, beyond a nick beside his nose that she stopped with a bit of cotton wadding. She grazed a small mole she did not see at his temple hairline, and he only commented that his regular barber—dead at

Toulouse—used to do that all the time.

He had to remind her once or twice that she needed to carry on some conversation, particularly since he was supposed to hold his face still. After several starts and stops, she told him about home in Devon, and their trip to London to find a suitable husband for Kitty, who was beautiful beyond words and entirely too gorgeous to waste on a red-faced, paunchy squire, or a mere vicar. She had never talked so much before, and she knew she was telling more than Mama would approve of, but for some reason unknown to her, she knew he did not mind. Nor would he store it up to pass it on. How do I know that? she asked herself. I just know it.

"Mama says if I am lucky, I might find a vicar, or perhaps a widower who is not too choosy," she said as she concentrated on that spot beside the major's mouth, where he had, drat it all, another mole. "Oh, do hold still," she ordered as she navigated the razor around the obstacle. "I do not know why you are so grim about the mouth. My job would be less onerous if you would relax. I have not killed you yet."

"Perhaps it is because I do not precisely understand why your mother has such a low opinion of you, my dear," he said, then tilted his head so she had a better view of the problem mole.

'Thank you. Sir, I am not beautiful enough for Mama to bother with," she concluded in a matter-of-fact voice, then stepped back. "I believe you are done, Major." She wiped the soap off his face, admiring her handiwork.

To her amazement, she heard applause behind her and whirled around to see all of the major's men who could walk standing or sitting at the entrance to the lady chapel. She blushed and frowned at Major Reed. "Sir! You could see them! Why did you not mention that my first-ever barbering had an audience?"

"Perhaps I wanted witnesses, in case you slit my throat, Miss Perkins! Well, lads, will I do?"

They cheered this time, which brought over the surgeon and one of the aproned matrons, who shooed them back to their cots. "You're next, lads," he called after them. "Mind you, behave yourselves!"

She laughed and cleaned his razor, then handed it back for him to strop again. He obliged her, then ran his hand over his face and sighed with contentment, to her amusement. "I am amazed what a difference this makes in my outlook. Anything is possible now. Perhaps I will even be able to walk upright soon, and not drag my knuckles like an ape."

"You will if you stay in bed and mind yourself," Lydia admonished him. She was still smiling as she patted his face with cologne, an overpowering lemon fragrance that no Englishman except a soldier would wear, and even then only on a foreign shore.

He sniffed it. "Better and better, Miss Perkins. I almost cannot smell myself now. Let us devoutly pray that the tin tub rumor is true, or I'll be out of my stash of Limon de Aranjuez much too soon, and you will run in terror."

"You may be out of it sooner than you think, sir," she replied as she stoppered the bottle. "I intend to use it on your men, too."

"Madam, it is two quid a bottle!" he protested.

"Thank goodness that you get a major's pay," she declared as she held it out of his reach and gathered up his shaving gear. "Now, take a nap and behave yourself."

There were ten wounded men in Battery B, and she took her time with each one, shaving him, and chatting such endless trivialities that she knew she was related to Kitty. The ones who were too broken to shave, she sat with, holding their hands if they had hands, or just resting her own hand on their chests when they did not. She knew she was boring them with her homely stories of Devon and the seashore, but no one objected. When she finished with Battery B's wounded, she continued down the next row, tending to the shattered men as best she could.

Other women were doing what she did, working quietly among the rows. She wondered at their serenity, then discovered late in the afternoon when her back hurt so much from bending over that she wanted to cry, that it was her serenity, too. She decided that it was a day's work to be proud of. "I have learned a trade," she teased when Corporal Davies came to find her. "Where have you been?"

"Finding tubs."

"And pine tar soap and fine-tooth combs, I trust," spoke up one of the other ladies. "There's not a man here who isn't lousy."

That gives me pause, Lydia thought as she returned to the lady chapel. If I bring home lice, Mama will not be placated, even if Major Reed were to buy every flower in Europe, Asia, and South America. The thought made her smile, where yesterday she would have trembled in fear.

Major Reed was asleep, so she tiptoed to his campaign trunk and replaced his much-used razor. The cologne was gone; perhaps he had another bottle. She looked inside the trunk, moving aside the letters, but could not find one.

Curious, she picked up a letter. I am such a snoop, she thought as she looked at the direction on one envelope. "Lord and Lady Laren, Major Sam Reed, Third Division, Battery B," she read to herself. This is odd, indeed, she reflected. Corporal Davies tells me yesterday that the major is not married, and yet here is a letter to the happy couple. How singular. One would not think him to be so absentminded as to forget a wife.

The thought made her smile. She looked at the major, who lay on his side, breathing steadily. He's not a handsome man, but he should show to better advantage with a haircut, she decided. She went closer. The afternoon sun was almost gone now, and the lady chapel was chilly again. She raised the blanket higher to cover his shoulders.

He opened his eyes, then yawned. "Well, are you a proficient barber by now, madam?" he asked, his voice thick with sleep.

"I am, sir, thanks to you. If I find myself a burden to my

parents, I shall strike out on my own and open an emporium."

He laughed and closed his eyes again. "You'll return tomorrow?" he asked.

"With scissors and comb," she assured him. "I already fancy myself good at cutting Kitty's hair, so you have merely to tell me how to arrange your ringlets, and whether that mass at the back of your neck would look better in a chignon or a top knot."

He opened his eyes in sudden alarm, then laughed. "You'll cut it army-straight, Miss Perkins! I'll send Corporal Davies in a carriage with you now. Lord knows, he's not as colorful as General Picton ...." His voice trailed off, and he was asleep again.

And that is precisely what you need, she thought as she took her leave with Corporal Davies. Some of Cook's good beef tea would be just the thing, Lydia considered as she sank with relief into the hackney, too tired to remove her stained apron. I wonder if I can wheedle her out of a gallon or two?

Lydia woke up when the hackney stopped in front of the house on Holly Street, and discovered that she had been leaning against Corporal Davies. "Do excuse my ramshackle manners!" she said. She reached up to straighten her bonnet, and realized to her dismay that she had left it behind on the altar in the lady chapel. "I cannot imagine what you must think of me," she said as the jehu opened the door to the hackney.

"I think you have made me the envy of Battery B, Miss Perkins," the corporal replied as he helped her down. "Do you know, for five quid, Corporal Jenkins offered to take my place!"

She gasped. "That is a lot of money!"

"Wasn't enough, though, was it?" he said with a smile. "I'll be by in the morning, Miss Perkins, provided that Jenkins doesn't mill me down and black my only eye."

Oh, heavens, she thought as she knocked on the door. Soldiers are certainly a breed apart. She looked back at the hackney, which was turning the corner. "I only hope I did not snore," she murmured.

Stanton let her into the house, a finger to his lips. "Miss Kitty is prostrated with anxiety because the flounce is not repaired on the dress she is wearing tonight to Almack's, and Lady Luisa is with her," he said.

"Oh, the flounce!" she exclaimed. "I was supposed to mend that this morning, wasn't I?" And now Kitty is in agonies, seeing her life slip away at eighteen, all because of a simple flounce that she could repair herself, Lydia thought. Of course, this is not to mention the other ball dresses she could wear instead. Lydia shook her head and went quietly up the stairs.

The dress was still draped across her bed, where she had left it that morning. Humming to herself, she removed her stained apron, scrubbed her hands and face until they hurt, then sat down with the dress and her sewing basket.

Usually she hated Kitty's mending, mainly because her sister was so careless with her clothing, but also because the material was always so much more lavish than anything Mama begrudged for her. Today was different. She kicked off her shoes (noting that her usually trim ankles were swollen from so much standing), propped her feet on her bed, and applied the tiny stitches that Kitty depended on. It was relaxing this time, a refreshing change from the pain and suffering she witnessed all day.

She finished the flounce, and just sat there, fingering the lovely fabric, pleased with herself to know that she was charitable enough to hope that Kitty wore it well tonight. Her peace was ended by Mama's sudden entry into her room.

"It is done, Mama," she said, holding out the dress to her parent. I suppose you can be furious with me because I was so slow in getting to this, or angry that I was not concerned, she thought, but to her surprise, she did not care.

To her further amazement, Mama barely glanced at the dress. "Lydia, I have such news," she said.

"Kitty is engaged already?"

"I depend upon that to happen this spring, but no, that is not my news." Mama wrinkled her nose. "Lydia, you have brought the smell of that dreadful place!"

"I suppose I have, Mama," she replied. "I was shaving the soldiers today, and that necessitated close quarters. I'll have the laundress boil everything."

Mama stared at her, and inched her chair farther away. "You *touched* those men?" she asked, her voice rising to unpleasant decibels.

Lydia waited for the familiar chills to travel up and down her back at Mama's dreaded tone, but they did not. I am either too tired, or I do not care anymore, she thought.

"I cannot think of another way to shave whiskers than to touch someone's face, Mama," she said with a slight smile.

Mama put up her hands. "Lydia, too little cannot be said about what you are doing! Granted you do not possess in the slightest degree Kitty's beauty, flair, or sensibilities, but I still feel that tending the wounded is not an occupation for a lady, especially when we need you so much here."

"Mama, anyone can sew Kitty's flounce," she said. "Even Kitty."

She waited for Mama's explosion, but it did not come. If anything, her mother's expression brightened. "Daughter, you remind me again why I came here. I must thank you for this opportunity you have given Kitty."

Lydia stared in surprise, unable to think of a time in her life when Mama had thanked her for anything. "I ... I don't understand," she said.

"This afternoon we received from General Thomas and Mrs. Picton these vowels to the banquet celebrating ...." She looked down at the card she had been carrying. "... 'The victory at Toulouse of the Duke of Wellington over Napoleon Bonaparte.' " She frowned. "Daughter, when did this happen? Where is Napoleon now?"

Oh, Lord, spare me from the disinterested, Lydia thought, feeling weary again through her shoulders. "It was in the middle of April, Mama. Everyone was talking about it. Don't you remember all the church bells in Devon ringing?"

Mama closed her eyes in thought for a moment, then opened them. "Oh, I know! We were putting the finishing touches on Kitty's wardrobe and probably packing her dresses in tissue. I *knew* there was something more important to claim my attention. But tell me, where is that beast Napoleon, then?"

"Mama, he has been these two months on Elba," Lydia explained patiently.

"I hear it is a lovely place for a holiday," Mama said. "So convenient to the Aegean."

"Mediterranean, Mama, and he is in exile, not on holiday!"

Mama shrugged and stood up. "Then, Elba will soon be fashionable. Perhaps I should suggest to Kitty that when she does make a suitable alliance this spring, that they honeymoon on Elba."

"I'm certain that would be a wonderful idea, Mama," Lydia replied, thinking to herself how loud Major Reed would laugh to hear Mama. I will tell him tomorrow, and he will go into whoops, she thought.

Mama gave her a kindly smile. "Lydia, it is so pleasant when we are in agreement on something." She took the dress from Lydia's lap. "I do think, however, that you need to offer Kitty an apology for delaying this mending and sending her into spasms." She left the room, closing the door quietly behind her for a change.

I would rather pull out my fingernails one by one than apologize to Kitty, Lydia thought as she took off her dress, sniffed it, and removed it to a far corner before she lay down. She closed her eyes in exhaustion. I have had a lifetime of Kitty this, and Kitty that. I can scarcely remember a time when I have not fetched and carried for my little sister, and all because she is a beauty, and I am not.

She pressed her hands to her stomach when it began to growl, reminding herself that luncheon at St. Barnabas had been a bowl of gruel, eaten on the fly. I am hungry, and it makes me cranky, she thought. Perhaps when I have eaten, I will feel more charitable toward my own family.

To her chagrin, she discovered during dinner that her charity was finite. Famished, she ate steadily, enduring Mama's remarks about young women who eat too much and never find husbands. My waist is as small as Kitty's, she thought as she took another helping of fricassee. She glanced sideways at her sister, who was dabbling with the sole in front of her. There are soldiers who would take her leftovers without a qualm. They need more than gruel and bread to recover, and we will only throw out course after course nibbled around the edges or ignored entirely. And do you know, Kitty, she thought, I rather believe my bosom is quite as elegant as yours. She smiled.

"I do not see how you can sit there and shovel in food with both hands, and smile about it," Mama snapped.

"It was a long day, Mama, and I ate only a bowl of gruel," she explained. She looked at her mother. Now I should be silent and hang my head, but I think I shall not. "Mama, tell me, what happens to the food that we do not eat at the table?"

"It goes to the servants, of course," Mama said.

"And if they do not want it? I know they have their own meals."

Mama rang her bell vigorously to summon the footman, who was standing right behind her. She shrieked when he leaned over to remove her plate. "They throw it out!" she exclaimed, her face red.

"Mama, could I take it with me tomorrow?" She indicated the laden table. "This is the kind of food that strong men need to recover from their wounds."

The silence around the table was monumental. Papa seemed to shrink in his chair, and Kitty's eyes grew wide with disbelief, and then disdain. Mama glared at her. "I would not dream of even *you* taking table scraps to those uncouth men! Come, Kitty, it is past time to get ready for Almack's. Really, Lydia, you have tried me to the limit. If it were not for this attention from General Picton and what it can mean to Kitty, I would put you on the mail coach back to Devon!"

That was certainly a snit, Lydia thought to herself as she returned her attention to the plate before her. Say what you will about her pretensions, Mama keeps a good table. How I would like to put Battery B around it, she reflected as she finished her own dinner, and leaned over to fork the sole from Kitty's abandoned plate. Major Reed would fill out and probably look almost handsome. Poor man. He should be on his way home to Northumberland, where people probably love him, instead of worrying about his men in a moldy chapel. It seems unfair.

"Papa, have you ever been to Northumberland?" she asked suddenly as the footman cleared the table and brought in the port for her father. "Is it dreadfully cold and primitive?"

Papa poured himself a drink, looked at the decanter, then pushed it her way, to her surprise. She added a spot to her empty glass.

"I was there once," he replied. "It was the summer I spent in Edinburgh. It is wild country, daughter. Why do you want to know?"

"Some of the men in Battery B are from there," she explained. "I just wondered."

He nodded and leaned back in his chair, after a wary look at the door through which Mama had exited in such a hurry. "Then, they are a long way from home, my dear."

Lydia sighed. "And some will never see it." To her surprise, she started to cry. She sobbed into her napkin, wondering at herself, knowing that she would scare Papa away from his after-dinner refuge over port.

To her further amazement, he left his chair and came to sit beside her. He put his arm around her and held her close until she stopped crying and blew her nose on her napkin. "Papa, I'm sorry," she said. "If I did that when Mama was around, she would forbid me ever to cross the threshold at St. Barnabas again."

"Perhaps it is too much for you, daughter," he suggested, tentative as always—a by-product of life with Luisa Perkins—but with a warmth in his voice that she had not heard in years. "I would not for the world have you hurt."

She considered her years of life bearing the lash of Mama's tongue and sometimes more, and overlooked that bit of fiction, content to feel his arm around her. "Oh, Papa, there is so much that could be done for those soldiers, if only someone cared enough!"

He kissed her cheek. "It appears that you do, my dear. Now, tell me about it."

She did, and he listened, as they both worked their way through the port. Mama pulled her away to arrange Kitty's hair, scold her for drinking port with Papa, and to animadvert on the subject dearest to her heart: the sore trials of running an establishment in London with too few servants. "Few people appreciate what we suffer," she grumbled, as Lydia worked her magic with the curling rod and judicious arrangement to cover Kitty's one flaw, fine hair.

Mama, there are so many worse off, she thought.

"At least you have achieved some skill in arranging Kitty's hair, and mending her clothes," Mama said as she sat later before her own mirror. "Now, position this turban and don't let me leave the house looking off balance, like you did last night!"

Yes, Mama, no, Mama, of course, Mama, she thought as she watched them leave in the carriage. What a pity that you have not a thought for others, Mama, you and your kind. She closed the front door. "But they are my kind, too," she murmured to no one in particular. "And Major Reed's kind, but he does something about it, even in his own pain."

She returned to the dining room, but Papa was asleep now—his head on the table, the decanter of port empty. I would wish again that you were more brave, Papa, she thought, and not for the first time. Perhaps if you were, I could be, too.

5

⌒

W HEN SHE ARRIVED AT St. Barnabas the next morning, Major Reed was sitting in a chair, waiting for her.

"Miss Perkins, you left your bonnet behind yesterday," he told her as she removed another bonnet and set it by the first on the altar. "I regret to inform you that a family of mice moved in after a brief reconnoiter during the night."

"Good heavens!" she exclaimed as she leaped back from the altar.

"Never fear, my dear Miss Perkins. After a skirmish, they were repelled. Your bonnet did suffer some structural damage, however."

She went to the altar again, cautious this time, and lifted the bonnet enough to see a hole in the crown. "This is indeed a casualty," she said.

"The battery owes you a hat," he said. "I'll add it to the bill."

She smiled at him. "I'm not sure there is enough money on 'Change to pay me for services so far, Major. Oh, you are wearing pants!"

He looked down in mock astonishment. "Good heavens, when did that happen! Actually, General Picton gave them back with a warning of more dire deductions from my person, should I show my face at Horse Guards. And no, we can never repay you for all you have done."

It was said simply, and she was touched. She realized that she knew next to nothing about Major Sam Reed, but with that realization came a sure knowledge that he was a man who meant what he said. For no particular reason, she thought suddenly of Kitty, her calculated search for a husband and her endless soliloquies on the qualities thought necessary for a husband. He should be rich and handsome, with enough intelligence to know when his tailor is cheating him, and have good manners, she remembered as one list. As she stood in the lady chapel listening to the major, Lydia wondered if perhaps honesty should figure somewhere on her own list. My demands are modest, she thought. I think honesty is enough.

"Miss Perkins, you are not listening."

"Oh! What?"

"Most of us have found our way out back to the tubs, and the pine tar soap, so you should not encounter too many unwelcome visitors."

She must have looked blank, because he laughed. "Fleas and lice, Lydia!" he said, using her first name. "A soldier's constant companions!"

"Oh!" She felt her face go red with embarrassment, whether from the use of her name, or the mention of vermin, she was not sure. He must not have noticed, she thought, so she knew it would be wise to say nothing. "Thank you, sir! If I were to carry those home, Kitty would have a hard time of it at Almack's."

"And not you?" he asked.

She made a face. "This is Kitty's year, sir. If I may quote Milton badly, I get to 'stand and wait.' "

He appeared to be thinking about that while she removed her scissors and fine-tooth comb from her reticule. "I have on good authority from a brother officer who was in here this morning, that Miss Kitty Perkins is cutting a wide swath at Almack's. He was there last night."

"I'm certain she is creating a stir. She has been groomed for it since birth," Lydia agreed as she removed a dishcloth from the basket she carried and tied it around the major's neck. "Kitty, eh?"

"So I assume. My friend said she was tall and blond and beautiful, with a wonderful laugh and ...." He hesitated, as if testing the wind. "... 'fewer brains than a leaf of escarole.' That last embellishment is a direct quotation, Miss Perkins, so do not bite my head off."

Lydia gasped, gave the major a severe look, and burst into laughter. "My sister," she said when she could manage speech again. "Kitty never did suffer education gladly."

"And you, Miss Perkins?" he asked.

She set down the scissors. "I like to learn. Mama declares that if I cannot find a husband somewhere in Devon's bogs, I shall surely be a first-rate governess. Hold still, now, sir, or your ear will be in danger."

He did as she asked, a slight smile on his face. "Devon's bogs, madam? Oh, *really*! You remind me of my two sisters, both of whom found husbands. And not in bogs, for God's sake. Where do women get their ideas?"

She laughed and combed his hair, quite liking its auburn color, and the flecks of gold here and there. "Not a speck of gray yet, Major," she said as she stood in front of him to part his hair.

"I should hope not! I am only thirty-one," he replied, his eyes on hers. "Probably close to your own age, eh?"

"Yes, I can tell that you have sisters!" she said her equanimity unruffled. She stood behind him to begin cutting. "I am far from thirty-one, sir, and no, I will not tell you my age!" She touched his shoulder. "I would have thought you slightly older. War does that?" she asked, not disguising her sudden sympathy.

"War does," he agreed, serious now. "Sometimes I ask myself what happened to that lieutenant of artillery who went to war only five years ago." He sighed as she began to cut. "His friends are dead on battlefields all over the Peninsula, the young ladies he kissed on the sly are married and mothers now, and his only talent is serving shot, shell, and canister on demand."

He was not feeling sorry for himself, she thought as she listened and snipped. "Are you remaining in the army, sir?"

"No. I have an estate near the Scottish border in dire need of my attention, now that Boney is on holiday. Don't forget that mole at my temple, Miss Perkins. If I bleed, it is on your dishcloth, remember. And your conscience. I have bled enough for England on foreign shores."

"Cook was happy to contribute to the war effort. She even sent me with beef tea for your men, and biscuits that she claims were languishing in the pantry, but which I suspect she made this morning," Lydia said. She smoothed back his hair with her hand on his temple until she located the infamous mole, then cut around it carefully.

"None for me?" he asked.

"When your hair is cut, sir," she replied. "You would not want hair clippings in your beef tea."

"Miss Perkins, when I think what I have endured on the culinary front for the past five years, I am scarce moved by hair, especially my own!"

She laughed and continued her efforts, pleased to see how well he looked, with his shave from yesterday and his haircut this morning. If only I could do something about the thinness of his face, she thought, and the way he hunches.

On impulse, she pulled back his nightshirt and looked at his back. The bandage was off, and she winced to see the long cut from shoulder to shoulder sewed, to her way of thinking, by an amateur with black thread. No wonder it pains him to stand up straight, she thought. I wonder he can stand at all.

"Nasty, eh?" he asked when she said nothing. "But you didn't have to look."

"I'm sorry," she said, contrite, embarrassed at her rudeness. "Is it red or puffy?" he asked. "No one tells me, and I cannot see it, of course."

She forced herself to look beyond the rawness of the wound. Imagine the pain, she thought. "No, it is neither," she replied, happy that her voice was steady. "I think the surgeon must have been working in the dark, however, or possibly he sent in his six-year-old son."

The major chuckled. "Actually, it was the regiment's barber, Miss Perkins, who specializes in sewing shrouds. The surgeon was busy."

She shuddered and looked again at the long, looping stitches. "Dear me," she murmured.

"Actually, miss, the major here told the surgeon to tend to me instead of him."

She looked up to see Corporal Davies, her morning escort, sitting at the entrance to the lady chapel with several of the more able-bodied gun crew. She smiled to see that the men had mugs of beef tea.

"Now, why would I do that?" the major growled. "I never met a more worthless crew."

The men only grinned at each other. Lydia found herself winking back tears. "Sir, I think you exaggerate."

"Only slightly, Miss Perkins, only slightly." He looked at his men. "All right, you sons of the guns. You're next, those of you who need haircuts. Bailey, you are bald, and I do not think you need to trouble Miss Perkins, beyond leering at her occasionally. I have been watching you, Bailey! Another leer, and you're on report!" He looked over his shoulder at her. "That is, you may cut their hair when you are done with me, Miss Perkins, if you truly wish to hack at these sorry specimens."

"I can manage it," she said. "You were my practice piece, Major."

He groaned in mock agony, and his men laughed, then moved back to their own part of the chapel. "Actually, Miss

Perkins, you had better do your utmost to make me charm personified. What day is it?"

"June fifteenth, Major," she said, mystified. "Why?"

"I am expected home in less than a month, Miss Perkins, and I must have a wife in tow by then. Do your best."

SHE COULDN'T HAVE HEARD him right. She stood there, scissors and comb suspended over his head. "Do be serious, Major," she said finally.

"I have rarely been more serious!" he retorted. "I never joke about the ladies. Well, seldom, anyway," he said with a grin. "After all, I do have two sisters, and they at least are fair game." He sighed. "And I have a mother, and an aunt, and they all figure in my desperation."

She combed his hair in silence, snipped at a few loose ends, then sat on his cot. "I must hear this," she said.

He shook his head, good cheer replacing his momentary melancholy. "Not now, Miss Perkins. My men are eager for their haircuts, and I must take a stroll to the necessary out back. Even the talk of so much exertion in less than a month's time, and me in a weakened state makes my bowels loose."

She knew she should be shocked, but she was hard put not to laugh. "Major Reed, may I make you a suggestion? You'll never find a wife if you are so blunt."

"Women do not like the truth?" he asked, watching her closely.

"I do!" she assured him, and promptly felt herself grow hot. "Oh, but that is not what I mean …."

"Then, say what you mean, Miss Perkins," he said crisply as he stood up, took the dishcloth from around his neck, and carefully gathered the corners together.

"I mean … well … but … sir, where are you going with the dishcloth?" her attention diverted by his actions.

"I am taking it with me, Miss Perkins," he said, his expression virtuous. "I noticed earlier this morning on a previous visit to the *pissoir*—there now, I know ladies like to hear French spoken—that there are nesting birds in the trees behind the latrines. They will have a use for hair clippings. See there? I am a philanthropist, *and* I speak French. Do not tell me that I cannot find a wife in four weeks' time!"

She watched him go, her mouth open. "I cannot believe that the army is going to turn him loose on an unsuspecting population," she murmured. "No wonder General Picton took his trousers yesterday."

Shaking her head, Lydia wiped off her scissors and comb, found another dishcloth, and ventured into the chapel. She was gratified to observe that the men who had been mere faces two days ago had by now turned into people. Not only was there Corporal Davies, her one-eyed escort, but also the only surviving powder monkey, who was much too young for the wound he bore, but proud of himself. In addition, two privates who had two arms between them played chess and another corporal watched, suffering a stubborn leg wound. They did not frighten her now; she had given them water, sat with them, and shaved their faces, and no one had been less than kind. I do so little, she thought as she cut Corporal Davies' hair first, and I am blessed far beyond my exertions.

Let us see if I can collect on some of my good deeds, she considered as she clipped and combed. "Corporal Davies, is your commander truly serious about finding a wife on short notice?" she asked, trying not to speak above a whisper, but capturing the attention of the chess players, anyway. The men laughed.

"Blame it on Lieutenant Percy Wilkins," Davies said. "I think it was his idea." He smiled. "Most of the mischief was his idea, but Major Reed, he got the blame."

He didn't say anything more. Patience, she thought, patience, but with little success. "*What* was his idea?" she asked, quite unable to let this conversation wither.

"Aw, I don't know, miss," said Davies, suddenly reticent. "He might not like it if I told you. Forgery, larceny, and highway robbery's different from talking about a wife."

"Forgery and larceny?" she asked. "I thought you were at war?"

Davies grinned. "Sometimes the biggest enemy seems like the Commissary Department, miss. T'major had his ways of squeezing blood out of that particular turnip." His expression was doubtful. "Still and all, miss, he might not like us talking about 'is troubles with the ladies."

"What he's not going to like is going home empty-handed and trying to explain to his mum how he misplaced a wife," said one of the chess players. "Checkmate."

Lydia put down her scissors. "Corporal Davies, I am not going to cut one more hair on your head unless you tell me what is going on. And believe me, you will look strange!"

The chess players started to laugh, and even the private with the troublesome leg managed a smile. "Lads, did'ye ever think half of that whole nonsense was for our own entertainment?" he asked. "T'give us something to laugh about, when nothing was funny?"

"Certainly was for Sir Percy," Davies agreed. "Don't know as I ever met a cove so ripe for a spree as Percy Wilkins. Remember the colonel and Sir Percy's ... uh ...."

"Another one you can't tell me?" she said as she picked up the scissors again. "Very well, Corporal, I will not insist on further elucidation. *And* I will even finish the haircut, because my charity is unbounded!"

"Good of you, miss," Corporal Davies said, kind enough to overlook her sarcasm.

She spent the morning cutting the hair of Major Reed's men, listening to their homely stories of life in the Peninsula, most of which seemed to revolve around Major Sam Reed. You are rare indeed, she thought, as she listened and glanced now and then at the lady chapel, where she could see the major hunched over a table engaged in paperwork. You do not seem like a man who would go to such lengths for a bunch of distinctly lower class, uneducated men, half of them felons and poachers with the choice of the army or Australia. Still, the respectful glances this way from the other wounded makes me suspect, Major Reed, that your 'men' of Battery B were fierce opponents.

When she finished her barbering among Battery B—and over their protests—she continued down another row, careful to avoid the area where another cluster of London's *bon ton* had gathered to gawk. She could tell how it embarrassed the soldiers to have them there, how they would turn away if they could to avoid being stared at, if their wounds were grievous. It pained her that those who could not move must only lie there, mute and exposed, on display to their betters who would never come near a firing line, or face a cavalry charge.

"I hate it," she whispered to Corporal Davies when he came to retrieve her. "I wish they would go away."

He took her arm and led her toward the lady chapel. "Doesn't it bother you, Corporal?" she asked as he hurried her along.

"Nah," he said, shaking his head. "Maybe we'll get lucky, and one of them gentry morts will stop to help. You did, miss."

Yes, I did, she thought, and I am ashamed of my kind. "I think I may be the exception, Corporal."

He only smiled. "We're sure o' that, miss." He nodded toward the major. "Don't let 'im worry you, miss. He may seem rough and strange, but I ... we'd all follow him anywhere."

The major was lying on his cot with the appearance of a man defeated by paperwork, which was strewn over his blanket. His eyes were closed. She smiled at him, then on impulse knelt beside him. "All you need is a lily in your hands, sir, and I am certain someone would return you to the family vault," she teased.

"I would gladly go, to avoid one more invoice, claim, or whine in print from the Commissary," he said without opening his eyes. "Madam, do you realize that there is a brass candlestick unaccounted for that has been following me since Talavera?

The accountants do not believe me that it dropped in a mud hole at a river crossing! I think their letters will follow me to Northumberland!"

She pulled up a chair and began to gather together the papers on his cot. "Sir, do you need some help with this?"

He opened his eyes. To her surprise, he looked feverish, so she put her hand on his forehead. "You are hot," she said, looking around for the surgeon.

He covered her hand with his own. "Just keep your hand there, Miss Perkins, and I will improve in minutes."

She leaned closer. "May I finish your paperwork for you?" she asked. "Will that help?"

"You cannot imagine, Miss Perkins. Words fail me," he said as he released her hand. "Draw yourself up to the table, madam."

She laughed and took the papers to the table. In a moment he was standing beside her, pointing out what needed to be done. "It appears that you want me to copy these documents onto these sheets."

He nodded, as he leaned heavily on her chair. "If things do not come to them in twos or threes, accountants get all tight about the mouth and … and diddle themselves behind bushes, for all I know."

"Major," she began, blushing. "You must become less colorful with your phrases, if you have plans to retire from the army and …."

"I know, I know," he interrupted. "Find a wife in a week or so." He lay down again. "Did my men fill you in on that exploit?"

"No, they did not …."

"Such restraint on their part."

"… which I thought rather beastly of them, since it sounds like an interesting story," she said as she dipped the pen in the inkwell and began to copy.

"It was a good story three years ago, I don't doubt," he

said, his voice wistful with remembering. "Somehow, I never thought I would live long enough to have to make good on it, Miss Perkins."

She put down the pen. "Well, tell me, or I will leave you to the mercy of the accountants!"

He shuddered. "It is not a pretty story."

"Major …."

He turned carefully onto his side. "Miss Perkins, in May of 1809, during the first siege of Badajoz, my father died and left me a title and an estate. I am the Earl of Laren."

"So I should have been 'my lording' you," she said as she continued copying.

"Please don't start now. I don't like it; never have. The estate is good enough, but it needed an immediate infusion of cash to make it much better." He made a face. "Especially since I have neglected it, and my father, too, only he did not have Napoleon for an excuse."

She turned to look at him, unable to hide the merriment that she knew was in her face. "Major, you not only need a wife, but you need a rich one, too? All this in less than a month?"

"Lydia, you are a trial," he said mildly, using her name again. This must be the tone he uses with his sisters, she thought, unoffended.

"My Aunt Chalmers lives with my mother, and she is richer than the Almighty," he continued. "In the same letter announcing my father's bad news and my title, she wrote that I would inherit her wealth. If I married, and soon, she would even let me draw on the principal to begin improvements immediately."

She frowned and put down the pen. "Why is marriage so important?"

He sat up and leaned forward. "My back still itches where the sutures were," he grumbled. "Miss Perkins, do I ask too much or could you …."

"Scratch it?" She put down the pen and sat next to him on

the cot. "I don't want to hurt you," she said dubiously.

He lifted up his shirt, exposing his back, and rested his elbows on his knees. "Just rub the skin lightly with your fingernails. Oh, God, that is perfection. Miss Perkins, you should be patented, duplicated, and issued to every hospital ward in the army! If you stop, I will cry."

If Mother sees me, she will make me cry, she thought as she gently ran her fingernails around the ugly wound. "Why didn't the Frenchman who did this sever your spine, Major?"

"I believe he was thinking more on the terms of parting my neck from my shoulders," the major replied. "One of my men clubbed him with a ramrod, so I got the backhand instead of the foreword thrust. I was lucky, indeed. Please don't stop yet."

"Only if you continue the narrative, sir.""Oh, yes. Aunt Chalmers harbors the notion that Laren men are not to be trusted around women." He sighed. "My father was one of them, I suppose. He wenched his way through Northumberland and one or two shires in Scotland, I believe. I probably have brothers and sisters I've never met."

She opened her eyes wide at this news, but said nothing. Perhaps I should be grateful for my own father, meek as he is, she thought for the first time.

"At any rate, Aunt Chalmers is quite loyal to Mama, and she has watched her cry over my father for years and years."

"If I may be practical …."

"By all means."

"Your father and mother were married, were they not?"

He nodded. "So why should it matter whether I am married or not, if my father was such a beast, and he was married, too?" he asked, following her thoughts. He shook his head. "I haven't a clue, except that I know she did not care much for my father. Could it be revenge? I do not know."

He was silent. She returned to her copying, then put down the pen again. "All right, what is the rest?"

"You're a nosy female," he teased, grinning at her. "Mama was determined that I should resign my commission, leave Spain, hurry home, and marry the daughter on the neighboring estate."

"You don't care for the lady?" she asked.

He shook his head. "She's pretty enough, I suppose, and if I recall, she can carry on a good conversation, but I am not interested. I could not leave my men, either, or my guns, or Badajoz." He reached out and touched her arm. "You have met my men. Do you understand?"

"Oh, yes. And from what they have told me, you are not one to leave someone in the lurch. I wonder that your mother and aunt thought you would drop everything."

"They have not seen war. How can they know?" he murmured as he took the page she handed him and shook sand on it. He poured the grains carefully into the shaker again and secured the lid. "It seemed like such a good idea to invent a wife."

"You didn't!"

"I did. Stupid, wasn't it? I blame it on the siege. When you're in the middle of one, it's hard to believe that it will ever end. And who knows? Maybe I would be killed, and not have to face my mother, my aunt, or the young lady on the neighboring estate, who I regret to add, did harbor some expectations in my direction." He peered at her. "I do not know that I have ever seen a more skeptical expression, Miss Perkins."

"I doubt you have," she agreed. "And who is this paragon you invented?"

"We—Percy Wilkins, I, and my gunnery sergeant—we created a daughter of the regiment. I believe we made her father a major from a very good family. After Badajoz, Percy found a miniature among the ruins, and included that with the letters and the marriage license, of course, so Aunt Chalmers would be satisfied."

"How did you find *that?*"

"Simple, my dear. We located a priest only too eager to help us, especially when it was pointed out to him that his head would look better on his shoulders. You should have seen it: all Latin, with gold lettering, and a seal something like what the lord chancellor must use. They really do it up right in Spain." He watched her face. "I can see that you are not impressed, Lydia. Wait, it gets worse."

"How could I doubt it?"

"Did you meet Percy Wilkins, my lieutenant?"

Lydia shook her head. "I have a feeling that I am going to be profoundly grateful that I did not."

"Percy's a bit of a romantic." For the first time in his narrative, Major Reed frowned. "I think this is where it started going wrong."

"You think *this* is the place?" Lydia asked in amazement.

"Percy decided it would be fun to begin a correspondence with my mother. He had rather delicate handwriting, so that was not a worry …."

She gasped. "He has been writing for three years …."

"Two, actually, with lots of help from almost everyone in the battery."

"… to your poor mother?"

"And my aunt. They can't wait to meet Lady Laren." He scratched his head. "Matter of fact, neither can I. I'm certainly ripe for suggestions, Miss Perkins." He took a long look at her, and she stood up quickly and started to back away, even before he continued. "Are you interested in getting married?"

6

❧

MAJOR REED LAUGHED AND motioned her back. "I did not expect a general stampede to the door!" he protested, his good humor intact. "You wound me."

She returned to the table, quite in charity with him, since he was so obviously joking. I can certainly respond in kind, she thought as she sat down again and folded her hands in front of her. "Dear Major, while I am not insensible to the honor which you do me, I must decline with regret," she said. "There now, I think I said that right." She dipped the quill in the ink again and continued her copying. "Seems a pity to turn down my first offer, Major, but I doubt that you and I would suit." She started to laugh again, and he joined in.

He lay back on his cot again. "You see my dilemma, Miss Perkins." He frowned at her. "Your first offer? I can hardly believe that. What is wrong with the men of Devon?"

It was her turn to frown. "Nothing," she replied, "once they see my sister. Kitty has had reams of bad poetry composed in her honor, and more proposals than are strictly legal, I am sure."

"No one's captured her heart?" the major asked, his eyes closing again.

"Of course not!" she replied. Kitty has no heart to capture, she thought. "Mama is convinced that someone so beautiful must only fall in love with a marquis or an earl, perhaps a duke. Do have a care if you should chance to stroll down Holly Street. You are fair game!" she teased.

He was silent quite a while, and she thought he had drifted to sleep again. I do not know why a little exertion won't help you find a wife, she considered, although I do not know that two or three weeks is precisely enough. While no jury would convict you of being handsome, I don't have any difficulty looking at you. Although I am no judge, you will probably look just as nice thirty years from now across the breakfast table. You are certainly friendly. And stubborn, she added to herself, considering how you have plagued Horse Guards. And honorable. What other officer would wear himself out for his men?

"Are you reconsidering, Miss Perkins?"

"No!" she retorted, startled into smudging the paper, certain that her face was red. "You cannot possibly succeed with this harebrained notion."

He thought about it. "I believe I would rather have the wife of my bosom meet with a fatal accident than have to admit that she was a figment of my imagination," he said frankly. "My friends would tease me past bearing, but if it were an accident, I think I could count on sufficient sympathy from them to help me bear up."

"You should have thought of all this when you were scheming in Spain," she told him, as she smiled at his wit and wondered why there were no men in Devon with a sense of humor. "Might I suggest another solution?"

"You know I am up for it."

"The truth."

He sat up and looked her in the eye, and she was hard put

to keep a straight face. "Miss Perkins, where is your sense of adventure? I was lying here wondering how to find a soldier of fortune who would be willing to murder my aunt. She has been at death's door for years and years, and I know she would really like to stick her spoon in the wall and continue plaguing my uncle, who escaped from her tongue twenty years ago! And all you can suggest is the paltry truth."

They laughed together. She returned to the papers before her, and in another moment, the major was sleeping peacefully. Well, you are no nearer to solving your dilemma, but I cannot believe you ever considered that a woman would just sit on your lap, she thought. She would have to be awfully desperate to shackle herself to a man she barely knew. I know I would never.

AND YET.... "TELL ME, Corporal Davies," she asked as he escorted her home again in the hackney. "Major Reed is not really serious about finding a wife on such short notice, is he?"

The corporal only grinned, and left her to her own thoughts. He helped her down when the hackney stopped at her house. "It took only one battle, miss, and I knew what kind of man I was dealing with. Never underestimate the major. I know I never do."

"I am convinced, Corporal, that finding a wife must be different from conducting a ... a military campaign," she said in protest.

The corporal only nodded, as though he indulged a child, and climbed back inside the hackney, seating himself with an air of complaisance that she found amusing. "Very well, I will own that your major is a remarkable gentleman, but ladies do not enter into marriage so lightly," she told him as the footman opened the front door for her.

"Oh, we'll see, Miss Perkins" was the last thing she heard as the jehu spoke to his horses and the corporal settled in for his return to St. Barnabas.

Her amusement carried over into dinner, where she found it remarkably easy to let her own thoughts entertain her. A smile or a nod occasionally in Mama's direction served to keep her parent at bay. I am becoming so good at this, she thought, as Kitty smirked and simpered her way through a commentary on today's fitting, and the receipt of a most-coveted invitation to a luncheon alfresco. Kitty even thinks I am interested in what she says. It would do Kitty no good to contemplate the hard fact that most of the world already eat their meals outdoors, and not by invitation. And probably without strawberries dipped in sugar.

Her mental picture of Kitty nibbling on raw meat plucked from the arrow point of a Mohican quite ruined any gravity she could have brought to the discussion, which by now had moved onto the fact that Kitty's host was the son of a viscount, somewhat spotty and rejoicing in a lisp, but worth a great deal, on his father's death.

"What do you think, Lyddy?" Kitty was asking.

Think? Think? When I am still diverted by a Stone Age vision of Kitty eating on the ground? This will never do. "Actually, my dear, I was not actually attending to your conversation," she confessed. "Do refresh my mind."

Kitty frowned. "Lydia, this is above all serious! I want to know if you think I should wear white or blue muslin to a picnic."

Lydia smiled and turned her attention to her plate. "I think you should send 'round a penny post to ask the viscount what he is wearing, so you can match."

Kitty's beautiful blue eyes grew even more round. "You cannot be serious!"

"Lydia, there is no hope for you!" Mama groaned, flinging down her napkin like a gauntlet. "You have put me off my feed!"

That can't be difficult, Lydia thought as she calmly continued eating, particularly since you have already consumed lamb, fish, and sirloin in the last two courses, not to mention soup and savories. "I'm sorry for that, Mama," she said cheerfully, pleased to feel no fear at her mother's combative tone. There is something about working—seriously working—for people who need my help that could go a long way to making me braver, she thought. She glanced at her father, happy to note his half smile.

But there is no sense in rocking anyone's boat, she told herself. "Kitty, I suggest that you wear something other than white, because of the possibility of grass stains," she said.

Her sister directed shocked eyes at her. "Lyddy, I cannot imagine we would be grubbing about on the ground!"

"It is a picnic, my dear," she replied calmly, wondering where, all these years, she received the strength to remain sober and upright when she wanted to laugh at Kitty's numerous stupidities. "That is, I believe, most generally where one finds grass."

Any botanical comment on her sister's part was canceled by Stanton's appearance in the doorway. "Sir Humphrey and Lady Luisa, there is a gentleman—or rather, a soldier of some sort—to speak to Miss Perkins. Shall I show him up?"

"Not if it is that common corporal who brings her home each evening," Lady Perkins said with a shudder.

The butler hesitated, looked around, and actually addressed Sir Humphrey. "Sir, I rather think it is an officer, but his uniform is so faded that it is only a conjecture."

"Why, show him in, Stanton," Sir Humphrey said as his wife stared at him. "Best to show a little courtesy to the men who helped keep Napoleon out of our salons and drawing rooms, my love." He spoke quietly but firmly, to Lydia's delight.

She knew it was Major Reed, and indeed, he came into the room even before Stanton could return to fetch him. She rose and left the table, then started to laugh. "Oh, Major, did I forget another hat?" she asked, quite overlooking that her mother and Kitty were watching.

Even wearing a uniform faded by the Peninsular sun and stooped by his injury, the major looked every inch the soldier, except for the two straw bonnets he carried. He smiled, and Lydia couldn't help but think that in a newer uniform, and standing more upright, he probably could find a lady to marry him, possibly even on short notice.

I do believe the men of the artillery have the finest uniform, she thought, and not for the first time as she observed the rows and rows of gold braid stretching across his chest. The fit is loose, though; I fear the major has lost weight during his illness. I did give him a good haircut, however.

With a smile of his own, he handed her both bonnets. "Miss Perkins, it won't do to be absentminded," he chided her. "My men and I are convalescing, and we cannot be expected to mount a guard over your hats to prevent mice."

"Indeed you cannot," she agreed with him. She took his arm, wishing that Kitty would close her mouth, and not look so astonished. "May I introduce Lord Laren, Major Reed, Commander of Battery B of Picton's Third?"

Her mother still sat dumbfounded, but her father rose and came to shake his hand. "I am Sir Humphrey Perkins, my lord. This is my wife, Lady Luisa, and our younger daughter Kitty. Won't you join us for the rest of dinner?"

The major shook his head. "Thank you, no, but I am on my way to General Picton's quarters." To Lydia's profound amazement, he took her mother by the hand. "Lady Luisa, may I congratulate you on your daughter Lydia? I can't remember when I have ever met a more useful female. I am certain the credit is yours." He turned next to Kitty, and flashed a smile that made Lydia's stomach ping about, for some odd reason. "Ah, Miss Kitty Perkins! Several of my brother officers have been lucky enough to see you at Almack's, and indeed, words do fail them, according to their reports. I understand why."

Considering that Kitty still stood with her mouth open, Lydia could not be sure if he were serious. She watched with some interest as he turned next to her father. "Sir Humphrey, you are lucky indeed to be the proud one in charge of three—three!—such gems. Surely you will not mind if I borrow Miss Perkins for the evening? I thought not. Thank you, sir! General Picton is most particular in wanting to see her."

Lady Luisa found her voice. "Lydia? Why would anyone want Lydia?"

The major laughed. "Lady Luisa, who would have thought you to be such a tease? I know I would not." He took a step closer to the woman, and Lydia was surprised to see her mother actually take a step back. Sir, you can be completely commanding when the occasion arises, she thought.

"Madam," he continued, "the general is interested in her opinion on tending the wounded. I knew you would not begrudge her service to our country. Miss Perkins, I recommend a shawl." He indicated the bonnets in her hand. "And one of these, preferably the one without additional ventilation. I will wait in the carriage. Good day, all. Grand to meet you."

He left the room, and it became so empty and still she wondered if he had sucked out the oxygen, too. I had no idea, she thought, then smiled. No wonder his men will follow him anywhere.

Mama made no comment as Lydia bid them good night and went upstairs for a better bonnet. There wasn't any need to pinch color into her cheeks. A glance in the mirror told her that her color was quite high enough, and her eyes even had a glow to them.

There was no time to change clothes. He would have to be content to shepherd her in a plain blue dress relieved only by a lace collar. She swung a shawl about her shoulders, snatched up another bonnet more suitable for evening, and hurried downstairs.

True to his word, the major waited in the hackney, clutching the strap. Once the driver helped her in and closed the door, she quietly took a handkerchief from her reticule and wiped the sweat from the major's face. "This is too much exertion," she said simply. "My hats could have stayed another night at St. Barnabas, and what is this hum about General Picton?"

He winced, and it wasn't all from the discomfort of his wound. "It is the unvarnished truth, or nearly enough so," he replied.

Considering that she had seldom felt a need to be stern around him, she fixed the major with a hard look. "Major Reed, I already begin to quake now when you qualify the truth. Tell me what I am really getting into."

She mollified her admonition with another wipe of his face, and he leaned back carefully. "I have been invited to the Pictons, but I know they will be gratified to hear your remarks. Now, don't look like that! Lydia, has no one ever told you that you are too suspicious by half?"

"It is Miss Perkins, and no, they have not," she retorted.

He smiled. "Besides that, I didn't want to waste this evening in a carriage by myself. If you cannot be charitable to me, at least consider the fineness of the evening and rejoice that I have sprung you from the house."

She did, thinking to herself that the night was uncommonly fine, even for late June. "What is Northumberland like, this time of year?" she asked suddenly.

He didn't answer immediately, and she was content to wait as he summarized Northumberland in his brain. She liked the way he thought through her questions because it meant he was listening. Only Papa ever listened at home.

"It's not to everyone's taste, and a far cry from the heat and general fervor of Spain," he said. "At home right now, everything would be going from that lime green look of spring into the full leaf of summer." He sighed, and she didn't even think he was aware of it. "I would be every day in the saddle now, looking over the work of my farmers and shepherds. The shearing would be over, and the wool on the market. I'd be late to bed every night, up early, and tired in between." He chuckled. "Do you know, I can't wait to be about it again. No one will shoot at me, and I understand the *patois* of the natives, because I can speak it, too. I can put my legs under a table, and my bed is soft in all the right places, unless Mama finally threw out that old mattress."

"You've been thinking a lot about it, haven't you?" she murmured.

"Only every day for the last five years," he said quickly. "No one was happier than I to see Boney take up residence on Elba." He was silent then, sitting beside her in the close hackney, their shoulders touching companionably. I like this, she thought. Perhaps when I return to Devon, I will make some exertion toward finding a husband. I am twenty-two, but surely there is a clergyman or a widower somewhere who wouldn't be disgusted with marrying someone past her first bloom.

"It's your turn," he said, when she had thought he was dozing. "Where do you wish to be?"

"Why, right here," she said without thinking, and then had the grace to blush. "Major, Mama says I am not possessed with much imagination. I suppose I am partial to the moment."

He touched her hand. "Then, you are probably more content than most of us who look ahead and are not so patient in waiting for the now to turn into tomorrow. Ah. Here we are, Miss Perkins."

She had to agree with him as they walked slowly toward the house. The night was fine, and truly too good to spend indoors. I do like the moment, she told herself in honest self-defense, and there is no real defect in that, even if Mama and Kitty call me stodgy.

She found herself in a plainly decorated hall, sparse of furniture, which made her suspect that Lady Picton was inclined to follow the army herself, and not invest much time in knickknacks and furbelows that required attention and careful packing.

Lady Picton was much like her husband, somewhat commanding in appearance, with a straight back and simple clothes. Lydia noticed with some amusement that she was also a good head taller than the general, who stood beside her, his arm around her waist. The general noticed her glance. "Miss Perkins, consider the folly of a youthful leg-shackle. Lady Picton and I were much the same height when we married at twenty. Alas, she continued to grow. Pick yourself a man like Sam here, who is as tall as he's ever going to be, and you'll get no surprises."

On the contrary, she thought as she curtsied and blushed with about equal skill, Major Reed is full of surprises and on the prowl for an instant wife.

"Tommy, I vow you have embarrassed our guest," Lady Picton said as she took Lydia's hand. "Thank goodness the war is over, my dear Miss Perkins, else men's manners would evaporate entirely. Do come in and meet the other guests. Sam, how good to see you again, and upright once more."

She was in excellent hands now, no mistaking. Lady Picton took her by the arm and led her around the drawing room, introducing her to officers with names familiar from the newspaper, their wives, and other ladies she recognized from St. Barnabas. It was easy to visit, and trade stories with the women who shared her tasks of nursing the wounded. It was a far cry from the trivialities of Devon drawing rooms, or even the few parties she had attended in London, which seldom advanced much beyond conversations about fashion and the trying royal family.

Lady Picton's last introduction was to an older gentleman, who had the military bearing without the uniform. "Miss Perkins, may I introduce Lord Walsingham? He has taken it upon himself to prepare a speech for lords to question the treatment of the wounded during the war."

Lydia flashed a smile in Major Reed's direction, understanding his reasons for including her in the gathering, and for the next hour, joined the others in describing their impressions of hospital conditions. She discovered that she had little to contribute, compared to those who had served in the Peninsula, and she listened to stories of great suffering, no supplies, poor conditions, and ill-trained surgeons. There is inadequacy everywhere, she thought as she watched the animation with which Major Reed and other commanders spoke to Walsingham.

Her estimation of Major Reed rose higher, the more he spoke. So you used your own money to send home the bodies of your men, rather than have them jumbled together in Spanish soil, so far from home? she thought. He was not alone in this, or in paying for medications from his own pocket. Others told similar stories.

"Major Reed, I do believe your mother and aunt will forgive your prevarication about a wife, if they learn how kind you have been to your men," she whispered to him as the discussion ended, and she found herself standing next to him again. "I still think you should take your chance with the truth."

He only nodded, tight-lipped. She looked closer at him, then took his arm without his permission and led him to a chair. "Sit down," she ordered, and went in immediate search of General Picton.

I am full of nerve, she thought as she interrupted a gathering of officers to pull her host aside, whisper to him, and ask him what to do. In another moment, General Picton was helping his major of artillery to his feet and motioning her to take his other arm. "Sam, it is upstairs for you, and bed," he said, with iron in his voice that allowed no rebuttal. "Help him, Miss Perkins, while I attend to my guests. Sam, you are the damnedest, most tenacious rascal it has been my misfortune to command—if I ever did command you, and I have some doubts. Take his pants, Miss Perkins, if he starts to animadvert, and make sure he stays in that bed. I'll see that you get home."

"But I must see her home," the major insisted.

"You are perfectly brainless if you do not think there are five or six officers who would like nothing better than to escort a pretty lady home!" Picton told him. "Help him, Miss Perkins, even if he is an idiot. I must return to my guests."

She did as she was bid, over the protests of Major Reed, who objected when she removed his shoes, took exception when she unbuttoned his uniform jacket, and nearly fainted when she helped him from the garment. "You shouldn't be wearing something this confining yet," she scolded him, even as her heart ached to cause him pain.

She feared that his wound had reopened, but to her relief there was no blood through the bandage. Without asking his permission, she pulled his shirt away from his back and peered under the bandage.

"Well?" he asked, and he was breathing hard, to her dismay.

"No blood, but oh, you aggravate me!" she exclaimed as she removed his shoes and helped settle him on his side. His eyes were closed, and she wasn't sure, but after a moment's reflection she unbuttoned the top few buttons of his trousers and then pulled the blanket over him. She sat down in the chair beside the bed.

"Well?" he asked, after a long silent spell.

"Well, what?" she asked in turn.

"When are you going to ring a peal over me, and scold and rail, because I haven't the sense to stay wisely on my cot at St. Barnabas?" he said, his eyes open now, but heavy-lidded.

She observed his face, already quite familiar to her now, and could tell that the pain was less, now that he was lying down. "You don't need a scold from me," she said quietly.

"But …."

"Sir?"

He smiled at her drowsily. "I know your own face well enough by now, Miss Perkins. Obviously there is something else you wish to say. Do unburden yourself."

It seemed too personal, what she wanted to say, so she

took a deep breath. "I only wish to add that I think your men are fortunate indeed to have such an advocate." She thought another moment, and knew he was expecting more.

"And … and if you can bamboozle some lady into marrying you on awfully short notice, she'll be well taken care of." It came out in a rush, and she knew she had embarrassed herself. "I mean it," she added, further discomfiting herself. "Now, go to sleep and don't worry about your men. I'll be there tomorrow as usual, and I will tell them where you are, and that you are destined to convalesce at the Pictons for a while."

He struggled to sit up at her words, and she pushed him down gently. "They will be fine, sir, and relieved to know that you are taking it a bit easier."

"I should be there. Lydia, no one cares as much as I do!"

He was raising his voice and starting to sweat again. Calmly she wiped his forehead. "It is Miss Perkins, Major, and I care about you *and* them."

"Oh, you do, Miss Perkins?" he said, and sounded formidable. "Then, help me up."

"No."

Amazed at her own effrontery, she pulled back the covers, unbuttoned his pants the rest of the way, turned her head, and pulled them off. "There, sir," she said from the safety of the doorway, with the pants over her arm. "Now, do as you are told." She closed the door behind her.

While she was upstairs, the party had dissolved. She watched from the quiet of the landing as the officers and ladies bid each other good night and went out into the fine evening. The general's wife noticed Lydia and came up the stairs, smiling to see the major's pants over her arm.

"The stubborn heroes are the worst ones," she said, taking the trousers. "I know, for I am married to one. He still suffers because he left his bed too soon after his wound at Ciudad Rodrigo. No one knows better than I." She smiled. "Perhaps you will be luckier with your major."

"Oh, he is not mine!" Lydia declared, quite unable to keep the confusion from her voice.

General Picton's wife only smiled and changed the subject.

7

HER WORD WAS AS good as the major's. She went to St.
Barnabas in the morning and informed Major Reed's
men that he was suffering enforced exile at General Picton's
house, and would remain there until he felt better. "It is
precisely as I told you it would be," she wrote that night after
her return to Holly Street. "They were relieved to know that
you were someplace where you might recuperate."

She set down her pen. Now, sir, if you were sitting across
from me, you would probably challenge that word "relieved,"
but I maintain that I am correct. There was disappointment
when she told them, but it was the relief she remembered, and
a certain satisfaction that someone was seeing to their major.

"I vow I would take it right painfully, if I thought he was
suffering," the corporal with the bad leg had told her.

What about you, she wanted to ask, but was too polite to say.
She was familiar by now with the fragrance of decay that rose
from his blanket, and she did not need to pull back the cover
and look at his leg, covered today at her insistence with a wire
basket to keep even the pressure of a sheet from it. Why was
it not amputated at Toulouse, she wanted to ask someone, but

the surgeons were too overworked to question, and she knew that they would only pat her arm and tell her not to fret herself. She could only watch the soldier's eyes begin to settle back in his head, and fret to herself at the inward look of him now.

She picked up the pen again, telling the major how each man was doing, and added, "I assure you, I will continue to visit them each day. If you wish, I could visit you, too, but that would take time from the men. Let me know how you are getting on, so I can tell your men. Yours respectfully, etc., Lydia Perkins."

He responded the next day, as she knew he would, and she took the letter to his men, reading it aloud to them. " 'I will return as soon as I am able,' " she concluded, and could not keep the laughter from her voice. " 'Do mind the surgeon, and the first man who troubles Miss Perkins will go on report.' There you are."

And there she was, as well. Major Reed had not addressed the suggestion that she visit him, too, so she mentally turned a page, and vowed not to think of him more than once or twice a day.

A week passed. More of the men in St. Barnabas had healed sufficiently to return to the ranks, at least according to the surgeon. She could not believe it, but her protests only earned her another pat on the arm, and the remark that only made her grit her teeth: "You needn't worry your head about this, madam. Let us be the judge."

Corporal Davies left at the end of the week, the bandage over his eye replaced with a patch that made him look like a benevolent sort of pirate. "Watch the rest of them blokes for me, miss," he said. "I don't like the looks of two or three of 'um, but what say do we have?" He shook his head. "And they keep bringing them over." He shrugged and shouldered his kit. "If you're ever in Belgium, Miss Perkins, look up the Third Battery there. Occupation duty is a dead bore."

She looked around her at the nave of St. Barnabas, as familiar to her now as her own room. The latest wounded from

Toulouse who had survived the rough hospital there were lying here now, far gone, many of them, with no place to go except a shabby church on London's dock.

"It is too bad, Papa," she said that night as she and her father sat together in the book room. Since that first night she had returned so discouraged from General Picton's, he had been waiting for her in the book room. "Think how everyone is celebrating here with parties and routs, while the men who made victory possible lie in a leaky church with bad drains, mice, and bat soil." Her voice hardened. "We are visited still— plagued is the better word—by fashion fribbles who come to gawk and point, as though the men had no feelings. It is not fair in the least."

"I am certain it is not, my dear," her father said. He held out his hand to her, and she sat beside him. "And are we not to be part of a celebration in two days' time? We can join our own hypocrisy to theirs, my dear."

She grimaced. "The Capitulation Banquet, Papa. How could I forget? Kitty has talked of nothing else, and I am not even sure she knows which continent Toulouse resides on, much less which country."

"Still, I am pleased to know that you are made of sterner stuff, and have rendered a service," he said.

She nodded, too tired to add more to the conversation. Oh, I have done my little part, she thought, with a certain bitterness that surprised her. I do not flinch at the worst wounds anymore, but I still jump when Mama makes a demand or Kitty verges on hysteria if I will not sew a flounce or do her curls. She sighed. "Papa, do you know, we are not really very brave here at home."

The moment the words left her mouth, she realized how rude they sounded, spoken to her parent. "Papa, I mean … I mean …." she stammered, quite unable to revise them. Sir Humphrey only shook his head and patted her hand.

"Never mind, my dear," he said, not looking at her, but with nothing but contrition in his already soft voice. "We sit here on the fringes, and hope that Kitty will make an eligible alliance ...." His voice trailed off.

"It never changes anything, does it, Papa?" she asked, driven by some demon of honesty. "I am never pretty enough, and you .... Oh, Papa."

They sat close together in silence until her father cleared his throat. "Daughter."

That was all. He could not bring himself to say any more. In a few moments, Lydia said good night and left the room. She had embarrassed him enough for one evening.

ALTHOUGH SHE WAS SELDOM allowed access to the newspaper, as the hackney drove toward the docks, she heard the news from the running patterers. The Capitulation Events were on everyone's lips. In the better part of the city, store owners were sweeping the streets with more interest than usual. An arch went up, and another, temporary structures on which to hang the greenery of high summer. When she returned that evening, tired and out of sorts, there were garlands and medallions with the Duke of Wellington's name prominent.

The victory at Toulouse, if not its full importance, had finally drilled itself into Kitty's brain, and she was full of cheer that evening at the dinner table. "Lydia, Edwin—I know, I know, Mama, Lord Allsuch—took me to a balloon ascension this morning, and what do you know but the man in the gondola poured out little tickets with Wellington's name? They were in all colors, and it was beautiful."

Lydia nodded, intent more on her dinner. She never took time for luncheon anymore, and indeed, had lost all appetite for a noon meal after spooning watery gruel down the throats of men who could scarcely swallow anymore. No one remained at St. Barnabas now except the worst cases. To her great distress, some of the men released too early were returned to St. Barnabas, where they died.

I could tell you stories, she thought, looking at her sister, but you do not wish to hear them. "We heard the music of a procession of some sort, I believe," she commented, as she nodded to Stanton to take away the half-eaten course, her appetite gone as quickly as it had come. She did not look at the butler; she knew he was displeased that she ate so little now. She glanced at him quickly—he is worried, more like, she thought, touched at his concern.

As tired as she was, she found some relief in sitting down with Kitty's dress for the Capitulation Banquet to take in a seam here and let out one there, secure in the knowledge that no one would plead for her to come quickly, for God's sake. She had only to sit in a sweet-smelling room, her stockinged feet propped on a hassock, and sew. How simple this is, she told herself. It could be that I am no better at nursing than anyone of my class. She sighed. Or it could be that I am worn down to a nub. Who would have thought it would take death in the afternoon, and suffering in all its forms to make me grateful for the peace and quiet of Kitty's work?

Simple and pale yellow, her own gown lay carefully folded in the clothespress, with yellow-dyed Moroccan leather slippers close by. It will look especially fine with my dark hair, she thought, and with a paisley shawl. And if Mama does not take the opportunity to comment on all my flaws before I leave the house, perhaps I can believe myself handsome enough for one night.

She returned to St. Barnabas in the morning, and was greeted at once by Major Sam Reed. She almost did not recognize him, because he was standing more straight, and he showed the effects of General Picton's dinner table. "I am so glad to see you," she said, her pleasure unalloyed by any thought to her forwardness. Mama was not there to remind her, and she was free to enjoy the moment. "Oh, sir, you will do now, won't you?"

He smiled back at her. "So the general's surgeon claims, Miss Perkins. I will do." He looked around him, then took her hand

and held it close to his chest. "Oh, Lydia, why didn't I tell you to quit coming here last week, before it reached this stage? We're at the mouth of hell now. It is always this way, and I didn't think to tell you." He made a face. "Sometimes I wonder why Horse Guards doesn't just tell the last dying man to blow out the candle before he pegs off, and pull the dirt over him."

She nodded, and made no move to pull her hand away. "No one remains now except the ones who will die?"

"Abominable, isn't it? Come along." He kept her hand in his and towed her along after him to the lady chapel, where his campaign trunk rested, strapped now, along with a duffle bag and what must be the box for his high-plumed shako.

"You're leaving?" she asked, seating herself at his table and removing her gloves. I wish you would not, she thought. This place begins to scare me.

He shrugged. "Today or tomorrow," he said, then went to the altar and returned with a hatbox, which he set on the table. "For you, Miss Perkins. I owe you."

"I am certain you do not," she murmured, but her fingers were already untying the white satin ribbon that bound the pasteboard box. She smiled at him. "If it is another bonnet, I will not be able to decline it as I ought. I have a vast, unsatisfied desire for bonnets."

He laughed. "Then, it was a lucky guess. I picked it out, madam. My taste is far from impeccable, but I gave this plenty of thought, and I was guided by the general's wife."

With a gasp of pleasure, she pulled out the bonnet, a ridiculous confection of chip straw au natural adorned with nothing more than the yellow ribbon tie and a bunch of cherries. It was incredibly understated, much too expensive ever to accept—unless one were Kitty, she reasoned—and too dear ever to decline.

"Here." He took it from her hands even as she stripped her own hat from her head, and then set it carefully on her hair, smoothing the tendrils that had sprung loose because of the warmth of the morning. "Oh, my. Lady Picton was quite right. Wait." He unstrapped his campaign trunk and pulled out his shaving mirror. "Have a look."

No matter which way she turned her face and looked in the small mirror, the hat was a wonder, and she was a wonder in it. All this from a hat? she asked herself. I vow even Mama would wonder at me now. After another moment's preening (which only made the major smile, she noted in the small space of the shaving mirror), she removed the hat and replaced it carefully in the box, as though it were blown eggs. "I cannot refuse it," she said honestly. She handed him his mirror. "How did you know?"

"I told you it was a lucky guess," he said as he replaced the mirror, "but I do recall each hat you wore, each a little different—flowers here, berries there—and worn with a certain—" he stretched for a word, looking at the vault overhead—"*élan,* as the French would have it. Miss Perkins, you have a flair for what becomes you."

"I'm sure I do not," she said promptly. "You need only listen to Mama animadvert upon the subject of my lacks." She replaced her own bonnet, tying it under her ear.

He sat himself on the edge of the table, and did not look at her. "Have you ever entertained the possibility that your mother could be wrong?"

She smiled at him, pleased to see him healthy enough to be clever, and funny. "You are quizzing me!"

"I don't quiz people very often," he replied, "particularly those who have helped me. I mean it."

"Then, I should blush," she replied, wondering where the conversation had taken this turn. "Actually, my family has high standards of beauty, so I think we can say that my mother is well-informed, sir." She held out her hand to him. "But I thank you for the gift, and yes, I will keep it. Wretch! I cannot resist it!"

"Excellent, madam." There was a pause; the mood changed.

He looked over her shoulder. "Miss Perkins, here comes the surgeon. I must have a word with him." "Very well, sir." She removed her cloak and put on the apron she had left on his bed the day before. As the surgeon approached, Major Reed took her arm.

"Miss Perkins, I really wish that you would leave now," he said, and she could not overlook the concern in his voice. "I suppose it is one thing to sit among the wounded, but these men are really desperate now, and ill beyond redemption."

"And therefore in more need than ever, sir," she said as she gently removed herself from his grasp. "I did not come day after day to ladle out broth, coo, and pat hands, Major Reed. It follows that I have not changed, now that they are all dying."

Brave words, Lydia, she told herself as she stood at the entrance to the lady chapel. She stood silently for a moment, her hands folded in front of her, gathering her courage.

"If you're determined to stay, sally forth, Miss P."

She turned around. The major was close by and watching her, solemn, but with just a glint of understanding in his eyes.

"I may need a push this morning," she confessed.

"Then, I will provide it." He came closer. "Miss Perkins, if you decide to marry me in the next day or two, I'm certain I can be found." He smiled and gave her a push. "It would certainly forward my scheme of inheritance, and give my aunt no end of pleasure to find out that I wasn't lying."

"But you were! Oh, bother it, Major Reed. I do not know you, sir, and it's quite out of the question."

He gave her another nudge, this time with his shoulder, and stood much too close. "I contend that you know me very well, Miss Perkins," he said, looking entirely too serious to suit her.

She shook her head and stepped away from him. "Depend upon it, Major. You now get to reap the rewards of a two-year-old joke on your relatives, unless an amazingly compliant female—which I am not!—can be found."

He nodded. "I suppose you are right. Lying on my stomach

at the Picton's certainly did not produce a wife, and my time is up here in London. Ah, well, Miss Perkins. Go to it."

With another shake of her head at the folly of some people, she went into the nave. The rows and rows of wounded were gone now, some men repaired, others released from the army, but most dead and buried. The stubborn ones, in whom the flames of life still refused to go out, were gathered together in an area closer to the main altar.

There was warm water in a pail beside the altar, so she took a pan from the altar, dipped some water, and added a touch of vanilla extract from the vial she had left there earlier in the week. Cook had given it to her. She took a cloth from her apron pocket and put it in the water. "Oh, this is puny remedy," she murmured. "Lord, help me."

If I were dying, what would I want? she asked herself as she went down the rows with the few other women who were as dogged in their duty as she. She wiped faces, sat and talked, where the soldiers were coherent, and just sat where others were not. I would want to know I was not alone.

It took her a moment to take the hand of the first man who looked close to death. Like the other women, she had busied herself in the last two weeks by cutting hair, shaving and washing faces, and attending to the most superficial of wounds that the surgeons would permit. There were no more men remaining to laugh and tease and flirt just a little as men did, no matter what their state of discomfort.

These were the dying now. They were silent, for the most part, beyond the world but still inhabitants of it in a curious way she could not explain, and which only left her in awe. Fear left her, and was replaced with a feeling of reverence. If mine is the last touch, their last connection with the only world we are sure of, she thought, then let it be a gentle touch, something perhaps like the one that ushered them into the world.

The man was not from Battery B, but as the census of veterans had continued to shrink throughout the week, she knew of him. He was a sergeant, one of the late arrivals from Toulouse. His hand lay hot and already lifeless on his rough blanket. She hesitated only a moment before she took hold of it.

Her grip was different from the surgeon's, who only took up a hand at the wrist to get a pulse. The sergeant's eyelids fluttered and then he opened them to look at her.

"Hello," she murmured. "You don't mind if I just sit here, do you?"

After a supreme effort, he shook his head. Another effort, and he spoke. She leaned far forward to hear him. "Tired, miss?"

How can you joke? she asked herself, her wonder far outweighing any squeamishness that remained. She smiled, surprising herself with how easy it was to do, and wiped his face with the vanilla-scented water. "Of course I am tired," she replied. "No one ever told me how exhausting soldiers are."

He smiled, and closed his eyes. She held his hand hour after hour, tightening her grip when he seemed to struggle with whatever was killing him, then loosening it when the pain subsided. He died at noon with a sigh that went on and on. The pain left his face, and his hand relaxed so completely that almost it felt part of hers.

She did not feel inclined to move, and she remained where she was. I am sitting in what is rapidly becoming a charnel house, holding the hand of a corpse, and I have never felt such serenity, she thought. Some part of her brain that was not intensely occupied with what was happening to her found a moment to think about Kitty and Mama, and their pouts and precocities over the most minute irritations. I recommend St. Barnabas' strange catechism, my dears, she thought as she stroked the man's hand one last time and let it rest on the blanket. I think even you would have to agree that we worry about the most trifling matters.

She stood, trying to lift what felt like blocks of wood from her shoulders, and remained in silence, looking down at the man.

"I know nothing about you, Sergeant, beyond your name, and the fact that some overworked surgeon should have removed your leg weeks ago instead of four days past," she whispered. "And I watched you face your last enemy with uncommon grace." His eyes were already closed, but she put her hands on them for a moment. "And you gave me some inkling how I should face death someday."

She turned away in tears. Major Reed sat close by with one of his men, watching her. He started to rise, but she shook her head. In another moment she was seated beside him, head bowed as she cried as quietly as she could.

"Here." He gave her his handkerchief. Beyond a close look full of sympathy, he said nothing more.

When the worst of her calamity passed, she blew her nose and calmly tucked her hair back in place. The major leaned toward her then, a slight smile on his face. "I know you are better now. After years and years of living with my sisters and other female relations, I have discovered that the moment a lady smoothes her hair again, and makes herself tidy, she is better."

Lydia nodded. "How do you get used to death?" she asked in a whisper.

"I never do," he replied promptly, "which is why I would say that my Peninsular service has been a trial, to say the very least. I take each death personally, Miss Perkins, and I hate it."

"Then, how do you manage?" It was a quiet question, but he seemed to be expecting it, as though he had begun to anticipate her. How odd, she thought.

"I used to get quite drunk, my dear," he said, "but on one of my sober days, I noted that the drunkards among the officer's corps seemed to have shorter life spans than I wished for myself, so I stopped." He sighed. "Now I think of home, and grassy meads, and the door opening at my manor house, and Mama coming out to meet me."

"You should be there now, sir," she said. "There isn't any

more you can do here. You've told me that much."

"And been ignored by you, I might add," he said, and she had the grace to blush. "You are right; I have been here too long." His voice hardened. "And done little good for these men, beyond adding my halfpenny's worth to a report that Lord Walsingham will present in all sincerity, and then file in some box and place on a shelf. I will go ...." He looked at the man lying on the cot. "... after he is gone."

She looked, too, chagrined to see that it was the private with the bad leg, the one who had joked with her that first day, and grown increasingly quiet as the infection spread. "I had not thought he would survive the night yesterday," she whispered, leaning close to the major. "I wish he had not. Look how even his face is now swollen with the infection from his leg. Oh, why did they not amputate?" She spoke more loudly than she intended, but she could not help herself. She gestured toward the body of the man she had just left. "And why was his leg amputated too late? Oh, I do not understand!"

The major did not release the hand of his private, but he took hers in his other hand. "Lydia, we know so little. I leave it at that, else I would become more bitter and cynical than I know I am already. You just have to let it alone."

"I cannot!" she said, and the ferocity of her voice startled her.

"You must," he insisted, and squeezed her hand before he released it.

She sat in silence beside him, wanting suddenly to lean her forehead against his shoulder, but knowing much better. After lengthy reflection and inward admonition, she turned her attention to the major, who was beginning to stoop over again.

"I thought you stayed at the Picton's for a rest," she accused him. "You need to lie down, don't you?"

He nodded. "General Picton's private surgeon decided to tinker with me. Were you aware of that portion by my right shoulder that was so red?"

She nodded, remembering how he favored it.

"He opened the wound again …"

"Oh, God!"

"… and extracted a portion of my uniform, which the saber had driven into my back. That was causing the infection."

She looked at him in horror, and he shook his head at her concern. "It's a common problem, Miss P, so don't get bug-eyed! My shoulder began to feel better immediately. I am certain I am almost well." He returned his attention to the private. "Unlike this poor devil, I had the advantage of a better man of science." He touched the soldier's cheek. "And now I go to one home, and he to another."

She sat a moment more in silence, then took a deep breath. "Major Reed, you will undo all your surgeon's good work if you do not lie down! I can sit here in your place. His name is Charles, isn't it? And he is from Bath?"

He nodded. "Yes. A workhouse there. There is much more, of course, but we are reduced to these essentials, eh, Charlie Banks?" he said.

There was no response, but from the major's tone, he had expected none. "Go lie down, sir. I can manage," she said, getting up. In another moment she was seated in the major's place, running the cool cloth over Charlie's face. When she finished, she took his hand in hers.

The major stared down at them both for a moment more, then made his way back to the lady chapel. She watched him go, making sure that he lay down upon his cot. As though I could do anything about it if he did not, she thought. She noted with amusement that he carefully retied the white satin bow on her hatbox before he lay down.

Men are strange creatures, she thought. Kitty regularly boasts that they are simple beings, but in this, as in other areas involving thought and observation, I think she comes up short. "Go home, Major Reed," she whispered. "You cannot do any more here. Nor can I, if ever I could."

The afternoon wore on longer than most afternoons. She had hoped to leave early, to get the smell of the hospital from her skin before she dressed for the Capitulation Banquet. Instead she sat in silence, listening to the sounds of revelry and bands playing in the streets outside as London went wild for the victors who had sent Napoleon to exile on Elba. Some fashionables came into the church for a look around, but they did not stay this time, driven out, she supposed, by the odor of putrefaction that was everywhere and unavoidable.

The sound of revelry faded as the shadows lengthened, and all she heard was the shallow breathing of Charles before her. It became more rapid, and she nearly called for Major Reed. I will wait, she told herself, even as she felt her own fears returning. Major Reed will never recuperate if he is continually jumping up and down to satisfy my own nerves, she reasoned. Willing herself into a steely sort of serenity, she carefully wiped the dying man's face and smoothed the hair back from his forehead. "You will do now," she whispered. "You are as clean and tidy as I can make you, and I will not let go."

To still her own anxiety, she hummed to him, and noticed that he seemed to relax. One or two times he forgot to breathe. She held her breath until he began again, but the rhythm was off now, and she knew he was close to death.

To her relief, she felt Major Reed's presence behind her. She did not turn around, but felt her own confidence returning. At least I do not have to walk this path alone again, she thought. At least, until the turn is mine.

Charles began to struggle for breath, and at last she turned around to motion the major closer. She stopped in surprise at first, and then in huge indignation.

Instead of the major, staring over her shoulder were two men in high shirt points, with fobs and seals. One of them held a cologne-drenched handkerchief to his nose.

"Oh, don't mind us," said the other, his tone as languid as the hand he waved at her. "We've never seen a man die before, and this is all so excessively diverting."

"Oh, God," she whispered, wanting to throw herself on the dying soldier to keep them from staring at him. "Please go away! He doesn't deserve this!"

The men only crowded closer. "He is only a common soldier, so how can it possibly matter?" said one, his voice muffled by the handkerchief. "You there, tell me. Do they all make such noises? I do hope he dies soon. We have another engagement"—he pulled out his pocket watch—"in an hour, but we do not want to miss something so promising."

"I thought they writhed about," said the other man, his tone disappointed. "He is merely lying there. We were expecting more," he concluded, and frowned at her as though such inattention to detail was her fault.

"Oh, you were?"

It was Major Reed, and he stood behind the men now, his uniform jacket off and his hair untidy from sleep.

Lydia stared at him. She thought she had seen the major angry before, but as she watched the way he stared at the two fribbles, inhabitants of their own class, she realized how wrong she was, how unenlightened. She had nothing except contempt for the human vultures who entertained themselves by watching Private Banks' death agony, but as she watched Major Reed's expression, she felt the smallest sympathy for the two men. "I think you two should leave now," she told them, her voice low.

"And lose a bet?" said the one with the handkerchief. "Lord Allsuch has one hundred pounds sitting on this one, and I intend to collect. Oh, do stand aside! He is doing something interesting now, isn't he? It's about time."

She turned back to the private, who in his struggle to breathe was attempting to raise up on his elbow. Keeping herself between him and the men who crowded close behind her, she elevated him with another pillow, then sat on the edge of his cot.

"You made a bet?"

Lydia flinched at the conversational tone in the major's voice. How can these men be so stupid? she asked herself in amazement. Major Reed had come closer now and was standing between her and the men.

"Yes! Yes!" said the other man impatiently. "Allsuch said we hadn't the rumgumption to watch one of the soldiers die at St. Barnabas. To prove we have been here, we are to take back some little souvenir from the dead man. You can find us something when he dies. I wish you would move."

"I'll find you something," the major said. "Let's be dears now and let Charlie die first, shall we?" He sat down beside Lydia and took the private's other hand. "It's all right, Private Banks. I order you to let go."

She thought he was beyond hearing, but the private opened his eyes one last time. "We did it, didn't we?" he gasped, and then he died.

The major sat in silence a moment and then he closed the private's eyes. "Yes, we did, Charlie," he whispered, tears on his cheeks. "From Vimeiro to Toulouse, by God. Shift a bit, Lydia."

She did as he ordered, and the major pulled the blanket she had been sitting on over his private's face. He turned around then, and still sitting on the cot, looked up at the fribbles. "Well, then, sirs, what can we do for you?"

His tone was so pleasant that she felt almost sick to her stomach. Go away! she pleaded silently, but the men were oblivious.

"To begin with, I am disappointed," said the man with the handkerchief. "I was expecting something more. Weren't you, Lindsay? I thought so."

"Really?"

"Yes, and this place stinks," complained the other.

Major Reed rose to his feet then. Lydia wanted to leap up and grab his arm, but she remained where she was. Reed sniffed the air elaborately, leaning close to the men until they backed up. "Funny. The only stink I notice comes from you two worthless hounds of hell."

He said it so calmly that it took a moment for his words to sink in. "See here!" declared one.

"Yes!" said the other. "Do you know who my father is?"

"No, and I doubt that you do, either," the major said. "You're not fit to stand with heroes," he continued, his voice rising slightly as he stepped closer and the men continued to retreat. "I could puke when I think that we—Charlie here and I— fought for dregs like you."

She could see fear in their eyes now as the men shuffled backward against the major's relentless advance. "I just need a souvenir!" insisted the one with the handkerchief. He gasped as he brushed against a pile of stained bandages.

"I have some proof for you. You can take it to Mayfair."

Before she could move to stop him, Major Reed bent down and picked up an earthenware jar covered with a cloth. With one swift motion, he threw the contents onto the two fashionables. Dripping, stinking, they screamed and clutched each other, then ran from the chapel.

His hand to his shoulder, the major sat down on a vacant cot. "I probably shouldn't have done that," he said after a long pause.

She thought of all the hot words she could throw at him about manners and decorum, and rudeness to possibly prominent people, but none of them seemed terribly important. She touched the blanketed arm of the private. Charles, you had an able defender, she thought, but you knew that, didn't you?

"No, you shouldn't have done that," she agreed, matching him calm for calm. "You might have hurt your shoulder again."

She stood up, noting how curious it was that the room seemed to be dipping and spinning. She waited a moment until the building stood still again, then crossed the dripping floor to Major Reed and held out her hand to him.

"Let us shake hands, sir. I am going now, and I will not be back. Do listen to your surgeons just once in a while. Oh, and I wish you luck in your matrimonial career."

He looked startled that she would leave, and this surprised her. "You have been telling me to go all day," she reminded him.

"I suppose I have." He shook her hand. "Mind that you wash your hands really well, Miss Perkins." He cleared his throat, and changed the subject in that drastic way of his. "If you won't marry me, would you allow me to write you?"

I would love to know how you go on in Northumberland, she thought, and whether you can find a wife, or even stand up straight again. "No, sir. That is rather too forward. Good day."

He seemed to take it in good grace, smiling and nodding as she picked her way across the floor. I will honestly miss him, she thought, and turned around for a last look.

He had not moved any closer, so he spoke to her in a loud voice, an artillery voice, one used to carrying over canister and round-shot. "As far as I can see, Miss Perkins, you have only one lack."

"I am an antidote?" she called back.

"God, no!" he said. "I don't know why you say that, and it irritates me." He held his thumb and forefinger close together. "Your spirit of adventure is a bit undeveloped. That is all."

She turned away. Thank you and good-bye, Major Reed, she thought.

8

⁓

LYDIA WAS QUITE ALONE with her thoughts as she rode home from St. Barnabas, and her thoughts were not productive. With a heavy heart she gazed out the window, seeing the arches and banners proclaiming victory, and wondering if anyone who cheered or raised glasses had even an inkling of the terrible price of success. I know I never did, she thought.

She stirred restlessly in the carriage, wishing that she could have walked off some of the agitation that festered inside. The war was over, and discounting renewed trouble in America, and the agitation that always simmered in India, England was more at peace than anytime she could remember. By the time the last man dies at St. Barnabas, she knew that few would even remember that anyone was there in the crumbling structure except bats and mice.

"What did you expect, Lydia?" she scolded herself. "You didn't know such places existed before your first visit." She wondered what she would do with her newfound knowledge. If Kitty does not contract a good alliance, we will return to Devon, and things will go on as before, she thought. Mama will scold and rail, Kitty will demand and pout, and I will be expected to soothe and placate each, while Papa retreats to his study. Life will go on as before, she decided and the fact did not fill her with any enthusiasm, even though it was the only life she knew.

She leaned against the glass and closed her eyes. I suppose I will always wonder about Private Charlie Banks, lowliest of men, a loader and rammer in the remarkable Battery B, where he had worth and family. I can pray he died peacefully, his commander with him, and not aware of the two creatures who saw him only as entertainment on a boring afternoon.

She took a deep breath and sat up straight, appalled all over again by what she had witnessed. You creatures are lucky that Major Reed only emptied the slops on you, she thought. How sad that the major and his men should have to fight through Portugal, Spain, and France, then come home to fight different battles no less painful.

What is my place, now that I have earned so much education? The question was high in her mind as she went into the house on Holly Street. I should probably say something to Mama, she thought. It will be an unpleasant interview, but I ought to advise her to warn away Kitty from the likes of those two—oh, I cannot call them men—those two unfeeling beings.

There was no time for conversation, she discovered, as she glanced at the clock, then hurried upstairs, where the overworked maid who worked for her and Kitty had already drawn her a bath. It was lukewarm, but she sank into it with gratitude, wondering if there was enough soap in the world to remove the disease and death that layered her like armor.

She knew Mama would never permit her to carry on any sort of philanthropic work at home. Lydia sank lower in the water. "I can hear you now, Mama," she said. " 'What would the neighbors think, Lydia, to find you grubbing in workhouses? A little soup at Christmas to the deserving poor, or some ox-foot jelly is all that is expected of a lady.' "

She washed thoughtfully, thinking of marriage, and reflecting on the vicar's wives she had known through the years; dour, practical women, for the most part, who were expected to do more good than their parishioners. I shall have to figure out how to snare a vicar, she thought. But oh, how I dread the idea of Sunday sermons!

There was no time for more reflection: the water was already getting cold. From habit, she dressed by herself, knowing that the maid would be entirely occupied with Kitty's needs. She smoothed down the folds carefully, her spirits rising a little. Papa had purchased the fabric for her when Mama and Kitty were in Bath, and the dress was commissioned and constructed before they returned. She clasped on the garnet necklace, then mentally kicked herself because she had left behind at St. Barnabas the beautiful bonnet that Major Reed had purchased for her. "Oh, I am stupid," she said, looking at herself in the mirror. "The dear thing would have been perfect."

Likely he is on his way to Northumberland by now, she thought. I wonder what he has done with the hat? I shall go back tomorrow and hunt for it, she told herself, even though she knew she would never return to the church.

How quiet the house is, she thought as she went downstairs to the drawing room and seated herself, careful not to wrinkle the fabric. St. Barnabas was quiet, too, she thought, unable to direct her mind along other channels. Death is charitable to come so quietly. One moment there is life, and in the next, Private Banks sees more and knows more than we do who remain behind. She closed her eyes. I must clear my mind of this, or it will overpower me, she thought.

Papa joined her in a few minutes, dressed formally and looking every inch a baronet. He ruined the effect by peering around the edge of the door before he came into the room. It is all right, Papa, she wanted to reassure him, but she merely smiled. How sad that we have almost nothing to say, after twenty-two years in the same family. "Papa, you look quite handsome," she said finally.

He started, as usual, then smiled back. "So do you, my dear. I believe yellow is most attractive on you." He cleared his throat, and glanced around again. "How was your day at St. Barnabas?" he asked, as he had every evening for the past two weeks.

Papa, they are all dying now, and it is quite hopeless. Vulgar men prey on the soldiers, and make a mock of their death struggles. I have seen such cruelty today that it will probably change my life. "It was as usual, Papa," she said after a long pause. "I … I think I will not be returning, though."

His vague look was replaced for the briefest moment by a glance of deepest concern, followed by an expression unfamiliar to her. Was it regret? She could not tell.

"Daughter, do let me tell you now while it is … quiet, how proud I am that you have done this thing." He said it quickly, as though afraid to be found out with an opinion.

It was a rare compliment, and filled her with unexpected pleasure. "I did so little, Papa," she said, apology high in her voice.

Another look around. He moved himself closer along the sofa. "You did more than any of us, my dear." He leaned closer to take her hand. "I do not know a man in London prouder of a daughter than I am."

"Humphrey, for once I am entirely in agreement with you!"

He started, and released her hand. "Yes, my dear," he said, turning to look at his wife in the doorway.

Kitty stood beside her, magnificent in pale blue. Lydia looked closer. *I wonder if she knows she has forgotten her petticoat,* she almost said, then changed her mind. *I suppose it is all the crack to appear half naked at these functions, and I am merely out of step,* she thought.

"Kitty *is* enough to make any father proud," Mama said.

Papa cleared his throat. "Actually, I was … I meant … Yes, my dear, she is lovely."

Poor Papa, Lydia thought. And poor Kitty, if I do not warn

her. "You need to know something," she said as she went to her mother and sister. "Kitty dear, it distresses me to tell you this, but do have a care around some of the young men of the ton."

Kitty stared at her blankly. "Whatever are you blathering about, Lydia?" she asked. "Do come out with whatever maggot has got into your brain." She glanced at the clock on the mantelpiece. "I am certain we do not have time for nonsense." She looked at her mother for confirmation, then back to Lydia. "We have already waited for you to return from that … that sewer where you insist on spending your days."

"And we would not have waited, except that these invitations came especially from General Picton himself, particularly to you!" Mama reminded her.

"I know, Mama, and I am sorry for any trouble." Lydia considered all of Kitty's sensibilities, and condensed her story into several sentences—leaving out Major Reed's impulsive reaction—as Kitty frowned at her and Mama listened, her face a study in irritation. Well, you should be angry, Mama, she thought as she finished. I know I would not wish the daughter I have so many hopes for exposed to such creatures. "I thought you would wish to be warned away from association with such people," she concluded, looking to her father for support.

To her amazement, Kitty laughed. "Lydia, you goose! That Lindsey you speak of is Lord Lindsey." She dimpled prettily. "Or more properly, I should call him Viscount Lindsey. Yes, his father is Lord Walsingham."

"More shame then," Lydia said quietly. "When I think of the trouble his father has gone to, preparing his report on medical conditions, I could shudder that his son …."

"Lydia, this is quite enough!" Mama said. "Lord Lindsey is all the rage this Season. See, you are wounding Kitty. How could you do that?"

She stared at her sister, who had begun to pout. Oh, Lord, she thought in disgust, in another moment there will be tears and a scene. I do not understand these people I am related to. She tried again. "Kitty, I'm only warning you. Probably the largest beast in this whole affair is someone called Allsuch. The whole wretched bet was his idea. And that other man, the one with the handkerchief and the languid air … I cannot think him fit company for demons."

Kitty drew herself up to her full height and glared at Lydia. "Lord Allsuch." She said the words distinctly, biting them off as Mama would have. "He is my particular friend. Indeed, Lydia, I have high hopes of him, so do keep your silly scruples to yourself."

Lydia gasped, as though her sister had struck her. She took Kitty by the shoulders. "Katherine Elaine, they watched a man die for entertainment! How can you …."

Kitty wrenched herself away and turned to her mother. "Mama, we will be late if we listen to much more of this. Lydia, I wish you would not take things so hard." She laughed, and the sound was brittle and hard to Lydia's ears. "Lord, Mama, we should never have brought her up from Devon. You were right, but I thought London would do her good."

"It did," Lydia said quietly as she turned away to gather her shawl from the sofa. Papa gazed at her with an expression of deep concern, but she did not trouble to return it. I have no allies here, she thought. Her head began to ache, and she knew it would be a long evening.

They rode in absolute, deafening silence to the Capitulation Banquet, each staring out a window of the carriage. I cannot look at them, Lydia thought. Kitty and Mama are no better than Private Banks' tormentors. She rested her forehead against the glass. No, they are worse. I have warned them of evildoings, and they choose to ignore it, all in the name of fashion. She closed her eyes. And Papa will do nothing to prevent their moral ruin.

The carriage was claustrophobic. She dug her fingers into the fabric of her dress, wrinkling the material and bringing down a fierce hiss from Mama to stop it, her only comment on the entire trip. Her panic increased the closer they came to the banquet hall and other carriages converged. Her eyes full of shock and disbelief, she stared at the other occupants, people as well dressed as the Perkinses, as well mannered, and probably with more wealth and position. Waves of humiliation washed over her. We are mushrooms from Devon, she thought, and not for the first time. Our title is small, even though our estate is well enough, and we have only one pretty face to recommend us. I am mortified.

After a wait that turned into another hour of excruciating silence, it was their turn to descend from their carriage. Lydia followed Kitty and her parents into the hall, wishing that she could vanish as Mama preened and looked around, and Papa cringed anytime someone jostled him. Kitty sailed forward with confidence, smiling and waving.

She stopped after a few minutes and whispered to Mama. In the press of people, Lydia was close enough to hear her sister's complaint, and she felt her bones chill. "Mama, no one is waving back to me! What can be the problem?" Kitty whispered. She looked down at her dress. "Surely I am à la mode!"

Mama whispered something in return to placate Kitty as Lydia took a deep breath and looked around. It was true. Some of the others were staring at them and whispering among themselves. No one smiled. I wonder, Lydia thought as the blood drained from her face. I wonder if that dreadful Lindsey or the other man recognized *me* this afternoon? She took a deep breath to counteract her sudden light-headedness. What did I say to either of them that wasn't the truth? She pressed her hands to her middle, suddenly queasy. And Major Reed's reaction would be hard to overlook. Put the two together ....

She wanted to sit down, but the tide of people bore them on into the banquet hall. The crowd thinned as people began to take their seats. She was almost afraid to glance at Kitty, who hung back now in an unaccustomed way, clutching her mother's arm, unable to account for the reaction of the young ladies and gentlemen she had teased and flirted with only that morning at a balloon ascension, or some other pointless, insipid gathering. As Lydia watched in growing concern, Kitty suddenly smiled and stepped forward.

Lydia groaned, then put her hand to her mouth. It was Lord Allsuch, and with him was that nasty tall man, minus his handkerchief, but unmistakable. With a highly artificial smile, Lord Allsuch beckoned her sister forward, then gave an elaborate, mocking bow that made her step back in surprise. Oh, please, no, Lydia thought. I have ruined us.

He spoke quite distinctly. There wasn't anyone within earshot who could not have heard him. Indeed, the anteroom had grown quite silent. "Kitty dear, let me warn your sister."

Kitty stopped in the middle of a smile.

"What do you mean, Edward?" she said, ready to put her hand into his, but hesitating now, as he did not offer his own. "My sister does nothing of importance here in London."

"She keeps dreadful low company in a charnel house." He took a deep breath and sniffed the air around Kitty's exquisite hair arrangement. "Dearest, dearest Kitty, I fear it has rubbed off on you! Such a stink."

Kitty stared in openmouthed amazement as Lord Allsuch bowed elaborately again and rejoined his friends. Everyone laughed, whispered among themselves again, and ignored the Perkins as they all moved forward to take their places.

White-faced now and trembling, Kitty leaned on Mama's arm and allowed herself to be led to a near table. No one else sat close to them. Lydia seated herself, and in a few words, completed the other part of the story—Major Reed's part—as her family stared at her. "I had no idea he was going to do that, Mama, really," she pleaded. "He was so angry, and there was Private Banks dead, an object of fun. You would have done …." Her voice trailed off. No, no one else in my family would have done what Major Reed did. "I am sorry, Kitty," she concluded quietly. "I know this is wounding to you, but you cannot want such low company. No one with true feelings would."

Kitty began to cry. The tears slid down her face in that wonderful way of hers without causing any blemish or ugliness. It was an art that she had practiced for a solid year in front of the mirror, with devastating results on the local Devonshire swains. There was no one to watch now, and sympathize. No family was as ignored as they were now.

Lydia shivered and drew her wrap close around her shoulders, trying to ignore the sniggers and pointing of fingers at Kitty, who was sobbing quite openly now. She thought Mama would rise and sweep out of the hall, with the rest of them to trail out in her wake, but she made no move at all. They sat close together, deriving no comfort from each other, afraid to call attention to themselves by leaving.

The dinner began. She tried to eat, but it was as though her throat were sealed. She put down her fork, scarcely daring to look around. General Picton, sitting several rows away, caught her eye and smiled at her, obviously unmindful of their ruin. If I were a man, I would take the king's shilling and follow General Picton to the next battle, she thought. I do not think Holly Street will be any better than this banquet hall. After everyone has had their fun with us, Mama will turn on me.

She sat rigid, scarcely daring to move. During the two hours spent not eating, Kitty managed to compose herself. Beyond an occasional sob that sounded like muffled hiccups, she was silent. Lydia could not bring herself to look at her mother.

She could have cried with relief when Lord Walsingham finally rose to speak. Some talks, some toasts, and they would be out of the hall. If they really hurried, no one would have any more opportunity to snub them. For no good reason, other than the fact that she was an optimist by nature, Lydia allowed her hopes to rise. Surely not everyone approved of evil schemes hatched by idle young men. Surely Kitty will be approached by her more discerning friends, she thought. I cannot believe that her Season is unsalvageable. A little time will make such a difference. People forget.

Later that night, lying in her bed perfectly miserable, she had time to think through the events of the next few minutes. If I had not *listened* to Lord Walsingham, it never would have happened, she thought. If I had not *cared* so much, she told herself. But she did listen, and she did care.

"In conclusion, honorables and distinguished guests, let me kneel for a moment at the feet of those noble among us who have taken of their valuable time to visit the sick in our hospitals," Lord Walsingham was saying. He gestured toward the assembled diners. "Some do not trumpet the good they do," he said.

"I know he means ladies like you, daughter," Papa whispered. "I am certain of it."

She looked at him, startled. She had forgotten he had even tagged after them into the hall. She started to say something then stopped, because Lord Walsingham was continuing, after a modest pause. His tone became warm, more intimate. "I call attention to my own son, who—when I dragged it out of him! Modest boy—was even paying such a call of sympathy today at St. Barnabas. All honor to such ...."

She heard a chair scraping back and someone rising and declaring in ringing tones, "Sir, you have been misled. He went there to do great mischief and watch men die for entertainment!"

Lydia looked around her for the voice and realized with sick horror that it was her own. Oh, God, she thought weakly, as her legs turned to pudding under her. She clutched at the table to keep upright, and then felt the great anger build even greater within her. Her indignation lit a fire that spread through her whole body like wind up an air shaft. She stood as straight and tall as she could.

"I know because I was there, my lord. On a wager, your son and another were sent by a weak mind named Allsuch to see if they had the stomach to watch men die, and then to return with ... with souvenirs!"

She spit out the last word like a bad taste. The hall was deadly quiet now, except for Kitty's sobs, and Mama's hisses for her to sit down. Papa seemed to have vanished. Some force within her kept her going. "Unlike you, sir, I can only sorrow at the great hypocrisy among us. We send men to war to fight and die for us. If they are not of our class, we ignore them, give them only the poorest places to lick their wounds, then send them back into the ranks only half well, if that."

The tall man next to Lord Walsingham rose to his feet and began to applaud her. She thought he was mocking at first, and she stopped in confusion; then she noticed the deadly serious expression on his face. She clutched the table to stay on her feet, for Mama was pulling at her dress now.

"Where are the hospitals for these men? Must they suffer in ruined churches with bad drains and more mice than sound masonry? My lord, I know that you care, but I am sickened by the hypocrisy in the rest of us assembled, who make sport of good men."Others were on their feet now, applauding her. She could see General Picton rise, and other men whose faces were familiar to her from depictions in store windows and on victory arches over London's major streets.

"It is time to ask questions in Parliament, my lord, about this neglect of those less gentled by birth than we are, but who fight our battles," she declared in ringing tones. "And then we should question those among us, who look upon the wounded as playful objects to while away the breathless tedium of boring, useless lives!"

She paused, struck finally by the effrontery of her action. Her anger had cooled itself into a little banked fire, and with the sickest of feelings, she knew she had just completed her family's ruin in London Society, even as England's greatest heroes applauded her. She sat down with a thump.

"Have you lost your mind completely?" Mama hissed at her. Mama's face was a sickly green color, and Kitty had withdrawn into that curious blank state preceding monumental hysteria.

"Mama, it is only the truth," Lydia said, when her lips would move again.

"I wash my hands of you!" Mama exclaimed, then turned to Kitty.

The applause continued, relentless, unimportant now in the reality of what she had done to her family. Without a word to her parents, she leaped up and fled the banquet hall, pursued by the approbation of the Peninsular veterans, but deeply aware of her own downfall. Mama would rather that we were hypocrites, she thought as she walked swiftly from the banquet hall, unmindful of the rain and its ruin of her dear dress. She shook her reticule for coins, then hailed a hackney, which took her swiftly home.

Stanton was astonished to see her: wet, fearful, and wide-eyed with disbelief at herself. "I do not know anyone more meek than myself," she told him later, when wrapped in a blanket and warming herself with mulled wine and sympathy in the servants hall. "I said all those things, Stanton! Mama is furious. I doubt she will let me stay here."

The servants exchanged looks; there was nothing they could say, which only increased her terror. It was true.

She was in her room, huddled into a ball in her chair by the fire, when the rest of them returned. Kitty was shrieking. In sick horror at what she had done, Lydia heard the front door slam again, and a few moments later, heavy steps on the stair. The doctor was here now. In a few more minutes, the shrieks ended. She closed her eyes, praying that her door was locked, as she heard her mother's footsteps.

"I will see you in the morning," was all she said outside her door.

"Yes, Mama." Lydia was on her feet now. I wonder how many things I can stuff into a bandbox, she thought as she went calmly to her chest of drawers. And more to the point, I wonder where on earth I will go in the morning?

9

⤫

LYDIA DID NOT SLEEP all night, but packed and repacked a bandbox until she had a petticoat, second dress, chemise, stockings, and shoes folded within. She would have liked to add a nightgown, but she thought a shawl more useful. Thank God it is high summer, she told herself. I will not be cold until fall, and who knows where I will be then?

She devoted that darkest part of the night between midnight and three o'clock to an appraisal of her abilities, and where they would get her. The result of her personal inventory of marketable skills only made her queasy. Perhaps things will appear more sanguine when the sun rises, she thought, remembering a moment at St. Barnabas when one of the surgeons took a moment to sit down and drink tea. He had told her that dying people seemed to fade fastest after midnight and before dawn. "Experience tells me it is a most hopeless time, Miss Perkins," he had remarked.

"You are right, sir," she said out loud around three o'clock. "I can knot a fringe, barber and cut hair, sketch a little, dance a little, play the pianoforte a little, sing a little." She sighed. "I know nothing about cooking—although I would be a willing student—and less about running a house. I do not flinch at open wounds, or removing maggots from high flesh." She rose and forced herself on another weary turn about the room. "Altogether it is an eccentric list of talents that will get me nowhere."

She almost dozed off at three-thirty, but a maggot of her own advised her to check her finances. In a moment she was on her knees by her trunk in the dressing room. Papa had given her five pounds before they left Devon, and three pounds were still there. "Thank goodness for that," she said, turning her face for comfort into the fabric of her favorite dress folded over the trunk. She shook her reticule again, and it was lighter, thanks to her hackney ride from the banquet hall to Holly Street. I will resolve to walk more, she thought, then shuddered, even though the room was warm. It is not a matter of resolution but necessity. Worn out with worry, she went to sleep as the sun was rising, only to dream of Private Charlie Banks dying over and over again, with those fops simpering and jumping up and down behind her, trying to see him. They would not leave, no matter how she pushed against them, and then Kitty was screaming and would not stop.

She woke up in a panic, her breath coming in short gasps that made her dizzy. She lay in her own sweat, her nightgown twisted around her like a wound-up top. With more dread in her heart than she could remember from other encounters with Mama, she listened for Kitty.

The house was completely silent, almost as though all of its inmates were holding their breath. She listened for the usual homely sounds of servants pattering to and from rooms with hot water, or tea. There was nothing. They have all gone to Devon and left me here, she thought, but knew that could never be. Mama would never miss an opportunity for a good scold. If only she will confine herself to a scold, Lydia thought with a shiver.

She got out of bed and went to the window, half expecting

to see that she had imagined daylight and it was still night. She blinked at the bright sunlight. Well, so much for my theory that I have dreamed this whole wretched business, she thought.

As she watched the street below, the postman stopped his cart in front of their house, rummaged around, and produced a collection of letters so large that it required an extra turn of the twine to contain them. Lydia sighed with relief. "There you are, Kitty," she murmured against the window glass. "More invitations."

It was a large collection, and then she remembered the invitations to their own rout that she and Mama and Kitty had labored over last week. There is nothing like a little notoriety to increase the RSVPs beyond one's wildest expectations, she thought. I wonder if we should increase our champagne order, as well. After Mama scolds me, I shall suggest that to her.

She dressed quickly, then tiptoed next door to Kitty's room, and let herself in quietly. The room was dark, but she could make out Kitty sleeping soundly. Lydia frowned, recognizing the slowness of her breathing as the pattern that always followed doctor visits. Kitty, I wish you did not require sedation after trying moments, she told herself. Perhaps in this pile of mail, there will be new inanities to attract your notice.

Satisfied that Kitty was sleeping peacefully, Lydia returned to her room to find Stanton waiting for her. Oh, dear, she thought, here comes Mama's scolding. If I am summoned to the blue salon instead of the sitting room, I know I am in for heavy sailing.

"Madam wants to see you immediately in the book room," he said.

"That is a new place for a scold," she said. "Wish me well, Stanton."

He did not smile. She had never seen him so serious, even allowing for his usual butler's demeanor. "Miss Perkins, it may be beyond that," he said finally as he held the door for her and followed her out.

She sighed with resignation. So it has finally come to that, she told herself. For my sins of Christian charity and righteous indignation, Mama is sending me back to Devon. After a moment's reflection, she could not say that the feeling stung her. This might be my opportunity to visit with the vicar's wife and carve out some role for myself in the parish. I will probably even be meek and biddable again by the time the rest of them return.

She knocked on the door. There was no answer. She knocked again, then pressed her ear against the panel to listen for a response. "Oh, dear," she whispered, and listened again at something unheard of: Mama was crying, but not the gentle tears one would expect from a grown woman. Not that Mama ever cried, Lydia reasoned. She had nothing to cry about. These were the noisy tears of a thwarted child. Lydia knocked again, less confident this time. Again there was no answer, but she squared her shoulders and entered the room anyway.

Mama sat at the desk, sorting through the invitations, tears streaming down her face. She ignored Lydia for the longest time, then blew her nose and wiped her eyes. Still she said nothing. Mama's tears had been replaced by an expression so cold that Lydia felt her blood run in chunks. As she watched, Mama gathered up the letters. She held them close to her breast for a moment, then stood up and threw them at Lydia.

"There is the result of your night's work, Lydia Perkins," Mama said. She turned her back to Lydia and went to the window.

Startled, Lydia picked up a handful of letters. "Oh, Mama, I certainly can't take credit for all these invitations," she said. "I just knew that people of sense and reason would rally to us."

Mama turned around to stare at her. Before Lydia even had time to take a deep breath, Mama strode across the room and slapped her. "These are all regrets, daughter! Every single one of them!"

Lydia gasped. She took her hand away from her burning

cheek and opened one of the letters that she held. She read it quickly as her insides began to churn. The handwriting was beautiful, well-bred, and the note was written on the best paper. Her eyes were watering from the force of Mama's blow, but still the phrases, "… want nothing to do with your family," and "We withdraw our invitation to you for Tuesday next," leaped out at her like imps. Her hands shaking now, she opened another letter. "… sever all acquaintance …" she whispered as she grabbed up another letter. "… worse than barbaric conduct …" And another. "… what can one expect …."

She knew her face had drained of all color because she felt suddenly light-headed. Lydia sank into a chair by the door, still clutching the letters. "Mama, these people have no feelings, no sense of honor! Surely you cannot want Kitty to …."

Mama was directly in front of her now, her hands like iron bars on Lydia's legs. "It is precisely these people of money and titles that I sought for Kitty!" She looked away, almost overcome with her anger. "*Poor* Kitty, I should call her now. You have ruined her chances! I wonder that we will not even be laughed out of Devon, and what could be less inconsequential than *Devon!*" She was shouting now, so loud that Lydia's ears began to hurt. "How could you stand there and wound those young men! Kitty all but had Lord Allsuch in her pocket! Sixty thousand a year and a marquis! Lydia, have you no sense at all?"

To Lydia's indescribable relief, Mama flung herself away, retreating to the far corner of the room as though she could not abide her presence.

"Mama, I am …."

"Sorry?" Mama sneered.

"Well, no, actually," Lydia said, stopping herself too late. "That is, I mean …."

She flinched and raised her hands to protect her face when Mama came toward her again, but her mother barely glanced at her. She went to the door instead, clutching the knob until it looked as if the bones of her hands would break through.

"Papa and I are taking Kitty back to Devon as soon as we can pack," she said, biting off her words. "If this ... this scandal doesn't follow us like a bad stink, perhaps we can arrange a marriage with the squire's son! The *squire's* pimply son, Lydia, when she could have had a marquis!"

"I ... can close up the house for you, Mama," Lydia whispered, "and follow later."

Quicker than Lydia would have imagined, her mother grabbed her by the hair and yanked her face hard against the door frame.

"I cannot think of anything you can do that would ever induce me to want to see you again, Lydia. Not anything," she added for emphasis.

That was all. After another yank for good measure, Mama released her and stormed from the room. Her stomach in complete turmoil, her face on fire, Lydia sank to the floor among the scattered letters. They rustled around her as she drew her knees up close to her body and cried. She cried quietly, not wishing to disturb her mother into a return visit to the book room. When she finished, she dried her eyes on the hem of her dress, then touched her cheek gingerly, wincing at the pain. Her lip felt swollen, too. She touched it, then sighed and wiped the blood on her petticoat, and rested her good cheek against her knees. Who are these people who have raised me? she asked herself in disbelief.

She sat there in silence for another few minutes, mainly to assure herself that Mama would not return. She nearly shrieked in fear when she heard footsteps, but they went quickly past the book room door, so she knew it was a servant. When the house was absolutely silent again, she left the room and tiptoed upstairs. Kitty's door was ajar, so she knew Mama was in there. She crossed quietly on the other side of the hall and let herself into her room.

She was almost afraid to look in the mirror, but she forced herself, and then drew back in dismay. A bruise—ugly and purple—stood out on her cheek like a carbuncle. This will never do, she thought as she went to the basin for a cloth and cold water. She sat rocking back and forth on her bed, the cloth pressed to her cheek and her lip, which was swollen. But only a little, she decided, after another look in the mirror. I doubt it will be noticeable tomorrow.

Her cheek was hopeless, however. Experience told her that in a week it would be just a fading greenish-yellow. But meanwhile …. "Oh, bother," she said. "Oh, bother. This complicates matters."

She sat back on her bed, wondering what to do. The decision was made for her when Kitty began to scream. Lydia clamped her hands to her ears, but the noise scarcely diminished. Mama, did you inform her that she was returning to Devon and destined for the squire's son? Lydia thought. Truly I am sorry for that, but Kitty, for all his spots and stammers, he is a far better man than Lord Allsuch, who makes devilish bets.

The screams continued, then turned into loud sobs, and finally subsided. The eerie silence that followed was twice as disturbing as the noise. Lydia sighed, remembering outbursts at home, and Kitty's stormy fits. "And my own 'punishments,' eh, Mama?" she said as she applied another compress to her ruined cheek. Servants had an instinct about silence around the manor. I wish my own were as good, she thought. I wish I knew when to keep silent. Mama is right; I *am* stupid.

She said it out loud, and then again, wondering why she did not believe it this time. "No, Lydia, you were right to stand up and say what you did last night," she told herself. "Evil of that nature should not be tolerated, no matter what Mama thinks."

She thought again of the men at St. Barnabas, both the sick and the dead, and their courage, and of Major Reed's numerous trips to Horse Guards on their behalf. I think he has been using his own money to get them settled elsewhere, she thought. He's not afraid to say what he thinks. Her hand went to her cheek. Of course, no one strikes him.

She knew what she had to do, but it frightened her, so she remained where she was for a few minutes more. I will count to ten, then I will be about it, she told herself as she started counting slowly. She reached ten, and still she did not move. She counted again, and this time she got to her feet.

Her traveling dress buttoned up the front, so she had no difficulty in putting it on. Sturdy shoes were essential, so she rummaged about until she found them. The hat would have to be a deep-brimmed one, to hide her bruised face. She put it on and frowned. It was better than nothing, but not by much. She drew on her best kid gloves, even though they were black and it was the wrong season for black. I do not know that I will be able to afford another pair like them for some time to come, she thought.

Her bandbox was full, but she knew she could carry it, since hackneys were beyond her price range now. I am leaving so much behind! she thought with regret. My books, my writing paper, my sketches. She paused at the desk, considering for a moment whether she should leave a note, then decided against it. I have nothing to say, she decided.

The ease with which she left the house astonished her. The upstairs hall was deserted. She heard Papa rustling about in his study when she passed it downstairs, but she felt no inclination to stop. Worse than useless, sad little man, she thought, tightening her lips together and wincing at the sharp pain.

She feared that Stanton would be stationed by the front door, but he was nowhere in sight. She was almost disappointed. It would have been nice to say good-bye to him.

Keeping her head down, she walked east toward the city, and did not look back at the house. When she turned from Holly Street, relief flooded her like warm rain. The feeling lasted until the next corner, where she stopped. During her rides to and from St. Barnabas, she had noticed an employment registry office. Which corner? she asked herself as she started moving again.

She saw it finally after a half hour's walk toward London's center, "open after luncheon," read the sign in the window. The sign seemed to trigger her own hunger, even though it was early in the morning. A bowl of an undetermined soup yesterday at St. Barnabas had been her only recent meal, she reminded herself. She had consumed nothing except great mounds of humiliation since then. She looked about, wondering where one went to eat in London. Another block took her past a public house, where she could smell onion soup and the sharp odor of new ale.

Working men went into the shop, but no women. She knew she dared not go in there, so she kept walking until she found a bakery. Standing in front of the window, she caught a glimpse of her own reflection in the glass and stopped. Her hand went to her cheek, and she lowered her head and turned away.

She found a small park a block over, and settled for a drink from the fountain, disturbed beyond words by her own reflection, and the dreadful thought that no employment agency would hire her with her face so bruised. It will be better in a week, but what will I do until then? She had no idea. She felt herself wilting inside. Panic started to rise, but she forced it down and compelled herself to consider her situation.

An hour's thought did nothing to change the reality that she was hungry, in pain, and without resources. I am too afraid to go into a public house, and right now, my face will never recommend me to a potential employer, she thought. I have three pounds to my name, and have no idea where to stay, or how to afford it.

She shivered, despite the warmth of the day, and looked around her. In another moment she was smiling. "Well, at least I am not lost," she said to a squirrel who sat on her bench, looking hopeful. "That is something."

She knew where she was. Another two blocks would take her closer to the docks, but in sight of St. Barnabas with its two spires, one of them stately, and the other falling down, probably a ruin since the War of the Roses. Who would ever have thought the old pile to look so good? she thought as she rose. I have nowhere to go, so I might as well see if I can do some good at St. Barnabas. "I have a hat there, too," she reminded herself. Just think, Lydia, if you can find your hat, you can pawn the dear thing, providing that you know where to find a pawn store. She picked up her bandbox and started off, resolving someday that if she ever married and was blessed with children, she would teach them useful skills, such as how to find a job, eat in public, and pawn things.

Her smile lasted to the doors of St. Barnabas, which were wide open, as usual. She peered inside, and discovered to her distress that the place was nearly empty. Surely not all those men died since yesterday, she thought in alarm. As her eyes accustomed themselves to the gloom, she saw a few cots remaining, and a surgeon.

"They're the ones who cannot be moved, Miss Perkins."

She looked around in surprise to see the other surgeon. "But where are the others, sir?" she asked. "I was hoping to help."

He smiled at her. "My dear Miss Perkins, you have already done more for them than anyone ever could! After your speech last night, and a visit from the Duke of Wellington himself this morning, those men were moved to better quarters." He gestured at the few remaining. "Poor fellows. We cannot move them, but they won't be long here."

"I am glad to have been of service," she said. "Tell me, do you know if there is a hatbox in the lady chapel? I left a hat there yesterday and …."

The surgeon laughed. "You were always leaving your bonnets!"

"I know, but this was a new one, and I want it."

Suddenly the other surgeon by the altar motioned to his colleague beside her, so he nodded to her and started toward the cots at a run. "You are welcome to look, Miss Perkins," he called to her over his shoulder. "Thank you again for all you did."

You're welcome, she thought with some satisfaction as she walked toward the lady chapel. She hoped, just for a moment, that Major Reed would still be there, but he was not. No, your bags were packed yesterday, she thought as she looked around the bare room. Although what use you have for a darling chip straw bonnet with cherries on it, I cannot tell.

She looked back into the chapel itself and saw him sitting— one shoulder still higher than the other—on a cot with one of his men. I can reclaim my bonnet at least, she thought as she came across the floor toward him. Perhaps he can tell me how to go about getting it pawned, although that is hardly a subject I know how to bring up.

He stood up when she came closer with a smile of appreciation on his face that faded as he saw her bruised cheek. He took her arm before she could protest and led her back toward the lady chapel, out of earshot of the others. "What in God's name happened to you?"

"That's no greeting," she replied. "It was dark, and I ran into a wall."

He sat her down on the cot in the lady chapel, untied the ribbons before she could stop him, and pulled back the bonnet. He held her chin gently with his fingers and turned her face toward the faint light from the clerestory window. "My God, Lydia, save your breath. That was no accident. That happened to me once in a taverna in Lisbon, when I had too much fruit of the vine."

You're not slow, she thought. Figure it out. Spare me the humiliation of having to tell you. "Whoever did this should be flogged," he said finally as he sat down next to her and stared straight ahead. He took her hand. "It must hurt, Lydia," he said, his voice soft.

She nodded, and winked back the tears. "It will be better in a week. It won't even show then." She put her hand to her mouth. "I mean, I suppose it will be better then."

His sigh was so big that she could feel it as well as hear it. "Not the first time, eh?"

She looked at him, then looked away in embarrassment. "My plain speaking—I suppose you heard about what happened last night—my plain speaking ruined Kitty's chances with that dreadful Lord Allsuch," she whispered, her voice so low that he had to lean close to hear. "I don't know how I ever had the nerve to speak out like that! I don't know what possessed me!"

He sighed again and released her hand. "I would like to think that my children someday would be as concerned as you are about the plight of others. I heard about it this morning from General Picton."

She dried her eyes, dabbing carefully around her cheek, then rose and reached for her hat again. "My plain speaking, as you so kindly term it, turned out to be a luxury I could ill afford, in my case." She replaced her bonnet. "Sir, do you still have that bonnet you gave me? I know you will think this dreadful of me, but I need to pawn it." She smiled, but couldn't feel any mirth. "Provided I can figure out where to take it."

A whole range of emotions crossed his face, none of which appealed to her. I should never have mentioned the bonnet, she thought with regret. I think I will just leave right now. "That's wrong of me, and terribly rude, isn't it?" she said. "I think I'll be on my way, Major Reed. So nice to have met you. Best of luck to you in Northumberland."

She turned to leave, except that the major grabbed her skirt and held her there. "Really, Major!" she protested.

He sat her down again, closer to him, if that was possible, and clamped his arm around her waist so she could not bolt. "Your parents have turned you out? Come on, Lydia, speak to me!"

"It's Miss Perkins," she said, then started to cry. He loosened his grip on her but did not let go. In another minute she pulled a handkerchief from her reticule and blew her nose, which only made her flinch from the pain. She knew she did not dare look at him, so she continued to stare straight ahead. "I do have a plan, so you needn't worry about me," she said.

"Good," he said. Then after a pause, "Would you mind sharing it with me?"

"I mean to go to an employment registry, and hire myself out as a governess, or a lady's maid. Heaven knows I've done enough of that for Kitty." She dabbed at her nose again, more careful this time. "My only problem is that I daren't go right now, with my face ... well, *I* would not hire me, would you?"

He shook his head. "Probably not, if I were a matron with hopeful children." He turned himself on the cot to see her better now. "Why did you come back here?"

"I thought I could work here for a week, and maybe just stay here ...." Her voice trailed off as she looked toward the main chapel and its few inmates. "It seems I have worked myself out of a job here, doesn't it?"

"It does. Thanks to you, the Duke himself, and Lord Walsingham—oh, by the way, his son the Viscount Lindsey is on his way to a well-earned rustication in Cornwall—and the first minister dropped by this morning." He nodded, real appreciation on his face. "Lydia, you must have opened up with a salvo worthy of Battery B!"

"Oh, don't remind me!"

He laughed and released her. "Oh, but I would like to thank you for what you did. Oh, yes." He reached under the cot and drew out the hatbox. "Here's your hat. I was actually going to take it by your house before I left."

"You would not have found much of a welcome," she said, opening the box for another look at the beautiful hat. She held out her hand to him. "Thank you, Major Reed. I really should be going now."

She got no farther than the entrance arch to the lady chapel, stopped there by one word.

"Where?"

She turned back. He still sat on the cot, regarding her with a kind expression. "I have no idea," she said frankly.

"Then, let me offer a suggestion—just a suggestion!—which you might consider."

She held up her hand, as if to ward off his voice. "Sir, you wouldn't be thinking of offering marriage again? I have certainly not forgotten your dilemma."

"Why not?" he countered. "I need a wife in the very worst way, and you appear to be a bit of a babe in the woods."

"No," she said, with what she hoped was a decisive tone.

It must not have been decisive enough, because he walked along with her as she hurried toward the chapel's entrance. "I contend it is an excellent solution to both of our problems. It will help me keep that inheritance that my aunt is so generously providing, and it will whisk you far away from London." His tone hardened, and she stopped. "It will certainly give you an opportunity for a pain-free life." He took her arm and pulled her around to face him. "Lydia, I do disjointed things at times, but I don't beat women."

They were at the entrance to St. Barnabas now. He sat down on one of the benches placed there earlier for recuperating soldiers and carefully leaned back against the sun-warmed stone. "Ah, that is good," he said. "Sit down, Miss Perkins, and give me a really good reason why this isn't a brilliant stroke of mine. I dare you even to think of three."

She sat. "Number one: I hardly know you."

"I contend that you know me very well," he said. "I'm a steady sort of fellow, except that I get an occasional wild hare." He peered closer at her, looking under the brim of her bonnet. "Which might be the sort of thing you need in your own life, by the way, Miss Perkins." He touched her cheek so gently that she did not wince. "Apparently someone's been trying to beat the spontaneity out of you, but obviously it isn't entirely gone, or you wouldn't be here. No, you know me by now. In essentials, I do not change."

Well, now, she thought, wishing that her face was not warm with a blush, even though she knew it was; he was too close. "Number two: I don't love you, Major Reed." There; she said it, even though it seemed so intimate, especially with men coming and going from St. Barnabas, even as they sat there.

He shrugged, and though a moment. "Do you like me?"

"Of course!" she exclaimed, "Who wouldn't?" then could not help herself. "And you have excellent taste in bonnets."

He laughed out loud, and it was a wonderful sound that warmed her down to her sturdy shoes. "Oh, my dear Miss Perkins. It appears that you are shameless in your love of hats!"

"I already told you that," she said pointedly.

"So you did, my dear. Miss Perkins, if you like me, that will do well enough." He leaned closer, so no one would overhear. "I was going to suggest an arrangement of convenience anyway, until we get to know each other better. It seems only fair. My, you can blush."

She turned away from him, only to see a grinning soldier on a nearby bench. She turned back to the major. "Number three: Mama says I am stupid and naive."

"Your mother is wrong, Miss Perkins ... oh, hang it ... Lydia," he said, taking her by both hands this time. "You're quite intelligent—smarter than I am, I think—and if you are naive, what is wrong with that? I know how to pawn things, and I can find a place to stay at night, and I'm certainly not afraid to tow you with me into a pub for luncheon."

He was speaking quite earnestly now, or she thought he was. I wonder, will I always have to guess if he is serious? she asked herself. "And besides all that, I have some salve for my back, which is still too hard for me to reach. You could put it on for me. Think of us as a team, Lydia."

She shook her head, but she was not unhappy with him. "And if this arrangement does not suit?" she asked. "You know that it might not."

"Lydia, we can arrange a quiet annulment. My aunt has been threatening to die for years and years, so I doubt I would occupy too many months or years of your time, if you decide I won't do. I'd see that you have sufficient income for a comfortable life. What about it?" He laughed again. "I am so prepared for a yes, Lydia. As a parting joke, Sir Percy even gave me a special license. It already has my name on it. You can't imagine how much exertion that was for Percy."

It was her turn to laugh this time, and she did. "I hear those things are expensive! You have strange friends, sir."

"Oh, I do," he agreed. "With any luck, you'll never meet him. What about it, Lydia?" he asked again.

Well, what about it? she asked herself. I should at least entertain the unimaginable. "You're sure there are no dark secrets you are holding from me?" she asked. "No surprises in store, beyond a little light nursing?"

"Cross my heart," he said promptly. "We'll have a peaceful ride to Northumberland. There's plenty of time for me to tell you all I know about Delightful Saunders, and …."

"Who?" she asked.

"Oh, that's your name. You don't really think we were sober when we hatched this scheme, do you?"

"No!" she declared. "But *Delightful* Saunders?"

"If it's any consolation, I believe Percy signed her letters as Della. Yes or no?" he asked. "If we hurry, we can get this done before noon and be on our way."

Don't even think about it, Lydia, she told herself. Just say it before you lose the last ragged remains of your nerve.

"Yes."

He kissed her hand. "You won't regret this, Lydia."

"I already do!"

10

❧

BEFORE NOON, SHE, LYDIA Lucinda Perkins, spinster, was married in the parish of St. Barnabas (the current chapel new since the Great Fire of London) to Major Samuel Elliott Howard Reed, bachelor, Lord Laren of Laren, Northumberland, by a special license purchased as a joke by Lieutenant Sir Percy Wilkins, second-in-command of Battery B. General Thomas Picton served as best man and his wife, who claimed she was never surprised at any stunt of her husband's officers, did what she could to hold up Lydia, who shook like blancmange, and whose stomach growled throughout the entire ceremony. The parish priest appeared to be hard of hearing, but even he paused once to look over his book at her.

There was even a ring, a pretty Spanish piece looted from Badajoz that the major had carried around for several years, for no discernible reason. To everyone's delight, it fit Lydia as though it had been meant for her finger all along.

The general and his lady were already late for another festivity associated with the victory celebration, so the major and his wife said good-bye to them from the steps of St. Barnabas. "If Boney should break out, I'll expect you in the battery again,

Major!" Picton called as he leaned out the window. Lady Picton pulled him in before he could continue.

As Lydia watched them go, her stomach growled again. Major Reed shook his head. "It seems I only married you just in time before starvation set in, my dear," he said. "This is a horrible neighborhood, but I know there is a public house around the corner where the beef and kidney pie should stave off famine. Shall we slum? I have been slumming for years and have acquired some expertise."

It was excellent food, served by an interested woman amid the clink of bottles and clatter of plates and shaking of dice. "Why does she keep staring at us?" Lydia asked in a whisper, leaning across the table toward her husband.

"At you, my dear, at you," he said cheerfully, wiping his mouth with a napkin surprisingly clean, considering the general condition of the dockside neighborhood. "You are quite pretty—Ah, now, don't object! *I* happen to think you're quite pretty—and that is a lovely bonnet, and I hate to tell you this, but your cheek really is impressive."

She gasped and lowered her head, then changed her mind. "I should fit right into this neighborhood," she said. "People will think you are a dreadful brute who beats his wife."

He nodded, and finished his ale. "We can only go up from here, Lydia Reed."

True, indeed, she reflected as he paid the bill. *I still cannot quite believe what I have done, except that my name is written on the registry in this parish, and I am most legally married. Lydia Reed will take some getting used to, however. I won't even contemplate how difficult Lady Laren will sound, but since Sam doesn't appear much interested in that part of his name, I suppose it doesn't matter.*

"What are we to do now?" she asked, and smiled at her husband. "I mean, 'What are we to do now, *Sam?* Now that you have so kindly married me, I don't have to worry about what I am to do." She clasped her hands in front of her. "Except that I would like to know."

He helped her to her feet, and took her by the hand to lead her from the tavern. "I directed my trunk to be taken to the King's Whistle Tavern, where the mail coach leaves, Lydia. It's not high style, but my banker is in Durham, not London, and we're going to economize at least that far."

She nodded, thinking of all the boring trips by post chaise she had made with her family, where no one ever had anything kind to say by the end of the first day's journey. "I have never traveled that way," she said as he hurried her along. "I hear it is quite interesting."

The mail coach was more than interesting; it was crowded. Lydia looked with some dismay at the current inmates, who stared back, as if daring them to find a corner to wedge themselves into. "H'mmm," said the major. "Madam, could you ...." The woman glared back and spread her skirts wider. "I suppose not."

Lydia caught the eye of an older gentleman. He grinned at her and gave her a broad wink. "Here, laddie," the man said. "You sit here and put your pretty missus on yer lap." He moved over six inches to accommodate them.

"Aye, then, very well," said the major. He eased himself into the narrow spot, which somehow widened enough for him to squeeze in his hips. He flinched as his right shoulder came in contact with the man, and Lydia could see the sweat break out on his forehead. Oh, we are walking wounded, she thought as she watched him. Calmly she took a handkerchief from her reticule and wiped his forehead.

"He has an injury from Toulouse," she said quietly to the older man who had made room. She sat herself on the major's lap, and his arms went around her, with his hands resting comfortably over hers on her stomach.

"No place else to put'um," he said in her ear.

"Can you stand this?" she whispered back.

His cheek was right next to hers. He kissed her quickly. "Lydia, my men would say I had died and gone to heaven. I've never suffered so well."

She blushed. "Hush," she whispered. She caught the eye of the older man and felt her face grow even more red.

The man nudged the major. "I didn't know women blushed anymore," he said.

She felt the major's chuckle. "This one does. Aren't I the lucky fellow?"

The woman across the aisle harrumphed and rearranged her skirts again. "I don't hold with men who beat their women," she said, her voice highly charged with disapproval.

Goodness, this is infinitely more interesting than the post chaise, Lydia thought in amazement. She straightened up a little and looked the woman in the eye. "We were married this morning over my parent's objections," she said. "They didn't think I should marry a common soldier."

"Common, eh?" he whispered in her ear. "You're a rascal." He shifted her weight slightly, then announced to the coach. "There was her da, deep in drink, and her mama wailing in the background. I knew she would be safer with me."

Lydia nodded. "We have been writing for years and years, all through Spain and Portugal. Thank God Napoleon is on Elba, and my dear Sam was able to rescue me from my own family." She kissed his cheek in turn.

All sympathy now, the woman nodded so vigorously that her bonnet tipped forward. "Mind that you treat her right, lad. She deserves a good life."

"My thoughts entirely," the major replied, tightening his grip on her.

"Dearie, if you can get some used tea leaves after dinner tonight, and pack that on your face before you go to bed, it'll make all the difference in the morning," the woman advised.

"Get out, yer old woman," the man next to them grumbled. "Didn't yer hear the lad, saying they were just married? Would *you* want tea leaves on yer face tonight?"

If she could have slid into the ground, Lydia would have. As it was, she had to endure the major's silent laughter behind her.

Unwilling to look at anyone in the coach, she began a serious examination of her gloves.

After a long stare at the old man, who glared back just as defiantly, the woman turned her attention to the lady seated next to her. By the time the mail coach started, they were deep in a discussion of the ratio of water to salt when pickling pigs' feet. The others in the coach turned their interests, variously, to a newspaper, a crying baby, and a greased paper which yielded fish so pungent that Lydia felt her head swim.

She thought the major was asleep, so she settled herself more comfortably in his lap. He kept his firm grip on her, and his lips were close to her ear.

"You can prevaricate almost as well as I can," he whispered.

"So pleased to hear it," she whispered back. She turned herself to be closer to his ear, enjoying the fragrance of cologne on his skin as a welcome antidote from the ripe herring that filled the coach. "I can only wonder what other taradiddles you have in store."

He considered her comment. "None that I can recall, Lydia. A wife invented to preserve an inheritance seems to be the best that I can do."

She smiled and removed her bonnet. "Was I sticking you in the eye with this thing?"

"Uh-huh," he murmured, his voice full of sleep now.

"Good!" she said with some feeling, even though her voice was low. "I still think you are a rascal."

"I will improve upon acquaintance," he said. In another moment he was asleep.

The mail coach stopped in Crosswich to change horses and deposit passengers. "A tea leaf poultice," the woman insisted to Lydia as she got off the coach. The old man only snorted, then returned to sleep.

Lydia kept their place as the major went inside the inn with the others for food. He came back with tea and two pasties wrapped in greased paper. "We'll stay the night at Mallow," he said, handing her a pasty and stretching his long legs in the coach.

"How is your back?" she asked as they ate.

"It hurts. I can tell you that I look forward to a bed tonight."

"Shouldn't wonder, lad," said the old man. "She's a pretty morsel. Coo, laddie, so you can blush, too? What a pair you are!"

Lydia looked at the major and burst into laughter. "And I will find tea leaves!" she said.

The coach was just as crowded when they resumed travel, except that a mother and child had to double up this time. Lydia sat beside the major and listened with interest—and some personal pride—to his battle narrative, sparked by a comment from a salesman about the victory at Toulouse. He never mentioned his rank, and dressed as he was in civilian clothes—in style six years ago—she wondered if the coach's inmates would have believed him, anyway. They would not imagine a major riding on the mail coach, either, she thought, as she sat hip to hip with him and absorbed his story of battle and army life. He is certainly no one to be ashamed of, she told herself. Late in the afternoon, he began to close his eyes, and fidget and suck in his breath every now and then. She put her hand firmly on his leg. "He needs to rest now," she told the listeners. "Would you mind terribly sitting over there, sir, so he could rest his head in my lap and put his feet up?"

No one minded. Without a word of objection, the major did as she said. He was even starting to shiver, so she spread her shawl over him, and put her arms around him. When he was asleep, she touched his shoulder and frowned. It was hot. She rested her hand against his forehead, and her frown deepened. Major Reed—Sam—you are not ready for this trip, she thought. I wonder how long it will take us to get to Northumberland?

Helped by their fellow passengers, Lydia and the major left the coach at Mallow as the sun was going down. "I know I can stand up," he insisted, even as he continued to lean against the salesman. "Sam, my dear, you can humor these nice people who want to help," she told him as she hurried ahead across the inn yard to find a room for the night. She forgot to be afraid or shy, even though she had never dealt with an innkeeper before, and in a few minutes the keeper and the salesman had helped him up the stairs and into a bed. "Thank you so much," she told the men. The keeper told her he would be back soon with soup and tea, and she turned to the major.

You would think I was an expert at this, she told herself as she helped him from his clothes, wincing when he did, and holding her breath as she removed his shirt. He obliged her by lying on his stomach, and she looked with some distress at his right shoulder. "You know there is more matter in this wound," she told him. "I had thought General Picton's surgeon …."

Wearily, the major shook his head. "He got what he could, but not all. I …. I just couldn't stand any more. More shame to me."

Lydia sat on the bed and rested her hand on his head. "No shame at all, Sam." His hair felt good and thick under her fingers. She massaged his head, and he sighed, then closed his eyes in sleep. "I don't imagine I will ever hurt like this," she whispered. "Bless your heart."

When the innkeeper brought Sam's campaign trunk, she rummaged in it until she found the salve that the surgeon had compounded, and applied it to the wound. She stood looking at him a long time, wondering what else she could do. She could think of nothing, so she covered him, took off her dress, and lay down beside him, careful not to touch his back, even though the bed was narrow. She was asleep sooner than she would have supposed.

WHEN SHE WOKE, IT was early morning and the bed was empty. She was on her feet in an instant, looking about in alarm. To her relief, the major was sitting in the chair by the window.

"You have not misplaced me, madam," he said, his voice full

of humor now, and not pain. "I own, I wish I had had subalterns in the Peninsula as quick to their feet as you."

"Wretch!" Her face on fire again, she quickly twisted her petticoat into its proper position and reached for her shawl, which she wrapped around herself to cover her chemise. "I had thought to be up long before you, considering your state last night."

"Well, you weren't," he replied. "I have been sitting here this last hour, vastly entertained."

"Entertained?" she asked, then shook her head. "I am sure I do not want to know."

"It was charming," he insisted. "You hum in your sleep. Did you know?"

I am mortified, she thought. "I did not know." She looked away, considered the situation, and came closer. "I suppose there is no point to my being embarrassed by all this."

"None whatsoever," he agreed cheerfully. "I feel better, too, by the way."

He had pulled on his trousers over his drawers, but his chest was bare. He turned around slightly, and she forgot her timidity to look at his shoulder. Much of the swelling was gone now, but the redness remained. Gently she laid her palm across the worst of the wound. It was still hot. "I tried to wish it away last night," she murmured as she ran her finger along the line of stitches, noting how tight the skin was underneath. "You know that it will be swollen again by evening."

He nodded, then gently took her hand from his back. "I know. Picton's surgeon told me that I would probably make it to Northumberland, if the trip is uneventful." He sighed. "Things always seem easier to bear in your own bed."

"You'll have to be physicked again," she said. She picked up the comb on the table beside the chair and began to comb his hair. "Thoroughly."

He nodded. When she finished combing his hair, he looked up at her. "Are you feeling sorry for me?"

"I suppose I am," she said, smiling at his question.

"Really sorry?"

"I said I was!"

"Then, sit down. I woke up early because I remembered one tiny wrinkle to the plot that I forgot to mention earlier." He waited as she got her brush from her bandbox, sat down on the bed opposite him, and began to remove her hairpins. He eyed her brush, a heavy silver thing. "In fact, if you feel inclined to throw that at me, let me remind you right now that I am a wounded veteran and your husband."

She laughed and began to brush her hair. "I cannot really imagine anything worse than this deception that we have begun for the benefit of your mother's feelings and your aunt's fortune. But, then, I have been told for years that I am not creative."

"You are extremely creative," he said. "Do keep a tight grip on that hairbrush."

He put on his shirt and buttoned it, looking about for his neck cloth. "Lydia, I blame it on Sir Percy."

"Why not? So far you have blamed everything on that singular gentleman. What could be worse than the tale you hatched already?"

He thought a moment, as though attempting to figure out how to begin. She watched him with growing suspicion. I am dealing with an inventive, intelligent man who is far more creative than I will ever be, she thought. Quite possibly my mission in life will be to rein him in—provided, she added hastily to herself, that I choose to continue this unusual marriage.

"Confess it, sir. I do not wear well with suspense."

To her amusement, he got up and went to sit farther away in the window seat. "Percy really threw himself into his correspondence with my mother and aunt," he began as he examined his fingernails. "Beyond sherry, it was his chief source of amusement. I remember one rather gushing letter where, as Delightful ...."

"Oh, that name," she interrupted.

"Ah, yes … he declared his love to me in quite resounding phrases. I intercepted that one in time, and reminded him that it was going to two ladies." He sighed again and slapped his hands on his knees. "There's no way to say this except to tell you right out …. Lydia, in the gospel according to Sir Percy, after nine months and some two weeks of wedded bliss, Delightful and yours truly had a baby."

Her jaw dropped. She stared at him. He looked back hopefully. "What could I do? He didn't tell me about that letter until after I returned from court-martial duty in Lisbon, and by then it was long sent. Oh, my dear, do close your mouth at least!"

"You cannot be serious!" she gasped, when she could speak.

"Would I *lie* about that?" He shook his head. "Percy assured me that it was the logical step, considering how deep my love was for Delightful."

"If you say that name again, I *am* going to thrash you," she threatened him. She got off the bed and came toward him. He may have been taller than she and well beyond her weight, even in his convalescent state, but the major retreated to another corner of the room. "You couldn't possibly have forgotten that little detail yesterday when you convinced me to marry you! Now, be honest!"

In the middle of her turmoil, she was at least gratified to see his own discomfort. "Well, I thought to do this a step at a time," he admitted. "I will confess this morning that such reasoning may have been a tad arbitrary."

"I think I have leg-shackled myself to a lunatic," she said. Without thinking about it, she threw herself down on the bed and stared at the ceiling. She could not help herself; in another moment she was laughing. She laughed until her stomach hurt, and she had to press her hand against her middle. Tears streamed from her eyes and puddled on the pillow. "Oh, Lord, spare me." She wheezed as she wiped her eyes with the pillow case and rose up on her elbow to look him in the eye. "Sam, are you aware that you are certifiable? You'd feel right at home in Bedlam. It would fit you like second skin!"

"No. Blame …"

"… it on Sir Percy," she finished in unison with him. She lay down again and stared at the ceiling. "Let me see: I reckon this baby of ours is thirteen months old now. Oh, how auspicious!" She reached over to the chair where he sat now, made a fist, and thumped his knee hard. "It appears that you will have to commit infanticide. When we arrive in Laren, you'll have to tell your mama that dear little …." She looked at him.

"Celia," he said promptly.

"Oh, we had a daughter!" She flopped back again and threw her hand across her eyes. "Sam, you will have to tell your mama that Celia perished."

"I could never!" he declared, his eyes wide. "Lydia, I am fond of children. We'll have to come up with something better than that."

"Sam! You are a blockhead!" She sat up, swung her legs around, and faced him, knee to knee. "Celia never existed! How hard can this be!"

"My mother will be vastly disappointed," he said after a long pause. He looked her in the eyes finally, and then started to laugh, too. "Lord, you are right, my dear," he said finally, his voice equal parts of contrition and high humor. "I *am* a blockhead." He took her hand then, running his finger over her wedding ring. "Can't we think of something? Percy really outdid himself on Celia. She is a wonderful little baby."

"Sam …." she warned.

To her surprise, he raised her hand to his lips and kissed it. "Didn't the priest say something yesterday about sickness and health, and a whole host of qualifications? I disremember; I was mostly scared."

"You, too?" she murmured. "There was no rider in our marriage vow about insanity, as I recall. If you're planning something, I think I will choose not to go along with it."

"I do recall something specific about 'obey' that you agreed to," he said with a grin. "And yes, I have an idea."

"Don't try me, Sam!"

He only smiled at her in that good-natured way of his that she was already familiar with. Whistling softly to himself, he turned away and found his neck cloth. He tried to stoop a little to see in the mirror, but all that achieved was a groan he couldn't hide.

Or didn't try to, she thought as she hurried to his side, turned him around, and took the neck cloth from him. I must be an idiot, too, she thought. So good that we found each other. "I'll do that for you," she said. "Hold still."

It was done in a moment, if a little crooked. He took a look in the mirror. "It'll do. I wish you would put on some clothes, Lydia," he said as he went to retrieve his shoes.

"I was only helping you!" she reminded him. "You are a trial."

"Yes, ain't I?" he agreed as he toed his foot into one shoe without bending down.

She hurried into her dress and knelt in front of him to put on the other shoe and buckle them. "You can't possibly bend over like that yet, so do not try," she scolded him. "Sam, I think I will like to murder you long before we get to Northumberland. The urge is on me now."

He nodded, his equanimity unruffled. He allowed her to help him into his coat, then he sat down as she continued to dress. She paused in front of the mirror, gratified to see that the swelling had gone down in her cheek. She touched it, and it felt no more than warm today.

"Does it feel better, Lydia?" he asked, his voice so gentle.

She nodded, and watched him in the mirror. I think I could have a hard time staying angry with you, Sam, she thought, but perhaps this is information I shall keep to myself. She finished braiding her hair, and wound it neatly into place with pins. She replaced the cameo at her throat.

"Neat as wax," he said. "Lydia, you do turn out well, even on short notice."

A hundred rebuttals rose to her lips. Beyond the occasional kindness from Papa, no one had ever complimented her before. My dress is wrinkled and worn from yesterday, she thought. I know I would like to bathe and wash my hair. My cheek is better, but I still look like an accident victim. "Thank you," she said simply. "Now, if it will not trouble you overmuch, my dear husband, do tell me how we are going to acquire a baby when we have been married only one day?"

"Simple," he said as he took her by the arm and led her to the door. "Let us call this a gesture in memory of Private Charles Banks and other men of my battery, who had rocky starts in life. My dear wife. Mallow is a prosperous community, and probably full of concerned Christian citizenry. We are going to locate a foundling home."

11

～

It was St. Catherine's Home, and located on a narrow street near the center of town. A sign over the door informed them that Sisters of Charity ran the place. The sister porter who opened the gate raised her eyebrows at Major Reed's request for a baby. "Usually people drop them off," she said. "This is singular."

I think I shall not say anything, Lydia told herself. It appears that I have married a master at manipulation. She tightened her grip on her husband. I am certainly along for a ride in this adventure that I will laughingly call marriage.

"Yes, Sister, we would like to adopt a baby," he was saying. He drew Lydia in close and brushed his lips against her ear. "We've had a tragedy of our own, dear Sister, and we are feeling a great void in our lives."

You'll feel an even greater void if your aunt ever gets wind of what you are doing, she thought. The picture of Sam trying to explain all this to his relations brought the handkerchief to her mouth to stifle her laughter. She choked and turned toward him. He obligingly held her close until her mirth passed.

"It is difficult," he told the porter.

"Follow me, please."

Was it possible for a man to charm *nuns?* She would not have thought so, but after a half hour closeted with the convent's mother superior, a stern, no-nonsense woman, Lydia changed her mind. No one is safe from this man, she thought. She watched the mother superior hunt in the depths of her habit for a handkerchief, when he finished his artless narrative about the loss of their little one, her own heart trouble that precluded any other child of their own, and their great longing for another one about the age of their dear little Nell, who went to sleep with the angels one night.

This man doesn't have a scrupulous bone in his whole body, she thought as he turned away to stand by the window, the picture of a grieving father. She stayed where she was until the nun burst into tears, and gave her a little shove. "Oh, go to him, my dear! See how he suffers!"

She did as she was bid, careful not to make eye contact as she hugged him. "You ought to be kept away from an unsuspecting public," she whispered. "Really, Sam!" she protested as he kissed her neck a little longer than she thought necessary, considering their surroundings.

"Thank you, my love, for your blessed consolation," he said as he turned back to the mother superior with a real effort. "I think I can pull myself together now," he said, with just a quaver in his voice.

Mother Superior nodded, then looked sympathetically at Lydia. "My dear, you seem to have suffered an accident yourself."

All right, Sam, you explain it, she thought, looking at her husband. "My dear, I cannot talk about it. You tell her," she said.

Sam shook his head slowly, after a look at her from under his eyelids that would have melted tile. He stood close to the nun and lowered his voice. "It is a rare nervous disorder." He leaned closer. "It is worsened by her present trial, I need not scruple to add. The doctor is certain that when there is a little one in our house again, she will stop running into doors and things."

"Dear me!" said the nun faintly. "We shall have to see what we can do about this. Mr. and Mrs. Reed, you are certain you wish a small child, and not an infant?"

Lydia nodded and dabbed at her eyes.

"Do follow me, then, and St. Catherine's will do what it can to assuage your grief."

The major, took Lydia's arm. " 'Doors and things.' Really, Sam," she scolded in a low voice.

"Well, you could help out a little here and there," he retorted as they followed the mother superior.

"And spoil your efforts?" she said. "Years and years ago, the government should have sent you to negotiate with Napoleon!"

The mother superior led them into a well-lighted, clean room with baby beds lining one wall. Children of various ages crawled or walked about, or sat at play. The room was austere in the extreme, but there was nothing of squalor or filth. She loosened her grip on the major's arm as she watched the young novitiate roll a ball to a little girl, who looked up when they came in, her eyes bright with interest.

"Oh, do let me," she said as she knelt beside the young sister. The woman smiled and moved away as Lydia rolled the ball to the child in front of her.

Like the others, her dark hair was cut quite short, but it was a riot of curls. Her eyes were brown like Lydia's. She was dressed in a simple, straight dress of sacking that came to her ankles. Sam squatted on his heels beside her and looked from her to the child and back. "She does look a bit like you. Pretty enough," he said. "Do let us look around, Lydia, before we decide." He reached out and touched the baby's curls. "She's a pretty minx, though, isn't she?"

Reluctantly, she allowed the major to pull her to her feet, and she followed him dutifully about the room. The little girl started to crawl after her, but her dress got in the way. Her face wrinkled up, and she scrubbed her eyes with her fists. "Oh, the poor dear," Lydia said, left Sam's side, and picked up the child, who promptly nestled against her shoulder.

The mother superior smiled. "Mrs. Reed, it appears that *you* have been chosen."

"How old is she?" Lydia asked.

"We do not know. She was brought here during the winter, when it was so cold, and none of the poor could sustain themselves. We found her beside the road." The nun fingered the child's curls. "There was no note. I do not suppose that her mother or father could write one. She will be walking any day, I am certain."

"Her name?"

"We call her Maria, but you may certainly name her anything you choose. Of course, there is another room of babies."

Lydia looked at her husband. "Sam, I do not care if there are ten more rooms. I'm not going to put her down."

He looked at them both, a smile on his face. "You're the manipulators, my dears. Lydia, you and this little minx are both looking at me with the biggest brownest eyes! What am I to do?"

"She is?" Lydia asked in delight. "Sam, I doubt I will run into another door or thing ever again. Oh, please!"

"I'm certain of that," he said. "Very well, then. Sister, we do believe we will be quite happy with Maria here. Do I sign some papers? Pay you anything?"

He did both while she held Maria, who had not loosened her grip about her neck. One of the sisters returned with a cloth bag of clothes and nappies. "She doesn't have any shoes, but it is summer," the woman said, her tone apologetic. "You are taking a great favorite," she said simply.

Lydia smoothed back the little girl's curls. "Then, why has no one claimed her before us?" she asked.

"Perhaps because few are as generous as you," the woman said quietly.

Oh, ouch, Lydia thought. She took the bag. "There is a towel doll inside," the nun said. She kissed the child quickly, then hurried silently down the corridor, not looking back.

In another moment, Sam was through. His face as serious as her own, he picked up the cloth bag. "Would you like me to carry her?" he asked as the porter showed them out and the gate closed behind them.

She shook her head. "She is light, but I do not think you should be carrying anything, Sam, not with your back the way it is." She stopped in the road, unmindful of the other people on the street. "Sam, we have just done something awfully big!"

He nodded, took her arm, and sat with her on a bench by the road. "We did yesterday, too, Lydia. I ... I think I am done with big things for a while." He smiled. "I suppose we should be grateful that the war was not longer, or Percy would have given us more children."

She didn't say anything, but they sat close together on the bench, Maria cuddled to her. I do not think I have ever felt so frightened in my whole life, she thought. She shivered. "Do you know, Sam," she said finally, trying to choose her words, but finding none. "Oh, I don't even know what I am trying to say."

"It will keep, Lydia. It will keep."

They sat together in silence until the major stirred finally and looked at his watch. "We could catch the mail coach and get into Warwich. I am thinking, Lydia, after we find some food."

She nodded, and held Maria away from her. "Are you hungry, my dear?" she asked. "Oh, heavens! I don't even know what you eat." He tickled Maria and took a close look when she smiled. "My dear, imagine yourself dining with seven ... almost eight teeth, and plan accordingly."

Sam was right, of course; she shouldn't have doubted it. Maria ate mashed potatoes with cream and a little applesauce, followed by milk with oil of peppermint stirred into it, "To keep her sound," the serving woman assured them. "All eight o' mine had a wee dram every day, and aren't they all healthy now?"

"We shall enter that in our catalog of skills for new parents, Lydia," the major said as they settled themselves on the mail coach. "When in doubt, take the advice of women with the most living children."

"Especially when they are emphatic," she added.

Wonder of wonders, the coach was not crowded, so they were able to put Maria between them. Covered with Lydia's shawl, and holding her towel doll, Maria went to sleep. "The sleep of the innocent," Sam murmured as he touched her.

"You're destined never to know what that is," Lydia said.

Sam grinned at her and closed his eyes, too. She watched them both, her hand on Maria to keep her from rolling off, but her eyes on her husband. I wonder, Sam, are you not aware how *bound* I am to you now by the addition of Maria, or are you so supremely self-confident that it would never occur to you? For no reason discernible to her, tears winked behind her eyelids. Yesterday, I think I entered into this marriage with the idea somewhere that I could wriggle out of it quite easily, even between here and Northumberland, she reasoned with herself. With Maria, I know I cannot, no matter what happens. She stared at the child in frank amazement. I cannot believe how rapidly she has become mine. One look at her, and I was gone. She gazed at Sam then. I wonder, sir, will you become mine, or am I the means to an end?

They stopped that night in a small inn outside of Coventry, to her relief. Maria was behaving well enough. Indeed, she had found her way onto several laps, and had earned a wooden horse intended for someone else's granddaughter, and a peppermint lozenge from travelers easily charmed by her sunny good humor. It was the major who worried her again. He became quieter and quieter through the long summer evening, doing his best to continue conversations with others in the coach, but unable to keep his attention fixed for long. He is in pain again, she thought. Surely he cannot make it all the way to Northumberland. We have only traveled a half day on the coach this time. How long will he last tomorrow?

They stopped briefly at a small village whose name she could not recall even a minute after it was announced. "Horse threw a shoe," the coachman announced. "We'll be fifteen minutes."

"We're stopping here tonight," she announced as she retrieved Maria from a vicar who had been entertaining her with a puppet glove.

"It's not a regular stop, Lydia. We'll have a hard time finding conveyance in the morning," the major said. His voice sounded almost normal to her ears, but she knew he had been gritting his teeth for the last ten miles at least.

"Here, Sam," she said quietly. "Don't argue with me, or try to tell me you do not hurt. I refuse to go another mile with you in pain."

He did not argue, but got down slowly from the coach. She followed with Maria and her cloth bag, and saw to it that the major's trunk and her bandbox were removed, too. "I know what I am doing," she told the coachman, who towered over her, and who would have frightened her to death, only two days ago. "My husband needs to lie down."

"Verra well, ma'am," the coachman said. "You'll forfeit the rest of that fare. It's only another twenty miles to Coventry."

"Then, I will take the loss," she said. "I am adamant."

Finding a room was simple, since the inn was not frequented by the mail coach route. After a quick dinner, she asked the innkeeper to help the major upstairs. "Does he need a surgeon?" the innkeeper asked her in a whisper.

"No, he does not!" Sam declared. "I am not deaf, you two! I just need to lie down, my good man. Thank you for your trouble."

WITHOUT A WORD, SHE set Maria on the floor with her doll

and helped him from his clothes again, almost dreading the sight of his shoulder, swollen and hot to bursting again. "Let the innkeeper go for a doctor," she urged.

"No," he said sharply. "I just want to get home."

It will take forever if we can only travel half a day at a time, she thought as she unbuttoned his trousers and pulled them off. Oh, Sam! I wish you were not so stubborn. "Very well, sir," she said, "but I am going downstairs to get a poultice for your shoulder, and if you argue I will ... I will ...."

"Will what?" he asked, his eyes teary with pain.

"Nothing," she said simply. "There is not a thing I can do, if you choose to be stubborn. But if you do not allow this little thing, I will sit on your back and make you keep it on."

He stared at her. "I believe you would, Mrs. Reed," he said finally. He lay quiet on his stomach while she went downstairs, carrying Maria with her.

The innkeeper's wife knew just what to do. "Now you go upstairs and put that little sweet one to bed, and I will have a poultice for your husband."

Almost weak with relief, Lydia went back upstairs. Sam appeared to be asleep, so she did not say anything to him. Silently she washed Maria as best she could, tied her into another nappie, and found a nightgown of sacking that was almost butter-soft with washing. She sat on the bed and held Maria close to her. "My dear, you have been well tended," she whispered. I hope I can do half so well as the Sisters of Charity, she thought. She looked at Sam, and then back at Maria. How odd, she thought. I who was useful to no one have suddenly become quite a necessity. I refuse to be frightened by all this responsibility. People depend upon me now.

After a couple of deep breaths, she put the drowsy baby down next to the major. "Sam, I am going downstairs for that poultice," she whispered into his ear. "Maria is here with you." He nodded, and she covered them both with the bedclothes.

It was a mash poultice, hot and steaming. The innkeeper's

wife helped her wrap it in a towel. "Just put it on his back for about ten minutes, taking care you do not burn him," she instructed Lydia. "Then take it off for ten more minutes, and then put it back on. It should be cool enough to stay on all night then." The woman smiled at her. "Do not look so glum! He looks like a healthy man otherwise. Soon he'll be up and about and bothering you again, miss, and won't you wish him elsewhere!"

She blushed, thanked the woman, and hurried upstairs. In another moment she had placed the poultice on the major's shoulder, careful to keep it covered with the towel. He flinched, then sighed as the heat went deep into the wound. She sat on the pillow close to his head, her hand on his hair, smoothing it back, and then just pressing firmly. He returned to sleep. By the time she had applied the poultice for the final time, he was snoring softly, Maria curled in his arms.

One more thing managed, Lydia thought as she took off her dress and petticoat, peeled down her chemise and washed herself. I think I would almost kill for a bath, she thought as she soaped herself. I would have hot water up to my neck and shampoo, and I would sit there until I was wrinkled. She dried off quickly and found drawers and a fresh chemise in her bandbox. There was a light breeze coming from the open window, so she closed it and looked down at the cot that the landlord had thoughtfully provided for Maria. It's a good thing I am short, she thought as she pulled back the blanket.

"Good night, Lydia."

She froze. Good Lord, was he awake and watching me the whole time I was standing there? she thought. She shook her head. I do not want to know.

"Good night, Sam."

HE WAS BETTER IN the morning, and she could only marvel at his resilience. The swelling was greatly reduced, but even to her inexpert eye, there was more redness. Oh, I do not like this, she thought as she touched the wound. "Sam, can we not …."

"No," he said firmly. "Two more days entire will see me home."

"You are unbelievably stubborn," she told him in a whisper. Maria still slept beside him, her arms and legs thrown wide with that casual abandon of the comfortable.

"I do not bend with every wind, Lydia, unlike …." He stopped, and sat up.

"Unlike me," she finished. "I know I am no bargain, Sam. It was what my mother said all along."

"Lydia, I didn't mean …." He looked at her. "I was rude. Forgive me."

No, you are in pain, she thought, and this is making you short-tempered. "Forgiven," she said simply. She took his hands. "Sam, please."

"No," he repeated. "I can make it home. Ho, there, Maria. You're a slugabed. I wonder that the Sisters of Charity tolerated you." He smiled at the little girl, who was looking up at him. She stretched in that stiff-legged way of the compact, and Lydia sat on the bed to watch her. "You're changing the subject, Mr. Reed," she said, even as she smiled at the baby.

"Oh, now I am Mr. Reed?" he asked. "Hand me my pants, Lydia."

"I should hide them like General Picton does," she said.

"Then, you would certainly be embarrassed to sit with me on the mail coach, Mrs. Reed!"

GETTING OUT OF THE village proved to be as aggravating as the major had predicted the day before. To his everlasting credit in Lydia's heart, he did not say, "Didn't I tell you?", but continued patiently to pursue all avenues, while Lydia and Maria sat in the kitchen with the landlord's wife. Luckily the woman liked to talk; with only a few judicious questions, Lydia was able to glean all manner of information about taking care of small children.

Her mind was also on Sam; she could not help herself. I think men are even more difficult than children, she thought, for all that they profess to know so much. She fell silent, thinking about the major, unable to get the sight of his poor back out of her mind.

"But you are worried about your husband, aren't you?" the innkeeper's wife asked, interrupting her own flow of conversation.

"Oh, I am," Lydia said. "He just refuses to consider any more tinkering with his wound until he is home." She fingered Maria's curls, and kissed the top of the baby's head. "I, for one, cannot blame him, but I wish I could convince him to let a doctor look at his shoulder."

The women looked at each other. "Lord, they are stubborn," the woman said. She found a tablet and stub of a pencil and wrote out the recipe for mash poultice, then gave it to Lydia. "At least get someone to mix this for you tonight."

It is such a feeble remedy, Lydia thought as she pocketed the recipe. She looked up then to see the major standing in the doorway.

"Good luck to us," he said. "I have arranged for a gig to take us to the next village …."

"Marbury Down," said the landlord's wife.

"Yes, that is it. There we will catch a smaller conveyance that will take us to Leicester, where the mail coach stops," he said. "Are you ready, my dear?"

She nodded. "At least I am not still Mrs. Reed," she whispered to the woman as she put Maria on her hip. "He does not like to discuss his ailments!"

An hour's travel in the gig—which Maria enjoyed enormously, but the major did not—they arrived at Marbury Down in time to catch the local conveyance to Leicester. Lydia eyed it dubiously. The vehicle may have been a mail coach in an earlier working life, but there was little to recommend it now, beyond wheels that turned, and horses approaching the geriatric.

The major startled her by putting his arm around her waist. "My dear Lydia, if the wheels fall off, we can always eat the horses."

She laughed, relieved that his irritation had dissipated. "I suppose you will tell me that was common fare in the Peninsula."

He nodded. "I've eaten horse every way except on the half shell. On a long fork over a fire is best, if the fuel is dried cow dung. It adds a certain piquancy not unlike the addition of pepper. May I give you two a hand up?"

He did, and she was charitable enough to overlook the pain that she knew it caused him. He also helped in an old lady with a bulging reticule, and a vicar who appeared to be suffering from prolonged contact with communion wine.

Lydia settled Maria on the seat with her toy horse and towel doll. The major closed the door after him but leaned forward to watch the coachman take his seat. He leaned back finally. "Interesting," he commented to no one in particular.

"What is?" she asked.

"The coachman has a man seated beside him with a pistol."

"Heavens," Lydia said. She leaned close to her husband to whisper, "I hope that does not startle this little lady across from us."

The lady across from them snorted and patted her reticule. "I always travel this stretch with a remedy for road agents."

"A bad area, eh?" the major asked, trying to make himself comfortable on the seat, which was slick from years and years of passengers' rumps. He winked at her. "Do you hit'um with your reticule, madam?"

She laughed and wheezed in equal parts, winked back and settled herself for slumber. In another moment she was snoring, to Maria's fascination.

The vicar stirred from his corner and spoke in a voice that almost sounded soggy. "The coachman swears he sees road agents, but I think he just drinks too much." He closed his eyes again.

"Well, you would likely know," the major commented. "Think of the adventure, Lydia."

She nodded, then looked at him shyly. "Thank you for not being angry about the traveling arrangements."

He gazed at her for a long moment, then shrugged. "What would be the point? You were right to make me stop last night." He put his forehead against hers for emphasis. "And I *do* feel better this morning."

"Very well, then," she said softly. "Mama would have scolded me for hours or …." She paused.

He took her hand and ran his finger over her ring in a gesture that was becoming familiar to her. "Those days are over, Lydia." She shifted her gaze and leaned back, unable to bear the intensity of his gaze. She opened her mouth to speak, then closed it and looked away.

"What, Lydia?" he asked finally. "You're miles away at the moment, and I know I am coming up short."

I sit in a carriage with people I do not know, and I have to tell you something so personal, she thought. I cannot do it, but I must. She took Maria in her lap so she could move closer to him. "Sam, I could tell Mama things and she would ignore me, or shout, or worse."

"I told you those …." he began, his voice as soft as hers, so she forgot her fear.

"They're not over, if you ignore me. I know that you need to see a surgeon now. If it angers you, I am sorry, but I tell you this from two or three weeks of actually *looking* at wounds like yours!"

"But…."

"No, listen to me!" she continued, taking his hands now while Maria squirmed. "I know you have seen countless more battle wounds than I have, but have you seen many *hospital* wounds? Oh, my dear, I fear there is a difference."

She stopped then. Such insubordination in Holly Street would have earned a back of the hand from Mama. She looked at him cautiously to gauge his expression, and discovered, in her concern and worry, that perhaps she had wandered into a better pasture.

"You are concerned," he said finally, with a tightening of his lips that made her momentarily uneasy. Oh, I am asking too much, she thought in dismay. This is where I should say I am sorry and promise not to tease him about it, even though I know I must. But I cannot.

"Sam, I am beyond mere concern now. You must *listen* to me."

She watched his expression, holding her breath at first. I know what I am used to, she thought; pray let this be different. She sat back then, overwhelmed by another feeling. I must love him to care so much, she told herself. When did this happen? She looked at him again, knowing that she had to make him understand. "Please, Sam" was all she could think to say.

It was his turn to hesitate. To her relief, he seemed to come to some decision of his own. He shifted Maria onto his own lap so he could move even closer to her and find some measure of privacy. Even then, it was a moment until he could speak. "Lydia, when General Picton's surgeon prodded about in my shoulder, I knew I could not stand another moment of that."

"You can, Sam," she said quietly, knowing with all her instinct that she was witnessing a most private side of him, one both devastating and human in a man sick of war. I doubt anyone else has ever seen this side of him before, she thought, both awed by the privilege and deeply aware of the responsibility that was hers now. "I won't leave you while it happens. You couldn't make me. If I could bear it for you, I would."

There were tears in his eyes now. "Am I a coward, Lydia?" he asked, his voice low.

She sighed, knowing that she had won. "You're the bravest man I know, and you are sick of death and war. You've been strong for a whole battery, Sam, and it's enough. You don't have to be strong for me. I'd like to think a wife would be mature enough not to require it."

Let those be the right words, she prayed when he was silent again. She opened her eyes and saw him smiling at her, even though his eyes looked suddenly older than the oldest things on earth.

"Very well, Lydia Reed," he said at last. "At our next stop, you can find a surgeon."

She swallowed back her own tears and opened her mouth to speak when the carriage lurched to a stop. Surprised, the major tightened his grip on Maria, but she slid off onto the floor and burst into tears at his feet.

Above her wails, Lydia heard the old lady across from her laughing and pointing out the window. "I told you, missy," she was saying.

"Stop now! Stand and deliver!"

12

❧

"ROAD AGENTS! OH, HELL's bells!" the major said in disgust, as Lydia retrieved Maria and held the sobbing child close to her. "Lydia, we can't afford this!"

"Hush, Sam!" Lydia kissed Maria and glanced out the window. Two masked men stood to the side of the carriage, pointing their pistols at the driver and his armed companion. The old woman seated across from her was bouncing up and down in her excitement. "I told you! I told you!" she exclaimed. "You two blaggards ought to be ashamed of yourselves, frightening old ladies!" she shrieked through the window.

"Please, madam, I suggest that you calm down," Lydia whispered, when one of the road agents pointed his pistol in the woman's direction.

Maria was whimpering now. Lydia watched one of the men gesture with his pistol to the coachman. In another moment she heard a gun thud to the road and then discharge, the ball whistling right past the major's head inside the coach. Maria cried louder, and the woman clapped her hands in her excitement.

"I was safer in Spain," the major growled. "Thank God we

had a guard along today for protection. Lydia, incompetents chafe me raw!"

She glared at him. "Am I the only one here besides Maria who is frightened?" she asked pointedly.

"It's possible," Sam said. "I am about to lose my temper at the prospect of becoming quite broke. You may have to sing and dance for our supper, Lydia. Maybe even show a little ankle." He glanced at the vicar, who was awake now and rubbing his eyes. "It appears your prophecy was correct, sir," he said. "We have been set upon by road agents."

The clergyman looked about, muttering, "Oh, my, oh, my," under his breath. He pulled a flask from his coat, unstopped it, licked his lips, and drank deep. Lydia watched in fascination as his Adam's apple bobbed up and down. Before he stopped it again, he looked at the major. "Would you like some?" He giggled. "It's a remedy for all evil."

The major shook his head slowly, amazement evident on his face. "No, thank you. I prefer to keep my head in emergencies."

The vicar seemed to think that was the most amusing riposte he had ever heard. He giggled some more, then burped. Even the old woman stopped her excited bouncing about at the window to glare at him.

The vehicle lurched as the coachman and his useless guard jumped down. One of the bandits jerked open the carriage door, only to have it come off in his hands. He blinked and stared at the door in his hands, then looked back at the other road agent for confirmation.

"Yer *tell* them to get out!" the other man said. "And drop the stupid door, yer light weight!" He promptly did as directed, and the corner of it landed on his foot. With a terrible oath, he leaped about for a moment on one foot. The old woman clapped her hands.

Her laughter brought him up short, because he stopped and waved his pistol at them. "Get out, all of you!"

With a frightened glance over his shoulder, the coachman

let down the step and helped Lydia from the carriage. "Just do what they say," he whispered. "These are bad customers."

She had no plans to do otherwise, but up close, the road agents looked less than formidable, despite their weapons. Shabby cloaks, shiny trousers, and boots that do not match, she thought as she clutched Maria to her and moved quickly from the carriage. "See here, sir!" she protested, when the man took her arm and pulled her away from the coach.

"Don't you lay a finger on her," the major said as he followed her out.

"It's all right, Sam," she said. She wriggled free of the road agent's grasp and tried to move closer to her husband.

"No, it isn't!" he declared indignantly. "She is my wife, and I will not have her treated that way! And look how you have frightened our daughter. Shame on you!"

Maria was sobbing in earnest now, clinging to Lydia's neck as the road agent took hold of her again and dragged her away from the carriage.

"Stand there, now," he ordered and released her. "And you over there."

"I'd rather stand with my wife," Sam argued. "It's my place to stand beside her."

The road agent's helpless look returned. He glanced around again at the other brigand. "You didn't tell me they would argue like this!"

"Oh, Lord!" snapped the man.

"Ah, yes!" thundered the vicar as he stepped from the coach. He pointed a finger at the road agent. "Woe unto ye hypocrites who call upon the name of the Lord as ye are about to rob us!" He jabbed his finger heavenward, then belched again. "H'mmm. H'mmm. Strange indeed," he murmured, and came to stand beside the major. He looked at Sam. "It seems there must be something appropriate to say at a time like this." He shook his head, as though to clear it. "I disremember whether it is in the *Book of Common Prayer*."

This can't actually be happening, Lydia thought as she held Maria close and quieted the child. Apparently we have been set upon by amateurs, Major Reed is inclined to argue, and the vicar is quite drunk. She looked around, her eyes wide, as the coach's guard began to weep. Oh, dear, and the guard is a ninny.

"If you've damaged my pistol by making me drop it, I will be in real trouble!" he sobbed. "My da will thrash me!"

"Ah, that is it!" said the vicar, gesturing dramatically. "Man is destined to trouble as the sparks fly upward!"

"Shut up!" Sam said, totally out of patience.

"Isn't anyone going to help me from the carriage?" asked the old woman, sounding like a disappointed child. "I don't want to miss a minute of this!"

She held out her arm for the coachman, who took her to stand beside Lydia. "Keep her quiet if you can," he whispered to her.

"Please, dear," Lydia said. "I think it best if we do not say anything." She looked at the nearer agent. "I do believe we are making him nervous."

The woman nodded and cackled. As the road agents ignored them and turned toward the men, she sidled closer to Lydia and opened her bulging reticule.

Lydia's mouth dropped open in surprise. A pistol even larger than the one the road agent carried lay, grip upright, in the woman's bag.

"My son's," the woman confided, patting it. "He doesn't know I have it.'"

"I am certain he does not," Lydia whispered, when she could speak. "Is it *loaded*?"

It must have been the funniest thing the woman had ever heard, because it set her off in a peal of laughter. "Oh, my, yes!" she declared between wheezes and gasps. "Aren't you a silly flibbertigibbet!"

"Silence, you old crow!" the road agent called over his shoulder.

Lydia looked at Sam, but he was in the middle of turning over his wallet to the road agent and she could not catch his eye. "My dear, perhaps you should give it to me," she whispered. "It might go off and hurt someone."

To her relief, the woman nodded and opened the bag wider. Shifting Maria to her other hip, Lydia reached carefully into the reticule and grasped the pistol. In another moment, it was heavy in her pocket. I will toss it in the bushes when I have an opportunity, she thought. I can't imagine what would happen if the road agents knew the woman was armed.

Oh, Sam, *do* stop arguing, she thought, pleading silently with the major as he gave the long-suffering road agent a generous piece of his mind. She set Maria down on the ground beside her, waited a moment to make sure that she would not cry, then started forward to deal with Sam. Husband, trust me when I tell you that there are times when it is best not to argue, she thought as she came swiftly forward. I have a wealth of experience in this.

She knew, even moments after what followed, that she would never have the sequence of it straight. All she remembered was the vicar spouting something nonsensical as she came closer, and then watching in horror as the younger road agent calmly turned and shot him.

She remembered stopping dead in her tracks. She must have made some noise because the brigand, his pistol still smoking, whirled about suddenly to see her close behind him and raise his weapon to strike her. She heard Sam shout at her to duck or move, and watched him run toward the road agent, ready to lean into him with his wounded shoulder.

"Sam, no!" She knew she said that, horror in her heart at the pain he was about to cause himself on her behalf. Quicker than thought, she dragged the heavy pistol from her skirt pocket, aimed, and pulled the trigger.

Nothing happened. Eyes huge with fright, and then ferocious anger, the man stood directly before her. His hand was coming toward the pistol to jerk it from her grasp when she pulled even farther back on the trigger and fired again. At that moment, Sam threw himself against the road agent.

She screamed as both men fell on the ground in front of her, blood gushing from the road agent's arm. He shouted even louder than she as he struggled to sit up, Sam a dead weight on him.

Pray God I have not shot my husband, she thought, horrified, as she tugged the major off the road agent. He sat up, his hand clutched to his neck, which was covered with blood and matter from his wound. "I have done this to you," she whispered in great remorse, as she saw the result of his exertions on her behalf. She dropped the pistol and threw her arms around him, patting him here and there for signs of a bullet hole, and finding none.

The road agent lay on his back now, pleading with his comrade to help him to his feet. The other brigand stood over his associate and calmly took Sam's wallet, putting it in his own bag. Quicker than thought, he snapped open a small knife and cut the strings on the reticule that dangled from Lydia's wrist, nodded to them both, and bolted for the woods. In another moment, they heard a horse galloping away.

"God, Lydia, help me lie down," Sam gasped. "I hear Maria."

She did as he said, lowering him gently to the road, sick with herself for being the source of his pain. She hurried to pick up Maria, who was crawling toward them and crying. "Hush, baby, it will be all right," she crooned, even as she began to cry, herself. She returned to Sam's side, kneeling beside him as he lay on his back with his knees up.

"He got all my money, Lydia," he managed to say.

"It doesn't matter, Sam," she said. "Please don't move."

It seemed like hours, but it was probably only a matter of minutes before the clearing began to fill up with horses and wagons, and farmers still carrying their implements who must have come running from their fields at the sound of the first pistol crack. The coachman, important now, was instructing them to bundle the vicar's body into the coach. It was followed by the wounded brigand, his arm covered in blood, held on either side by two especially stalwart members of the farming fraternity.

"He's reopened a wound on his back, received at Toulouse," she found herself calmly telling a farmer, who bent over her husband. "Please, sir, do you know of a good surgeon?"

"Happens I do," the man said. "This one is going to the inn at Merry Glade."

"Ealing is closer," argued the coachman. "That's where I'm headed."

"Have you ever seen the surgeon in Ealing?" countered the farmer. "I wouldn't trust him with a split haricot. *I'm* going to Merry Glade."

The major opened his eyes. "Merry Glade? Oh, excellent," he murmured, his voice dreamy, which alarmed her even more than the blood that oozed steadily from his wound.

"Do have a care," she pleaded as the farmer and his two young sons picked up the major and settled him in the back of the wagon. They helped her and Maria in, and she sat as close as she could. One of the young boys took Maria and cuddled her to him. Lydia smiled her thanks, settled herself, and rested the major's head on her lap, turning him slightly so he was not lying on his wound.

"Can I do something, ma'am?" asked the other son as his father called to the horses and they moved forward at a spanking pace. She thought a moment. "Do you have a knife? A sharp one?"

He nodded, his eyes wary. "I do, mum, but …."

"Don't worry. Just slit his coat up the back. Mind that you are careful around his neck."

Without any questions, he did as she asked, working swiftly, his expression serious. When he finished, he sat back on his heels.

She had finished unbuttoning his coat. "Take hold of the sleeve and tug it off," she said.

In a moment the coat was off and the blood-drenched shirt exposed to view. "Oh, Sam," she murmured, bending low over him. "You didn't need to do that for me."

"He was going to hit you," he said without opening his eyes, his voice slurred in its dreamy state. "I told you when I married you … no more hitting. I take what I say"—there was a long pause—"seriously."

I don't deserve that, Sam, she thought as she rested her hand on his matted hair. He said nothing more, but his face was serene, his expression composed, as though he derived comfort from the softness of her body.

They came into the small village on a dead run. The farmer called to his horses, and they slowed enough for a son to jump off the wagon and hurry to a nearby house. "The surgeon," the farmer explained as he slapped the lines along the horses' backs and urged them back to their former pace.

In another minute they pulled up before the Mill and Glade. The farmer shouted to the innkeeper inside, and he appeared promptly in the doorway, a cloth and glass in his hand. He cast them aside without a qualm when he saw the major in the back of the wagon. He climbed in and called for help, which brought several customers from the public house. As Lydia bit her lip and worried, the men carried the major between them into the inn. She took a moment to hold Maria and steady them both before she followed them inside and up the stairs.

I have fallen among kind folk, she thought with gratitude, willingly surrendering Maria to an older woman who held out her hands for the child and promised to clean her up and feed her. "And then she'll need a nap, dearie, so don't trouble yourself." Someone else handed her a damp cloth for her hands and face, which were splattered with Sam's blood, or the road agent's, she was not sure which. There wasn't anything she could do about her dress. The coach with her bandbox and

Sam's campaign trunk must have continued with the dead and wounded to its destination in Ealing. She thought about her beautiful bonnet, left in the dust and blood, then put it from her mind.

"Here, Mrs., Mrs.—"

"Mrs. Reed," she replied, holding out her hand for the apron offered her by a woman who must have been the keeper's wife. It wrapped around her waist twice, but it was clean and white, and hid the worst of the bloodstains. "This is Sam," she said, indicating the major, who was stretched out on his side now. The keeper was pressing gently on his back with a towel to stop the blood. "Mr. Wilburn will be here soon," said the farmer who had brought them.

"I can't thank you enough," she said as she sat down on the bed close to Sam's head, touching him so he would know she was there. If he knows anything, she thought. "I wish I could pay you …."

The farmer shook his head. "Mrs. Reed, we've all been in tight spots before. There's no remedy for it except to do a good turn for someone else. Did you say Toulouse?"

She nodded. "He was a major of Battery B, Picton's Division."

"Another Toulouse hero in Merry Glade?" said the farmer. He ruffled his son's hair. "And here we were saying only this morning that nothing ever happens, lads, eh? Today is enough to keep us in conversation until the frost at least."

"There is another veteran of Toulouse here?" she asked, but no one answered. The people in the room were looking toward the door now.

"Unless I am mistaken, mum, that will be Mr. Wilburn." He gathered his sons to him, an arm on each. "We'll come back later to see how he does." She must have looked worried, because he reached across Sam to pat her cheek. "Don't you worry, now. Your lad's in good hands."

My lad, she thought, as the responsibility for Sam Reed plopped onto her shoulders with a force that would have staggered her, had she been on her feet. A clarity borne of extreme anxiety brought to her mind, clear as water, the words she had said only two days ago. "'Wilt thou obey him and serve him ….'" She leaned over Sam and spoke in his ear. "Mr. Reed, I am not obedient, but I can serve you," she whispered.

"Mr. Reed?" he replied, opening his eyes for the first time since the farmer picked him up from the dust of the road. "Still angry with me for arguing?"

She kissed his temple, appalled at the strong smell of blood, but unwilling to be far from him. "I should be, Lord knows. Hush, now, Sam."

She looked up, and there was the surgeon. She sighed with disappointment, unable to hide her chagrin. He was older than anyone in the room, with eyes milky from cataracts. His bulk was impressive, too, and he seemed almost as tall as he was wide. He smiled at her, and extended his hand to her across the body of her husband. "Edward Wilburn, ma'am," he said. "And this must be our poor unfortunate."

She took his hand and felt the heart go back inside her body again. His fingers seemed to belie everything else about him. They were long and handsomely veined, and his grip tight. These are surgeons' hands, she told herself, and felt tears of relief well up in her eyes. "Lydia Reed," she said quickly, hoping to speak before she cried. "This is Sam."

Mr. Wilburn nodded, then looked around the crowded room. "Dave and Maudie, you'll bring me hot water and towels, won't you? Have ye an old sheet in the ragbag? I could use it." He looked at the others, and shook his head. "I'd love you to stay, laddies, but ye know I work best when I have room to swing my elbows." He bowed elaborately to them, with surprising grace.

The others laughed and left the room, nodding to Lydia. Soon just the three of them remained. She touched Sam's head, feeling protective of him.

Her gesture was not unnoticed by Mr. Wilburn. "Don't

worry, my dear. I'll take as good care of him as you would."

She looked at him, wondering how delicately to broach the situation. "Sir, I do not doubt your abilities. Indeed, everyone in the room seemed quite comfortable with you. Mr. Wilburn, this is a war injury, and I doubt your expertise extends to much battle in Merry Glade. Forgive me if I am rude, sir, but ...."

"You love him, don't you?"

It was simply asked, but it took her off guard. I suppose I do, she thought in quiet surprise. "Oh, my" was all she managed to say before the responsibility of that piece of news settled right alongside her other newly earned stewardships.

"Help me off with his clothes, and we will wash him when the Innises—good people, by the way—return with water and towels," Mr. Wilburn said as he removed his coat and rolled up his sleeves.

Impulsively she took his hand again. "I must know if you can do what he needs," she asked, not even trying to disguise her anxiety.

He kept her hand in his firm grasp. "Mrs. Reed, thirty-five years ago, I was surgeon to Banastre Tarleton, possibly the worst British officer who ever ravaged through the Carolinas. It's even possible that we hated him more than those pesky Colonials."

"The American war?" she asked. "But that was ...."

"Years ago?" he said helpfully, supplying the text. "Aye, Lord bless us. I was awfully young then, but I learned awfully fast." He let go of her hand. "I have not always lived in Merry Glade! Help me now."

Swiftly the removed the major's clothes, Lydia gritting her teeth as they pulled away the blood-clotted shirt. The Innises returned with water and towels, and left just as quickly. Sitting on the bed again, she watched the surgeon wipe carefully around the wound, exposing the length of it.

"A saber cut to the back, eh?" he asked, more to Sam than to her. "Oh, laddie, I know your problem. Lord knows, I saw plenty of these."

"You … you did?"

He pointed a finger at her. "You are amazingly skeptical! I suppose I must heal the sick here before you will believe me!"

"Well, I, yes, actually," she said. She touched Sam's back where Picton's surgeon had operated. "This was done over a week ago. He … he said he could not bear any more. He wanted to hurry home to finish it there."

The doctor washed the area around the wound, up into Sam's hair. "See that?" he asked, pointing to the red rash spreading up his neck. "Ill humors. He would not have made it home, lady. I don't think I am too late, but I need to go to work now. Stay or go, madam."

"I will stay."

He beamed at her, the picture of good nature, except that his hands were red with Sam's blood. "I knew you would. You must allow me to tie his hands to the bedpost."

"*No.*"

The doctor looked down in mild surprise at the major, whose eyes were open again. "I don't recall inviting you into the discussion, lad. It's between me and your lady."

"Don't tie me down," he pleaded, and her heart went out to him. "Just let me rest my head in her lap. Oh, please."

The doctor looked at her, and she found the strength from somewhere to nod. "You'll have the best seat at the cockfight, missie," he warned her. "And if you move, I'll tie your hands, Major Reed."

"I will be fine, if Lydia is here."

I do not know why I was so wild to be away from Holly Street, where I had no responsibilities, she thought as she settled onto the middle of the bed and rested Sam's head in her lap. Heaven knows, life was not pleasant there, but I never was called upon to make decisions, or exert myself.

"Put your arms around her, laddie," Mr. Wilburn said as he dumped some evil-looking instruments into the hot water.

"With pleasure," Sam replied. He draped his arms around

her, hissing in his breath with the agony of it, and then unable to keep from groaning with the pain.

"Excellent! Excellent! I do not know a surgeon with a better view"—he winked at Lydia—"or a prettier restraint." He selected a scalpel and dried it on his shirt. "You know what I have to do now, since you've been down this road before, lad. Cover his eyes, Mrs. Reed."

She did as he said, clamping her hand over the major's eyes, but unable to take her own from the spot where the wound had not broken open, but still bulged with infection. The major screamed, and she grabbed his hands behind her back and held them there, wondering if it was possible for her bones to break through the skin from the ferocity of his grip. In another breathless moment, he fainted with a sigh and relaxed his hands.

"Excellent!" said the surgeon cheerfully, his face close to the nauseating wound that oozed milky white infection. He squinted his poor eyes, changed the scalpel for a probe, and worked around in silence for long, long minutes.

When she thought she could not take another moment of the mess and blood in her lap, he set aside the probe for long-handled forceps. After another concentrated effort, during which Sam, still unconscious, began to stir restlessly, he pulled out an unidentifiable, rotting mass that made her stomach turn.

With a grin of satisfaction, Mr. Wilburn spread out the mass on a corner of her apron that was still clean. "Looks like a piece of blue shirt, and a bit of red wool." He bent close to his unconscious patient. "Any more of your uniform in there, laddie? Shall we hunt about? Ah, yes. I knew you would agree, considering the alternative."

He poked about some more, going deep into the major's shoulder until he seemed to be in up to his forearm. Dizzy with nausea, Lydia watched, unable to take her eyes away, reminded of the Christmas goose, boned, laid bare and ready for stuffing and trussing. She willed him to finish, but still he poked about, finding the most minute scraps with his poor ruined eyes. Thread by thread almost, he pulled out the last of Sam's shirt, driven deep into his own shoulder by a French dragoon's saber thrust.

"Shall we reassemble your husband, and hope that we do not have any parts left over?" he said at last, when a clock somewhere downstairs chimed four or five. She could not be sure, so weary was she with watching.

He called loud for some more water. Mrs. Innis must have been right outside the door because she hurried in, took one look, and sank to her knees. "Up you go, Maudie," the surgeon cajoled. "The major here needs some more water."

The woman gasped and rose to her feet, her face red with embarrassment. She hurried out and came back with a bucket of warm water. "Thank you, my dearie," the surgeon said with a smile. "Now, be a good girl and hand Mrs. Reed a damp cloth." She did as he said, then hurried from the room. "She's a real good'un, as you'll likely learn tomorrow," Mr. Wilburn commented. "If it's not too much, my dear, would you wipe my face?"

Touched, she did as he said, taking off his blood-dotted spectacles to clean them, and put them back on his nose. She squeezed out the cloth and began to wipe delicately around the gaping wound. When she finished, the surgeon realigned the flesh he had pulled back, working slowly, continuing his hunt for the smallest stray bit of fabric that would only suppurate and cause pain and further infection.

"There may be bits and pieces that will fester and rise to the skin, but the wads that would kill him are gone now," Mr. Wilburn explained, ever the teacher, even as his shoulders drooped with weariness. "He's young; he looks healthy. If you can keep your hands off him for a few weeks and make no strenuous demands, your major will heal."

He smiled at her and winked, despite his almost palpable

exhaustion. Quietly he began to close the wound, expertly winding the suture around the forceps and tugging just right. How could I have thought you were unequal to this? she thought. Oh, Father in heaven, when I get silly and tight-lipped, remind me not to judge so quickly.

Sam's shoulder was a map of black lines now, each stitch orderly. Clutching his spectacles so they would not fall off, Mr. Wilburn looked closely at his work, frowning and squinting, and then nodding in satisfaction. "You'll do, laddie." Tears came to her eyes when the old man quickly kissed the major's cheek. "Brave lad. When you are conscious again, I will tell you how much I hate war," he whispered.

It took him a moment to straighten up, and he was generous enough to overlook her tears as she sobbed quietly into the wrung-out cloth. When she finished, she helped him into his coat.

"My dear, I will return in the morning." He fumbled in his pocket and pulled out a packet. "Here are some fever powders."

"I doubt he will let me give them to him."

"Then, do it anyway," he said. "Be the benevolent despot that most good wives are." He fished the instruments out of the long-cooled water and dumped them in his satchel. He rummaged in it and pulled out an odd-shaped earthenware container.

"I don't want him getting up for anything, not even to piss. Use this instead." He patted her cheek. "You can certainly blush over the ordinaries of life, missie. The major must find you refreshing."

He left then while she stood there holding the urinal. She set it down and walked slowly to the window, feeling older than the oldest person in the world. In a few minutes, the surgeon was out in the street, starting off with a purposeful waddle that would have made her laugh, if she had not been so tired. She opened the window and leaned out.

"Oh, thank you, sir! From the bottom of my heart!"

He looked up, squinting his ruined eyes. "Think nothing of it, my dearie. Just wait until you get my bill. I will be in Bath this winter, thanks to you!"

She sank down in the window seat, her stomach in turmoil again. An operation and at least two weeks in bed at the Mill and Glade, she thought, seeing again in her mind's eye the road agent grinning at her as he snatched her paltry resources and grabbed Sam's wallet. "And how are we to pay for this?" she asked her husband.

She looked at the ring on her finger, twisted it, and shook her head. "'With this ring I thee wed, and all my worldly goods endow,' eh, Sam? That was what you said. Ah, well. Maybe I will think of something tomorrow."

Weary to the marrow in her bones, she lay down beside her husband and closed her eyes.

13

SHE THOUGHT SHE WOULD sleep for a few moments at least, but she could not. For a long time she rested herself against the major's comforting bulk, but her mind would not stop spinning like a top. She worried about him when he seemed to breathe too deeply, or when it was too shallow for her liking. She thought about Maria and knew she should go find her. She wondered what would happen if there were more uniform fragments hidden deeper in his shoulder.

Always through verse after verse of her worries was the chorus: You have no money; no worldly goods to endow anybody with. Even people as kind as the Innises need paying guests at their inn. Few of us can live long on goodwill. She shuddered and imagined the Innises booting them downstairs and out the door, and then Mr. Wilburn pulling out each painstakingly applied stitch when told that she could not pay.

She sat up in a perfect sweat. Lydia, you are a fool, she scolded herself. These are good people who will help you, if they know of your present dilemma. She sighed and leaned against Sam's hips, staying far away from his shoulder. "Sam, you would probably have a thousand solutions," she said softly, "but I do not think you are in any condition to suggest anything right now."

She lay down and tried to sleep again, but it was hopeless. Making sure that Sam's bare body was covered against the slight breeze of early evening, she went downstairs. Her hair was a tangled mess, but her hairbrush was in the bandbox and probably in Ealing. The small comb she carried in her reticule was in the possession of the other road agent. "And my three pounds," she grumbled out loud.

The public room was occupied by a fair number of the local constituency, drinking, rolling dice, smoking, and playing cards. She hung back at the entrance, too shy to go in, until the innkeeper saw her and set down what must be his perennial glass and rag to hurry to her side. "Mrs. Reed, you're looking lively!" he said. "How is the major?"

The room was quiet, and all eyes turned in her direction. I'm sure this is the most exciting thing that has happened in ages, she thought. "He is unconscious still, but he is breathing well. I have every hope that he will recover," she said, loud enough for everyone to hear.

It seemed straightforward enough to her, but as she dared herself a look around the room filled with men, she noticed, to her surprise, that several of them were dabbing at their eyes, or coughing and turning away. "Oh, I do not mean to make any of you melancholy," she said, clasping her hands in front of her. "He's a brave soldier and a stalwart one." She looked down in confusion at their reaction, and noticed her bloodstained apron. Oh, dear, I hope they do not think I am soliciting anyone's sympathy with my sad plight, she thought as she removed the apron, then hastily put it back on; the stains underneath on her dress were worse.

"If there is anything we can do for you, Mrs. Reed, you only have to ask."

She looked at the speaker, and recognized him as one of the farmers who had come upon the coach that afternoon.

She gave what she hoped was her bravest smile. "I thank you for what you have done already." Oh, dear, she thought as she turned away. Some of them are even sniffling.

Mrs. Innis was in the room now. She took Lydia by the arm. "Come to our quarters, Mrs. Reed," she urged. "I think I can safely say there is someone who would like to see you."

Maria sat on the floor in the cozy sitting room behind the public room, concentrating on blocks. She looked up when Lydia called her name, and crawled over to be picked up. With a sigh, Lydia picked her up and held her close, enjoying the sweet smell of her, and the feel of someone sound and whole, and without a worry. "I hope she was no trouble," she said to Mrs. Innis as she seated herself on the sofa with Maria on her lap.

The innkeeper's wife shook her head. "I don't know when I have seen a more pleasant baby. My daughter Suzie here has quite enjoyed this afternoon."

The young girl nodded and shyly came to sit beside Lydia. "I can watch her anytime you like, Mrs. Reed, if it will help with the major."

"It is a relief to me to know that," she said simply, touching Suzie's arm. She looked at Mrs. Innis. "I do not know how to thank you for your help thus far." Or how I can possibly pay you, she thought, but I will trust your goodwill to get me through this day and night, while you still feel sorry for me.

Mrs. Innis only nodded, then turned away to blow her nose. I do believe this is the most softhearted village we could ever have wandered into, Lydia thought. Either that, or I look more pitiable than I imagined. "Oh, dear, I don't mean to cause you distress, Mrs. Innis," she said. "I should go upstairs and let you get on with your own concerns."

Suzie touched her arm and took a deep breath. "Mrs. Reed, you don't need to go anywhere! It's almost like a fairy story, with you so pretty and fragile-looking, and so much a lady; and then Mr. Wilburn tells everyone how brave you were during that whole medical ordeal; and there is the major so handsome and courageous, defending your virtue from those dreadful road agents, and how you killed the road agents single-handedly to save the major's life; and there is little Maria, so sweet and looking so much like her dear papa, and what a shame it would be if he did not live to see her grow! Oh, it fair takes my breath away," she concluded, her eyes shining with the excitement of it all.

Oh, my, Lydia thought in amazement. Already this tale has exceeded its boundaries! I am not pretty and have never been accused of fragility, and by no stretch of anyone's imagination is Sam handsome—although he does possess a certain something that makes my stomach feel warm when he looks at me—and as for the road agents, and defending my virtue .... I am only grateful down to my toenails that I did not shoot Sam, too! Like an idiot, Sam was arguing, and my virtue was never in much jeopardy.

"I only wounded one of the road agents, and the other one got away," she said, deciding that it would be best to leave the rest of the tale as Suzie told it. "And there is that poor vicar," she added.

Suzie and Mrs. Innis glanced at each other, and burst into laughter. When Lydia stared at them in surprise, Mrs. Innis did look a little uncomfortable. "You must forgive us, but we are thinking that the road agent who shot him must have been a member of our congregation."

"His sermons were so dull," Suzie explained. "I fall asleep before I ever get inside the church."

"But we should be charitable," Mrs. Innis said, although Lydia could discern no contrition in either her voice or expression. "Mrs. Reed, may I get you some soup?"

The subject change suited everyone, until Lydia sat down at the table. Mrs. Innis served cream soup, and it looked so much in color and texture like the infection in Sam's shoulder that she could only stare at it and shake her head. Without any questions, Mrs. Innis whisked it away and brought tea and toast instead. She ate until she felt herself too tired to lift the toast to her mouth, or manage one more sip.

Mrs. Innis was there watching her. "You should go to sleep now, my dear," she said, her voice low and kind. "I have a nightgown for you. You are much Suzie's size, and I am certain that this dress of hers I have here will fit."

"Oh, I couldn't," Lydia began.

"We know it is not what you are used to," Mrs. Innis said in apology, "but Davey is going to Ealing in the morning to retrieve your luggage."

"It isn't that …." she said as she accepted the loan of the clothing. It is just that I am not used to such kindness, she thought as tears came to her eyes again. "I dislike being a trouble to you."

Mrs. Innis only smiled and helped Lydia to her feet. "Mrs. Reed, you cannot imagine our own pleasure at doing our little part to help the soldiers who defended our shores from invasion."

Lydia took Mrs. Innis's hand. If you could only see how people—vultures really—worked their way through St. Barnabas, looking for soldiers to entertain them in the agony of death, you would be amazed at the way others feel. "I am certain that everyone feels the way you do," she lied.

"I'm certain they do," Mrs. Innis said, returning the pressure of Lydia's grasp. "Let me help you upstairs. We hope you will let Maria remain here with Suzie. You need your rest, and so does the major."

The nightgown was surely made of flannel and comfort, she decided as she dropped its folds around her. She washed her face in the basin, pausing several times as though trying to remember what it was she was doing. I have never lived a longer day, she thought, as she looked in the mirror and brushed her hair with the brush on loan from Mrs. Innis. Perhaps I do look fragile, she thought. I feel fragile right now, and so much in need of comfort.

Sam lay on his side as she had left him. She crawled into bed beside him, backing herself up against his chest and legs. He sighed and settled his arm around her and inched closer until she could feel his breath on her neck. With a groan that made her freeze in worry, he threw a leg over her, and then settled back into deeper sleep.

She was warm now, and embraced into sleep by someone who was really too ill to have any idea what he was doing, she told herself. She closed her eyes, ready to let the mattress claim her, too.

"Lydia."

Wondering if he was awake or asleep, she waited for him to say something else. She was almost asleep when he moved closer. "I think I cannot sleep if you are not here." At least, she thought that was what he said. His words were still slurred and the pauses so great that she wasn't sure. Suzie would call that extremely romantic, she thought as she settled against him and went to sleep.

The major woke her once in the night with his restless turning, and muttering. She sat up and watched him, remembering how the surgeons would administer fever powders to men who fidgeted, even if they did not appear to be awake. She got up and mixed the powders and brought them back to the bed.

"Sam, hold still," she said, speaking distinctly into his ear.

He opened his eyes. Oh, how you suffer, she thought in shock. Even the tiny light of the candle she had lit did not soften the dull look of pain.

"I ... don't ... need ... that," he said with great emphasis, even if he could manage no more than a whisper.

"Yes, you do," she said. "Hold still and behave yourself, Sam." She rose up on her knees on the bed and got a good hold on his lower back, enough to prop him up slightly. When he would not open his mouth, she pinched his nostrils closed until he did, then poured down the drug.

She was afraid he would try to spit it out, but the liquid went down without a murmur. You know you need it, she thought, as she lowered him carefully to the bed again and tried to reposition him on his side, with a pillow at his back again. How grateful I am that women are not as stubborn as men.

He was still restless, and moving his hands toward his privates, so she found the urinal and held it for him. When he finished, all without opening his eyes, he nodded and she took it away. When she turned back to the bed again, he was soundly asleep, his breathing slow, regular, and more normal to her ears.

"Thank goodness for that," she whispered, as she worked to arrange the pillow again and position him onto his good side. She sat cross-legged on the bed for a while, both hands against the small of her back. You really are too heavy to roll over, she thought. Sitting there with Mrs. Innis's nightgown comfortably up around her knees, she assessed her husband and found him not wanting in any way, except for the business with his shoulder. She touched his chest, pleased with the feel of him.

"For goodness sake, Lyddy, cover me .... Go ... sleep."

She squeaked in alarm. He still had not opened his eyes. She tugged her nightgown down and covered him with the sheet. "Sam, are you awake?" she asked.

He nodded slowly. "Too much trouble ... open my eyes."

"Does it hurt?' she asked.

He nodded again. She lay down beside him, not as close this time. "Closer," he said.

She inched herself back into his embrace again. He sighed as her back rested close to his chest, and said nothing more until morning.

He still slept when dawn came and she edged herself out of his embrace. Mr. Wilburn had decided not to bandage his shoulder, so she rose up on her knees again to get a better look at it in the early light. "Drat," she said softly, seeing the rash on his neck still. Is it higher? she thought. Am I borrowing trouble? After all, the light is poor yet. She knew she was not when she saw the spots of high color in his cheeks, and felt his forehead. "Oh, Sam, no," she whispered.

Moving quietly, she got out of bed and came around to the other side for a better look at his shoulder. It was red, and the stitches were pulled tight. She touched the skin, and he flinched. As she watched, he began to pat the space where she had been. In another moment, tears began to pool under his cheek.

Touched beyond words, she leaned over him and hugged him as carefully as she could, then rested her cheek against his. Could I possibly mean so much to one person? she thought in stupefaction. This one? It must be the pain. "Poor man," she whispered in his ear. "All you want to do is get home, don't you?"

After a long pause, as though her words had to filter through miles and miles of passageways, he shook his head. "No?" she asked in surprise. "What can I get you?"

"You," he whispered finally and patted the bed again. "Sickness and health," he said quite distinctly, his memory making a strange parabola from the effect of the fever powder.

She returned to bed, feeling honored and shy at the same time. His eyes were closed, but she knew he was conscious because he smiled slightly when she jiggled the mattress as she laid herself down next to him. With an effort he put his hand on her stomach and prodded her to move closer. She turned to face him this time. Lydia, I wonder why you never thought he was handsome before? she asked herself. Even with fever branding holes in his cheeks, he is handsome. Any ninny can see that. She smoothed his hair back from his face. You need another haircut, Sam, and a shave, and a good shoulder, and some money to get home. I can supply the first two, you must do the third, and I think the fourth is my task, too.

"Will you get well soon?" she asked him, not knowing if he would answer. It was probably a complicated question for someone involved in pain, circled about with it, throbbing with it.

"Soon," he said after the long pause she expected now. The word came out more like a sigh, his hand became heavier, and she knew that the fever had pulled him under again. She twined her fingers through his hand as it warmed her stomach and slept, too.

HE DID NOT WAKE up when she left the bed an hour later, dressed, and went downstairs. Maria was sitting in what must have been a high chair left from a smaller Innis, finishing a pear that Suzie was feeding her piece by piece. Lydia kissed her. "How nice not to worry about her," she said to Mrs. Innis as she accepted a bowl of porridge. "Sam is so hot now. Should I send for Mr. Wilburn?"

"He stopped in earlier and said he would be back after he paid court on the miller's wife and her rheumatism," Mrs. Innis said. "There are others in the public room who want to speak with you when you finish breakfast."

"Oh?"

"The magistrate." She made a face. "He told Dave that he wants a complete report, though why he needs to be bothering you, I am sure I do not understand."

"Probably because I was the one who pulled the trigger, Mrs. Innis," Lydia replied. She thought about the road agent: the anger in his eyes, followed by bewilderment, then excruciating pain. "Poor man," she murmured.

Mrs. Innis stared at her. "I hope you are not feeling sorry for that ... that dreadful man!"

"I am a little," Lydia replied honestly. "I don't think he was much used to robbing people." She touched Mrs. Innis's arm. "And really, Mrs. Innis, my virtue was never in any danger. It seems that this story is being embellished far beyond its reality. I'm only grateful I did not hit Sam, instead. My hands were shaking. Oh, Mrs. Innis, I could have!"

She didn't mean to cry then, but just the thought of the damage she could have done set her off. Mrs. Innis's arms were around her immediately, and she cried until she felt better.

"You needed that," the innkeeper's wife declared as she handed Lydia a second handkerchief. "There's nothing worse than hanging onto tears." She gave Lydia another pat and released her. "And don't canker over what *didn't* happen, my dear. Most days have enough trouble without adding more. Your major is in good hands with Mr. Wilburn … and yours, I would imagine."

My major. "Oh, I hope so," she said, almost surprised at her own fervency. "I will feel better when the surgeon has seen him this morning."

Feeling the need of Maria, she took the baby with her into the public room, which was empty now of customers, if one did not consider the magistrate a customer. He did have a pint of ale in front of him, and there was Mr. Innis, beaming his encouragement at her from behind the bar.

"You have requested that I speak to you?" she asked from the doorway.

The man rose, nodded to her, and indicated the chair opposite him. "Have a seat, Mrs. Reed. I am Reginald Barton, the magistrate's solicitor," he said. He drew pen and paper form the voluminous coat that draped the back of his chair. "It is my duty to take your statement regarding yesterday's incident," he intoned, as though he stood in the magistrate's office.

She held Maria close on her lap. "Sir, will you tell me, what is the condition of the man I shot?" she asked, discovering how hard it was even to say the word.

He glanced at the notes before him and became a little less gloomy. "It appears that the ball fired from that pistol broke his arm, which was amputated at Ealing last night."

"Ah, me!" she said, making no attempt to keep the remorse from her voice.

"Never fear, madam," he replied as he dipped his quill in the ink bottle. "He will have ample time to heal, and then he will do a rope dance."

She frowned. I know it cannot be any other way, she thought, but, oh, to be involved at all is something I do not find appealing. "What are the charges against him, sir?"

"Attempted robbery, attempted assault, attempted murder," he said, referring to the paper. He dipped his quill in the ink again. "Now, madam, if you would …."

"Attempted murder?" she asked. "You are saying he did not kill the clergyman?"

In some exasperation, the magistrate's solicitor put down the quill. "He merely creased the man's leg, although apparently the clergyman was quite convinced at the time that he had been killed." He put his fingers together, and she saw the ghost of a smile around his mouth. "Mrs. Reed, it appears that you are the better shot, only I pray you, do not consider a life of crime."

I suppose he does not wish me to rob coaches to earn money, she thought. She smiled down in Maria's hair, and could not resist. "Mr. Barton, are you a member of the vicar's congregation?"

The smile vanished. "I am, indeed." He looked around and leaned forward. "Do you realize that this means there will be dissections and cross-references from the pulpit of this incident enough to last him until the twentieth century at least?"

"Oh, I *am* sorry," she replied, grateful that this was not her parish. "Let me give you my statement, sir, and then I have a request."

He nodded, and she told the event again, which troubled her more than she would have thought. He interrupted with a few questions to clarify the situation, but soon the subject was exhausted to his satisfaction. "Very well, madam, that will do." He capped the inkwell and returned it to the overcoat. "You said you had a request?"

"I wish that you would be lenient. Surely he should not hang," she said in a low voice. I must be crazy, she thought. Sam lies upstairs wounded and in pain, and I would wish the law to be kind to the man who had certainly increased the difficulty of our journey? I cannot understand myself. Couple this with my bold statement at the victory banquet, and I could be accused of indiscriminate charity running unchecked. And it does not trouble me. I doubt it will even trouble Sam. "Please, sir," she added, testing herself, and finding her conviction unchanged. "What if I choose not to press charges of attempted assault?"

"There remains the attempted murder charge, and robbery," the solicitor said. "He could still hang.""Could you send him to Australia instead?" she asked. "No one died, although we are all poorer. Mr. Reed's injury was brought about at Toulouse by Napoleon, and I was not harmed at all. I think the road agent fell in with bad company, sir, which is unfortunate, but hardly a crime punishable by death, for goodness sake. The clergyman would have provoked anyone. I know Sam wanted to throttle him," she said frankly.

"Did he? Your husband is to be commended for his common sense, then." The solicitor held out his hand to her as he rose. "Mrs. Reed, you are too kind." He permitted himself a smile. "Were such things not impossible, you would have made an eloquent advocate at the bar! I will certainly give your recommendation to the magistrate. You can still expect a visit from the justice of the peace, however."

"Very well," she said as she rose with Maria asleep in her arms. My family would never recognize me, she thought as she watched the man leave. I have become an eloquent, persuasive crusader. I wonder what the justice of the peace can possibly want? Lord, apparently it is hard to shoot someone and keep it quiet.

"Mrs. Reed, you are a kind, kind woman," said the innkeeper from his place behind the bar.

She smiled at him and returned Maria to the crib in Suzie's room. I think I was never anyone before I was Mrs. Reed, she thought. How odd this is. Now I must become an entrepreneur, if I am to save the Reeds from financial ruin. She laughed softly as she bent over the sleeping baby, unable to leave her alone. "The Reeds," she whispered, liking the sound of it. Nothing in this entire situation puts me at ease, but I must admit that nothing is boring about it.

Assured that Maria slept, Lydia climbed the stairs to her room again. Mr. Wilburn was there. He put a finger to his lips as she entered the room, and she sat quietly while he did all those things she had done earlier. He stared for a long time at the major's rash, smoothed his hair to feel his forehead, walked around to look at the stitches, and ended up by the window, rocking back and forth on his heels, regarding the market street below.

She felt a chill, and shook it off. Can you do no more than I have done? she thought in sudden alarm, as she hurried to stand beside him at the window.

"Tell me, sir," she said quietly. "You know that I can take it." I cannot, of course, but you expect me to say that.

He clapped his arm around her. "Mrs. Reed, this is the interesting part of medicine," he said.

She felt herself crumble inside. I will not be a ninny, she thought fiercely. "Interesting?" she repeated putting all the backbone she could spare into the word.

"Yes, my dearie. I have done all I can, and it is good work. You appear to be doing everything you can. I doubt a man was ever in more capable hands."

"I feel so incapable," she confessed.

"Well, it does not show, dearie," he said, giving her another comfortable squeeze. "Now we have to see what Sam Reed is made of."

It was as though a giant hand had whooshed all the air out of her. She sank onto the window seat and put her forehead on her knees, staying that way until the surgeon sat beside her. "Mrs. Reed, I did not mean to frighten you ...." he began, alarm in his voice.

She took a deep breath, sat up, and hugged him, to his

surprise and hers. "Mr. Wilburn, he will be fine, then. I *know* what Sam Reed is made of! He is the strongest person I know." She could have cried with relief, so good was this news.

He absorbed her news, then shook his head. "I bow to your better knowledge of your spouse, dearie, but let me venture to suggest that he is the second strongest person in the Reed family."

She let his words soak all the way into her heart, where they felt like balm of Gilead. They sat together in companionable silence then, listening to the major breathe. "He's not really wakened yet, sir, but he talks to me sometimes. Why does he do that?" she asked. "Next to the fever, I think it is my biggest concern. I mean, is he all right?"

"Healing is hard work, Mrs. Reed," the surgeon said. "Your good husband—and he must be good, if he had the sense to marry you—has shut down everything that is not essential. Is he at least voiding?"

She nodded.

"No blood in the urine?"

She shook her head.

"Excellent! Try to get him to eat, if you can. Just watery gruel. The fever powders?"

"I had to hold his nose until he gave up and opened his mouth."

Wilburn laughed, then covered his mouth with his hand when Sam stirred and muttered something. "Sorry, laddie," he murmured. "Does he *know* what a lucky husband he is?"

Such a question, she thought. I would like to know the answer. "Sir, you will have to ask him," she said, suddenly shy.

He sat with her another moment, then slapped his knees. "What a month this had been for Merry Glade, dearie, a regular beehive of excitement! First, the midwife delivers triplets—triplets—for the butcher's wife; the village's only barber drops down dead during the middle of shaving the squire; a cat has a litter of six-toed kittens; and now there is a wounded Toulouse hero with a lovely wife and daughter, and road agents. We will be discussing you at table long after you have left us." He rose and took another thoughtful look at the major. "I'll be by tonight again, if that will make you happy."

"You know it will," she said fervently. She looked at him shyly. "I suppose what you are saying is that I am managing?"

He nodded. "You are managing."

She walked him down the stairs and into the street. She turned to go back inside when what the surgeon said hit her like a brick between the shoulders. She sat down on the bench outside the door to catch her breath, and was joined a moment later by the innkeeper.

"Mrs. Reed, are you well? I saw you from the door. Is all this too much for you?"

She thought a moment, her excitement barely contained. He will think I am certifiable if I jump up and down, which I want to do, she thought. "I am fine," she said, and took a deep breath. "Mr. Innis, do you know how I can make arrangements to open the barbershop?"

He stared at her, his mouth open. She gave him what she hoped was her most radiant smile. "I think I am about to go into business here in Merry Glade. Do let me explain, and while I am at it, make a slight confession."

14

∽

SITTING THERE IN THE sun, warmed by the genuine concern of the Innises, she spilled her budget. Reasoning that there was no possible benefit in going all the way back to Genesis, she told them merely that the Reeds had lost all their traveling money when the other road agent appropriated Sam's wallet and her reticule.

"I know that my husband has a banker in Durham, but I confess to little interest in his finances and I do not know the name of the business," she said.

Mrs. Innis patted her husband's knee as they sat close together on the bench. "Remedy that, my dear, when your husband comes to himself. A wife should always know where the money is." The Innises looked at each other and laughed.

You dear people, Lydia thought as she watched them. "I know how true that is now," she said, feeling contrition at the tale she told.

"Don't take it so hard, my dear," Mrs. Innis said. "Davey called me out here to tell me that you have a scheme to change your financial picture."

"Indeed I do," she replied. "I propose to open the barbershop.

When I met my husband … met him after Toulouse, he was in the hospital in London. I have some talent with hair, so cutting his was no difficulty. He kindly let me practice on his face."

The Innises looked at her with some concern. "That's not much practice, my dear," Mrs. Innis said.

Lydia laughed. "And what was I drafted to do then but shave all of his men who were invalided there with him, and cut their hair, too! You know how husbands are, Mrs. Innis, I daresay." More than I do, I am sure, she thought, but I have discovered how coercive the male sex can be.

The innkeeper's wife nodded. "I would say that you are a regular proficient now."

"I am," she declared. She cast a critical eye at the innkeeper. "I would be happy to demonstrate on you, Mr. Innis. Do you have any scissors? A comb?"

Mrs. Innis did. While her husband was still thinking about it, she went inside and returned with the scissors. "He's too much of a shagbag for me, Mrs. Reed," she said as she handed Lydia the scissors, a comb, and a dish towel.

Lydia put the towel around Mr. Innis's neck and combed his hair, praying for the best haircut she had ever given. She snipped in silence until Mr. Innis put up his hand to stop her.

"Mrs. Reed, this will never do," he said.

Oh, please, she thought. This is my one talent. "Sir?" she asked, determined not to cry.

"You are supposed to carry on a conversation with me, tell me the latest news, and complain about the government," he said with a grin. "What did your husband's soldiers talk about?"

She continued clipping, her heart light. "Mainly they told me all kinds of stories about the major. I believe I have sufficient information in my possession right now to get my way anytime I want." She stood in front of him to compare the sides. "Beyond that, I fear I am not given to much small talk."

He shrugged. "Inconsequential, Mrs. Reed, inconsequential. There is a wonderful old mirror in the barbershop. They'll use it to admire your beauty and be struck dumb anyway. I know the lads in Merry Glade."

"I am not beautiful!" she exclaimed.

"You are far easier on the eye than the last barber," he retorted. "He was bald and had only one eye."

"If you are trying to put me at my ease … you have succeeded," Lydia said as she removed the dish towel and shook the hair into the street. "What do you think, Mrs. Innis? May I be taken seriously?"

To Lydia's amusement, the innkeeper's wife made a slow circuit around her husband, surveying the haircut from every angle. Finally she stopped in front of him and gave him a loud smack of a kiss on his forehead.

"Davey, you haven't looked this good in years," she said, then grasped Lydia's hand. "My dear, what a difference it makes to have his ears covered a little!"

"Well, they *are* a prominent feature," Lydia said, trying to keep her voice serious.

"Of course, this will mean less of a breeze for him, without all that flapping, and that could be a trial in the heat of summer," Mrs. Innis teased. "Oh, Davey, you're a sight to behold now! Mrs. Reed, let us take a walk to the barbershop while he admires himself in the mirror."

She put her arm through Lydia's, and they strolled down the market street. "Are things truly in a bad way with you?" she asked in a low voice.

Lydia nodded. "All our money is gone, and we … I must find a way to pay you and the doctor." She took a deep breath, relieved to unburden herself. "Since Sam must convalesce here, obviously, I can easily occupy myself as a barber." She stopped and took Mrs. Innis's hands in her own. "Is it too wicked? Too forward? Will anyone come? Please tell me if I am being silly. It is just that I cannot think of anything else."

Mrs. Innis squeezed back. "It is different, I will allow, but since the whole village is caught up in the story of the gallant major and his brave lady, I think you will have every success. Come now, we are almost there."

It is amazing to me how quickly a place can get shabby, once the owner quits the premises, Lydia thought as she peered in the dusty window of the barbershop. She could make out a barber's chair, and there was the striped pole inside the front door.

"I believe he should have pulled in the pole several years ago," Mrs. Innis was saying. She smiled. "His hands shook so bad that I told Davey to quit going there for a shave!" She rubbed at a small space on the pane of glass. "Oh, look! You can still see everyone's shaving mugs on the shelves."

Lydia looked. She smiled at all the mugs. "It is certainly fortunate for me that most men of a certain age and heft accumulate whiskers on a daily basis," she told Mrs. Innis. "Tell me: Who do I see about renting this place for at least two weeks?"

"It can only be his widow, Mrs. Broadbent," the innkeeper's wife said as she changed directions and took Lydia with her. "If you don't mind shouting to be heard, I predict success."

LYDIA LEFT MRS. BROADBENT'S house an hour later in a less sanguine mood, her ears still ringing from so much shouting to be heard. I wonder the neighbors did not call the constable on us, she thought. She and the innkeeper's wife walked along in silence past the apothecary's and the wig maker's.

"Five shillings! It might as well be the crown jewels," Lydia said at last. "Who would have thought someone so old, dried up, and toothless—not to add deaf—would be so shrewd?"

"Five shillings," Mrs. Innis echoed. "It seems like a fortune. What are you to do now?"

What, indeed, Lydia thought as she went upstairs to the bedroom with a bowl of soup. She opened the door hopefully. I need someone to talk this over with, she thought, someone with right good sense who will take me seriously. The only one I know is my husband.

The major had scarcely moved since she left him. Absently she twisted the wedding ring on her finger. "What am I to do, Sam?" she asked. "Five shillings will rent me a shabby little barbershop, where I hope men will appear for shaves and haircuts. Never mind that such a thing is unheard of, and their wives would probably rise as one to smite me. I will never know, because I cannot lay my hands on five shillings!"

The major muttered something, and she was instantly sorry for disturbing his curious sleep. She washed his face with cool water, hoping to wake him sufficiently to eat. By tugging him here and there, she managed to work him into a half-sitting position. Armed with a spoon, she perched on the bed and brought some soup to his mouth. "Oh, please, my dear," she whispered. "You simply have to eat. What will I do, if you won't?"

His eyelids flickered. He opened his mouth when she put the spoon directly against his teeth. Remembering something she had seen at St. Barnabas, she stroked his neck to remind him to swallow. To her relief, he swallowed more soup without the reminder until the bowl was nearly empty.

She was an expert with the urinal now, keeping him modestly covered, wishing he was not hot everywhere. Her own anxiety mounting, she wiped him with a cool cloth, then lay down beside him. She stared at the ceiling. "I do not know what to do, my dear," she said, moving as close as she could. He sighed, turned his face into her hair, and sighed again, as though he was relieved at her return.

She closed her eyes, and woke an hour later with the sun slanting across the bed. She sat up, sweating from contact with the major's feverish body and the heat of early July. Even the braids she wound around her head felt heavy with heat. In another moment she had pulled out the pins and was brushing her hair forward. I should cut off this nuisance, she thought. I tell myself that every summer, but my one vanity persists.

She sat on the edge of the bed and brushed her hair, enjoying the feel of it, soothed somehow. It was not the beautiful blond of Kitty's hair, but a dark brown the color of old wood. Soon it was hanging straight and shining down her back. I have a wedding ring, she thought. Perhaps …. She looked at it, letting the light catch the gold and set it winking, then shook her head. I cannot sell this.

She went to the mirror and stood there a moment. She stared at herself, then quietly put on her shoes again. With fingers that shook, she braided her hair in one loose plait, kissed her husband's hot forehead, and let herself out of the room.

Lydia returned to the Mill and Glade an hour later as the sun was going down, in vast need of consolation. She hurried past the public room and knocked on the door to the Innises' private quarters. Mrs. Innis opened the door, gasped out loud, and pulled her inside, closing the door behind her. She reached out her hand tentatively to finger the remnants of Lydia's hair.

"Oh, my dear, your pretty hair," she said finally.

"It was, wasn't it?" Lydia said, holding out her arms for Maria. She cuddled her close. "It will grow again, Mrs. Innis."

"Did you get enough money?" the innkeeper's wife asked. Lydia shook her head. "Only two shillings. Mrs. Innis, I had three pounds in my stolen reticule, and you cannot tell me that a road agent ever needed it more than I do!" She had cried all her tears at the wig maker's, so she sat and hugged Maria to her. "This means I must pawn my wedding ring in the morning."

She closed her eyes against the physical pain her words brought, even as she wondered why it meant so much. It's just a ring found after a grubby siege and carried around and stuck on my finger to signify a marriage that is half joke and half bargain, she thought. I hardly know the man who gave it to me, and yet I know him well. I wonder: do I love him? Is he trusting me to solve our problem? How many people do I have to fail before *I* am a failure? Mama would say I am already well beyond my limit.

"Suzie, bring a bowl of soup," Mrs. Innis said quietly as she sat beside Lydia. "My dear, perhaps something will happen."

"I do not know what it will be, then," Lydia whispered into Maria's curls. I continue to be a disappointment to myself. Silent now, she ate the soup put before her, looking quickly at Mrs. Innis to see if she gave it grudgingly, but seeing nothing in the woman's eyes except concern. Her cup ran over, and she could scarcely swallow. Maria ate every other bite, leaning against her as if she belonged there. How am I to care for Maria, much less Sam? she asked herself in perfect agony.

"My dear, it will grow," Mrs. Innis reminded her as she took away the empty bowl. She looked back at Lydia. "But that is not your concern, is it?" She set down the bowl and took Lydia's hands in hers. "Lydia! You've already solved your problem! You're going to pawn your ring in the morning, and you will have enough money to open the barbershop."

"It was not the solution I wanted," Lydia said in a voice so small she could hardly hear it herself. She held out her hand. "It's just a ring, isn't it?"

"Yes, dear, it is. When the major feels better and you return home to—to Durham was it?—he'll buy you a better one. Now give Maria back to Suzie tonight and get some sleep! I know things will look better to you in the morning."

I think there are some things that cannot be cured by a good night's sleep, she thought. After a long moment of resting her chin on the top of Maria's head, she nodded. "Love doesn't have anything to do with rings, does it?" she asked.

Mrs. Innis smiled. "No, it does not, Mrs. Reed." The smile left her face. "My dear, are you afraid that the major will not make it, and you won't have a ring, either? Is that it?"

Was it? she wondered. I will be almost where I was before, she thought. "I don't know," she said. She handed Maria to Suzie, nodded to Mrs. Innis, and hurried upstairs. She opened the door quickly, not knowing what she expected, but relieved to see the major lying quietly, his breathing strong. He was on his back now, which surprised her. She came closer.

With the sun down the room was cooler now, but he was sweating. She touched his chest and took a deep breath. His skin was cool, his face relaxed. She leaned over him. The fever spots in his cheeks were fading, and she could see no new rash on his body. The stitches no longer strained to contain his wound. She took a towel and returned to the bed to dry him, patting him gently, then covering him so he would not be too cold. "You're better, Sam," she said. "I know you are."

She hoped he would open his eyes, but the effort was still beyond him. He nodded and tried to edge himself closer to her. She accommodated him by moving closer instead and taking hold of his hand. She lay down beside him, feeling the tension leave her for no discernible reason other than that he was there and he had never made her feel anything but comfortable.

She took his hand and rested it on her stomach. "Sam, I did something that my relatives would declare quite distempered." He said nothing, but she thought his hand moved slightly on her stomach. "I arranged to open a barbershop, and I cut off all my hair to pay for it, but I still don't have enough." She sighed and tightened her grip on his hand. "I have to spout my wedding ring in the morning to raise the rest. I hope you are not upset with me, but I think I can raise all the money we need." Lydia moved closer to him, grateful that he was cool now. "If you have any hidden sources of wealth, do tell me please."

"Trunk."

He said it quite distinctly, too distinctly for her to ignore. She sat up and looked around the room. The major's campaign trunk lay in the corner next to her bandbox. Bless Mr. Innis's heart, she thought. He did promise to fetch them from Ealing. "The trunk, eh?" she asked as she got up and knelt by the battered trunk, probably a veteran of as many battles as the major himself. She opened it, shy at first because it was not hers, then bolder when he repeated the word again.

"Very well, sir," she murmured as she carefully pulled back

a layer of shirts and uniform trousers, each one worse than the one before. "Heaven knows why you saved such rags, Mr. Reed." She smiled at him. "Are they too comfortable to part with? I can see that you are going to be a difficult husband."

The next layer held a uniform case, and she opened it. Goodness, but the artillery certainly has it over every other service, she thought, as she ran her fingers over the rows and rows of handsome gold braid tacked horizontally across the bosom. "Elegant, but not the answer to our problems, sir."

Another probe of the trunk unearthed his razor of Toledo steel, which she snatched up with cries of delight. "Oh, very good, sir," she exclaimed. "I can shave everyone to a hair's breadth with this wicked thing. Let there be a strop, too." There was, and an extra cake of Spanish soap. She put the items beside her and continued her search. She glanced through several books of geometry and trigonometry, as applied to the science of artillery, and shook them, in the hopes that banknotes were hidden somewhere within. "You *are* intelligent, Major Reed," she said to him. "My compliments, certainly, but we are still as poor as Job's rooster."

There remained only a nightshirt that she would not have used to wipe off a wet dog, a towel so full of holes that it would have been useless for all but the skinniest of men, and a tablecloth with a chessboard drawn onto it, and what must be chess pieces knotted into one corner. "Sam, whatever treasures you once possessed, they are long gone now," she said as she carefully replaced the items in the proper order. "I will keep your shaving gear, though."

"No treasures," she told him as she took off her dress and petticoat and lay down next to him in her chemise. "Oh, well. I can manage tomorrow. Come put your arm around me again, and say something sweet and tell me not to worry, that you will solve all my problems," she said. He was deep asleep now, and did not move, and she knew he had no power to help her at all, but she went to sleep with a sigh of considerable contentment, resting close beside him.

HE WAS EVEN BETTER in the morning, able to hold the urinal himself, even though he still did not speak or open his eyes. "What an effort you are going through," she said to him when he finished and she helped him lie back on his side this time. She kissed his forehead, and she smiled to see him purse his lips at the same time. "You're getting better every day," she told him as she washed his face. "Your sickness is turning to health, but I am afraid we are still poorer instead of richer." She looked at the wedding ring. "I have the remedy, Sam. Lie here and get better please."

She picked up her tearfully earned two pounds from the bureau, counting it again to make sure that it hadn't grown magically overnight, like Jack's beans. Combing her hair took no time at all, and truly, because her hair was inclined to curl, it didn't look too dreadful.

Mr. Innis was sweeping the floor in the public room when she came downstairs, with Maria fenced off by a ring of chairs on their sides. "Ta' missus and Suzie had a small errand this morning," he explained as she retrieved the baby. "I promised to watch."

She sat with Maria. "Will it be forward of me to come in here tonight and announce that I will be offering shaves and haircuts tomorrow?"

"I think everyone will be happy to hear you, Mrs. Reed," he said as he swept up the dust and deposited it behind the counter. "You would be amazed how many people have been inquiring after your husband. This whole adventure has caught everyone's fancy."

She smiled at him, and set Maria down, balancing her against the chair. "I have discovered something about adventures, Mr. Innis. I suspect they will seem much more exciting five years from now, when viewed from a distance." She looked at her ring. And some will never be right, no matter how many years pass.

"I don't doubt it," he said, leaning on his broom. "Well, here come my darlings, Mrs. Reed. Tell me what you think."

She turned around when Mrs. Innis and Suzie came into the room, and her greeting froze on her lips. There is nothing I can say, she thought finally, when her brain started to function again. There is nothing I can do to repay the kindness so visible before me, except succeed at my attempt. If there is a stronger bond than the love and confederacy of women, I do not know it yet.

She got up slowly and came toward Mrs. Innis first, putting out a shaking hand to touch her shorn hair, and then putting both her hands on the woman's cheeks, which were now as tear-stained as her own. "Your hair," she said. "Oh, what have you done for me?" And then her arms were around Suzie, too, a girl-almost-woman who already knew more about kindness than Mama or Kitty could ever imagine. These are my sisters, she thought as she kissed them both, wept with them, and laughed at the same time.

"Oh, my dears," she said. "Oh, my dears."

Suzie burst into loud sobs and hugged her tighter. "We couldn't have you pawn away your ring, not with the major so ill," she said. "It was only hair, Mrs. Reed. It will grow back."

Mrs. Innis reached into her reticule and pulled out four coins. "With what you have, this makes six shillings. I believe that is enough for the rent, plus any supplies we need." She smiled at her husband and blew him a kiss. "Davey had already promised to ride to Ealing today for any special soaps or creams we cannot purchase here. Take it, Mrs. Reed, with our love."

Lydia did, looking down at the money in her hands, and knowing in her heart that no offering in church or chapel was ever more sacred than that which she held. "I will pay you back, of course," she murmured, "except that I can never really do that."

"We know you will," Mrs. Innis said, and hugged her around the waist. "This is our investment, and we expect a good return."

Lydia nodded. I am loved, she thought in wonder. I think now that I can do anything. "Very well," she said as she pocketed the money. "I am off to Mrs. Broadbent's house. If you want to compound the felony, I would welcome your help in cleaning that shop. You say Mr. Broadbent only had one eye, Mr. Innis? I am certain there will be dust and grime enough for us to see."

Mrs. Innis was looking beyond her with her mouth open, so Lydia turned around in time to see Maria—hands upraised, eyes fierce with concentration—stand by herself before waving her arms about and plunking down. "Mrs. Reed, what a day this is!" she declared as Lydia picked up the baby and kissed her. "We are shorn like sheep now, and ready to dig into a dusty barbershop, and Lady Maria has favored us with progress of her own. Tell me please that the major is better, and I will be full enough for one day."

"He is better," Lydia said. She went to the door, her step light for the first time in days, her mind clear. "I hope you will not stand around all day! Our investment awaits. We have a barbershop to open!"

15

❦

SKIRTS HIKED UP, SLEEVES rolled to their shoulders, they toiled like Turks all day in the barbershop. There wasn't a single surface that didn't need cleaning, and nothing that escaped their attention. "You know, of course, what the amusing thing is about all our effort," Mrs. Innis told Lydia after she had removed two wigs that looked remarkably like dead things. "A man would never even notice this dirt. Essentially, my dear, our labors are in vain."

Lydia worked steadily, stopping only long enough to return to check on the major. The first time, Mr. Wilburn was there. "Delightful, delightful, Mrs. Reed," he said, gesturing to his patient, who stretched out in comfortable sleep. "We even had a couple words of conversation."

"Then I envy you, sir," she said, sitting beside her husband.

The surgeon shook his head, even though none of the merriment left his eyes. "It was a strange conversation. Something about chess."

"He has a tablecloth with a chessboard drawn on it," she said, her hand on his foot. "And look! You have got him into a nightshirt. You must have discovered that his shoulder is better."

"Much better." The doctor rose to go. "Mrs. Reed, I predict that his eyes will be open tonight, but I would not hold out for too much sensible conversation yet." He kissed her cheek. "But, then, my dear, how many men engage in sensible conversation when they have no excuse of a morphine pick-me-up? Good-day!"

How many, indeed, she thought, as she pulled his nightshirt neatly below his knees and wondered if this was a loan from the shorter Mr. Innis. As she watched him, alert for any change, he opened his eyes and slowly stretched out his good arm.

I know an invitation when I see one, she thought as she lay down beside him and rested her head on his outstretched arm. "It's been a long day, Sam, and here we are only at noon," she said. "I am cleaning out a barbershop, and I will go into business tomorrow morning." She turned her head to watch his expression, and to surmise that none of this was making any sense to him. "The only thing of value I found in your trunk was your shaving razor, my dear Mr. Reed, but that was quite enough."

He lay watching her, his expression blank. In another moment, he closed his eyes and slept. Taking her turn, she looked at him, sorry to see his cheeks so sunken, but gratified by the evenness of his breathing. Soon you will be robust again, she thought, a state in which I have never seen you. She kissed him, rested her cheek against his for a brief moment, then hurried downstairs to feed Maria. In a half hour, she was scrubbing shelves in the barbershop again.

She had never worked so hard before, not even at St. Barnabas, spurred on by the unwearying efforts of Mrs. Innis, who obviously took her investment seriously. She was ruthless with dust. If this venture fails and I am left to sit outside on the road with a tin cup, at least I will know that I did everything I could, she told herself.

Her fear of failure turned dinner to sawdust. I might as well nibble on the tablecloth, she thought as she carried on what she felt was sparkling conversation. She could have saved her breath; after fifteen minutes of witty repartee, she stopped to see both the Innises grinning at her.

"What? Am I making no sense?" she asked.

"None whatever," the innkeeper replied cheerfully.

"We don't mind, if it makes you feel better, dearie," Mrs. Innis said.

The only thing that will make me feel better would be to dump all my problems in someone else's lap, she thought. With a sigh, she excused herself and looked in on Maria, who already slept under Suzie's watchful eye. "I confess, I wish I could sleep that peacefully," she whispered, her hand on Suzie's shoulder.

"You will, Mrs. Reed, tomorrow night when you have made pots of money," the girl said.

Everyone is confident but me, Lydia thought as she left the public house and breathed deep of the cool night air. Unable to help herself, she walked back to the barbershop and scrutinized their day's work through a window so clean it was nearly invisible. Mentally she ticked off all the soap, shampoo, and pomade which lined the shelves. There was the stack of barber's linen, basins, and combs and brushes, and Sam's Spanish razor, honed to a wicked edge.

"Hello, Mrs. Reed! Ready for business tomorrow?"

She gasped and leaped back from the window, her hands behind her back like a child in a china shop. It was only the constable, out for his own evening stroll. If he noticed how fine-tuned she was, he chose not to remark on it, but only tipped his hat to her. "I'll be there tomorrow," he assured her. "And tonight, I'll try all the doors all over Market Street and look out for evildoers who might be after pomade or talc." He looked around elaborately and gave her a slow wink that banished the terror from her mind.

"I will look forward to giving you a haircut tomorrow, sir," she said, then gasped again when he whisked off his hat and exposed a bare scalp. "Perhaps a shave, instead?"

He grinned, wished her good night, and continued on his rounds. She returned to the inn, and steeled herself for one last ordeal that night.

The public room was full. Well, Lydia Reed, you have tended fearful wounds, harangued a whole banquet hall of lords and ladies, wounded a road agent, and turned short hair into a community fashion. Put one foot in front of the other and go in that room. They may be rough and uncouth, and Mama would spit nails if she could see you, but there is not an enemy in the bunch. They want you to succeed.

She went in and stood in front of the bar. The pub fell silent so quickly that she knew the inhabitants could hear her stomach thud down to her ankles and bounce back. She cleared her throat, a sound so puny that she blushed. "I just wanted to announce that the barbershop will be open tomorrow morning and every day thereafter for the next two weeks, excepting Sundays," she said.

Several of the men nodded and smiled at her. The rest returned to their pipes, drinks, cards, cribbage, and conversation. I could almost use a pint of ale, she thought. Now, wouldn't that dumbfound these men? She smiled at Mr. Innis and walked quietly up the stairs.

The room was dark, but she did not need a candle, considering that the moon was full and seemed to be stopped right outside their room. She admired the night for a moment, resting her elbows on the windowsill to absorb it all. It's a moon to share with someone, she thought, and glanced at Sam. Mr. Wilburn has great confidence in you, Sam, and so do I. Maybe we can admire next month's full moon?

She unbuttoned her dress and stepped out of it, wishing for a bath again, but contenting herself with a thorough wash in the basin, after making sure that Sam Reed slept. From habit, she went to take the pins from her hair, then stopped. I must admit that short hair is simple to deal with, she thought. I wonder if Sam will like it. A few pulls of her hairbrush sufficed, and then she was lying next to her husband. He was turned away from her, and she lay down with her back against his.

"Lyddy?" he asked.

"If I am not, then we won't tell her," she teased, relieved to hear his voice again. "Oh, Sam, can you talk now? I wish you would talk to me."

"Move a little."

She obliged him, and he slowly turned onto his back. "Wrong side, Lyddy," he said. She got up and walked around the bed to lie down next to his good shoulder. He had stretched out his arm for her again. When she lay down, he hugged her to him with more energy than she thought he possessed. I wish I could adequately express how good that feels, she thought. She put her arm across his chest, resting her hand on his heart. "I'm scared to death," she confessed.

He didn't say anything, and she wasn't even sure that he had an inkling of what was going on tomorrow. It was enough that he could hold her. "If no one comes to have a haircut tomorrow, we will probably be sharing a cell with our favorite road agent," she whispered into his chest. "The doctor and the innkeeper will shut us in debtor's prison and swallow the key. Only think what terrible examples we are as parents for Maria! The mother superior would smite us on the spot. We will probably receive a free ocean voyage to Australia and all the stale bread and moldy water we can consume twice a day."

"What else could possibly happen?" he murmured, tugging her closer, speaking in that slow, dreamy way.

She sat up and touched his face. "You could follow all that silliness?" she asked, less afraid now.

"Some of it," he said, but he did sound like he was registering information more slowly than usual. His voice was lazy-sounding, unlike his ordinary crisp delivery.

I will take whatever he offers, she thought. "Can I get you anything?" she asked.

"No." He took her hand and pulled her down beside him again. "All I want … is here." He patted her arm slowly, as he seemed to be doing everything. "I wish …."

Thank you, God, and Mr. Wilburn, and the Innises, and everyone else involved in this miracle, she thought. She rose up on her elbow. "You wish you could help me tomorrow?" she asked. "I can't tell you what that means to me, just knowing."

He shook his head. "No."

"Oh, I like that!" she teased. "Here I thought you wanted to help me cut hair and raise the money to pay the doctor for your emaciated carcass."

He shook his head again. "Better idea … tonight." His voice was more drowsy now, even though he had not relinquished his surprising grip on her. "Want to love you."

She knew she had heard him right. "That's how Major Reed solves problems?" she asked, unable to feel embarrassed, and equally unable to hide her amusement. "My word, husband, you are three parts dead, wasted, crosshatched together with black thread." She felt his forehead. "Well, you are cool, at least, and possibly your derangement is only temporary."

"Works in all crises." His eyes were closing again. "However, not quite"—he was silent a moment—"able."

Interesting, she thought, digesting this bit of news and quite forgetting her fears. More shy now, she rested her hand on his chest again. He grunted softly when she ran her foot down his shin, enjoying the softness of the hair on his leg. "I shouldn't worry, then?" she asked finally, long after she thought he was asleep. "I won't if you say so."

Contented, she was about to turn away and compose herself for sleep when he gave another tug and pulled her half onto himself. She knew he was trying to kiss her, so she obliged him by inching up a little and kissing him, instead. Then he was gently kneading her back with his good arm as she put her hands under his head, careful not to touch his stitches.

He can't be enjoying this, she thought. I must be hurting

him. She tried to rise up, but he seemed quite disinclined to permit it. I am amazed what fever powders can do to a sensible gentleman, she thought as she returned his kiss with enthusiasm. As she kissed him, he began to relax slowly in her arms until he slept. She smiled, kissed him quickly on the cheek, and slowly disentangled herself. No more fever powders for that man, she thought, as she put her leg back over him again and settled herself quite comfortably against his side.

"I love you." She said it quite softly, not wishing to wake him. She knew how tentative it sounded to her own ears, and she wondered about herself. She rested her hand on his chest again, liking the feel of him, and the pleasant odor of the oil of wintergreen, which Mr. Wilburn patted on his shoulder at every visit. Let us see now, Major Reed, she thought, so far in our marriage you have been little but work and worry, and some considerable exasperation. You could have told me about the necessity for including a year-old baby in the bargain. She nestled closer. No, that would not have served a purpose, she told herself. I would never have said yes to your outrageous proposal, if I had known everything that lay in store.

I wonder if anyone knows anything before they marry, she asked herself as she lay so close to her husband. I suppose Papa would never have married Mama, had he known what a shrew she would become. Why should I presume to think that knowing more about Major Reed would have made the slightest difference? I have still to discover if he leaves the lid off the tooth-powder tin, or drops his clothes everywhere, or belches at the table. I do know that he is quarrelsome and irritable when things don't go his way, vulnerable to pain like all of us, unflinchingly loyal to those soldiers to whom he was committed, and brave beyond all reason. I wonder if he loves me?

She woke in the morning to a still dark room and rain thundering down, then flopped onto her back in the worst sort of misery, mourning the downfall of her plans. No one will come on a day like this, she thought as her eyes filled with tears. She turned onto her side to stare out the window. As usual, the major had filled up most of the bed in that way of his, so she clutched the edge of the mattress and added that complaint to her darkest thoughts.

I would not go out in a rainstorm for something that could wait for better weather, she told herself. Why should the men in this village care whether their hair was cut or their faces shaved, when some have done without since the barber dropped down dead? Perhaps their wives are reluctant to surrender their men to a rather mysterious young woman no one knows? And why do I listen to myself when I am like this?

"Out you go, Lyddy," her husband said.

"I did not know you were awake," she said quickly, sitting up to take a good look at him.

His eyes were open, but he still looked a bit dreamy to her. "How am I supposed to sleep when you are revolving like a top, snatching the covers, and … oh, I can't remember."

She was instantly contrite. "Oh, dear, I do that when I worry," she told him as she felt his forehead.

He took her hand off his head and pressed it to his chest. "Dear Lyddy, my bed at home is wider. You'll be able to stew and fret to your heart's content there." He paused, and brought her hand to his lips. "If that is what you choose to do. Although why you think that will help matters, I cannot quite fathom."

She nodded, then got up to look out the window. "It *is* a bad habit, isn't it?" she said, watching the rain thunder down.

He patted the spot she had vacated, and she returned to bed. "Put your arm under my neck like you did last night," he said. "I like that."

"I'm so afraid to hurt you," she said.

"I'll let you know. Ah, that is much better. Lyddy, I am not prone to giving advice, but let me give you some right now," he said. His voice was clear. She could tell by his eyes that he was in pain, but his mind seemed his own again.

"Tell me, then," she said, resting her head on his chest.

"The night before a battle, I get my battery in place. Water is in the tubs; the shot and shell are lined up where they should be. The horses are far back, but not too far, in case we need to move fast. God knows we've pulled the guns ourselves at times. We eat a good meal, if there is food available. We sometimes play chess. I always pray before I retire. Then I lie down and sleep and let the morning come. I am ready for it, no matter what."

"But it's raining and…."

He put his finger to her lips. "No, wife, don't. I cannot remember quite what is going on, but I know it is important to you. Have you done everything to be ready?"

She nodded, thinking of the hours of scrubbing and redding up. She saw again in her mind the rows of shaving mugs all gleaming and preparing for lather. "I have."

"Then, go do it. Let go of my neck and get out of bed, and go do it."

She closed her eyes for a brief moment, steeling herself for the day. She slid her arm out from under his neck, watching him closely. He did not wince, but he bit his lip. She pressed her own lips close together, but she kept her voice normal when she spoke. "Do you need some more fever powders? I would prefer not to give them to you, but you are the judge of that."

"Let's not, Lydia. I can manage, if you'll just help me with the needfuls."

She did, then dressed quickly, making sure her hair was fluffed out and curled here and there around her fingers. No point in claiming I can do hair, if my own is a bird's nest, she thought. Sam was quiet now, exhausted from so many coherent thoughts. She put on her best muslin dress and one of Mrs. Innis's long aprons.

"You'll do, pretty thing."

He sounded so tired. She sat on the bed a moment until he

nudged her with his hip. "Go on now."

She hung back another moment at the door. "You'll think of me?" she asked, feeling foolish, but wanting to know.

"I always do, wife," he whispered.

Tell me you love me, she thought, willing him to speak. He closed his eyes. She stood there until he was asleep, then went quietly downstairs.

Breakfast was pointless. She fed Maria, but shook her head when Mrs. Innis offered her porridge. Mr. Innis was standing at the window. "The public room's empty," he said, his eyes on the rain. "Even my regulars are having breakfast at home." He turned to her, and she knew he had more on his mind.

"That is all very well, Mr. Innis," she said before he could speak. "I said I would be at the barbershop, and so I shall be. Mrs. Innis, will you look in on Sam occasionally? I anticipate that Mr. Wilburn will be by. And now, may I borrow an umbrella?"

Mrs. Innis insisted on a cloak, too. She put it around Lydia's shoulders, hugged her, and handed her the umbrella. "The rain may slow down in a few hours. We can hope."

Lydia nodded. She stepped outside and opened the umbrella, then patted her pocket where the key rested. She hesitated. Mama would be home now, and over the worst of her anger. I could apply to them for passage home, and I know they would send it. "No, Lydia," she said out loud. "Too many people are depending on you."

The rain showed no sign of letting up. She took a deep breath and left the shelter of the tavern. Just two streets over, she thought. One foot in front of the other. I've done all I can. I can't go back. I could never face Sam again if I quit now.

She turned the corner, and frowned. How odd, she thought. I wonder if there is a funeral. There was a line of people down the short block, some with umbrellas, others bareheaded. She looked closer. It couldn't be a funeral because the line extended past the church and just around the corner. She noticed that they were all men, too.

"How odd," she repeated, and then the impact of the line struck her like a blow to her body. She hurried faster, crossing the street, unable to reach the corner fast enough because the rain slowed her down. She turned the corner and burst into tears.

The line stopped at the door to the barbershop, and heading the queue was Mr. Wilburn, cheerful as ever, even though the rain pelted down. "Mrs. Reed, you'll have to work fast," he said cheerfully.

With hands that shook, she opened the door. The men hurried inside, the first two lifting the barber's pole out beside the door. She ran to the stove and lit it. The water was ready in the tub. She blew her nose on her apron and wiped her eyes. Brushes, combs and razors, pomade and talcum. She went to the door and told the first man waiting outside. "Pass it down, please. Tell the others to wait in the pub. When this group is done, one of them will tell you, and you can send more."

She turned to the men in the shop, took Mr. Wilburn by the arm, and led him to the chair. "Sir, you don't have much hair, you know."

He patted his head in mock surprise. "Good Lord, I believe she is right!" The men laughed, looking at the floor in their shyness. "Then, trim that fringe, Mrs. Reed. And I am ready for a shave." He nodded as she settled the cloth around his neck, then winked at her. "Better work fast, Mrs. Reed, so you can see what handsome dogs we are here in Merry Glade. You'll wish you had never leg-shackled yourself to a grumpy major, when you see how lovely *we* are! Right, lads?"

She worked steadily all morning as the rain drummed down and the barber's chair began its regular creaking as one man left the seat and another sat down. She knew her own shyness in the presence of so many men would keep her from much small talk, but these friends and neighbors supplied their own text. They were rough men, yeomen and crofters mostly, but they kept their language seemly, looking at her for approval when someone made a witty remark. It was easy to smile her approbation, and to realize that no matter where she went in the world, that these simple souls had taught her a valuable lesson.

The only emergency came as noon approached. Out of breath and wet, Suzie ran into the shop. "Mrs. Reed! You have to come quick! It's the major! Mama wants you now!"

Her heart dropped to her shoes and did not rebound. He was fine when I left, she thought in sudden alarm. She set down the shaving mug and turned to the man she had just lathered.

"You go right on, Mrs. Reed. I'll keep. Hurry now," the man urged, his expression as concerned as hers.

She did hurry, running through the rain, outdistancing Suzie. She pulled up her dress and apron and gave the whole village ample opportunity to observe her legs, if anyone had felt inclined to gawk.

She took the stairs two at a time, her mind a perfect jumble, and burst into the room. Sam Reed lay on his side, his lips set in a tight line. Mrs. Innis stood next to him, the urinal in her hand, her lips equally compressed, every line of her body expressing disapproval.

"Mrs. Reed, your man is devilishly stubborn," she announced, her words clipped. "He refuses my help." She glared at him. "I am certain he is about to pop, but he won't let me touch the covers, let alone him."

Lydia sank into the chair by the door, out of breath. "I thought ... a terrible emergency ... Sam, you are certifiable! I would like to brain you over the head with that thing!"

Mrs. Innis shook her head, but she was smiling now. She handed the urinal to Lydia. "He says he's your man, and he won't have some strange woman fumbling with his privates." She was laughing as she left the room.

"For heaven's sake, Sam," Lydia scolded as she pulled back the blankets and helped him. "Not a minute too soon! You are a trial."

He sighed with relief and was silent for a long moment, concentrating on the matter at hand. "Lydia, they call them privates for a reason," he said finally.

She started to laugh, and he had to remind her to hold still, or she would be changing sheets, too. "One more day and I'll be on my feet," he promised her. "I really don't enjoy doing this lying down. Or having to sit up to turn over. Or the smell of wintergreen."

"I rather like it, Sam," she said as she removed the urinal and carried it to the commode. "Makes you sweet. I was hoping you'd keep dabbing it on here and there when you feel better."

He frowned, as if trying to decide whether she was quizzing him. He looked at her and laughed. "I should change the subject, shouldn't I, before you thrash me for being an idiot. Lydia, I am shy about some things. Maybe more than I should be."

"You amaze me, Sam. Here you've fought the length and breadth of Spain and Portugal, crossed the Pyrenees with your guns, fought in France, and endured years of privation and toil, seen disease and death in its most dreadful forms, and you're squeamish about kind Mrs. Innis, who has certainly seen … well, if not yours, then Mr. Innis's. I doubt there is much variety." She thought of her waiting customers, covered him again, and sat down on the bed. "Just get better, Sam. I'll come back in an hour or two, so you needn't run the risk of exposing yourself to Mrs. Innis."

He kissed her hand. "Lydia, am I an idiot?"

She nodded. "Completely certifiable. And you're getting grouchy." She kissed his cheek. "I have someone waiting for me with his face lathered. He's not as handsome as you, but he's paying me for my time and talents, while you are not."

He nodded. "Mrs. Innis told me about the barbershop. You've been telling me about that, too, haven't you? I am sorry that it did not register."

"Apology accepted. I think you have had more on your mind

than Lydia Reed and her enterprises, even if they are created to keep us from the poorhouse."

"I know I'm foggy, but didn't I tell you to look in the trunk?"

She started to rise, but he would not let go of her hand. She squeezed it. "I did, and I thank you so much! Your razor is far and away the best one I have. How clever of you to remember that much, even though I know it was a strain."

"But …."

She kissed him again, shaking her head at the bewildered look on his face. "I'll see you in a few hours, Sam. Do try to behave yourself."

WITH ONLY BRIEF INTERRUPTIONS to tend to Sam's needs, she worked steadily through luncheon and beyond the afternoon. The rain never let up any more than the customers did, to her continued amazement. Before she asked the last man to pull in the barber pole, the men she had not had time for came in one by one to tell her that they would return tomorrow.

When the last one left the shop, she pulled down the shades and sat in the barber's chair, her back on fire and her arms throbbing from holding them up all day, cutting hair and shaving faces. I don't dare take off my shoes, she thought as she raised her skirts to look at her ankles. I'd never get them back on. I wonder if anyone would miss me, if I just stayed all night in this wonderful chair?

When she found the energy to rise, she quickly cleaned up the shop, swept the room, stopping to lean on the broom when her feet refused to hold her. She was stealing herself to go outside and pump some water for tomorrow, but the constable came by and did it for her. When he finished, he nodded to her and straightened his uniform jacket. "This is an official visit, Mrs. Reed."

"Oh, dear! Are you going to arrest me for causing men to loiter about Merry Glade all day?" she asked, unable to resist.

"None of that, Mrs. Reed!" he said, shocked. He must have

noticed the twinkle in her eyes then. "You're quizzing me!" He threw back his shoulders. "I am here to escort you and your money to the Mill and Grange. I'll even carry it, if the sack's too heavy."

It was, and she let him gladly, taking his arm and limping in triumph to the tavern. He bowed elaborately to her, even though the men in the public room pointed at him and made rude noises. "I am the law," he reminded them with all his constabulary dignity, and said good night.

She sat with the Innises and Maria, carefully counting out the money she owed Mrs. Innis and Suzie for the sacrifice for their hair, and then paid for their lodging up to the present. The sack was almost empty now, but her heart was at ease. "I will have the rest soon enough to cover our meals and Maria's tending," she assured them. Listen to me, she thought as she sat with Maria asleep against her bosom. I shall have to thank my husband for his good advice. There was the surgeon to consider, too, and the fare on the mail coach to Northumberland, but she did not doubt that she could earn it.

The stairs were almost more than she could manage, but she took them slowly, her hand heavy on the railing. I am decrepit, she thought. Lord, remind me that when we are on Sam's estate and I have servants, that I remember how hard they work for me, and treat them better than ever my parents would.

Sam was sleeping. Automatically she went to him first, feeling his forehead, and touching his shoulder lightly. He was blessedly cool. She was too tired to do anything but stand there and appreciate the fact. Move, Lydia, she told herself finally. You were reluctant this morning, and now you are simply tired; tired hurts, but it is better.

With a groan that surprised her, she unbuttoned her dress and stepped out of it. She wanted to stick her feet in the washbasin, but that would have meant bending over to place it on the floor, so she washed her face instead. The nightgown was where she had left it, so she put it on, groaning again.

Sam was spread out in his usual fashion. She thought about claiming the window seat instead, but it was too far to walk. She lay down and pushed him gently, then resigned herself to the little space it created.

"Tired, Lydia?" he asked her. He moved over slightly to accommodate her, then put his good arm around her, stopping when she flinched. "Everything aches?"

"Everything," she assured him. "I have never been so tired. Sam, it was wonderful. We still owe a lot, but I know I can raise it."

He was silent a long time. As tired as she was, when he spoke again, she noticed something different in his voice, something almost joyful, she thought, but that was silly. She was just tired, and it had been a long day. "You sound quite certain," he said.

"I am." Wearily she turned onto her stomach. "Sam, if it's not asking too much, will you rub my back before it breaks into two or three pieces?"

She thought she would scream when he began to knead that spot between her shoulder blades which had been troubling her since before noon, but the pain quickly yielded to immense relief. "You are good at that," she murmured.

"I can make it better."

She was too tired to object when he reached under her nightgown and continued to rub her bare skin. "Nice," she whispered, wanting to carry on some polite conversation since he was being so kind, but her brain seemed disconnected from the rest of her. When he reached under her to massage her breasts, she thought she ought to make some remark or other. They don't ache, she wanted to tell him, except that they did, in an odd sort of way that was making other parts of her ache. I really ought to do something about this, she thought, and then it was too much trouble to think what. She slept; she probably even snored.

16

～∞

SHE CUT HAIR THE next day and the next, with a certain single-minded goal: I can rest my feet at night. Able to sit up in bed now, Sam very kindly massaged her bare feet at night after Maria was asleep, then entertained her with stories of the Peninsula while she soaked them up to the ankle in Epsom salts and warm water, a remedy much favored by Mr. Wilburn.

The second day had been as busy as the first. The rain had not abated appreciably, but she woke this morning with the fear of failure gone, replaced by the sure knowledge that she would be fully occupied. She felt disinclined to stir from the warmth of her husband's arms, wanting another back rub, but too shy to ask for it in broad daylight.

He did not wake up when she left the bed. She sat on the edge of the mattress a moment, admiring him as he slept, and wondering why it was that some men were blessed with long eyelashes. She nearly kissed him when she left the room, but that same shyness prevented her. Lord, I am a goose, she thought. When I went to sleep last night, he was making me extremely comfortable, and here I am shy about a kiss. I wish he would tell me how he feels.

The day settled into the routine that would be hers until Sunday, and then again on Monday. Lydia even ventured into a little small talk, which embarrassed the men of Merry Glade as much as it pleased them. She clipped and shaved efficiently and quickly, wasting no one's time, pacing herself to prevent yesterday's exhaustion. She took time out for Sam's personal needs, played with Maria, and spent the rest of the day at the barbershop.

She liked the evenings less as the week passed. She was quite ready for her husband to kiss her again, and suggest another back rub, but he did not. He was alert now, and enthusiastic about her small successes, even as she wondered at his surprising lack of interest in her. The other night's brief pleasure might not even have happened. She was tired; she could have dreamed it.

"You're enjoying this, aren't you?" she asked on the third night as she sat cross-legged on the bed, counting coins and determined to regain the ground she had so mysteriously lost.

"Why wouldn't I?" he asked in turn as he fished under her leg for a coin that had escaped. "If farming, cattle, and sheep get slow in Northumberland, I can send you out into the working world to earn our keep. Lyddy, add this shilling to that pile by your ankle, and I believe you will have covered our board and Suzie's kind care of Maria. Well-done, wife."

And that was it. He did not offer to rub her back again. In the morning he assured her that he could manage his own personal business now. "Think how much time you will save, if you do not have to see to my needs, Lydia," he told her as she tied on her apron. "You might even have time to sit down, yourself."

"I haven't complained," she said quietly. She could almost feel her old uncertainties creeping back into her mind like that tenth plague sidling around Egyptian doorposts.

"That's the wonder of it," he replied. "I cannot imagine another woman being as kind as you have been."

His statement, delivered in his usual stringent way, passed judgment on her as sure as if he had banged down a gavel. She looked at him. *You think I have done all this because I am a creature of duty,* she thought, trying not to frown at first because it wasn't polite, and then not caring much what he thought. She turned to leave, the adventure gone now from the long day of work and ultimate exhaustion that stretched before her. Her inclination was to say nothing; no one had wanted her opinions before. *I love you and I care what happens to you, you wretched man,* she thought.

She paused in the door, looking back at him, and the change in his expression. "Mr. Reed, if you think that no woman would be this kind, then obviously you were woolgathering when the priest read our marriage vows! Good day."

I am married to an idiot, she thought. While she did not precisely slam the door, she did close it firmly enough to set a vase in the hall shivering. She hurried to the barbershop, winking back tears, and thinking up all kinds of horrendous fates for the major, should the Lord request her suggestions at some later date closer to Judgment Day. *He has no idea how it terrifies me to chatter with strangers, and thrust myself into what is a man's world, and all to raise money to pay his doctor bill, feed and house him, and return him to a better life somewhere in godforsaken Northumberland. Useless, useless husband!*

Her anger cooled as the morning passed, especially when she gave a shorter haircut than the vicar had really wanted, and nicked the mayor several times during a shave. She looked at the clock at mid-morning, uncertain whether to return to their room, even though he had told her he did not need her help. *No,* she told herself as she snapped the barber's towel loud enough to make the sexton leap from his chair as though she had shot him. *Sam says he does not need my help, and I won't bore him with my company.* Still, she reminded herself as she over-lathered the sexton, *I know that urinal was not placed* anywhere near the bed. He will hurt himself if he tries to get up. I should be there.

She wavered through two more haircuts, arguing with herself, even as she smiled at her customers and gushed forth with some nonsense about life in London versus life in small towns that would have astounded even Kitty. Drat the man. No wonder Sir Percy Whoever had to invent a wife for him in Spain. No real woman in her right mind would come close to him. Except me, she concluded mournfully. I am an idiot, too.

In her frame of mind, lunch was out of the question. She put up the "BACK IN TWENTY MINUTES" sign, sat herself down in the chair, and indulged in a hearty bout of tears and self-pity of the variety that was almost, but not quite, comforting. She was drying her eyes on her apron and looking about for a handkerchief when someone rapped on the glass.

"My next money-making scheme in this village will be lessons in literacy," she grumbled as she went to the door. "Or else this one is so shaggy that his hair is covering his eyes and he cannot read my sign."

Her husband stood outside the door, bracing himself on the doorsill, pale as parchment but with a look of premeditated contrition in his eyes. She gasped and opened the door, taking him by the arm and leading him to the chair, too worried to say anything.

He sank into it with relief, and closed his eyes. "My word, Lydia, I cannot believe that only months ago I pushed and pulled cannons over the Pyrenees," he said at last, when he caught his breath. "I doubt I could nudge a canister of case shot with my foot today. I started out with your lunch, but the sandwich was so heavy I left it with a beggar on the church steps. Oh, Lydia, you are married to a fool."

"I know," she said softly. "So are you."

He touched her face, and she felt a mountain roll off her back. "Then, perhaps it is a good thing we discovered each other at St. Barnabas, that least romantic venue in London, with its unspeakable drains, and rats enough to keep as pets and serve for dinner, too," he told her as he took her by the hand. "Lydia, I am sorry. You've been working harder on my behalf than any gentlewoman I ever knew." He blushed and looked down at the floor. "I've given you precious little in return."

"Oh, opportunity," she said with a smile. "You've given me such room to maneuver!" She took him by the hand. "If I were Kitty, I would probably pout and scold and never ever forgive you until you had done something marvelous to make me forget how irritated I was."

"I have every intention—eventually—of causing you all manner of astonishment," he replied with a smile of his own that made her blush and look away. "Lydia, you tell me what Kitty would do. What about you?" He ran his thumb over her wedding ring. "I mean, other than slam the door this morning."

"I didn't! … Well, perhaps it was just a little slam."

"Lydia, how on earth can you slam a door just a little bit?" he asked patiently, then grinned at her. "My word, but wives are interesting! Who would have thought it?"

She tried not to smile back, then thought a moment. "Sit still. You look like a stray dog whom no one will feed." She put a cloth around his neck and picked up a comb. "I don't know how to answer your question, because I was never allowed to be angry."

She could tell from his thoughtful reflection in the mirror that such a consideration had never occurred to him. "Kitty could have her megrims, and Mama was forever berating Papa with his numerous shortcomings, but I was supposed to be usefully quiet," she said. She combed his hair. "Do you want your part lower?"

"No, it's fine there. But … what are you saying, my dear?"

She let go of his hair and stood in front of him so she could look him in the eyes. "You know what happened when I spoke out."

His glance did not waver. He reached up and touched her

cheek, where the bruise was nearly gone. He took a deep breath. "Let us get two things straight." He chuckled and pulled her close, his hands on her face. "By the Almighty this is odd, but it's the very same two items I told my men in the battery when they came to me as recruits."

"I think there are those who would argue that marriage and war have their similarities, Sam," she said, perfectly in charity with him again. Lord, but I am easy to cajole, she thought. How dreadful if he ever finds out. I will have nothing to bargain with. Perhaps I will not need to bargain with this man.

"Oh, so I am Sam again? I think I may come to cringe at 'Mr. Reed' from you, delivered in that crisp, inimitable style reminiscent of … could it be your mama?"

She had the grace to laugh. "It could be. I must have learned something in all those years, Mr.—Sam." She pulled herself gracefully from his grasp and began to snip. "Do divulge your treatise delivered to soldiers and now wives."

"Well, we cannot duplicate the scene, and thank God for that. You certainly smell better than they did, and you're so much easier on the eyes," he said, relaxing in the chair as much as his injury would allow. "I would sit them down and tell them that I would never beat them, and that there was nothing we could not discuss."

Startled, taken aback, and deeply touched, she continued cutting. "I do believe you mean that," she said at last, when even the dust motes seemed to hum in the silence of the shop.

"I never meant anything more."

It was said quietly, with all the resolve of a strong man. I am flattered, she thought. She touched his good shoulder lightly and continued her work. "I have never doubted the former item," she said.

"Thank you, madam," he replied. "I never could understand those commanders who sought to instill loyalty—love, if you will—by beating the men their very lives depended on." He swiveled slightly to look at her, paying for it with a sharp intake of breath that made her hold her own. "I expect it is the same with wives. I believe my life has already been in your hands, and you have been most kind, for no particular good reason."

Other than that I do believe I love you, she thought, amused at him. "Yes, we did make a rather odd bargain to begin this marriage, didn't we?" she asked as she cut and trimmed. "You are to have an accomplice to smooth things with your aunt and your inheritance, and I am to have … what? A safe place to live? I want more."

How quiet it was in the room. She looked at him in the reflection of the mirror, and he gratified her by returning the look, and with the same smile that was on her face, she was certain. I believe we have a right good understanding, sir, she thought, her eyes brimful of amusement.

He turned his head to look at her again. "Well, I did give you Maria, didn't I?" he said, his grin broader and broader.

"I can't even imagine what other surprises await," she replied, perfectly in charity with her quixotic husband. She looked closer, watching the blush rise in his face. "Oh, no! There is more?"

He nodded.

"Don't tell me, then," she said. "Let us muddle along until you feel much, much better, and I will not be accused of doing injury to a poor war hero when I find out what else my future holds. Hold still, now; I am at the dread mole. There. But, then, I am also unlikely to cause you any physical harm." She laughed and touched his face, enjoying the way his eyes closed when she did it. "I think cold, implacable irritation and silence are far more effective. You forget that I have trained with masters, Sam."

Another long silence. "I hope you are quizzing me," he said at last.

"Of course I am," she answered, then took a deep breath. "But all this is tease and banter. I do have something of a personal nature to unload from my shoulders, if you care to listen."

"I care to."

"When you are feeling excellent again, I expect more than a back rub from you, Samuel Reed," she began, felt brave, and continued. "Since we have acquired Maria, and neither of us, I expect, would ever abandon her now, and since I have seen all there is to see of you and not run screaming into the night, and since I confess to much pleasure in both your back and your front rub, I have no intention of annulling what we have recorded in the parish. What a waste of a good special license, ink, and paper." To relieve the huge silence in the room, she hummed as she undid the towel and brushed his neck. "You owe me, Sam," she said as he got out of the chair. "A lot."

"More than you know," he replied. "Put your arms around my waist and don't squeeze too hard."

She did as he said, and enjoyed a kiss so satisfactory that she could only stamp her foot in irritation when someone knocked on the door, then rattled the knob, which her husband had so wisely locked. She started toward the door, and he pulled her close against him again. "When I am feeling in the trim, you'll be the first to know it," he said, his lips practically against hers as he spoke.

Well, she thought, as he released her and allowed her a moment to fluff up the curls he had managed to twine rather too tight in his hand during that kiss. Well, I am speechless, and having waited this long, I am surely good for a few more weeks, if that is what the major requires, she told herself.

There was already a line outside the door. Sam nodded to her and turned to go. "Do have a care, my dear," she called after him. "Sit down on the church steps if you tire."

"You are so solicitous," he said.

She laughed. "Not especially, Sam. If you sit on the church steps in your present wretched condition, perhaps some kind soul will think to toss a coin or two your way. Why should I be the sole wage earner?"

So it went for the remainder of her tenure in the barbershop. Just when she thought—and the Innises agreed with her—that she must have shaved everyone in Merry Glade, others turned up from surrounding towns and villages as the story of the gallant, wounded artilleryman and his even more gallant wife spread out like ripples on the smooth lake of a rural society. No one needed to be reassured that she could cut hair, too. Even the most cautious of men sat in her chair, as though they had known her a lifetime.

"I do believe that my fame has spread throughout at least three districts. I am amazed what notoriety does to ordinary people," she told Sam one night as she sat, nearly asleep, her aching feet in his lap for their nightly massage.

"What it does to you is give you a corn on your last toe, Lyddy," he said. "I can see that you will not be much further use to me without shoes better suited for standing all day in a shop."

She smiled at him, moved her feet from his lap, and lay down while he tugged up the covers around her and sat himself upright against the headboard in the stretching exercise that Mr. Wilburn had recommended. She noticed that he could do it now without wincing, even though he still held one shoulder higher than the other. Perhaps he will always be that way, she thought, without any diminution of her appreciation of him. Ah, well.

"People treat me as though they know me, even though they do not," she said, continuing her thesis even as she composed herself for sleep. "The magistrate's solicitor—you do not remember, but he interviewed me that first day after the robbery—was a customer today. From his address, you would have thought we were comrades in the law, or something." She closed her eyes and moved her hip against Sam for his warmth. "I like it, actually. I can talk so easily now with men that I am certain I can hold my share in the Northumberland grain market, should you take sick, die, and leave me a grieving but wealthy widow."

She enjoyed his laugh. "I will do nothing of the sort," he protested. He rested his hand on her hip and was silent for a long moment. "Actually, Lyddy, speaking of that—or something like—Mr. Wilburn has put it forward to me that tomorrow would be a good time to remove the stitches." The weight of his hand increased on her, and she turned to look at him, knowing what she would see.

She took his hand. "Then, I will send Mrs. Innis to the shop with a sign saying that we will open at noon. I will be here with you, Sam."

She was, of course, making no comment to him when he cried even before the surgeon began, but pressing his face against her bosom and consoling him for pain real and imagined, as she would a child. How frightening it must be to hurt just because you know you will hurt, she thought as he sobbed. Sam, you are the bravest man I know, and possibly the most honest.

He fainted before the doctor was partly through, a heavy weight on her that she lowered carefully to the bed. "Is he really in pain?" she asked Mr. Wilburn, as he snipped and gently extracted the sutures.

"No, lass, I think not. This part is not so onerous. It's his mind that is weary with it all," the surgeon replied. He sighed. "And who can blame him? I know I do not." He surveyed his handiwork, then rested his hand on Sam's back. "This, child, is glorious war. Which bears it worse, the mind or the flesh?"

Sam regained consciousness in a few minutes, embarrassed and choosing not to look at either of them, but out the window instead. "You are not married to a brave man," he said at last, when Mr. Wilburn left.

She sat next to him and put her arm around his waist. "A coward would never have soldiered through Portugal, Spain, and France, Sam. You don't like it when I am hard on myself, so do not charge yourself with crimes you didn't commit." She nudged him and handed him a folded piece of paper. "If you want to suffer, look at this bill Mr. Wilburn has just left us. I own my courage lacks right now."

"Silly nod," he murmured as he opened the paper. He looked at it for a long time, then kissed her on the head suddenly with a loud smack. "Lyddy, many of my relatives are from Scotland, considering our proximity to the border."

"And? I suppose this is leading somewhere."

"Certainly! When have I ever danced you down a primrose path? Oh, don't answer!" He looked at the paper. "You already know that we lords of Laren are eccentric."

"Without debate."

"We are also clutch-fisted and prone to pinch farthings until they gasp for breath. What do you say, when we have babies that we send for Mr. Wilburn? He is a great economy." He shook his head in amazement at the bill. "Lyddy, he has charged us so little!" He looked at her. "I would tell you to run after him and get the full reckoning, but all my Scots ancestors would probably clutch at you with skinny-boned fingers."

She took the bill from him, blessing Mr. Wilburn from the bottom of her heart. "This will mean I can afford a post chaise for you, Sam. One more day will do it."

One more day was all she had, anyway, according to the terms wrung from the barber's widow. That is it, she thought, as she finished the last haircut on the last customer and the sun was going down. I cannot say I am sorry to see the end of this, but I am grateful for the opportunity to do for Sam what he could not do for himself. She swept the shop until the floor almost gleamed in the last light of day. She did not leave until the ashes in the stove were cool and bundled outside to the ash can. Each cup was again in its place. She admired them one last time, pleased that she had met most of their owners, tactiturn, hardworking men whose time she had not wasted, and whose esteem she knew she had earned. She stood in the doorway, looking inside. "I know I will not see any of you again," she whispered. "Thank you for what you all did for me."

She waited for the constable's nightly escort, knowing enough about him now to wish him well with his pigs and cows, and to offer the hope that his mother would soon be healthy again. She knew better than to offer him a gratuity for his faithful nocturnal escort. She had already embarrassed him, and knew better than to do it again. "Will you be leaving soon, Mrs. Major Reed?" he asked as he stopped outside the tavern door.

"Soon enough," she said. "I would like another day or two here for Sam … for the major to recuperate before I put him into a jolting coach for the journey home." She held out her hand, knowing it would cause the constable agonies, but unable to stop her own gratitude of him and his services. "Thank you."

She doubted he had ever shaken a woman's hand before, but he rose magnificently to the occasion. "I accept this in honor of our whole village, Mrs. Major Reed," he said, breathless with delight as he pumped her hand up and down. "If you ever want to come back, why, we won't even make you cut our hair or shave our knobby faces!"

She was going to stop in the Innises' quarters as usual to visit and play with Maria, before seeing to Sam, but she had only opened the door when Mrs. Innis came to her in a hurry. "Is Sam …." she began, wondering if there was ever a time in her life from now on when any quick movement or excitement wouldn't compel her to sudden fear.

"Mrs. Reed, he is better than we are! Heaven knows he has had more rest in the past week or two than you, what with your work and worry on his behalf," Mrs. Innis said. She touched Lydia's arm, her eyes bright with interest. "Mrs. Reed, the son of the justice of the peace is upstairs! He said he wanted to see you in particular, so I cannot imagine why he is still plaguing Mr. Reed, but some men don't know about convalescents, do they?"

"Indeed they do not, Mrs. Innis," she declared as she started immediately for the stairs. "If he is exhausting Sam, I will be disturbing *his* peace."

She came into the room quickly, then stopped in surprise. Sam was resting, as she had expected, but the other man had propped his long legs on the bed with a familiarity that amazed her. They must have been enjoying a huge joke, because Sam was wiping tears from his eyes, even as he wheezed with laughter. She stared.

"Oh, hullo," said the man, regarding her with nothing less than real interest. He looked at Sam. "Major, you never spoke truer words. She *is* a looker. How did you manage?"

"I couldn't get her sister!" Sam said, then started off in another spasm of amusement that had him pressing his arm against his shoulder. "My dear Lydia would have it that she is not the handsome one in her family, so I am pleased that she can hear some contradiction, Percy, from an unbiased source! She *is* a looker."

Lydia frowned and looked from one man to the other. This is such a casual village, she thought as she slowly removed her bonnet and set it aside. Sam even calls him Percy, as though …. She paused, her eyes widening, as the men looked at each other with the easiness of old friends. Somewhere in the back of her brain, a bell rang, and then another. Soon her whole head felt as though it were a jangle of noise.

"Sam," she began, her voice heavy with suspicion.

The other man laughed and tipped himself back even farther in the chair. "Major, my knowledge of the ladies is even less than yours, I think, but I do know that tone of voice. I think you have landed yourself into the basket." He tipped the chair up and rose just as quickly to tower over her. "Should I wait outside until you have greased your way through what I suspect is going to be a delicate introduction?" He started to laugh. "Lord, but this is amusing. Don't you wish General Picton were here?"

"Not especially," Sam said. He patted the bed. "Do have a seat, Lydia."

She sat.

"And do put down your bag of coins. I don't want another injury just now."

She kept it firmly in her lap.

"May I have the honor of introducing the son of the justice of the peace? Lydia, this is Sir Percy Wilkins. Now, I know what you are think …."

"*Lieutenant* Percy Wilkins?" she asked, interrupting him. She glared at Sam, then turned her attention to the lieutenant, who was still on his feet. "He of Battery B?"

Percy nodded and extended his hand to her. "Yes, indeed, madam, Picton's finest."

"You live in this district," she stated, making every effort to keep her voice conversational. She shook his hand. "And Sam, of course, knows that you live here."

"Mercy, he has always known I lived near Merry Glade. Just forever! Oh, dear." He hesitated, even as Sam winced. "That seems to be the delicate matter at this moment, mum, wouldn't you say? I know I would, and heaven knows I just stumbled onto this situation. Dear me, Sam, am I talking too much?" He ran his finger around his collar as she continued to look from one man to the other.

"It would seem that way, Percy," the major said, his eyes on the bag of coins. "Do shut up."

Lieutenant Percy giggled. "Oh, sir, I think we are 'way beyond that." He turned a kindly eye on Lydia. "Wouldn't you agree, mum?"

17

⚬⚬

"CERTAINLY," SAID LYDIA. "Do sit down again, Sir Percy."
She turned slightly to regard her husband. "Husband, you are in such trouble."

"I thought perhaps I was," he agreed.

She was silent then, thinking about the events of the past three weeks, even as she knew her husband was regarding her with considerable anxiety. As she observed him, she was struck by the fact that this was an expression she had not seen too often in their short history together, and this, she was forced to admit, provided her with some secret amusement. It's nice to know that you are not always supremely confident, she thought, especially where I am concerned.

"You knew from the moment we were rescued from the road agents, didn't you?" she asked finally, as she considered the matter.

To Sam's credit, he looked at her with a frown. "I really don't remember what happened during the robbery."

Percy laughed. "Lord, if I know the major, he was probably arguing with the road agent! Sam, do you remember the time in Valladolid...."

"Not Valladolid," Sam said in a hurry. "Percy, do be silent before I am standing deep in my own ... well, do be silent."

Lydia thought herself quite charitable to not question him about Valladolid. It could probably wait. "Yes, indeed, he was arguing. As I remember now, when our rescuer said he was taking us to Merry Glade, you said, 'Oh, excellent.' Sam, Sam!"

Apparently silence and Percy were not well acquainted, she decided. The lieutenant leaped into the conversation again. "That farmer is one of my tenants, Mrs. Reed, and he rehearsed all these events with me." He gazed on his former commander with such a look of benevolence that Lydia was hard-pressed to retain her composure. "Really, Sam, you know how nice the accommodations are at my place! Mama will be quite put out when I tell her you passed up nearly a month at her home to stay in a public house," he chided.

Lydia raised her hand to stop the flow of words. "Sir Percy, in all fairness, I am not sure that Sam had another coherent thought for a week, beyond that one. He was so ill." She rested her hand on his blanketed leg and gave Sam a brilliant smile. "And some would probably argue that he hasn't had a coherent thought since! Husband, why didn't you *say* something? Just a word or two, and you could have been in more comfortable surroundings."

"You, too, mum," Percy chimed in. "I'd have been glad to loan you a packet to pay the surgeon and sent you on your way rejoicing." He glared at his major in mock distress. "Sir, you should have known that. You *must have* known that!"

She stopped. It was true, of course, but then she would never have met the Innises, and their kindness that extended to sacrifices few would make on behalf of strangers. The villagers would be strangers to her yet, and she might not ever have learned what she could do for herself, when she had no choice and everything depended on her.

He knew. At least, from the moment he regained his senses again, he knew, and he said nothing. He had let her worry and contrive, and solve her own problem, and wear herself out, and know the satisfaction of success. She increased the pressure of her fingers on his leg, even as she bowed her head and let the tears slide down her face, to Sir Percy's horror.

He leaped to his feet again, wringing his hands, as she cried quietly and Sam did nothing. "Major, I say! You're a heartless brute! Mama will be so disappointed that you have not turned out better!"

"Percy, do excuse yourself for a moment," she heard the major say in a low voice. "Get us some ale from the public room and take your time returning."

She heard the door close, but she could not stop the tears. After a few minutes, Sam handed her a handkerchief and she blew her nose.

"Come a little closer, Lydia Reed," he said, and she heard uncertainty in his voice. "If you must clutch me, clutch a part more substantial."

With another sob, she threw herself into his arms, and continued her tears until none were left. She let him wipe her eyes this time. "Blow now," he told her, and she did.

She realized where she was then, and tried to sit up. "I hope I am not hurting you," she murmured, worry and embarrassment competing with her feelings.

"I never felt better," he assured her, and did not relinquish his grip on her.

She sighed and nestled closer. "May I say that I never…." She could not continue, so deep were her feelings. She shook her head and returned to silence.

Sam kissed the top of her head and then rested his chin there. She listened to the steady beat of his heart and struggled to subdue the tears that threatened again. Even though my feet ache, I am hungry, and my head is starting to pound, I cannot imagine that I will ever feel better than this, she thought. But I must tell him.

She sat up, but did not remove herself from his arms. She

looked into his face, taking a moment to admire his brown eyes and the pleasant sprinkling of freckles across his nose. He was still too thin, but she would see to that. She took the handkerchief from him and dabbed at his eyes. "Mustn't let your ridiculous lieutenant see those," she scolded.

"He's seen them before," he told her. "And he's not so ridiculous when the French are charging. Far from it. Oh, Lydia."

She put her hand to his lips. "Sam, thank you from the bottom of my heart," she said simply.

She could hear Sir Percy moving restlessly from one foot to the other outside the door, so she got up and opened it, taking the pint in his hand and giving it to Sam.

Percy obviously had time of his own to think, and the words poured out. "Sam, I imagine you did not even tell her about the valuables in your trunk, did you?" he accused him, then drank deep. "Lord, but Innis has good ale. I had forgotten. So wise of you to hole up here, even though Mama will be chagrined."

Lydia laughed, and resumed her spot on the major's bed, although not quite so close. "You are wrong there, Sir Percy! He told me to look in the trunk, and I did find a treasure, considering the venture I was engaged in. A wonderful razor," she explained, when the other man stared at her. "You know, for shaving. Well, *I* thought it was a valuable treasure."

Percy set down his cup, tipped back in his chair again, and started to laugh. He laughed until he had to press his hand to his stomach. Lydia stared at him, and then at Sam, who was smiling. Without a word, she rose and went to her husband's campaign trunk. As Percy's laughter returned to a lower register, and then to helpless, intermittent yelps, she looked through the trunk. She sat back on her heels and stared at Sam.

"Husband, unless dirty shirts and pants full of powder burns are valuable, you will have to enlighten me. Obviously I have missed something."

"You have," he agreed, smiling at her with such fondness

that she blushed. "And once you had found the razor, and I understood what all this meant, I did not press it."

She looked back at the trunk in bewilderment. "I dare *anyone* to find a treasure in this … this midden!"

"Mum, find the chess game," Percy said.

Mystified, she dragged out the worn and dirty tablecloth with the chess pieces knotted in one end. "This, for heaven's sake?" she asked, holding it out to her husband.

"Come back here," he said.

She sat beside him again and handed him the small bundle. With practiced effort, he untied the twine that held in the pieces and tumbled them into her lap. She gasped and stared, open-mouthed, jerking up her apron to keep the pieces from spilling onto the floor.

With hands that shook, she picked up the pieces she recognized. They were of some heavy wood, and much battered from use. She set them aside, then ran her fingers through the small gold coins.

"Pawns," Sam explained, his eyes merry. "I had to have something uniform, of course, and these little pieces of eight answered. Wouldn't you agree?"

Stupefied, she nodded. She picked up a lump of gold, and looked at him, a question in her eyes.

"I found it that way after the siege of Badajoz. Don't know what it was. Just some finery that melted in the fire," he said. "It sits level, so it became a knight." He poked his fingers among the treasures. "These earbobs were bishops, and that louis d'or was a king." Gently he touched the wedding ring she wore. "A queen, of course." For some reason his voice was rusty then, and she had the good grace not to look at him.

In silence, his face unreadable, the major picked up the pieces from her lap and restored them to their place in the shabby tablecloth. He looked at her then, a long, measuring look that made her palms start to perspire. "Forgive me, Lydia?" he asked softly.

"There isn't anything to forgive," she replied, her voice just as soft, as she dismissed weeks of swollen ankles, shyness around strangers, and more worry for another human being than she had ever suffered through before.

"I should think there is!" Percy said, leaping into the conversation with indignation that made his eyes go a little wild. "Major, you will be lucky if your convenient matrimonial arrangement doesn't just … just leave you!"

Now I am a matrimonial arrangement, she thought in surprise. Well, of course I am. At what point did I forget that? Was it when I was holding him while the surgeon cut, or was it even back at St. Catherine's when I knew I wanted Maria, and had only to look at him for his approval? Or even when my hands were shaking so badly and he held my arm so steady to put this ring on my finger? I wonder when it was.

"Would you?" the major asked her.

"What?" she asked, startled out of her own discomfort.

"Would you leave?" There was the slightest frown on his face, and it pleased her just a little to know that even he had some doubts.

"Never," she said promptly, forcing down her misgivings. She took his hand and held it in her lap. She smiled at the two of them, feeling no pleasure in her thoughts, but determined that Percy should know no more. "I could murder you, perhaps, and no jury in this district would ever convict me. No. I would never leave. I am intensely curious to find out what kind of demented people have had the raising of someone so devious, husband!" She hated her glibness. It was not what she wanted to say, not the way she was feeling now.

Percy laughed and stood up, shaking his head. "Major, she is so good at that!"

"Good at what?" he asked.

"Calling you husband as a real wife would, and taking your hand as if this were a serious arrangement!" He looked at her then, his expression kindly, "Mum, I don't know who you are, but you certainly will be a success in securing the inheritance in Northumberland! Sam, without question you found a lady. What a pleasant diversion this has become! Sorry I missed the proposal at St. Barnabas—God save us—and the wedding. How on earth did either of you keep a straight face? And look at you now, holding hands. Lord, I am diverted. This was well worth the price of a special license."

His words hung in the air like a bad smell. Lydia felt her face grow hot. She released Sam's hand, but he did not lift it from her lap. He kept his hand on her thigh, applying enough pressure to keep her courage fixed. When she felt braver, she looked at her husband's lieutenant, searching for meanness, or animosity. There was none. A kindly face looked back at her, one used to amusement, his questions remaining.

"Percy, someday I will explain the whole series of events to you, and we will all have a good laugh." Sam said at last, when the silence had gone on too long for politeness.

"Promise? Sam, I want you and your lady—oh, Lord I am amused—to come to Quavers for the rest of your recovery. Mama will be pleased to see you both, and you can plan out the rest of your deception," Percy said, his eyes bright. "I only wish I could come to Northumberland and see how this all plays out …." He paused, his eyes hopeful.

"No, Percy. It is out of the question," Sam said firmly. "And as for your kind invitation …." He glanced at her. "I think not. We'll just stay here and rub along as best we can. Thank you, though. Another time."

Percy did not attempt to hide his disappointment. "Oh, I am sorry! This amusing joke would have been just the antidote to Papa's gout!" He put his hand to his head in a gesture that would have seemed theatrical if anyone else had done it, but to Lydia's eyes, was appropriate for anyone so intent on entertainment as Sir Percy. "I am reminded, Mrs. Reed—Oh, gadfrey, you are Lady Laren, are you not?—Sam, I am beyond diversion now!"

"Collect yourself, Percy," Sam said. "I am feeling quite tired and need to go to bed. *What* are you reminded of? Do come to the point."

"The reason for my visit in the first place! I come in Papa's place as interim justice of the peace, I suppose. Papa's gout did not permit, and didn't that turn out to be our good luck?" he said. With a flourish, he pulled an envelope from his coat. "Mrs. Reed, there is a reward for the capture of that miserable man you shot." He looked apologetic. "This is not really a flush district, so it is a small stipend. Now, if you had shot the other one, that would have earned you more. He is a *really* ugly customer." He giggled. "Perhaps we should issue pistols to all the fair women who ride the coach. Just a small reward."

"How small?" she asked, swallowing her uneasiness at his relentless good cheer, and wanting to stop his endless flow of words.

"Only twenty pounds, but…."

"That is a fortune!" she exclaimed, amazed all over again at this sudden turn of fortune. She looked at the bag of coins, paltry now, that she had earned in ten hours of work today. "I can pay for a post chaise now, and at least another week's stay here."

Sam's lieutenant nodded as he handed her the envelope. "My offer of a stay at Quavers still stands, and I know Papa would be happy to give you the loan of his coach and horses to Northumberland." He looked from Sam to her, and back to Sam again, his eyes cheerful, even in the defeat of his plans. "I think you are being foolish, Sam. Why, at Quavers, you wouldn't even have to share a bed! It must be an awkward situation, considering this whole arrangement." He started to laugh again as he held out his hand to Sam, and then went to the door. "Do at least give me your permission to tell my father about this whole escapade."

"If you say one word about it, when I feel better I will carve you into chewable pieces and have you for breakfast, Percy," Sam replied, his voice just as pleasant.

Percy held up his hand. "Major, I am undone! What good is a practical joke if it cannot be shared?" He looked hopefully at his superior officer. "No?"

"No. Go away."

With another laugh and a bow in Lydia's general direction, Sir Percy left the room. Lydia was about to speak when the door opened again.

"Do at least write me from Northumberland and tell me how this whole adventure ends!"

"Go away, Percy," Sam repeated.

There was noticeable iron in his voice this time that Lydia could hear, and the door did not reopen. She sat another moment on the bed, then got up and put the coin pouch on the dresser with her other earnings.

"I'm rather sorry that happened," Sam said at last.

Lydia had been so occupied with her thoughts that she almost jumped when he spoke. "It probably doesn't matter," she replied, keeping her voice calm. "Sam, if you would be more comfortable there at his estate…."

"No. Lydia, sit down again and quit fiddling with those coins. Could you take out one of these pillows and help me lie back?" He smiled. "I like Percy well enough. He is a better officer than you would think, but I can safely conclude that conversation with him can be exhausting when one is in a weakened state." Her solicitude returned. Drat that man for wearing Sam down to a nub, she thought, as she removed her pillow from behind the major's head and placed it next to his. Gently she helped Sam stretch out again, smoothing the blanket and too shy to speak.

"I didn't want him to know about Maria," Sam said, then letting out his breath, he turned himself more comfortably onto his side. "I do not think I could recuperate in peace if Percy is continually reminding me how strange this whole arrangement is."

It is, isn't it? she thought as she prepared for bed. She took her time. Sam had closed his eyes almost immediately, and she knew, with a pang, how tired his lieutenant had made him. Dressed in Mrs. Innis's extra nightgown, she stood beside Sam a long time. Mr. Wilburn had paid her a visit in the barbershop that morning to suggest to her that quite possibly Sam would never have full use of his left arm again, not with such gouging as he had been forced to do in his shoulder and back. He says I am to tell you that you will probably look a trifle lopsided, Sam, she thought, raising the blanket higher. You will be a long time recovering. I wonder that you will be able to manage your estate without some frustration, the kind that could turn you bitter.

She lay down beside him, weary in her heart and mind, and settled as close to him as she could. She had discovered how much she liked the scent of wintergreen. His back was no longer bandaged, but the fragrance remained in his nightshirt. She breathed deep, thinking about Northumberland, and wondering if she could drive him about in a gig, and learn something about the Corn Exchange herself, if he needed her help. He has only to ask, she thought as she closed her eyes. Will he?

SHE CONTINUED HER QUIET work of coaxing her husband to good health, making sure he ate, even when he said he was not hungry, and slept when he said he was not tired. She didn't have to tell him what the surgeon had recommended to her. One evening after bathing Maria and then herself in the security of the Innis's laundry room, they had returned to find him standing and frowning in front of the mirror. Her heart nearly broke when he frowned into the mirror and said to her reflection, "I am not really symmetrical anymore, am I?"

"No, you are not," she said. She set Maria on the floor, not sure whether to jolly him, or cry with him, or just put her arms around him. With no more thought, she chose the latter, wrapping her arms carefully around him as she rested her head against his poor back.

"Do you mind?" he asked, after a long pause, then chuckled, even though she knew without seeing his face that he was not laughing. "You're the one who has to look at me. You, and Maria, and my mother and aunt, my crofters, my neighbors, everyone in my district, and shire, and my God, if I ever go to Parliament to Lords …."

"Stop it. It isn't that bad, and I'm sure your tailor can add a little extra shoulder padding on that side," she said, and pushed him away from the mirror. She sat him down in the window seat, and not caring if everyone on Market Street was staring up at them, hiked up her skirts and sat on his lap. Before he could say anything, she kissed him.

If she had ever wondered where her skills lay, she wondered no more. Kissing Sam Reed on the mouth was more pleasant than any nursing techniques that Mr. Wilburn had recommended to her so far. Years of staring into her own mirror, plus Mama's barbed reminders, had acquainted her with the fact that her mouth was a shade too large for beauty. As Sam returned her clumsy efforts with enough polish and enthusiasm for them both, she knew it wasn't a defect—far from it. She hadn't suspected that a kiss could be so *involving*.

Breathing was not a problem, at least until her husband put his hand on her bare leg and moved it up under her skirt. She could have sighed then with impatience that she had adopted French drawers. It's not as though I need them in high summer, she thought as his hand stopped. Drat fashion.

Still kissing her, his hand went to the waistband of her drawers at the same time she felt another hand pat her ankle. Startled, she pulled away from Sam with a homely smack that made him smile, then stared down at Maria, who was standing beside them and patting her leg.

"Oh, you dear!" she said.

"In all modesty, thank you," Sam replied, and the laughter was genuine in his voice now.

She kissed him again, then moved from his lap when his

hand came out from under her skirt. "Maria, not you," she said. "I'll have other things to call you."

"Oh, I hope so," he replied as she picked up Maria, cuddling the baby to her. "Come here, Maria," he said, and took the baby onto his lap. "Tell me what you think of your deformed papa. Oh, my." He did cry then, as Maria nestled against his chest with a sigh of her own. Lydia said nothing until he finished, beyond finding him a handkerchief when her legs felt firm enough to hold her, and telling him to blow his nose.

"What if I cannot ride a horse?" he asked as he set Maria down finally and motioned her closer.

"You will," she assured him, serene in her own confidence.

"Until that happens, I do not know why I cannot drive you here and there in a gig." She dabbed at his face with the handkerchief. "And I have always wanted to know all about sheepshearing and horseshoeing, and lambing and …."

"Liar," he murmured, playing with Maria's curls as she bobbed up and down beside him, grinning and displaying her teeth.

"I am wounded," she replied.

"No, *I* am," he said with amusement. "Or was. Will I do, Lydia? Pardon me if I seem anxious. Possibly it matters."

She touched Maria. "She seems to think you will do, and I suspect the same."

He grinned at her, and as much as she felt embarrassed by the look in his eyes, she also felt relief and peace. I have become so confident, she thought, even though I am no closer to being a real wife.

"Can you wait to find out?"

It was a quiet question, with no one but Maria and her to hear it. I think that talking about their own prowess must embarrass men, she thought as she nodded, then blushed. Of course, it is not every day that I leap into a man's lap and acquaint myself so thoroughly with his mouth.

"I ... I think I am not precisely the same Lydia who agreed to marry you on such short notice in London," she said. Or am I? she asked herself. I wonder when I will know for sure?

18

MARIA WALKED THE NEXT morning, her hands up and her stomach pooched out for balance, her eyes fierce with concentration. Lydia brought her upstairs so Sam could watch, as the little one walked and fell, pulled herself up, and walked again until she was wringing with perspiration.

In another day, she could even turn herself around and go in another direction. To Lydia's enjoyment, Maria would not allow anyone but Sam to hold her hand and walk with her.

"Such a determined little poppet," Mrs. Innis remarked that evening as they sat outside the inn in the cool evening and watched Sam and Maria walk slowly toward them. "She certainly takes after you, Mrs. Reed."

"Thank you," she said. You would not have known me five weeks ago, Lydia thought as she stood up at their slow approach. I could hardly say boo to a goose then.

"She looks like the major, though," Mrs. Innis said, rising, too. "Wouldn't you say so, Major Reed?"

He stopped, and Maria looked up at him, impatience stamped on her face. "I rather think she resembles my wife, Mrs. Innis," he said as he crooked his arm for Lydia to take hold of him. "I never saw two prettier ladies."

Mrs. Innis stood a moment, observing them both. "I would say she is a nice blend of the two of you, and isn't that the pleasant thing about one's children?" She laughed and followed them into the pubic house. "I am only grateful that my children did not inherit their father's ears!"

"Don't you own to just a twinge or two when Mrs. Innis declares that Maria looks like us?" she asked that night in their room as she stopped Maria long enough to whisk her dress over her head.

"You're becoming quite an expert at scooping people from their clothing," he commented as he leaned back against the headboard and watched them from the comfort of his bed. "Hush, now, Maria. Your mama is most efficient with us! I never argue when she helps me from my trousers."

She blushed and would not look at him. "You can probably take care of yourself now," she murmured as she stopped Maria from another circuit around the room, to the baby's intense displeasure. Pinning Maria under protest between her knees, she held her long enough to pull on a sleeping shirt. She put her on the bed for a fresh nappy and soakers, then turned her loose to crawl across the mattress. She laughed as Maria flopped herself against Sam's leg. In a moment she was tugging at her eyelids, and then she was asleep, exhausted from the business of the day.

Sam watched her, his hand on Maria's back. "No, I do not feel any qualms when Mrs. Innis sees Maria's resemblance to us. Not even a twinge. She'll have a much better life with us than she ever would at St. Catherine's. Of course," he pointed out, "I do not have your finely honed conscience, do I?"

She bent over them both to pick up Maria. "I believe you do, Sam." Holding her burden close, she sat down when he moved slightly. "I do not recall any other officers investing themselves so thoroughly for their men in the hospital." She could not help the slight shudder that passed through her and caused

Maria to stir. "I think your solicitude at the expense of your own health almost killed you. Do not quiz me about being the only one of us who cares, Sam. Maybe I learned from you."

He was silent then. Deftly she transferred Maria to the pallet on the floor that Suzie and Mrs. Innis had devised, when Maria had decided that she would not sleep unless the major was close by. I can appreciate that, she told herself. Already I seem to require his warmth and that pleasant odor of wintergreen to see me to sleep.

With a sigh, she sat in the window seat and combed her hair. The street below was quite empty of traffic, even though it was not yet dark. She could hear the low murmur of voices in the public room below, with the occasional punctuation of laughter. It was August now, and still the welcome warmth of the sun lingered. She would remind Sam to sit outside again tomorrow in the side yard where Mrs. Innis hung her laundry and let the sun work its own healing on his bare back. He will be as well as I can make him, she thought, satisfied with herself.

She stood up to remove her dress, then stopped in modest confusion. Sam was not asleep; far from it. He was observing her with a half smile and a degree of watchfulness that made her pause with her hand on her top button.

"I thought you were asleep," she said, realizing the moment she spoke that it sounded so stupid. Obviously he was wide awake. Swallowing her own shyness, she sat on the bed beside him, and took a good look. For the first time in their acquaintance, there was nothing in his eyes but admiration. While caring for the wounded at St. Barnabas, she had been struck by the preoccupation in their eyes, no matter how hard she worked to distract them. She doubted whether the wounded were aware of it themselves, that inward turning of expression as though they looked upon pain from the inside out. She did not see that look in the major's eyes now. This was not to say the look would not be there again, but for right now, this evening, his eyes were free of it, and she knew he did not hurt.

He hadn't answered her inane question. It didn't appear to have even registered in his brain. He lay there watching her, and when she continued to unbutton her dress, his smile widened. "Mr. Reed, you realize that if anything we do tonight causes you a medical problem, Mr. Wilburn will give you such a scold," she said, hoping that she sounded more serene than she felt.

"I'm all aquiver about Mr. Wilburn," he said.

She removed her dress, and placed it over the chair, making sure that Maria slept. While Sam watched, she slipped out of her petticoat and stood there in her chemise and bare feet, with toes suddenly cold and a brain full of indecision.

Her husband sat up and held out his hand to her. She needed no other encouragement. In another moment she was in his arms. "I'll take my chances with the surgeon's wrath," he whispered, and then he kissed her.

She wanted to put her arms around him, but she was afraid to touch his back. In a moment he pulled her arms around him, settling them just above his waist, and she knew her boundary. He was too thin; she could feel his ribs under his nightshirt. "You need to eat more," she fretted, even as she pulled her chemise over her head and tossed it somewhere.

"Not now, please," he said as he unbuttoned his nightshirt. "I can pull this arm out if you will take it over my head and off my other arm. I can eat later."

She laughed softly and did as he asked, hampered because he explored her breasts with his free hand and then his mouth, which seemed somehow to affect her breathing in a marvelous way. This is odd indeed, she thought. When both of his hands were free of the nightshirt, she discovered that his breath was just as ragged. She also discovered that she was so busy trying to make sure that she did not hurt him that she forgot to be afraid or nervous for herself.

Whether he was careful of himself, or mindful of her, what she felt was the greatest relief she had ever known. As inexpert as she was, Lydia knew he was trying hard not to be a dead-weight, even as his shoulder still tyrannized him. She pulled him close, and he understood, allowing himself to relax on her. Whatever pain she felt in this first encounter was promptly swallowed up by the enormity of her love for her husband. She knew she could bear him gladly; his pleasure became hers in a rush she had not expected. Lord, I will summon the night watchman, she thought in some embarrassment, then it didn't seem to matter much.

Sam rose up on one elbow so she could take a good breath. "I really don't aim to smother you," he whispered. "My goodness, that would be a dreary end to my future as a constant husband."

"I'll die smiling," she replied, and pulled him close again, wrapping her legs over his in a way that quite soon caused her to worry about alerting the night watchman again, and then dismiss him forever.

"I had no idea," she said finally when he left her but settled close by, his leg draped over her body. "Mama did talk about this sort of thing once to Kitty and me, but she called it a duty."

His hand was warm and heavy on her stomach, then he rested his head on her breast, to her total enjoyment. "I think I can safely say that your mother, in this matter as in others, has all the accuracy of a Congreve rocket," he murmured, his voice quite muffled. "Of course, one should not speak ill of the in-laws. If what we just enjoyed was your interpretation of duty, then I can hardly wait until I am well enough to survive your wild abandon."

She laughed, her hands gentle in his hair. She kissed him, familiar with his mouth now, and the homey little sounds he made when he returned her kiss. "I do astonish myself," she said softly, "but, then, I have been astonishing myself for weeks now. Sam, I love you. Sam?"

He was asleep, his mouth still parted, as though for another kiss. She kissed him, then got up to tidy herself and find her chemise. She stood for a moment in front of the mirror. I look the same, she thought, but I am so different. In this, and in other ways, I have changed. She looked back at her husband, stretched out on his back, his hands open in that perfectly relaxed way she had not seen before tonight. How comfortable I have made you, she thought in awe over so much power. She smiled to herself as she pulled on her chemise. And how comfortable you have made me. I think I could purr, if I tried.

They made love again before the sun rose, and she was pleased that her first attempt had not been just a happy chance. Could it be that this will get even better, she asked herself when they both lay spent and sweating, even in the cool of morning. "This could become a habit," Sam said as he drifted back to sleep again.

She washed and dressed and intercepted Maria before she could march over to the bed and demand that Sam pick her up and coddle her. "Let him sleep, dear," she whispered as she dressed Maria and took her downstairs to breakfast. She hesitated at the Innis's door, wondering if they would notice a difference in her. Beyond a cheery hello from Suzie, and a nod from Mr. Innis as he looked up from the columns he was adding, it was just another morning.

She was wiping the last spoonful of porridge from around Maria's mouth when Sam came downstairs to join them. He sat next to her, resting his hand on her shoulder. While he chatted with Mrs. Innis, he ran his thumb just under her ear in a way that was making her restless, even as Maria demanded to be lifted onto his lap. Dear me, husband, you might as well announce that we were not heavily engaged in sleeping last night, she thought, enjoying his hand, but mindful of Mrs. Innis's smile.

"I think we will leave tomorrow morning, Mrs. Innis," Sam said as she passed him a bowl of porridge.

"You're feeling fit enough?" Mrs. Innis asked, a smile in her eyes that made Lydia blush and wonder if any carpenter could be found who made bed frames that did not creak.

She marveled that Sam could be so straight-faced about the whole thing. "I am fit, indeed. It is high time I took Lydia home to meet my mother," he said. "We have been these three years in Spain, and she has never met Lydia. Or Maria, of course."

"Then, she is in for such a treat," Mrs. Innis said as she returned to her duties at the dry sink.

"I almost forgot about our Banbury tale," Lydia whispered to her husband, leaning close just to enjoy the fragrance of his skin.

"I haven't forgotten," he replied. "That is the whole reason for all of this, remember?"

He had not removed his hand from her neck, but suddenly the warmth was gone. *I suppose you are right*, she thought. She shifted in her chair, and he removed his hand. *For whatever reason, we each made an impulsive marriage*, she told herself, feeling like an idiot. *Perhaps beyond the enthusiasm of lovemaking, I am to be reminded of this regularly.* She got up to help Mrs. Innis with the dishes, wanting to put distance between herself and the man she had loved so fiercely last night. When she turned around after the last dish was dried, he and Maria had left the room.

The inn was too small for her feelings, and she was relieved to discover that she had left Sam's razor in the barbershop. She mumbled something to Mrs. Innis and left, hurrying to the barbershop. She stopped in the church on the way back, for no other reason than to sit in the dark and the cool, breathing the fragrance of incense and letting her mind go blank. She wanted to pray, but decided it would be best not to trouble the Lord about her marriage, which had originated in motives less than lofty.

She did kneel and rest her forehead against the pew. *I wonder how many parishioners have knelt here and pleaded for this or that through the years?* she asked no one in particular. *I am certain we have all thought that our petition was the most important. I know that mine is not. I have made my bed, and* now I am lying in it. She rested her cheek against the wood and closed her eyes. I love him. Quite possibly this is the biggest folly of all, if I am just an arrangement.

THEY LEFT IN THE morning after the confusion of tears and kisses, and good advice from the Innises. To her embarrassment, Mr. Wilburn insisted on one last look at his patient's back. She hurried downstairs during the surgeon's perusal and hid herself in the kitchen, not wanting to think about the nail tracks on Sam's back, and any raised eyebrows from Mr. Wilburn. They were fresh, too, put there early this morning when she realized she would always be helpless to resist her husband, even if she was only a convenient arrangement. I have made my bed, she thought, even as he was lying on her, satiated and peaceful. I want this man, and I will give him all I have. Perhaps someday he will love me, too. Stranger things have happened.

She could not avoid Mr. Wilburn. Her face red, she paid him the last of her barbering money to settle accounts. She wanted to tell him how grateful she was, but she could not look him in the eyes. She started to leave the room, but he took her hand and held it in a firm grip. "My dear Lydia Reed," he began, his voice soft, "I am so glad to leave your husband in such capable hands."

"I'm so embarrassed," she whispered, her humiliation complete.

To her surprise, he hugged her, then held her away from him, but close enough that she could not avoid his eyes. "Lydia, I fought in the Americas, and I can tell you that there is only one remedy for war." He smiled, then pulled her close for a last embrace. "It is love. How lucky you two are! Now, write me from Northumberland, and let me know how you, Lydia Reed, get on."

She was so close to tears that it took a moment before she could speak. "Don't you mean, how Sam gets on?"

He shrugged. "Sam will always get on, as long as you are

there. I want to know how *you* are. My dear, if you bloom, so will he. That is why my whole dependence is on you."

"I do not know that I have that much power," she said. She wanted to say more, to tell him that she was only a convenience, a woman of no influence, but he had released her, and was hunting for his handkerchief.

"You have only to believe in yourself, Lydia," he said, after a productive moment with his handkerchief. "No one can do that for you."

"But …."

"Good day, Mrs. Reed, and *bon chance,*" he said. With a deep bow that turned his face red, the surgeon nodded to Mrs. Innis and left the tavern.

After more tears, and a stiff-armed salute from her protector the constable, they left Merry Glade in a post chaise paid for with part of the reward money. To her relief, Maria was content to sit on the major's lap and watch the countryside change as they traveled the Great North Road. Lydia could think of nothing to say out loud, even though her mind was busy with half a hundred apologies, and doubts, and dredgings from old wounds of her own, less healed, she was discovering, than the visible ones on the major's back. She stared out the other window, wondering how she had ever thought that anyone as wonderful as Major Sam Reed could ever love her. She called herself a fool in all the ways her mother and Kitty had called her, unable to wrench her mind beyond her own unableness.

Maria occupied her sufficiently when she began to fuss, and then fell asleep in Lydia's arms. Lydia closed her eyes in the quiet as the coach swayed. She opened her eyes when Sam began to tell her about life in the regiment in the Peninsula.

"This is information you will need to know, if we are to pull off this deception," he reminded her. He took Maria from her arms and placed the child on a nest of blankets Mrs. Innis had arranged on the chaise floor. He laughed softly. "And I promise most faithfully to call you Della, and not Delightful." He shook his head with the memory. "We were so drunk that night, and there was Percy, weaving this whole imaginary genealogy while the battery listened and offered suggestions! Lydia—I mean Della—you have an adventurous past!"

She listened, hearing little of what he said, in a perfect agony of love. If his mother should ask, I can be utterly convincing of my love for her son, she thought as she watched the animation on her husband's face. But I am an invention only. She stirred restlessly, and focused her attention out the window even as he continued to speak. He stopped finally, when it was obvious that she was not attending. I do not understand any of this, she thought in misery. Less than a week ago, he was cheering me on to find out what I, Lydia Reed, could do. And now I am an invention, a convenience, and an arrangement. If I did not love him so much, I would hate him.

He was quieter the next day, and the silence was great between them. She thought of what Mr. Wilburn had said, how Sam would take his lead from her, but she knew it could not be so. He must be quiet because he was contemplating a long life with Lydia Reed, someone he hardly knew. That must be it, she decided, and the thought only drew her deeper into silence. Luckily there was Maria to distract them both.

Her confusion only deepened with each night, when he turned to her and she refused him nothing. It was beyond her power to deny him anything, or to feel less pleasure herself, even if she knew he meant nothing by it beyond the comfort a body could give and receive. She gave her whole self; she would have turned herself inside out if he had asked.

HE WAS IN PAIN the next morning, and she was grateful all over again that her earnings had enabled them to travel by post chaise. "We will just stay here this morning until you feel well enough to travel," she told him as she applied a hot towel to his back. "Could it be the weather, I wonder?" she asked, after a glance out the window to the rain sliding down the glass in a steady sheet.

The major lay on his stomach, his chin propped on his hands. "That's a dismal reflection, considering how stormy the weather can be at home," he said, then rested his cheek on his hand to look at her. He watched her in silence for such a long time that her face grew as warm as the towel she pressed to his back. "I think I would feel better if I thought you were more enthusiastic about this final stage of the journey, Lydia."

She could think of nothing to say beyond the truth, but even then, it was only the smallest part of what she wanted to say. "I don't know that I can deceive so many people."

"Of course you can. You fooled a whole village, and with very little help from me." He laughed, then sucked in his breath when she pressed harder on his back. "My God, Lydia, must you?" he gasped.

"Mr. Wilburn said heat and pressure," she reminded him, even though it smote her soul to cause him pain.

He was silent then. He narrowed his eyes, and she knew how he hurt. I know every clue, she thought, from the way you narrow your eyes to the way you make a fist. I wish you were so perceptive about me. You have been, she amended, remembering the chess pieces residing still in the trunk. Now we are close to your home, and your interest is elsewhere.

The moment passed and with a sigh, he relaxed again. She let up on the pressure. He took several deep breaths, then glanced at Maria, who slept on a pallet on the floor. "Sit a minute, Lydia, and I'll tell you about my mother and aunt; things you should know about the neighborhood, too."

She draped Sam's back with another towel from the basket of towels the concerned innkeeper had warmed for her, and sat close to him. "Can't we just tell the truth?"

He shook his head wearily. "Lydia! I told you my aunt will cut off all the money, and probably demand back what she has put into the estate, if she finds out I have been telling such a tale for two years! Making fools of them, I suppose. I wonder why we didn't think of that at the time. I wish you could …."

He stopped, his lips in a tight, thin line.

You wish I could get it through my thick head? she asked herself, finishing the sentence for him. Just play along as we agreed? Remember your share of the bargain. "I'm sorry," she murmured.

"I wish you could trust me," he finished. "That's all."

She touched his back, wanting to kiss his head, and then his ears, and other places she had overlooked last night when they had wanted each other so much that it was hard to wait for Maria to get to sleep. Instead, she rested her cheek against his for the briefest moment. "Sam, I hardly trust myself," she whispered, amazed at her own daring.

To her relief, he smiled at her. "I know," he said, his voice just as soft. "You'll change."

Will I? she wondered as they started out in early afternoon. Will I even recognize myself, especially if I am someone named Della with a baby and a husband, and years of experience in the Peninsula, and whatever fiction Percy created through the years and mailed monthly to two unsuspecting ladies? Lord, this is a strange brew. All Sam wants now is someone different than who I am. Who is to say that either of us will recognize me when I get there?

The rain stopped as the afternoon yielded to nightfall. Sam had been quiet all afternoon, with that inward look of pain that she dreaded, and the silence of someone hoarding his own thoughts, even as she did. They stopped at a crossroads; the coachman leaned down to ask directions, then started the horses in motion again.

Sam took her hand then, but he was squinting out the window at the gathering darkness, looking ahead even as he pressed hard against the floorboards with his feet.

"We'll be there soon enough, Sam," she said. "You can't make the coach go faster."

He looked down at his feet and smiled. "Lydia, I have been waiting for this moment for years. Maybe it won't be much of an estate to you—I don't know what you came from in Devon—but it is my special place. I can't explain it."

She nodded, even though she did not understand; there was nothing in Devon that she missed, except one or two of the servants who were kind.

"Ah ...."

She pulled her attention back to her husband, who was squeezing her hand now. Maria squirmed in his lap, and he set her to one side, his whole energy concentrating on the view outside the travel-muddied window. The exhaustion in his eyes seemed to lift like a window shade as he gazed on what she knew must be his own land, in its own way more bone of his bone than she could ever hope to be, even if he loved her.

She saw a deep valley, like so many they had bowled through in this rugged part of England, a valley cut and measured millennia ago by glaciers and harsh climate. The trees of summer were leafy, but the trunks and branches were bent and braced against the wind. A small river tumbled through the valley, the rush of water so precipitate that she could hear the sound through the glass. Sheep grazed on a distant hillside, and there were cattle in another field. The grain in another quarter was a particular green that she did not know from Devon; perhaps it was oats.

The house came into view as the post chaise rounded a bend, and Sam Reed sighed again. She looked with interest at the building, noting the weathered stone and the cheerful white trim around the windows. It was no more than two stories tall—the dower house was larger on her father's estate—but looked firmly rooted, enduring, and able to withstand centuries of weather and border politics. She glanced at her husband. Rather like you, my dear, she thought.

As they neared the house, his grip slackened, as though he forgot she was there. They were only at the head of the lane when the front door opened and people hurried down the broad steps, the servants to line the walkway, and the others to come quickly up the lane. She saw two older ladies, but younger people, too. Lydia looked at her husband, a question in her eyes. "Are they all your relatives?"

"What day is it?" he demanded, not taking his eyes off the house or its inmates as the coachman began to slow the horses. "Why, it is Wednesday," she said. "Who …."

"Of course it is Wednesday," he echoed. "And how many years have the Averys been coming for dinner and cards? Quite possibly some things never change. Oh, Lydia, I am home."

She wanted to help him from the carriage, but there was no need. As soon as his foot touched the ground, he was surrounded. "Oh, do not jostle him," she whispered as she held Maria. Shyness overwhelmed her, but she pushed aside her own qualms in the face of the larger danger to her husband. She gathered Maria close and hurried from the carriage to try to protect his vulnerable back. "Oh, please, he was wounded," she said finally, raising her voice for the first time since that dreadful banquet. "Do stand back a bit."

The crowd around him parted. "My ablest champion," her husband said as his relatives backed away slightly. "May I introduce Lyd—my little Della? And of course Celia. Della, this is my mother, Lady Laren, and my Aunt Chalmers."

She would have recognized Lady Laren anywhere, with the same brown eyes as her son and the freckles so charming on a lady of gathering years. "Oh, my dear," she said as she smiled at Lydia. "You are so welcome. And this is my granddaughter?" She looked at Maria, appraising her, and then at Lydia. "Sam, you've certainly outdone yourself this time. Without question."

That is an odd thing to say, she thought, but then she was gathered into the woman's embrace. And then there was Aunt Chalmers, she of the fortune in question, who wanted a share of her. Funny, but she does not look like a woman with a foot in the grave, even if Sam did assure me, she thought. And here is ….

Still in the grip of her mother-in-law, Lydia stared over the woman's shoulder. There was Sam, his arm around a young lady even more beautiful than Kitty, ten times more beautiful than Kitty. Lydia didn't mean to stare with her mouth open. It was rude of her beyond belief, but from the placid look of the young woman in Sam's grip, obviously an expression she was used to.

"Della, you'll catch flies!" her husband was saying. "Look who I have here? Anna Avery! Anna, when did you turn into such a beauty?"

Lydia groaned inside. Anna turned impossible crystal blue eyes on the major. "Silly! It was during all those years I waited for you!"

19

~⁘~

THERE WAS NO DIFFICULTY in pleading a headache, and an early retreat upstairs. Her head did pound in earnest. Thank goodness Maria was tired, and she could sit in the quiet of the nursery holding her little one until she slept, knowing that nothing short of the guillotine would stop the throbbing in her temples.

Sam had brushed through Anna Avery's comment with that adroitness of his that Lydia had previously marveled over, and which now made her want to thrash him. He had skillfully detached himself from the lovely woman and bowed to her. "My dear, you are too late! This is my wife Della and our daughter Celia. I hope that you two will become the best of friends."

Over my corpse, Lydia thought as she put Maria into the crib someone had thoughtfully prepared. With no idea where to go in the house to find her own bed, she lay down on the cot in the nursery, weary beyond words. She knew no one downstairs would miss her. Even the servant who had showed her to the nursery had been in a pelter to run back downstairs and listen around a door or alcove to Lord Laren's exploits in the struggle against Napoleon. Every now and then she heard laughter. I only hope Sam does not burn himself down to a stub tonight, drat his miserable carcass, she thought as she closed her eyes. I have worked hard to get him to a state of health where he can return to his family and friends and ignore me completely. She was irrational, and she knew it, but that much common sense did nothing to assuage the pain in her heart.

She was about to sleep when there was a tap at the door. She lay where she was a moment, confused, then she got up quickly, with a glance at the crib to make sure the child slept.

Aunt Chalmers stood in the doorway, her eyes bright with interest. Lydia marveled again at Sam's inaccuracy. There was nothing remotely fragile about this woman. She will live forever, Lydia thought as she smiled at her new relative. I do not see our charade ending anytime soon.

"My dear, I have the deepest suspicion that you have a raging headache—a gathering of Reeds and Averys will do that—and nowhere to lay your head!" the woman said, taking Lydia's hand. "Oh, such a lovely ring!" she exclaimed, keeping her voice low. "Is this the one you wrote about that the King of Spain himself gave to dear Sam in partial thanks for his role in the storming of Madrid?"

Lydia gulped. Storming of Madrid? King of Spain? she thought wildly. I will kill Percy when I see him next, and it will be a slow, agonizing death. "Yes, it is," she managed, turning it over to catch the light from the hall.

Aunt Chalmers sighed with pleasure. "Oh, we would love to have seen the Duke of Wellington himself give you away to our Samuel."

So would I, she thought grimly. She wanted to take the woman by both her hands and describe her own wedding at St. Barnabas, how her hands shook and her knees smote together …. "How much I loved Sam then," she said softly. Oh, Lord, I am a far bigger fool that Kitty.

"We trust you still do," the older woman teased as she drew

her arm around Lydia's waist and walked with her into the hall. "I have already advised Meigs to mix up a potion for you. Let me show you to Sam's room while we wait for her."

She opened the door and motioned Lydia in. "I know you will work wonders in here, my dear niece—Oh, how I adore the sound of that! Naturally this is not so grand as your own estate and extensive lands in … in … where was it?"

She paused, looking at Lydia so expectantly that her mouth went dry and her headaches went from a throb to a clang. "Devon?" Lydia asked.

Aunt Chalmers frowned. "Dear me, somehow I remember something about the Lake Country …. I must be mistaken." She laughed and kissed Lydia's cheek. "You would certainly know where you lived, wouldn't you?" She sighed, and hugged Lydia closer. "And how totally gallant of your mama to give up a quiet life in …."

"Devon?" Lydia said, trying to mask her own desperation.

"Ah, yes … in Devon to follow the drum through Portugal and Spain." She went to the window and pulled open the draperies. "We cannot promise anything but a peaceful life here in Northumberland, my dear. Nothing exciting ever happens." She motioned Lydia to join her.

Sick in her heart from such a compound of lies, Lydia went to the window. The sun was setting now, casting a honey glow over the fields. A distant figure led a line of cows toward a milking barn. Aunt Chalmers opened the window, and Lydia breathed deep of the clover-scented air.

Aunt Chalmers touched her sleeve. "My nephew has always enjoyed the best view. Even when he was young, I could find him here in the early mornings before his mama was up, looking out the window." She sighed and sat herself in the window seat, patting the space beside her. "He has such plans for this little estate—Lord knows his father tried to run it into the ground—and I have been working to help Sam achieve redemption. Ah, here is Meigs. Thank you, my dear. Drink this,

Della. I guarantee a sound sleep." She nodded to the servant, and the door closed quietly in a moment. "You have a whole lifetime here to sort out our stories. We have certainly been delighted with yours! Welcome to Laren Hall, my dear. I know you will be happy here."

When Aunt Chalmers left, Lydia looked around the room. It was without question a man's room. She sat on the bed, wondering why her new aunt had not showed her to a lady's room. Surely there was another bedroom, not that any woman married to Sam Reed would ever want to use it, she thought, and blushed a little. "It is almost as though they did not expect me," she murmured as she tried to take off her shoes without bending down and increasing the drumbeat in her head. "Strange, indeed."

She was standing in her petticoat when there was another knock at the door. "It is your mother," said the voice on the opposite of the door, and Lydia gave a start, then relaxed. "Do come in, Lady Laren," she said, "and excuse me, please."

Her mother-in-law came in, carrying Lydia's bandbox. "Perhaps you would like this," she said. Her eyes opened wider as she approached. "Tomorrow when you feel more able, you must tell us how you lost all your clothing and possessions in a fire in Toulouse, set by Napoleon himself as he retreated! And how you saved dear little Celia from the flames." Lady Laren sat herself on her son's bed, shaking her head. "Your last letter was read and reread until we could not see the writing for the creases! My dear, you will simply have to let me help you put down on paper your reminiscences of the Peninsula." She leaned forward to take Lydia's hand. "I know this is grossly ill-mannered, but wouldn't your young life make a splendid novel?"

"I would certainly love to read it myself," Lydia said honestly. She ached to crawl into bed and draw herself into a ball and disappear. Murder is much too good for you, Sir Percy, she thought. I think I would have you naked and lustful in a roomful of clergy and their wives, to get some inkling of the vast discomfort I feel right now.

Lady Laren patted her arm. "You have such a frown on your pretty face, my dear daughter. I am sure that you want nothing more than to sleep. I imagine this has been a trying day for you, but not as exciting as that time you and Sam escaped from certain death at the hands of Marshal Soult."

Lydia's eye widened, then closed. "That was exciting," she agreed as she thought up yet another torture for Percy. She did not protest when her mother-in-law helped her from her petticoat and found Mrs. Innis's nightgown in the bandbox. In another minute she was tucked in bed, with Lady Laren seated beside her, her face kind with welcome.

"You can have plenty of time to tell us that whole story tomorrow," Lady Laren said as she kissed her good night. "You only alluded to it briefly in your letter, and we have waited this whole year to know more! You are so welcome, child. Good night now."

Whatever Meigs had put in that potion was doing the job. Lydia could barely raise her head from the pillow. "Lady Laren," she began.

"I insist on being called Mama, my dear," her mother-in-law said. "You cannot imagine how many years I have waited for a daughter."

"Mama," Lydia began again, "do send Sam up here soon. He is not strong yet." She shook her head. "I do not mean to sound so managing, and protective, but …."

"I will send him right up, my dear daughter," the woman promised. "And do not apologize for your concern! I think, more than ever now, that Sam needs a woman firmly in control." She bent to kiss Lydia again, then left the room.

Lydia closed her eyes. *I have no business sleeping*, she thought, even as her brain began to shut down. *I must concoct a fiction about estates in the Lake Country, or was it Devon; how the Duke of Wellington came to give me away at my* wedding; how I lost everything in a blazing fire and managed to save my daughter; and how on earth Sam and I came to be in Marshal Soult's control. Dear me. That is probably only the smallest part. These good women seem to have memorized Della's letters.

I have to think of something, she told herself as she drifted off. She was only dimly aware of Sam when he came to bed, although she knew she heard the draperies again, and knew that he must have opened them to stand and stare at the view, even as she had. When he got in bed, he pulled her close as usual, kissed her, and settled his leg across her. She could sleep now.

Sam was up before her in the morning. She missed his warmth, and his usual early morning inclinations that left her breathless. She sat up and stretched. Her husband had got no farther than the window, where he sat comfortable in his nightshirt, one bare leg doubled under him and the other stretched out casually. He must have sensed that she was watching him, because he looked over his shoulder at her.

"You cannot imagine how many mornings I have lain in my tent trying to recall that exact shade of gold across the front lawn." He gestured out the window, then returned his gaze to the view. "Come on over here, Lydia."

"I would rather just lie here and be out of sorts with you," she replied frankly.

His shoulders shook, and she thought she heard his laugh low and barely audible over the wrens bickering by the wren box under the eaves. "Mrs. Reed, do come here so I can fondle you just a bit and try to jolly you into something resembling good humor."

She shook her head, but left the bed and joined him at the window. He pulled her down to sit between his legs and lean back against him. This is fraught with peril, but quite agreeable, she thought as she closed her eyes and enjoyed the moment. "You are a complete scoundrel," she scolded, even as she sighed when he touched her. "Your Aunt Chalmers is as healthy a woman as I have ever seen."

He was silent, and she felt some satisfaction in knowing that while her face was nowhere the equal of Anna Avery's, at least her body was here and seemed to have his entire attention. "Could we carry this discussion to the bed?" he asked finally, a bit breathless himself. "I'm a little large to attempt this in the window seat, and I wouldn't want to scare the goose girl down there."

The discussion ended then. He took her back to bed, and while she wondered at her own fragility in maintaining a serious irritation with her husband, it was only a brief wonder, before she forgot everything except the business at hand, which occupied her fully.

She lay in his arms when they finished, careful as always to rest against his better side. "Aunt Chalmers," she prompted, when he sighed and rested his leg over her again.

"Somehow I never pictured a discussion with a naked woman about my aunt," he teased. He kissed her neck, where she was sweaty now. "Mama told me last night that Aunt Chalmers recovered from years and years of ailments with the first receipt of Percy's damned letters."

Lydia edged out from under his leg and sat up. "Those letters! Apparently Percy has taken great license with what must be a fervid imagination." She told him what his aunt had mentioned last night and watched his eyes grow wide with dismay. "I cannot possibly think up enough stories! Sam, we cannot continue this. I won't. You must tell her."

He turned carefully onto his back. "I can't just yet, not when she is taking such pleasure in telling me about all her improvements—the ones I suggested and the ones she paid for. We're going to have to muddle on a while longer, Lydia."

"And then what?" she asked, getting up to hunt for her clothes. "Will it be so terrible if she withdraws her money?" She pulled on her chemise and petticoat, and stood still while he buttoned her dress up the back.

He returned to bed, sitting there with his nightshirt in his lap, looking at her with a frown. "Lydia, I kept alive in Spain by planning what I would do here. When my brother officers were screaming in nightmare, wenching or drinking themselves into a stupor, I sat at my desk and planned pages and pages of improvements to this place. My razor and your scissors won't get me what I want now. Even my chess set won't be enough. I need my aunt's total approval, because I need her money. I can't make it any plainer, Lydia."

"No, I suppose you cannot," she murmured. "It seems that all our discussions circle right back here, don't they?"

"Only when you drag them there," he said.

She stood in the doorway and looked at her husband. I would tell any lie for any length of time, if you could bother to tell me you loved me, she thought. "I remember something about 'all my worldly goods endow,' " she said quietly. "Am I not part of your venture now? I've seen your view out the window. I could love this place." Oh, and you, too, only please won't you tell me first, she thought?

He took a long time answering. He tried to put on his nightshirt again, but he could not raise his arm high enough over his head. She made no move to help him this time, even though she ached to.

"Mrs. Reed, so far all you have done is try to get me to end it! We made an agreement," he reminded her.

She thought of St. Barnabas. "Husband, we made a larger agreement when we married! I am certainly your wife now."

"And you promised to obey," he said quickly, with enough ice in his voice to frighten an entire battery, let alone a wife.

His words came at her like a slap across her face, and she stepped back in surprise and hurt.

"Oh, wait, Lydia, I didn't …." He stopped. "Well, I did, actually. Lydia, I am certain that once my aunt is pleased with you and Maria, she will not be upset when I tell her."

I suppose I should ask in which decade that will be, she

thought, her mind almost numb with humiliation. Perhaps I have said enough. She gathered up her shoes and stockings as he struggled to put on his nightshirt, then wrenched the door open. "Husband, you puzzle me," she said from the safety of the open door. "You were so pleased that I stood up and spoke the truth the night of that dreadful banquet. I ruined myself. I want to tell the truth now, and you won't hear of it. Mr. Reed, I call you expedient, for now *you* are ruining me."

Her heart breaking, she stayed in the nursery with Maria until she heard him leave the house. With Maria clasped in her arms, she looked out the window. Aunt Chalmers was driving the gig, while Sam sat beside her. As she watched, she saw a figure ride toward them, a figure on a side saddle. Lydia sighed as the gig slowed and the horse pranced alongside it. "Well, Maria, I have cooked our goose, I fear," she whispered into the child's hair.

Her misery lifted only a little when Maria clapped her hands on her face and came toward her for a kiss. Lydia gladly complied. "But you are a treat!" She could not help looking out the window. "And you, Miss Avery, can drop into the first convenient hole."

SHE SPENT HER MORNING in total panic, her stomach twisted into a thousand knots, as her mother-in-law showed her around the house, pointing out the part of it that had been standing since the days of the first Bishop of Durham. They looked at chests and chests of linens and old furniture, and all Lydia could think of was her husband.

She paused during Lady Laren's recitation to hand over Maria to the servant for a nap. Her mother-in-law was frowning when she returned. "Do you know, my dear, I am wondering if dear Celia has a hearing problem," she said, her voice hesitant, as though she thought it might not be her business.

"Oh, I don't think so," Lydia said.

"My dear, she does not answer when I call her name!" Lady

Laren said. "You saw her earlier, playing with the spools there. She did not turn around when I called to her."

Lydia smiled, relieved and hopeful of an explanation that would satisfy. "Mum, I am in the habit of calling her Maria. It is her second name, the name of my dear dead mama, who perished after the battle for Salamanca in the general troop withdrawal." There, Sam, that ought to be enough lies for you, she thought grimly.

To her dismay, Lady Laren stared at her. "Della, how can this be? In your last letter, you referred to your dear mother who had returned to Lisbon to await your father, who was still in Toulouse! And she was there with your two sisters ... or was it brothers? Never mind." She closed the linen drawer with a bang, jumping back because the noise must have been louder than she anticipated. "How comes your mother's resurrection?"

Lydia stared back. She looked into the mirror beyond Lady Laren and watched her face drain of all color. Sam, I cannot raise people from the dead, she thought in desperation. I cannot do this. Slowly she removed the apron Lady Laren had loaned her for the tour of the house's dustier regions and folded it neatly over the chair back. "I do not know, Lady Laren," she said, her voice calm and quiet. "Please excuse me."

She walked slowly from the room, knowing that if she started to run, she would panic. Without a word or nod to any of the servants, she went up the stairs, her back straight, her eyes thoughtful. She paused outside Maria's door, wanting the solace of her good humor, but not willing to wake her. She let herself into Sam's room. The bed was made, the room tidy. Without thinking, she took off her wedding ring and placed it on the bureau next to his pocket watch.

She knew there were back stairs, and she found them, moving quietly, unwilling to see Lady Laren again. It was a relief to be outside again, especially with her face so warm now, and the house stuffy and closed in. Walking purposefully, even though she had no idea where she was going, she skirted the stone outbuildings and walked through the orchard, where the apples were still green. The grass was high between the trees, and she sighed with the pleasure of being in the country again. I know I cannot return to London, and Devon is out of the question, she thought as she plucked a stem of grass and chewed on it. Perhaps I can rent the barbershop in Merry Glade again, but that, too, will require the truth.

The river was beautiful. Sam had called it a beck, or was it a burn? All she knew was that the water was cool when she took off her shoes and stockings and sat on the bank with her feet in the fast-moving stream. Soon they were so cold that she could wiggle her toes and feel nothing. When her feet were limber again, she walked on down the bank until she found a convenient crossing place. Three jumps onto stones and then one splash that wet her dress to the knees took her across the beck. She climbed higher and found a sun-warm rock set back into the trees.

It was a giant's chair. She leaned back in satisfaction, enjoying the warmth of the rock. Her view took in the whole valley, and as she sat there, she began to understand how someone could think it was heaven, especially someone in the middle of war so terrible. "I wonder what it is like in the winter," she asked out loud. Is the air so cold that it almost cracks? Are the streams quiet with their burden of ice? "Never mind that," she said. 'The walls are thick on the house, and Sam probably has considerable foresight in putting away wood, or coal, or whatever they use."I do not aim to leave this valley, she thought, even though I must tell the truth today. Sam will be furious that I have come up so short. "Or have you, Lydia?" she asked herself. "You are not afraid of hard work, and Sam is hard work. He probably fancies himself in love with Anna Avery, but I am his wife, and I do not intend to cry foul and run. Someday I will hear him say he loves me."

It sounded good to her ears. She closed her eyes, enjoying the sun and the prospect of years and years ahead of her in this valley. She would just rest her eyes for a few minutes.

When she woke, the sun was quite gone and the rock was cold. She sat up in alarm. No, it was not gone, but merely cloudy now. She sniffed the air. Soon it would rain. Lydia clambered down off the rock and retraced her steps, leaping farther this time to avoid the splash into the beck.

Her shoes and stockings were gone. "This is odd, indeed," she said, then smiled. I suppose some urchin is complimenting herself on her good luck, she thought. Well, I can be charitable. Sam owes me a wedding wardrobe anyway. She walked back through the orchard in no real hurry, confident that bad news would keep another minute or two. I almost do not know where to begin this, she thought. I shall have to suggest to my mother-in-law that she call for a large pot of tea.

She came into the house the way she left it, noting how quiet it was. She was starting up the stairs to find another pair of stockings when the housekeeper came around the corner, shrieked, and backed into the little 'tween stairs maid, who was following her with a plate of biscuits.

"My goodness, let me help you!" Lydia said, hurrying back down the stairs, her hand held out. To her amazement, the woman shrieked again and threw her apron over her head. "Do tell me what is wrong!" she asked as she tugged at the apron. "Sharon … Sharon, is it? Whatever is her problem?"

The maid's eyes were wide as saucers. "You're not dead!"

"Of course not," she replied with some asperity. "I just went for a walk and fell asleep. Goodness, what a strange household." The housekeeper lowered her apron. "You're living and breathing?" she asked in awe.

"The last time I checked. Mrs. Appleton, this is outside of enough," she said firmly. "Do let me help you up. Where are Lady Laren and her sister?"

"I believe they are in the sitting room." The housekeeper paused for what she must have thought was dramatic effect. "The best sitting room, what is used for funerals and other untidy events, Lady Laren."

"Well, this certainly qualifies as an untidy event," Lydia said. "Lead on, then, and let us hope they are not as skittish as you were!"

They were worse, far worse, worse to the point of trembling and staring until she gave them each a hug, and her deepest apologies for falling asleep. "What on earth has happened here?" she asked, when the women were calm again, and calling for tea, that blessed British restorative.

"My dear, when you did not return, we sent out the servants to look for you. The goose girl came back with your shoes and stockings from the beck, and Sam ...."

"I thought he was ... well, you are here, Aunt Chalmers. Wasn't he with you?" she asked, reaching for a cup of tea. "Oh, no! Did someone actually think I had *drowned* myself?" She took a gulp of tea, wincing at the way it scalded down her throat. "Please don't tell me that Sam ...."

"He has organized a search party, and they are even now searching every inch along the river," Lady Laren said.

"Pray he is not on horseback," Lydia said, leaping up to look out the window. "Sam, you idiot!"

"Of course he is on horseback!" Aunt Chalmers said. "He had someone throw him into the saddle."

"He will hurt his back," Lydia said. She shook her head and managed a little laugh. "He is far more trouble than he is worth, ladies."

"Quite possibly," Aunt Chalmers said. She patted her sister's hand. "Laren men are such a trial. I did hope that Sam had broken the link, but do tell us, my dear, what kind of a scoundrel he is. That is, if you have something to tell us?"

Both ladies looked at her expectantly. Lydia looked back, seeing nothing in their expressions except interest, and perhaps a little impatience that she begin. She filled her teacup again, sat down, and propped up her bare feet on a hassock. "It's a long story, and I am not entirely sure where to start."

"Begin somewhere," Aunt Chalmers said, sitting forward on

the edge of her chair, her eyes bright. "Don't leave out a single detail."

She began at St. Barnabas, but that wasn't the right place, so she started over in Devon with her own family, and how beautiful Kitty was, and how Mama could never treat her with anything but impatience and contempt. She took a sip of tea now and then, and scanned her rapt audience for any sign of boredom. There was none, only a certain expectancy bordering on the giddy. The ladies became almost indignant when she told of her impulsive declaration at the victory banquet and her subsequent exile from the family. They sobbed into their handkerchiefs as she recounted Sam's desperate wound, and how brave he was with the road agents (she did not tell them how he argued with the bandit), and courageous during his terrible operation. She told them how hard she had worked to raise the money to pay their bills in Merry Glade, the visit of Sir Percy, and then right down to her arrival at Laren Hall, and the fact that she was even now sitting barefoot in their best sitting room, while her husband—drat his hide—scoured the water for her body.

The ladies were silent for a long moment. Lydia leaned back in the chair, exhausted with the telling of so much truth. The tea was long cold, but she swirled what remained in her cup and drank it. "Aunt Chalmers, I know you are disappointed that he did not precisely keep the agreement he claims he did. I know he means well, but that promise of the inheritance meant so …."

She stopped in mid-sentence; it was her turn to sit, open-mouthed. As she stared, the ladies looked at each other and began to laugh, not little chuckles, but guffaws that made her smile, in spite of her own amazement. Aunt Chalmers even beat her feet on the carpet like a child, then wheezed and gasped so much that she called for her sister to loosen her corset strings.

Lydia stared from one woman to the other as the truth began to strike her somewhere between the eyes. "You two have known all along, haven't you?" she accused them, even as the laughter swelled up inside her.

"Oh, my, yes, dearie," said her mother-in-law, when she could speak.

"Who?" she asked. "It couldn't possibly have been Sir Percy."

"Della—no, no, what *is* your name? We went into positive whoops over 'Delightful,' and figured that had to be something dreamed up while crawling from a vat of rum."

"Quite possible. My name is Lydia, and Maria is Maria." She blew a kiss to her mother-in-law. "Her hearing is quite acute, my dear," she said, "but she will never answer to Celia."

"Lydia. I do like that. A pretty name for a pretty wife," Lady Laren said.

"But you haven't told me who let the cat from the bag," Lydia said, when the two of them threatened to go off into another fit of laughter.

"It was General Picton's wife," Aunt Chalmers said. "Apparently the general wrote to her, and she felt bound to tell us."

"I'm sorry you had to be party to such a joke for two years," Lydia said.

"Oh, I am not!" Aunt Chalmers insisted. "I had been feeling unhealthy for years, but once I knew what Sam had concocted, I didn't dare die! I simply had to get better to see who he would bring home." She smiled and leaned close enough to pat Lydia's knee. "He did rather better than he deserves, I believe." She clucked her tongue. "And he has *never* told you he loves you? Laren men continue to be blockheads."

Lady Laren stood up then and left the room. She returned in a moment with a miniature, which she handed to Lydia as Aunt Chalmers began to laugh again. "My dear, this came in that first letter from Sir Percy. I believe it is supposed to be Delightful Saunders." She collapsed into her chair again, carried off by another fit of the giggles.

A handsome blond woman with prominent eyes and a

beauty mark smiled back at her. She wore hoop earrings, and looked decidedly Peninsular. Lydia smiled at the unknown woman. "Something found in a siege, like my wedding ring," she said softly. She gasped, and leaped to her feet then. "Oh, my ring! I left it on the bureau in Sam's room! I was so angry with him. You can't imagine."

It was Lady Laren's turn to frown. "He came downstairs with it on his little finger. I have never seen him look so bleak, my dear." Lydia sat down. "I suppose we will just have to wait until he returns."

They chatted another hour, punctuating their conversation with a burst of giggles as one or the other took the notion. They all trooped upstairs while Lydia fed Maria and got her ready for bed. There was one thing more she had to ask her mother-in-law. "Mum, I hope that you can love Maria as much as we do," she murmured, holding the child close. "I will not be happy if she is less favored."

"I would not be happy, either, my dear," Lady Laren said. "Rest assured that as much as we have enjoyed this perfectly delightful diversion for the last two years, we have kept it to ourselves. No one will know that Maria is not your own baby, or that you were not married to Sam all that time."

When the baby slept, they went downstairs in perfect charity with one another. Lady Laren had just called for another pot of tea when they heard horses thundering toward the house. "Thank goodness," Lady Laren said. She smiled at her sister. "Come, Hermione, and let us retire to my room. Quite possibly Lydia has a few words for Sam. I think our little news can wait until he at least realizes that he still has a wife."

IT WAS REALLY A small bruise, and not likely to turn into anything ugly. "I thought ladies were supposed to faint, my dear," she told her husband after he had been carried upstairs, made comfortable, and propped into bed with a hot compress on his shoulder and a cold one against his forehead. "I would have caught you, except that you surprised me and that dratted umbrella stand was in the way."

He said nothing, but would not let go of her hand, so she perched herself beside him on their bed. "And now you have worn yourself out on this wild-goose chase." She smoothed his hair back from his eyes, then lay down next to him. "Sam, I would never leave you! I couldn't possibly."

He nodded, his eyes weary, but took her hand and held it. He removed her wedding ring from his little finger, and put it back on her hand, where it belonged. "Don't take it off again," he ordered. "And for the Lord's sake, if you feel like a walk to work off irritation—I'm not saying it won't happen again—let me know where you are going. Lydia, you cannot imagine what I thought."

She looked into her husband's eyes. "Sam, do you love me?" she asked. "I have to know before I am one minute older, and you have never told me."

He closed his eyes, and in a moment she was dabbing at his tears, and then her eyes. She kissed him, his mouth as familiar to her as her own, then rested her head on his chest.

"Lydia, I have loved you since your first afternoon at St. Barnabas."

She remembered all the terror of that afternoon, holding the gunnery sergeant's hand while the other gentry left, one by one. "I was so afraid."

"You were magnificent," he said. "I could have kissed the ground when you said your name was Miss Perkins." His laugh was shaky. "That meant I did not have to call out your husband and kill him in a duel, so I could run away to Brazil or … or somewhere with you. Lydia, you smelled like sugared violets, and you were so tidy and pretty, and … and grimly brave."

"I never felt pretty until you said I was," she told him. "If I am brave, you have made me so."

"You've always been beautiful to me," he said simply. He touched her breast. "Bravery comes from somewhere inside. I had nothing to do with that."

"Why didn't you tell me you loved me?"

He ruffled her hair. "I was sure you would think me deranged. We didn't really know each other well. Besides, my love, I am shy about speaking of matters so intimate." He sighed. "And then Percy Wilkins was so stupid to remind both of us how … how *calculated* this whole marriage was." He kissed her. "I was going to tell you so many times, and then I said that awful thing about obeying. You could have told *me*," he pointed out. "That is, if you do love me."

"Amazingly," she said, "I think I have been in love ever since I cut your hair. Such nice hair! Or it might have been when General Picton stole your pants so you could not pester Horse Guards. By the way, your hair needs a trim tomorrow, providing you are feeling well enough to leave this bed. Sam, I warned you about riding a horse when your back is not entirely healed yet. At some point you will simply have to start listening to me. What are you grinning at?" she asked.

"You. Do be serious and let us return to the original concern. You do love me," he stated.

"Yes. Absolutely," she said. "I wouldn't scold you or nag you if I were indifferent. I love you so much that if I see Anna Avery again on this property, I will smite her."

Her husband laughed. "Silly! She stopped our gig to tell me that she accepted a proposal this morning from a landowner just over the border. A good friend of mine, by the way. Lydia, she's a beauty, but I want *you*. You can doubt me, but it would be a waste of time, as most doubts are."

"I need to hear it, Sam," she said, nestling closer to him, comfortable with the way she fit on his better side. "Husband, I have been thinking today about what I learned."

"And what have you learned?" he asked, then jostled her. "Come on, Lyddy, you can tell me."

"I am self-reliant, dependable, courageous, somewhat prone to speak my mind …."

"Oh, never that!" he teased, then kissed her again. "What else?"

"You are a distraction," she said. "I have doubts about myself, too, Sam. I hope they go away eventually, but I am going to require you to tell me quite often that you love me."

"I hardly think that is onerous," he said, "particularly since I do." He held up her hand, then kissed it. "Keep that ring on, will you?"

Lydia nodded. She got up and began to prepare for bed. "You know, of course, that you will have to face your mother and your aunt tomorrow," she reminded him as her dress came off. "I told them the whole story, and they let me know that two years ago, General Picton's wife wrote to them of your invention of a wife from the regiment, and Sir Percy's misguided enthusiasm."

He stared at her, then started to laugh. She took off the rest of her clothes, washed herself, and found a nightgown while he gave himself over to mirth. "I suppose I am not the clever fellow I thought I was," he said finally as he wiped his eyes with the hem of the sheet.

She sat on the bed again. "It wouldn't appear so, Mr. Reed. Here, let me have that compress. There now, the swelling is almost gone. I have infinite hope that someday you will be in excellent health." She returned the cloth to the basin.

"Lydia, I almost forgot," he said. "There in my coat pocket. While we were organizing a search party at the tavern in the village, the postman delivered that to me. You might find it interesting."

She took it from his pocket, sitting beside him again, relishing the warmth of his hand on her leg. "It is from my father, and addressed to you!" She stared at him. "How did he … well of course he knew. I had said your name often enough."

"Read it, Lydia."

She read, putting down the letter when the words became blurry. She waited a moment to compose herself, and then read the rest.

"You bolted from Holly Street too soon, Lydia," Sam said.

"Another few hours, and you could have been the toast of London, according to your father. Think of the ugly customers you could have avoided. Me, principally."

She could only look at him in profound love.

He tapped the letter. "I imagine your mother was dumbfounded when the afternoon mail contained many more letters, those in praise of your actions." He took the letter from her numb fingers. "I like this most of all: 'My dear Lydia, thanks to you, questions have been raised now in Commons about the infamous medical treatment of soldiers. Dearest Lydia, every door is open to you in London in those houses that matter. Please do come home.' "

She traced her finger over the signature. " 'Your loving Papa,' " she said softly. She put the letter aside, blew out the light, and got under the covers. She smiled as Sam gathered her close into his usual embrace. "This is the only house where I care about the door, but I do think it's time to paint it, Sam. And I noticed when I walked down to the river …"

"Burn," he corrected, nuzzling her neck.

"… the burn, that you need to send someone to cut the grass in the orchard."

"Sheep will do. Lord, but you are managing! Hush so I can go to sleep. I need all my energy to … to …."

"Refresh me in the morning?" she teased, reaching behind her and caressing him until his breath came in ragged chunks.

"Face my mother and Aunt Chalmers, more like!" he declared when he could speak. "Give a wounded husband some peace, Lydia! Eventually."

Epilogue

◦◦◦

May 16, 1815

General Sir Thomas Picton
Third Division
Allied Headquarters
Ostend, Belgium

Dear General,

It is with considerable reluctance that I must decline your offer of a recommission in Battery B. I do not decline lightly, and my reasons are two.

First, I am not the battery commander I was. My wound has healed to the point where I can expect nothing better. Since February, I have been able to mount a horse by myself, so you have some idea how difficult this has been for me. Lydia insists that I am getting better still, but she loves me fiercely, and in her case, that seems to cover a multitude of malignancies. It pains me to send you my regrets. I would like nothing better than to serve the guns against Napoleon again. Sir Percy Wilkins will do you well. I trained him; I trust him, at least in this matter. Are you still laughing over the letter that Lydia wrote to you last fall? I am.

Second, I could not leave Lydia now, even if my back were in excellent shape. She is due to be confined within the month, and I will not abandon her at this time. She never left me during my medical trials, and I owe her that much, and likely more.

We anticipate a son or a daughter, as Lydia would tell you, if she were writing this. I had no idea what a tease she is, and how funny she can be. Of course, your wife would probably say that a cheerful disposition is one's best ally in marriage. Maria is well, and eager to be of help. We love her.

We both wish you well. My God, those words are paltry! You and the division are in our prayers. We expect good news from you when you return, and the hope that you and your excellent wife will visit us this summer when the war is won for the last time.

I remain, yours truly,
Sam Reed
Major Samuel E. H. Reed, Lord Laren,
Late Commander, Battery B, Third Division

Bryner Photography

A WELL-KNOWN VETERAN OF the romance writing field, Carla Kelly is the author of thirty-one novels and three non-fiction works, as well as numerous short stories and articles for various publications. She is the recipient of two RITA Awards from Romance Writers of America for Best Regency of the Year; two Spur Awards from Western Writers of America; two Whitney Awards, one for Best Romance Fiction, 2011, and one for Best Historical Fiction, 2012; and a Lifetime Achievement Award from *Romantic Times*.

Carla's interest in historical fiction is a byproduct of her lifelong study of history. She has a BA in Latin American

History from Brigham Young University and an MA in Indian Wars History from University of Louisiana-Monroe. She's held a variety of jobs, including public relations work for major hospitals and hospices, feature writer and columnist for a North Dakota daily newspaper, and ranger in the National Park Service (her favorite job) at Fort Laramie National Historic Site and Fort Union Trading Post National Historic Site. She has worked for the North Dakota Historical Society as a contract researcher. Interest in the Napoleonic Wars at sea led to a recent series of novels about the British Channel Fleet during that conflict.

Of late, Carla has written two novels set in southeast Wyoming in 1910 that focus on her Mormon background and her interest in ranching.

You can find Carla on the Web at:
www.carlakellyauthor.com.

CAMEL PRESS

The All-New Spanish Brand Series

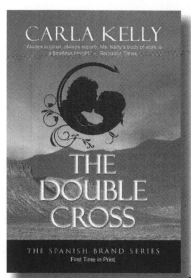

At the end of the 18th Century, during the decline of the Spanish Empire in the New World, a brand inspector saves a lovely orphan from her cruel relatives and sets out to solve the mystery of her lost inheritance.

Marco and Paloma fight the scourge of smallpox by bravely venturing onto the Staked Plains, stronghold of the Comanche. As part of a devil's bargain, they must put themselves at the mercy of these dangerous enemies and try to inoculate them.

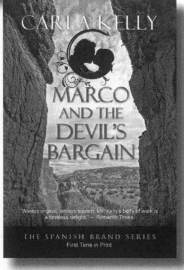

Maria Espinosa is "La Afortunata." First she survives the 1679 cholera epidemic in Mexico City, then an Apache raid on the caravan transporting her to Santa Fe. Rejected by her sister, Maria goes to live with a ranching family living uneasily among the Pueblos and inspires a rivalry between Diego and his half-Indian brother Cristobal. When the Indians revolt, will Maria's good fortune hold?

Other Camel Press Editions of
Regency Romances by Carla Kelly

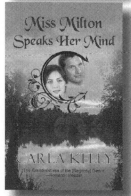

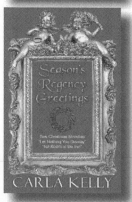

Made in the USA
Lexington, KY
19 April 2015